A
Garland Series

VICTORIAN
FICTION

NOVELS OF FAITH
AND DOUBT

A collection of 121 novels
in 92 volumes, selected by
Professor Robert Lee Wolff,
Harvard University,
with a separate introductory volume
written by him
especially for this series.

THE MINDER

THE COMING
OF THE
PREACHERS

Frederick R. Smith

Garland Publishing, Inc., New York & London

1975

Library of Congress Cataloging in Publication Data

Smith, Frederick R
   The minder.

   (Victorian fiction : Novels of faith and doubt ; no. 66)
   Reprint of 2 works, the 1st published in 1900 by
H. Marshall, London, and the 2d published in 1901 by
Hodder and Stoughton, London.
   1. Smith, Frederick R. The coming of the preachers.
1975. II. Title. III. Series.
PZ3.S64724Mi3 [PR5453.S684]   823'.8   75-1517
ISBN 0-8240-1590-8

THE MINDER

Bibliographical note:

this facsimile has been made from a copy in the
British Museum
(012641.C47)

THE MINDER

THE MINDER

THE STORY OF THE

COURTSHIP, CALL AND CONFLICTS

OF

JOHN LEDGER

Minder and Minister

BY

JOHN ACKWORTH

AUTHOR OF

"Clog Shop Chronicles," &c.

LONDON

HORACE MARSHALL AND SON

TEMPLE HOUSE, TEMPLE AVENUE, E.C.

1900

BRADBURY, AGNEW, & CO. LD., PRINTERS,
LONDON AND TONBRIDGE.

To the Memory of

ROBERT KELLY KERMODE

AND

WALTER JAMES CANNELL

(MY FRIENDS)

CONTENTS

PART I

THE MINDER

PART II

THE MINISTER

THE MINDER

CHAPTER I

HOW ONE GOOD KISS BEGOT ANOTHER

THE engines of the Bramwell new mill had just stopped for the night, and the hands were streaming out through the great gates near the boiler-house. As it was nearly dark, and a drizzling, sticky sort of rain was falling, the workpeople were all making homewards as fast as possible, and there was a clatter of innumerable clogs on the flagged sidewalk. Most of the hands were going in couples, but there was one young fellow who was walking by himself, and had his head down. There was nothing in the least remarkable about him, except that his dark hair was a little longer than usual, and suggested amateur and not too frequent barbering, whilst his greasy old hat was soft and round, and looked as if it might once have been a parson's wide-awake. He had a plain, open face, a little sharper perhaps than it ought to have been, and that seemed to indicate that he was already finding life somewhat hard. His clothes, too, shiny with wear and mill-oil, hung somewhat loosely upon him, and created the impression that the body they covered was not so well nourished

M.

B

as it might have been.   Of medium height, and uncertain, almost sallow complexion, he was just such an average young factory lad as could have been found in any Lancashire town.   A second glance at his face shows that pleasant thoughts are moving in John Ledger's mind, and the fingers of his left hand drum merrily on the lid of the breakfast can he is carrying.   Now he raises his head, turns his face upwards and smiles, and you note that if his face wore that light upon it always it would be really worth looking at.   Then he mutters something to himself and draws down his brows, but the lips and chin seem to have escaped control for the moment, and joy lurks in the corners of his mouth. Joy was such an uncommon thing with him that he was shy in its company, and afraid, and even a little suspicious, but though he pulled the wayward mouth tight again the fingers only drummed the more rapidly, and before he had gone many yards he caught himself actually humming.

By this time he had reached the end of the street and turned into the Market Place, still musing.   All at once he pulled up, and staring hard at the church clock, suddenly burst into a laugh that made the lamplighter turn round and stare at him resentfully. John looked surprised too, and ashamed, and plunged across the Market Place into Shed Lane, where he stopped again in the twilight to call himself names and pull himself together.   He seemed to have himself well in hand when he started down the lane again, but though the expression on his features was stern enough, there was a tell-tale light in his eyes, and the corners of his lips would not keep straight. Suddenly he pulled up again, his whole face one delighted grin.   Another thought, in which pleasure and mischief seemed about equally blended, had got possession of him.   He looked up the lane and down, and then turning his face toward the dim gravestones in the churchyard, he shook his fist and cried—

"I will! I *will!*"

But mill girls were coming down the lane, and were just beginning to observe him; and so starting off once more, becoming serious as he walked, he dismissed the great idea, whatever it was, with a grunt of stern rebuke. But the joy within him was not so easily put down, and so fifty yards from his own door, and speaking apparently to the bills of a great hoarding, he cried—

"H-a-y! wouldn't she like it!—she'd cry!"

By this time he had become quite excited, and also a little embarrassed; he was so near home that he already felt its influence, and his great resolve began to look foolish. Propping himself against the hoarding, he looked up the lane and down, and then, shaking the breakfast can until it jingled again in his hands, he cried—

"I will! I'll kiss her!"

He looked very resolute and very serious as he said this, but he stopped twice before he reached the little cake and bread shop where he resided; and when he finally got up to it his heart suddenly failed him and he walked past. Then he grew ashamed, and checked himself: "I will! I *will!* I never have done, but I will!" and then, lest his shyness should once more get the better of him, he darted back and hastily pushed open the door of the little shop. But here, to his confusion, he found a small customer getting her pinafore filled with oat cakes and crumpets, and he strode nervously forward and stood on the hearthrug. Many a time during the short period it took to dispose of the little one, he resolved to put off his rash resolve, but the idea had taken possession of him, and he could not move it; and so before the door had been closed a moment, and whilst the tall pale woman of the shop was putting back some cakes into the window, he suddenly sprang at her, and seizing her round the neck imprinted on her wan cheek a rousing kiss.

It was his mother.

"Hoo! Ha! Save us, John! whatever's to do?"

But though there was alarm and protest in the tone, the face told another story; a sweet light rose into the faded eyes, and a blush, soft and beautiful as any girl's, spread itself over the colourless cheek, whilst the chin dropped upon the breast and she hung her head like a naughty child. And John, who had skipped awkwardly back to the hearthrug, and now stood with his back to the fire, was blushing too. He was utterly ashamed of his unprecedented act, and yet so glad of the news he had to tell, that though he dare not look into the eyes that were shining so unwontedly, he was delighted to see them so, and hastened to explain himself.

"I've got 'em, mother! I've got my wheels at last! Cheer up, mother lass! I'm a minder now!"

"Thank God! Oh, thank the Lord!" and she dropped into the low iron-rockered chair, and great tears of relief and gratitude welled up into her eyes.

"That's it, mother. Thank the good Lord we're all right now. 'Sorrow may endure for the night, but joy cometh in the morning.'"

For a few moments "mother" sat still in her chair, and then commenced absently to rock herself. Her face was lighted with uplifting emotion, and her lips moved uneasily, and at last, as she began to finger nervously the hem of her apron, raised her eyes to one of the pot dogs on the mantelpiece, and repeated—

> "Judge not the Lord by feeble sense,
> But trust him for His grace."

For several minutes longer she continued to rock

herself, and then, in sudden self-recovery, rose to get her son his tea.

John was her eldest child and only son. Her husband was one of those unworldly souls who, though they possess more than average intelligence on most questions, can never be made sufficiently to understand the absolute necessity of bread and butter, and can never for the life of them concentrate their energies on mere commercial matters. He was at once the admiration and the cross of his ambitious and practical wife, who in her struggles to keep her head up had made a confidant of her beloved son from his earliest days, so that he was by this time already old in his knowledge of the world, at least on its sterner side. There were two children besides John, both girls, but the secrets of the family life were always kept from them, and John and his mother did all the scheming and pinching.

These experiences had prematurely sobered him, and, as he was of sensitive nature, they had left their mark even upon his body; and so, though old in sorrow, he had dropped behind his competitors at the mill and been outstripped by younger but better-developed fellows, and still remained a "big-piercer" at about fifteen shillings per week. At last, however, his turn had come, and he had received a sort of certificate of manhood by being appointed minder of a couple of spinning mules, with a bobbiner and piecer under him. This meant an addition of ten or more shillings per week to the family income, and as mule-minding was piecework he was not without hope of exceeding the average. Circumstances, rather than natural temperament, had turned him into a serious stay-at-home fellow, and outside his own home he was regarded as shy and uninteresting. At the time of which we write the struggle of life had become somewhat easier for them, and John and his mother had begun to indulge in ambitious hopes for his young sisters, who, he declared again and again, should never go to the factory. It had been hard work keeping them at school so long, and now Annie, the eldest, had turned out delicate, and so they had started the shop in order to be able to allow her to remain at home in her mother's care. Lucy was a pupil teacher, but did not care for the profession, and was anxious to get something more congenial; but as yet nothing had presented itself, and of course her wages at school were next to nothing.

Now, however, things would be better. With a full man's wages and their other little sources of income they were not likely to be in any immediate want, and if only John's father, who was a painter, would not spring any of his own financial troubles upon them, as he had an awkward habit of doing when they least expected, they would be fairly comfortable.

And so John finished his tea with a light heart, and a face that beamed in sympathy with his mother's grateful sighs.

Later on John washed himself and put on his evening clothes and sat down to a book; but he did not read much. His eyes wandered again and again to his mother, who went about the house humming a tune, a thing almost unheard of in her. From his mother his gaze returned to his book, and then to the fire, into which he stared with widening eyes and pleased, contented smile. Then he would suddenly remember himself, and puckering his brow with stern resolution, bring his eyes back to the volume in his hands, and, before he knew where he was, he was day-dreaming again.

The house was spotlessly clean and the fire-irons shone with their week-end polish, the little swing lamp cast a cheery light, and the kettle hummed drowsily on the hob, and John's heart was warming in sympathetic joy and gratitude when the door opened quickly, a gust of wet wind swirled into the house, and a voice that went through him like an electric shock cried—

"Good evening, Mrs. Ledger. Oh, what a night! Isn't it?"

"Sallie! You! Whatever have you come out a night like this for? John would have brought the bread down. Come in and get to the fire."

"Oh, I had to come this way. Yes, I *will* sit a minute or two. Never mind my cloak, John."

But John, at sight of the visitor, had jumped to his feet, and with hands that shook a little, had drawn the rocking-chair near the fire, and was now engaged in helping to remove the waterproof from the visitor's shoulders.

She was a young person of about twenty-two, and as she handed her cloak to John, throwing back as she did so a coquettish little veil, she revealed a remarkably pretty face. Her features were so formally regular as to be almost uninteresting of themselves, but at this moment they were wreathed in bright smiles, and flushed with conflict with the elements outside, whilst her fine dark eyes flashed with points of light. She was rather below medium height and inclined to *embonpoint*, and her dress indicated that she belonged to a class a little above that of John and his mother. A cynical person might have said that the young lady was evidently quite aware of her attractions, but John Ledger was neither cynical nor critical, and at that moment she appeared to him a ravishing embodiment of bewitching womanhood. She did not talk to John, of course, though his book lay on his knee and his face wore an inane company smile.

She had come for the week-end cakes and bread,

and to talk with Mrs. Ledger; and though she did now and then flash a look at John, it was only because, being there, he could not in politeness be altogether overlooked. She spoke of the weather and the storm that had overtaken her, and seemed so animated about that stalest of topics that John found it wonderfully interesting. Then she had to tell her woman friend about yesterday's sewing meeting, and she looked so very pretty as she talked that the male hearer forgot that small scandal was his pet abhorrence. Then she grew suddenly confidential, and in low, earnest tones expressed her fears that the new Circuit stewards were not hitting it with the super., and John would really have become very uneasy about this kind of tittle-tattle, only she every now and then rolled her eyes round to him, and arched her brows in such an altogether irresistible way, that he could think of nothing else. Presently she discovered that it was on the stroke of nine, and she must, of course, be going. But the bag she had brought for the bread proved on examination to be sodden wet, and her order was larger than usual, and her arms had not been made for carrying heavy burdens, and—well, Mrs. Ledger said that John must go with her and carry the parcel. Of course Miss Sallie would not hear of this for a moment, but John, being in most unusual spirits, and feeling that he must make amends for not having offered before, became quite bold in his urgency; and so, in a few minutes, with the loaves and cakes wrapped in an old newspaper, and hugged to a thumping heart, he was going down the lane by Miss Sallie's side.

It was three-quarters of a mile to the old-fashioned stone house where she resided, but the time passed so rapidly that John was quite disappointed when they reached the gate of what had once been a farmhouse. Sallie, still talking brightly, did not stop at the gate and relieve him of his load; she simply pushed it open before her, and still chattering, led the way into the house. Opening the door, she took the bread from his laden arms, and thanked him with a look and tone which he, shy fellow, found delightfully embarrassing. Then he must sit down and rest a moment before returning; and though he said it was getting late, he allowed her to pull a chair towards the fire for him, and sat down in it, scarcely able to believe that he was not dreaming.

Sallie carried the bread into the back kitchen, and was so long in returning that John had time to realise that they were alone in the house. Oh, if only he had been in any position! But she returned just then, and set before him a steaming glass of blackberry tea, which was so good for keeping the cold out. John required pressing, but when he did accept, either he was unduly nervous, or else she retained her hold upon the glass longer than was strictly necessary, for their fingers touched, and the contact thrilled John through and through. An awkward silence fell upon them as John sipped at his glass; but as Sallie still stood over him he grew more and more embarrassed, and declaring that he really must be going, he gulped down the hot liquid and hastily rose to his feet. They shook hands quite shyly, and John's susceptible and timid heart went pit-pat again, and he felt that she did not withdraw hers as promptly as mere courtesy would have prescribed. And then she came with him to the door, and as she held it open with one hand she snatched a little shawl from a nail behind it, and accompanied him to the gate.

" The ' sneck' was rather awkward," she explained.

But John's experience of life had made him cautious almost to suspicion, and he had learnt to distrust appearances that were . more than usually propitious, and so he was growing a little uneasy under this gracious treatment. It was too good to be true. Sallie took quite a long time to explain to him the mechanism of the gate latch, and, perhaps because the rain had now stopped, he seemed to forget his hurry and to be most curiously interested in this branch of mechanics. As, however, they bent down at the same precise moment to inspect the latch their heads collided. John drew back with a cry of alarm, and wildly threw out his arms; Sallie tossed her head up with a merry laugh, but without stepping back, so that he might have caught her in his embrace by "accident," only he daren't. With another anxious hope that he had not hurt her, he got out of the gate, and was turning round to say good-night once more, when something seemed to strike her, and, putting the gate between them, she leaned over it and said in a loud whisper—

"John! Here!"

John returned, and she drew so near that he could look right down into her deep, dark eyes.

"Hey, I am glad you came with me to-night, John; Sam Kepple was watching for me."

John, with those dangerous eyes still upon him, felt that he was expected to look astonished and shocked, and he did his best.

"I cannot think why he bothers after me. I'm sure I don't encourage him."

It occurred to John that here was a chance for an honest compliment, but he could not for the life of him think of the right word, and so he answered huskily—

"Of course not."

"I'm not *that* sort of girl, forward and running after fellows, now am I, John?"

John was absolutely sure of that, and tried to say so; only those eyes seemed in the darkness to be looking into his very soul, so he only made a stammering sort of answer.

Sallie turned her head away, and John thought he caught a little sigh; but before he could speak she had leaned against the gate again, and, looking right at him, she said—

"Of course, it's different with you, John, isn't it? We are *old* friends, aren't we, John?"

She seemed quite anxious about this matter. Her little head was thrown back, and she was looking earnestly up at him, with her red lips parted, in eager desire to hear his reply. And John was only human, and he was unusually elated to-night at the sudden brightening of his worldly prospects—the ordinary ambitions of men were possible to him now—and so, looking down upon her with hungry, gloating eyes, an overpowering impulse suddenly rushed upon him, and, ducking his head, he kissed the two lips so temptingly turned up to his, and then with sudden and violent reaction broke away from her, and without even a "Good-night," plunged madly into the dark lane, and ran as fast as his legs could carry him.

CHAPTER II

A KISS MAY BREED A COMPLICATION

WHEN he had travelled about a hundred yards a sense of the utter ridiculousness of the situation and its compromising possibilities came upon the fleeing lover, and he was just pulling up to collect his thoughts when a tall figure stepped out of the hedge backing, and planted itself in the path before him, whilst a high falsetto voice cried—" Hold ! "

John did not require a second bidding ; the suddenness of the thing pulled him up dead, and his heart was in his mouth before the figure spoke.

" Come on ! Show thyself ! What have you been doing as you're feared of being seen ? "

John stepped uneasily forward, but before he could make out who had accosted him the man in front, turning half round and flinging back his head to address the shadowy hedge rows, cried, " Well I'm jiggered ! " and then, springing back with a gesture of repudiation, he went on, " Nay, nivver, nivver ! That would be a mank ! " and once more breaking off, he rushed forward, thrust a long narrow face into John's, and shouted squeakily—

" It's nivver John Ledger ! "

" Yes it is, Sam," replied John wonderingly. " Whatever's to do ? "

Sam towered over him in silent amazement, and then, moving a step backward and looking him over from head to foot—though, in the darkness, he could see little—he turned away, and, apostrophising the hedges, he cried—

"Didn't I tell you? Isn't it always so? Isn't it t' way o' t' wold?"

"Sam, whatever is the matter?"

But Sam was still glowering into the darkness and tossing his arms about in tragic gestures; and as John watched him in dire perplexity, he suddenly smote on his breast in melodramatic intensity, and then, in thin piping tones that greatly heightened the comic effect, he cried—

"If it had been a henemy that had dun this! But it is thou! *Thou*, my own fameeliar friend, thou!"

Sallie had hinted not many minutes before that Sam was "after her." Here was a pretty state of things! He had been trifling with another fellow's sweetheart. Sam was a minder like himself, and had been kindly trying to get him his "wheels" for some time, and it was to some degree to his influence that he owed his promotion. Moreover, Sam was a member of the same class, and a prayer leader, and it was through words spoken by him to the super. that John had first been encouraged to try to preach. He heaved a long sigh, and drew himself together. After all, he had more experience in fighting his way through difficulties than in sustaining prosperity, and the emergency steadied him for the moment. He must first see exactly where Sam was, and how much he knew. Had he seen that utterly reckless kiss? He could not imagine that the bright Sallie, who was twenty-two, could ever think seriously of this thirty-year-old fellow workman of his; but if she had simply been playing with Sam—but he would not allow himself to think of that.

"Sam, old friend, I was——"

"Friend! Friend, he says!" cried the other, appealing once more to the darkness. "The sarpent bites, an' then licks. Friend! Aye, I'm wounded in the house of a friend," and then breaking off abruptly, he plunged forward at John again, and thrusting his long face into his, he cried with wild, pathetic, wailing tones, "Three year come Good Friday I've gone after that wench, an' I've never hed so much as a little kiss yet."

John was about to offer a soothing remark, when the distracted fellow plunged off again. Turning his back upon his friend and shaking his fist at the hedge, he cried—

"I will! I'll let him! I'll watch him dance like a carlin' pea in a frying-pan—like a weasel at a rabbit hole! She'll lift him up and flop him down—like me; she'll fry him o' one side an' freeze him o' t'other, an' I'll let her! Aye, I'll let her! It'll do me good."

Touched by his friend's distress, and always ready for self-accusation, John felt half inclined to offer to withdraw in his friend's favour; but a new jealousy for Sallie's honour got the better of this unloverlike feeling, and he cried—

"No, no! Sam. She's not cruel, at any rate."

"Cruel? Who said she was cruel? The man who says a word again that girl will get my fist in his face. What is it to thee if she is cruel?"

John felt this was getting beyond him. It was no use talking to a fellow in a state of mind like Sam's, and so he took him gently by the arm and began to move forward. Before they had gone many steps, however, Sam pulled up, and, looking earnestly into John's face, he said—

"They say as matches are made i' heaven, don't they?"

"Well!"

"Well, if they are, I'd rayther go to t'other place."

"Sam!"

"I would! After what I've gone through, hell 'ud be a holiday."

In tones of low, husky sympathy, and with feelings which frightened him as he felt them rising within him, John said—

"Do you really love her, Sam?"

But the touch thus given to Sam's lacerated feelings sent him off at another tangent, and jerking his arm out of that of his companion, he shouted—

"Love her? I hate her! My blood's afire wi' hate of her!" And then he paused, gazing wildly about him as he did so, and at length, with a moving break in his voice, he wailed out, "Yea, I *do* love her! She's spelled me, John. Oh, John, she's my doom, lad, she's my doom!"

John's brain was buzzing into his ears, and his heart jumped spasmodically. One thing, however, was clear to him. At any cost he must put himself right with his friend; there must be no further concealment.

"But, Sam!" he said, in a sort of sad dismay, "I like her myself, but I didn't know! I never guessed——"

Sam's arms dropped limply to his side, a long struggling groan escaped him, he stared distressfully into the other's face for a while, and then, in low husky tones, he murmured—

"Aye, an' she'll tak' thee, lad—now!" and then, with a long quivering sigh, he concluded, "God help poor Sam!"

The cry went through John. Sam's characteristically inconsequent, coals-of-fire sort of treatment scorched his very soul, and he proceeded almost with passion to reiterate that he had never dreamed that he was in love with Sallie, and that he could not think for a moment of entering into competition with him; but as soon as ever the last statement had

been made, he would have recalled it, only he could
not think of anything better to say, and so he stood
there and stared helplessly at his companion. Eye
to eye they remained there for several moments, and
then Sam, drawing a reluctant breath, said—

"Johnny, lad, she'll nivver have me—that I know.
I'm not good enough for her. But, lad, if what
they're sayin' about thee be true, she'll have thee ;
aye, she'll have thee ; but, Johnny, she's not good
enough for thee—specially now."

"Now! How now ?"

"If thou doesn't know thou soon will do ; but,
Johnny! mark what I say. I know her through an'
through, and she's not good enough for what thou'rt
goin' to be ; be careful, lad, an' God help thee," and
before John could stop him the strange fellow had
darted down Sandman's entry and disappeared.

John's father was reading a leading article to his
reluctantly listening wife when he entered the house,
and waved his hand to prevent his son from inter-
rupting, and so, glad enough of such a chance, John
slipped off his boots and stole quietly upstairs, his
mother following him with inquiring eyes.

His bedroom was on the third storey at the top
of the house ; the bed occupied the middle of the
room, the only position in which the old four-poster
could stand upright. Against the wall near the
door hung a small amateurishly-made book-shelf
containing Wesley's notes, some volumes of the
Cambridge Bible for schools, Banks' " Theological
Handbook," and a few home-bound volumes of " The
Preacher's Magazine," whilst near to it, and almost
immediately under the skylight, was an old desk,
upon which were pens and pencils, a penny ink
bottle, an open Bible, and a copy-book. He put
the little benzine hand lamp upon the desk, and fell
heavily into a chair. He was tired, damp, and

harassed. A wan smile curved about his lips as he absently unbuttoned his coat and vest. How very like life this was! at least life as he had so far known it. Hitherto, every piece of good fortune he had had invariably proved the forerunner of some great trial, and here was another example of the same perverse fate. He had that day achieved one of the great ambitions of his strenuous young life, and it had already plunged him into complications. He rose mechanically and hung his wet coat upon the spike of the bed post, and then suddenly checked himself. No, he was slandering Providence! The blessing had been given graciously enough, and he had proved unworthy of it. He had allowed himself to be so carried away by his suddenly brightening prospects that he had, by a reckless act, placed himself in a very invidious position. Yes, it was his own doing. No wonder he had received so few Providential favours; he was not to be trusted with them, he used them to his own hurt. He had sat down again by this time, and with folded arms and chin on chest he began to review the adventures of the night. The first discovery he made added to his contrition; the old Adam in him was still revelling in that hasty kiss at the farmyard gate, and threw it up so vividly that he could think of nothing else. The slender little hand on the gate, the ripe lips, the dark, enslaving eyes seemed at that moment more real to him than they had done in the mad moment he was recalling. He had rushed away out of a sudden sense of his presumption and the resentment it might provoke, but now, strange as it seemed, all doubt on that point had left him, and he realised the amazing fact that, to Sallie at any rate, his conduct had not been distasteful. The thought filled his brain like an enslaving mesmerism; his blood tingled again and his eyes sparkled. For some time now he had felt that Sallie Wood was different to other girls in his eyes, but the insignificance and uncertainty of his future had kept him within the bounds of secret admiration, but now he realised that he was possessed by a great overmastering passion, and for the moment the consciousness was a delicious, intoxicating dream. But the very strength of his feeling alarmed him as he thought of it, and the difficulties at once began to present themselves. He took serious views of life, and marriage was to him the most solemn step that could be taken. He had never yet gone so far as to ask himself whether Sallie was suitable for him, and when he did so, the answer added to his perplexities. No man, he felt, ought to allow his passion to over-ride his judgment, but he had done so, and now he had more than one misgiving as to whether they were suited to each other. Sallie was light and gay, and, in fact, these, sad to say, were the characteristics that most attracted him in her, and she belonged to a family which had a reputation for over-keenness in commercial matters. John had his full share of that odd contempt for riches which so often characterises the hopelessly poor, and he imagined it had a spiritual origin. Sallie, he felt sure, would have earthly ideals, and would try to infuse into him her own low but practical ambitions. Then he recalled with another pang what Sam had said, and he could not disguise from himself that his own observations of her gave him too much reason to suspect that she was quite aware of her attractions, and somewhat unscrupulous in her use of them. But flirtation was utterly abhorrent to him, and he realised that their courtship, if it did proceed, would be a tantalising and uneasy experience. By this time he had worked himself into a state of restlessness, and was pacing the little room with uneven steps. His mother had entered the room below, and now called to him to get into bed, and so he put out the lamp and threw himself, half-dressed as he was, upon the bed, and once more surrendered himself to his tormenting perplexities. Poor Sam's agitated looks came back to him as he lay in the darkness; of course his passion was an utterly hopeless one; Sallie, he felt sure, would never think seriously in that direction, but the big man's pathetic warning alarmed him, and his own temperament and the deep, though narrow, theology he believed made it easy for him to blame himself for that compromising kiss; and he did so, muttering bitter self-reproaches as he tossed about upon the bed. He had played the fool; he, a local preacher, had allowed a sudden and altogether fleshly passion to overcome him, and stood committed to the consequences. He could not draw back, and—oh, awful situation!—he did not really wish to draw back. Self-sacrifice came easy by long practice to him, but now, when he fairly faced the question, his whole nature rose in rebellion. Again and again his deeper manhood grappled with the enemy, but each time they "clinched" it was thrown, and a sense of helplessness came upon him, and he had a cowardly, unregenerate longing to let go and drift.

The church clock at the end of the lane struck twelve, and he had to rise a few minutes after five, but he still lay tossing there, tortured with the consciousness that he had lost self-mastery, and—oh! terrible situation!—did not want to resume it. Then a new thought entered his mind, and he rolled off the bed, and was just dropping upon his knees when he drew himself up again. "What? ask God to deliver me! Why, it would be asking Him to condone sin! It is something I have done myself, and only I can undo it." Turning away, therefore, he began to pace the room, but remembering presently who was underneath he desisted, and upon fresh impulse sank upon his knees at his bedside. With bowed head and writhing body he poured out his whole soul to his Maker, stopped, and began again, paused once more, and then plunged into a long, impassioned supplication. Then he leaned further over the bed, and buried his face in the clothes, and was still. Presently he rose to his feet with set, stern face, and crept into bed. He had won, or thought he had won, one more battle. He had not slept much when he rose next morning, and as he walked to the mill, breakfast-can in hand, he was able to review his position. The hope and love born last night were to be resolutely crushed out. It was not absolutely necessary for people in their condition to explain or apologise for a kiss, and though he would greatly have liked to know what Sallie thought about his ridiculous running away, he must leave that and see her no more. He had acted without due thought, he had placed himself in rivalry with an old friend, and though he realised that the course he was taking was neither very lover-like nor very courageous, it was certainly safest. In the meantime he would watch and wait; he would study, as circumstances might allow, the character of the girl he now knew he loved, and would also ascertain what were Sam's chances, though he already guessed them. He did not see, as the reader will, that his resolution was not quite consistent with itself; he had a sort of instinctive feeling that the most painful course must necessarily be the right one—there was present safety in it at any rate—and he must be content with that.

All Saturday afternoon he was strangely uneasy in spite of his resolves. He wondered whether Sallie would call on Saturday evening as she sometimes did, and he spent his time, now trying to settle to his books, and now resolving to go to the band-meeting and thus avoid a possible *rencontre*. In the end he fetched downstairs a magazine and tried to interest himself in an article on "Open-air Preaching." The hours passed, however, meeting time came and went, but Sallie did not appear and he stole off to bed at last, out of love with himself for feeling so disappointed. On Sunday morning he had an appointment at a little mission-room on the outskirts of the town, and so missed the service at the chapel. He was early at school, however, and stole many a sly look across at the young women's class, but no Sallie appeared, and by this time anxiety was fast getting the better of caution, and he so far relaxed his original resolution as to decide to get a word with her that night if at all possible. The Woods sat three pews behind the Ledgers under the gallery of the chapel, and as, of course, he was too well-behaved to turn round, he found himself listening to the banging of pew doors and imagining the entry of Sallie and her father. Once or twice during the service he thought he caught the sound of her contralto voice in the singing, and whilst the sermon was being delivered he felt as though his sweetheart's black eyes were boring holes into his back. When the service was over he moved, whilst waiting for the commencement of the after-meeting, into the corner of the pew, and turned half round to get a hasty glance behind him, and lo! the Woods' pew was empty.

He felt he was going cold; something certainly must be the matter at Fidler's fold, and when the first two prayers were concluded, he took up his wide-awake hat and stole out of the chapel.

Twenty yards down the street he heard himself called in a husky panting voice, and turning round came face to face with old Zeph Wood, Sallie's father.

"Hold! Hold wi' thee! Art walking for a wager?" tried the old fellow, puffing hard, and pushing his Sunday hat back on his head as he came up.

Zeph was a short man, and thick-set, with arms and feet disproportionately long for his height; his eyes were as dark as Sallie's, but small and restless, whilst an overhanging nose and long drooping mouth to match gave an almost whining expression to his face. He was a leader, and had a somewhat numerous following among the more demonstrative of the members; but his record was stained by instances of over-shrewdness and trickery.

" This is a bonny mank," he cried, pulling up and staring hard at John, whilst he rubbed his perspiring face with a blue-spotted cotton handkerchief, " Dost know that yond wench is bad?"

" Bad!" cried John, with a sinking heart.

" Ay, bad! This is wot comes o' stannin' at t' fold gate with young fellows like thee!"

" I'm awfully sorry," began John confusedly, but Zeph broke in upon him again.

" Sorry! wot good'ull that do, if she's gotten her deeath o' cold? Stir thy pins an' cut off to Black Jacob's for some cumfrey herbs an' camomile, while I go and fetch Aunt Pizer. Hay, dear! young folk ne'er has no sense."

John was not in a state of mind to see this new incident in its true proportions; so, full of fear and self-reproach, he darted off to the herbalist's, which was a mile or so on the other side of the town. When he reached Fidler's fold Zeph and Aunt Pizer were already there, and Sallie, with her long dark hair hanging in wavy masses down her back, and a soft cream-coloured shawl on her shoulders, looked, John thought, lovelier than he had ever seen her. Mrs. Pizer took the herbs and soon had them bubbling in the pan and giving forth a pungent savour, whilst Zeph walked about the room, snapping and snarling at everything and everybody, in his muttered disgust of young people's thoughtlessness. John would have expressed his sorrow and retired, but Zeph drew him nearer the big chair in which Sallie was sitting, as though he wished him to realise the enormity of his transgression by beholding the condition of the sufferer. Sallie did not smile as he approached; she simply looked very solemnly at him, closed her eyes, and put on a suffering and resigned expression. John, consumed with sympathy and contrition, stood awkwardly, first on one leg and then on the other, and when Aunt Pizer asked for a mug, Sallie, without opening her eyes, told her father where he would find one, and when he had disappeared into the kitchen, and Aunt's back was turned as she inspected the boiling herbs, she slyly put out a moist little hand for John to take. In spite of all his resolutions he grasped it eagerly, and then discovered, with an embarrassing mixture of joy and alarm, that she did not want to withdraw it. Even when her father returned she still held it in his, and he felt his scrupulous prudence vanishing before the strong risings of pleasure and passion. He tried to say something sympathetic, and Sallie put her soft fingers between his and drew him nearer. Both Zeph and Aunt Pizer saw the position of things, and whilst Aunt turned her head away, with a sort of apologetic little cough, the father looked dreely for a moment at John, and then snorted out a half contemptuous grunt, as if to say that he thought the situation very ridiculous, but he supposed he must accept it. John went hot and cold; they were all, Sallie included, taking his supposed relationship to the invalid as a settled thing, and evidently regarded him as possessing the privileges of a lover; and with that soft little hand laid

so confidingly in his, it would be the meanest of all
mean things not to accept, at least for the moment,
his happy fate. What was that dull, heavy feeling,
which lay underneath all the keen pleasures of the
moment? Was not this a position he had long
desired, and had it not come to him almost without
an effort? and by that peculiar series of circumstances which he had always been taught to regard
as providential. Now that his highest ambition in
earthly things was suddenly and wonderfully realised,
why was he so suspicious and shy of it? Still holding that little hand, and allowing his greedy eyes
to wander over that mass of rippling hair and the
margin of white neck below it, his struggles of the
night before looked like the morbid imaginings of
an introspective ascetic; he was only frightened at
the ease and suddenness of his own success, and so
he gave the lissom fingers a gentle squeeze, and
began in nervous manner to recommend certain
simples much believed in by his mother. Then
Sallie withdrew her hand to put back a stray lock
that would droop over her brow, and as the clock
just then began to strike ten, John remembered
himself and prepared to make his departure. Sallie
did not move, but she opened her eyes and looked
at him as he drew nearer, and put out his hand for
leave-taking. She did not appear to see his action,
but turned up her face and raised two ravishing
lips to be kissed: and to crown all, as he was with-
drawing his burning face from hers, she whispered,
"Come again to-morrow night."

How he got out of the house and into the lane he
never knew; for the time all fear and doubt were
swallowed up in the glow of a great delight. What
a wonderful thing! Sallie had evidently secretly
loved him for many a day, and he had gone on
thinking about her without ever imagining that she

held him in any special regard. How confiding and innocent she was! As soon as she had seen what he meant she had accepted the situation without a trace of the finessing so common with young women. She understood him better than he understood himself, and knowing his serious ways, she had fallen quietly into his possession as soon as he had really shown his heart. What an open-minded, loving, beautiful girl she was, and oh! how happy he felt.

CHAPTER III

BRAMWELL was a small town of some six or seven thousand inhabitants, and had a somewhat curious appearance arising from the fact that whilst it was now almost entirely given up to cotton manufacture, it had formerly been a somewhat important market town and the centre of an agricultural district. The old market square, which was any shape but the one indicated by its name, was now almost at the extreme end of the town and contained a certain mysterious stone erection in the centre, about which local archæologists grew wrathful or enthusiastic, according as their descriptions were accepted or otherwise ; but which the up-to-date vandal vicar laughingly declared was the burying-place of such of the ancient Bramwellians as had perished in the time of the Great Plague.

The church, a low squat example of Tudor-Gothic, stood at the west end of the square and was covered with ivy that was black with layers of soot from the mill chimneys. Half-way down Lumley Road, which ran due west from the square, was the Wesleyan Chapel, an ugly brick building with a flagged yard in front and a disused burying-ground at the back. At the eastern end of the square was a small enclosed cattle market, and beyond that long rows of workmen's cottages running at right angles to Station Road, with three or four mills in the background, and the railway station, which old-time prejudice

had prevented coming near the town, still further
down the road.

Between the cattle market and the square, just
where the latter ran into Station Road, there stood a
row of dilapidated one-story buildings used by small
local tradesmen. The third and most dingy-looking
of the lot was evidently devoted to the business of
painting, and had over the door a drunken-looking
signboard, on which was written in sprawling old
church-type characters :—

SAMPSON LEDGER,

Gilder, Decorator and Artist's Colourman.

On the time-honoured principle that the cobbler's
children are always the worst shod, this building was
entirely devoid of paint, and when close inspection
revealed here and there slight traces of the presence
at some by-gone date of that excellent preservative, it
was utterly impossible to decide what had been the
colour originally used. As compensation, however,
the back of the shop door was bedaubed in all the
colours of the rainbow, and so thick were the layers
that the middle of the door must have been nearly
half-an-inch thicker than the other parts; for this
was the place where the proprietor dried his brushes.
The inside of the windows and the walls were covered
with dust of ancient date, and various implements
of the painter's craft, most of them appealing patheti-
cally for instant superannuation, were lying about
here and there in careless disorder. In the middle
of the floor stood a small stove perfectly innocent of
varnish, but splashed here and there with various
colours of paint. Near this stove was a round block,
at one time evidently part of the trunk of a tree, and
about twenty inches high, its polished top giving
ample evidence that it was usually used as a seat;

whilst against the wall were dirty-looking bags of painter's colours, old and useless stock ; across which was laid a whitewasher's plank, which thus formed a seat.   This resting place bore signs also of frequent occupation, for the painter's shop was the general rendezvous of the left or radical wing of the Bramwell Wesleyan Church.   The proprietor of the establishment was John Ledger's father, a rattling, graphic, anecdotal local preacher of the old school, whose gifts and shortcomings made him at once a fearful delight and an unhappy burden to his friends.

On the Monday morning after the events described in the last chapter, Sampson was standing at the bench-like table under the window absently grinding paint on a slab, for he had a supreme contempt for the "ready made trash they sold in tins," and adhered stubbornly to the ways of the good old times.   He was rather tall, with long greyish hair turned back without parting over his head, and hanging down with a slight outward curl behind. He had high cheek bones, a narrow, though lofty forehead, sharp grey eyes, a dogmatic chin, wide, loose mouth, and thin Dundreary whiskers.   His greasy, green-black coat of clerical cut was covered with a long apron that now, as usual, was twisted round under his left arm.   Behind him, seated on the bench near the stove, was a man who even in that position appeared to be a dwarf.   He had a full, corpulent body, a big, long head, short, ungainly legs, and a shrewd, almost intellectual face, of pugnacious expression.   He wore a thick showman-like silver watch-chain hanging over a waistcoat that had once been imitation sealskin, but which now only retained its nap in out-of-the-way places.   He was smoking a long clay pipe, and every now and again got off his seat and stepped close to the stove, where he had a full view of the little dingy broker's shop opposite, of which he was the proprietor. Wilky Drax, or Robert Wilkinson Drax as he signed himself, though he had been in the shop for fully ten minutes, had never spoken, as the ordinary courtesies of greeting were dispensed with between such old friends. Just now he has wriggled off the bench and is standing with his pipe stretched out and his back to the stove watching a stray customer who is scanning the contents of his shop window across the road. The stranger, however, moved on, and Wilky, as he waddled back to his seat, removed his pipe from his mouth and remarked in hard, crackling tones, as though he were resuming a conversation which momentary attention to business had interrupted—

"A second-hand shop, an' a secon'-hand church, an' a secon'-hand wold, and nowt doin' i' none on 'em! It's sickenin'!"

As this was a distinct challenge to discussion, and as controversy was meat and drink to the painter, he stopped his rubbing, and turning round and leaning his back against the edge of the slab, he demanded—

"Second-hand?"

"Second-hand!" and Wilky punctuated each syllable with a defiant nod. "Secon'-hand preaching, secon'-hand sermons, secon'-hand services, an' secon'-hand revivals!"

The momentary perplexity vanished from the painter's face, he pushed his open fingers through his hair, blinked his grey eyes, and answered in the pulpit phraseology he never dropped except under great excitement.

"Thou speakest as one of the foolish—a—a—men. Thou looks at the world through the smoked glass o' thy own worldly callin'. Thou'rt for the new, the cheap, the flimsy, bogus new. Thou'rt bitten wi' the vice o' the age, brother! No man having drunk old wine straightway desireth new, for he says the old is better."

"Old! Ay! Oldey an' mouldy!" and with eyes that glistened at his own unexpectedly brilliant alliteration Wilky continued: "New times, new men. New men, new methods! New methods, new Methodism, that's my motty! We nivver gets a new toot out of an old horn;" and gripping the stem of his pipe with his forefinger, he glared defiantly at Sampson and all the world besides.

"Wilky!" replied the painter, rubbing his hands on his apron and approaching the stove. "Thou rushes like the unthinkin' horse into battle! All the great things is old. The cheap things nivver gets old. Where's the old power? Where's the old times of refreshin'? Where's the sons of thunder now?"

"What about the super. then? He's old enough, surely to goodness! leastways his sermons is, they smell o' Wesley's saddlebags—regler green, mouldy second-handers."

"Speak not evil of dignitaries, brother! Honour them that's over us in the Lord. Isn't he a managing man? Doesn't he abide by the stuff? He's a horganizer, he is! What we want i' these times is horganization."

But Wilky could listen no longer to "Bosh" like this; thrusting out his chest and jerking the words forth like bullets from a pistol, he cried—

"That's it! That's it! We axes bread an' you gives us a stone! We wants power an' you gives us machinery! We calls for life an' you gives us a corp! Can you organise life into a corp? Can you horganize the Sperit? We shall hear as Pentecost was horganized next."

"Methodism declines, sir, because the Newtons an' Punshons is gone," cried Sampson, now thoroughly roused. "There are no men to lift up axes on the big trees; there are no giants in the land in these days! What we want is more Boanergeses an' not misnancified striplings wi' little sermonettes! Our fathers, where are they? An' the prophets, do they live for ever?"

"Ay, an' if young men would do, we canna get 'em," chimed in a strange voice; and as the debaters turned they were joined by old Zeph Wood with a newspaper in his hand. "Summat's wrong, somewhere. We want young men an' they don't come forrad. Listen to what t' *Times* says."

"T' *Times*," snorted Sampson, throwing back his head in contempt, for the mention of that publication was like shaking a red rag at a bull. As there was not much light, and Zeph's eyes were not as good as they had been, he stepped to the door and commenced reading a paragraph which expressed a fear that the supply of candidates at the approaching March quarterly meetings would not be equal to the needs of the Church, and calling upon young men of talent and education to resist the temptations of mercantile success and consecrate themselves to the service of their fellows.

"Just so; just so!" said Sampson reluctantly, for this once only acknowledging the wisdom of what he had heard. "T' old preachers is dyin' off an' t' young uns can't do nothin', an'—an' we can't get 'em if they could."

"T' chat!" rapped out Wilky, overlooking the inconsistency of Sampson's remark. "We've brains enough i' Methodism to manage a—a—t' universe! They can have five hundred candidates if they'll open their mouths."

"Ay! we could find 'em one or two i' this circuit if they were fast," and old Zeph nodded significantly at Wilky, but avoided the eye of the painter.

"This circuit! why we haven't even a decent local-a-a a—'mong t' young uns," he added, as a cover for himself and Wilky.

" Hav'n't we? We 'ave that. We've one or two as 'ud make rippin' ministers," spurted out the broker.

Sampson looked very doubtful whether " rippin' " was a proper term to apply to the cloth, but his curiosity was stronger than his taste, and so he asked cautiously, " Well, who are they ? "

And Zeph with a glance at the diminutive furniture dealer for support, turned his face to the painter and said boldly, " Well, your Johnny for one."

To say that Ledger was taken aback by this suggestion is an utterly inadequate way of describing his appearance. He gasped, opened his mouth, threw back his hair, and then after a long stare at Zeph, shook his head; but all these signs did not conceal from his friends the look of eager pride that rose into his eyes and puckered his face into a sort of painful smile.

" Whist ! brethren, whist ! Don't trifle with a subject like this ! Our John's a good lad, but *that*— why it would be rank presumption." All the same he glanced inquiringly at Wilky to see how he was taking the idea.

John had none of the ready volubility and demonstrativeness of his father, and was made in an altogether different mould, and Wilky had declared again and again in that shop that he would never be the man his father had been.

" No, friends," Sampson went on. " He's my own lad, an' as good as goold, but he hasn't the gifts, though I say it myself—he hasn't the proper gifts."

But this was the opportunity for which the contradictious little broker had been waiting.

" No," he jerked out, " he hasn't the gifts, as you call 'em, an' thank the Lord he hasn't."

Both his companions turned upon him with astonishment, and rising to his feet and glaring at them defiantly whilst he drew himself up to the utmost of his four feet something he repeated—

"Thank God, I say, he hasn't! We don't want the windy washy blethering tub-thumping of the 'good old times.' We want hideas, we want thoughts, we want arguments an' brains, that's what we want, an' that lad shall be brought forrad at t' Quarterly meeting or I'll know the reason why."

As both the friends looked the little man over curiously, he hitched himself up upon the stump seat and began dangling his little legs against the sides.

"I suppose it rests wi' the super., after all?" said Zeph, feeling his way to something definite.

"The super. must move first, an' we must move the super.," cried Wilky oracularly, and then dropping suddenly into a loud whisper he added, "an' by George here he comes!"

The painter's shop was an institution in Bramwell; the new ministers as they arrived began by suspecting and disliking it, then they came to tolerate and fear it, and generally ended by accepting and making the best of it. It was a sort of left wrist of the body ecclesiastical, where the pulse of the circuit might be felt. It was also the best place to procure or at least to hear of supplies for vacant pulpits, and its proximity to the cattle market made it a convenient place for the leaving of parcels of circuit plans, magazines, and messages for country officials. Superintendents, therefore, made use of it somewhat frequently, and all the more willingly, perhaps, because they could always pick up there the latest circuit gossip and the first mutterings of ecclesiastical thunderstorms, with the comfortable knowledge that the trouble, when it did come, would certainly not be worse than it had been represented at the paint shop.

"Morning, brethren! Still cold, isn't it?" and the super., a florid, well-groomed man of fifty-five or so, strolled into the shop and made his way towards the stove. Wilky immediately slipped down from the stump and retreated to the bench, whilst the painter carefully dusted the top of the seat and obsequiously invited the super to accept the stool of honour. Mr. Haley protested against dethroning Wilky, but as everybody insisted that he must occupy it, he sat down, and leaning his arms on the top of his stick turned his face towards the door as everybody else did, so that they could sit and talk and still watch the street and the passers-by going to the station.

"Well, Methodism's comin' to somethin' now, Mestur Super.," said Zeph, who seemed strangely interested for him in the question of the supply of the ministry.

The super. knew his men too well to be easily drawn, and so he enquired in his easiest manner—

"Why, what is the matter now, Mr. Wood?"

Zeph, who had dropped upon the bench alongside Wilky, gave his companion a sly nudge to invite his assistance, but the little broker was thinking hard, and earnestly watching the minister, and so did not feel the jog.

"Hav'n't you seen that piece in the *Times*? It seems we cannot get no ministers."

The super. laughed.

"Ho! ho! that's a new idea! I think I've heard brother Drax say we have too many already 'of the sort.'"

As both his friends knew that this was one of Wilky's favourite positions, but that it would not exactly fit in with their present designs, they looked to see how he was taking the home-thrust; but he simply stared steadily before him, blinked his eyes rapidly and puffed away stolidly at his pipe, which had long since gone out.

"Still if there *is* a scarcity, sir," began Zeph——

"Tut! tut! no such thing. We want quality, not quantity, eh, brother Drax?"

Wilky puffed away at the useless pipe more stolidly than ever.

"It's a great while sin' we sent onybody out fro' this circuit," said the painter in a cautious, tentative way.

"They canna' send thersel's out—they've to be brought out," said Zeph, who had, evidently, difficulty in restraining himself.

"Steady, brethren! Don't let that paper alarm you! There's nothing worse than getting up a scare and dragging in all and sundry; we've suffered from that before."

Wilky's tight mouth emitted an indescribable sort of snort, and Zeph looked apprehensively round at him, fearing he was going to say something personal to the dignitary present, and the painter turned and stared glumly through the dirty window.

"There were one went out o' this circuit every year as Mr. Pyewell were super.—but that's a deal o' years sin' now," persisted Zeph.

"But you can't bring them out if you hav'n't got them, brother Wood; we cannot *make* preachers, you know," replied the super., who began to suspect there was something behind old Zeph's most unusual persistence.

"No! an' when God makes 'em and sticks 'em under our stupid noses we cannot see 'em," and having shot out, bullet-like, this unexpected fling, Wilky threw one of his diminutive legs on the bench and lolled back with the air of a man who has, at last, said his say.

The super. began to rise from his stump seat; these men were evidently after something, but he was not going to be dragged into a ridiculous position just to please them, and so he thought of beating a retreat.

"Well," he laughed, conciliatorily, "if some of you

brethren had been younger something might have been done, but——"

"Instead of the fathers shall come up the children," rapped out Wilky sententiously, and the super., who was already on the move, turned round in puzzled surprise and looked from one to the other of the companions.

"The children! But none—ah! oh! do you mean young John Ledger?"

Nobody answered, and the minister, to whom the idea thus unexpectedly presented appeared perfectly absurd, moved a little nearer the door. It was the last thing he would ever have thought of, but whether to get away before he was cornered or say something that would nip the notion in the bud at once he could not quite decide.

"The standard is so very much higher than it used to be, you see, and it rises every year," he said dubiously at last.

"What standard?" demanded Wilky with a snap.

"The standard of education and general culture, you know."

Wilky was evidently expecting this answer and waiting for it. Everybody anticipated an explosion, but to their surprise he seemed to change his mind all at once, and staring hard at a pile of wall papers on the other side of the shop he said, in slow musing tones—

"Ay! t' Almighty makes some terrible blunders sometimes."

Every man present uttered a shocked ejaculation, but Wilky had evidently not finished. Giving himself a little twist, as though to assist the processes of thought, he went on in mock apologetics—

"But I reacon *He* isn't heddicated neither."

They were all used to extravagant things from Wilky, but this seemed to border on the blasphemous, and the super. was just about to rebuke him when he went on in the same pitying apologetic tones—

"You see he hadn't Conference to keep him right i' them times."

"Drax! whatever are you driving at? What times?"

"T' Bible times. You see, we have no account o' t' prophet Elisha's examination marks, an' we don't know as t' apostles even preached trial sermons."

The minister laughed, with a curious mixture of amusement and irritation.

"Well! well! but you see we must have educated men, when all's said and done."

"Sartainly! an' t' Almighty were wrong when he called Elisha, the ploughman, and Peter, the fisherman, and Bunyan, the tinker, and Peter Mackenzie, the collier. Why didn't he consult t' Conference?"

The super. began to feel that he was demeaning himself by arguing with men holding ideas like these, and he threw up his head and started to leave.

But just before he reached the door the painter, who was still staring hard through the window, asked without turning his head—

"What's t' Hinstitutions for, Mr. Super.?"

"Yes! oh yes!" cried the super., turning round again a little irritably, "We can give them education if they have got decided gifts. Has young John got gifts, that's the question, and does he feel called to the work?" and he glanced enquiringly towards the painter.

Sampson waved his hand grandiloquently.

"Respecting gifts, I'm his father, he is of age; ask him, he shall speak for himself."

Mr. Haley stood in the doorway meditating.

"Well," he said at length, "I certainly never thought of such a thing myself, but I'll think about it and make a few enquiries and see, and in the meantime let nobody say a word to the young fellow

himself," and with a cautionary nod and a curt
" Good morning," he disappeared.

Before he had got many yards away from the shop
Zeph rushed at the painter, and smiting him heavily
on the back he cried—

" It's done, lad! it's done! Yond fellow always
puts the worst side out."

But Sampson was now on his dignity; the idea
they had been discussing had never entered his head,
but it was already realized to his sanguine mind, and
imparted to his manner some of the dignity which he
imagined became the father of a minister. Then
another idea possessed him; parents who had sons
in the ministry were always supposed to have made
some great sacrifice in giving up their beloved ones
to the service of the Church, and so, whilst his
companions were discussing the situation, he was
conjuring up suitable emotions, and when Zeph
turned round to congratulate him he was met with a
look of martyr-like resignation, and Sampson, with
a doleful face, shook his head, and heaving a
prodigious sigh groaned out—

" It'll be an awful wrench."

Wilky gave a snort of disgust, whilst Zeph
demanded in amazement—

" What 'ull be a wrench?"

Sampson shook his head again, gave his long nose
a hasty upward wipe, drew in his lips with sorrowful
but relentless resolution, and then, disregarding the
question just asked, he snivelled—

" But I'll take up my cross! I'll take up my cross!
Lord help me!"

And Wilky, the uncompromising hater of all
humbug, stuck one of his little legs upon the stove
and snarled out contemptuously—

" Ay! take it hup, lad; it 'ull be a change for
thee, anyway."

CHAPTER IV

IN WHICH THE SUPERINTENDENT SURPRISES AND IS SURPRISED

THE Reverend William Haley was a strong man, and not the least likely to be unduly influenced by the things he had seen and heard at the paint shop. He held strong views, also, on the absolute necessity of an educated ministry. But he was a Methodist, and shared to the full the democratic belief that God was as likely to call a plough-boy to the ministry as a University graduate. He knew, also, that some of the strongest men in the brotherhood were of the lowliest origin. But he held, also, that obscure youths must give evidence of the possession of unusual gifts, and that if they had such endowments they would evidence them by surmounting, by some means or other, mere educational difficulties. But young John Ledger had not attracted his attention in any way whatever, and he could not remember to have heard a single thing about him indicative of special talent. There was no man on the plan, in fact, of whom he had heard less, and the only things he could recall at all were remarks made by country hearers that John was not the least bit like his father ; and as the older man was notoriously popular, and the remarks were somewhat regretfully made, he was forced to the conclusion that John was a very ordinary young fellow. Well, he was not going to be forced into bringing forward an unsuitable candidate, either by

impetuous "locals" like the little broker, or anybody
else; but as it was Monday morning, which he
generally spent in working off little odds and ends of
business, he would see what other people thought
about the suggestion and act accordingly. Bulwood,
the senior steward, "did not even know the young
fellow by sight," and Raskelf, the ex-steward and a
Conference man, said "John was a pious, well-
meaning young fellow, who had got further than he
ever expected him to do when he was promoted to
'full plan.'" Then the super. remembered that John
had never preached at the circuit chapel, and that,
therefore, it was unfair to him to consult those
who had never heard him. Consequently, he next
applied to Parbold, the saddler, a strong, sensible
local preacher, who, by reason of his business con-
nections with the Methodists of the country places,
and his keen interest in young men, would be able
to tell him all he wanted to know.

Parbold had great respect for John, but he could
say nothing very encouraging about his preaching.
It wanted more of his father's "go" and sparkle.
For the first time during these enquiries, the super.
ventured to hint at his reason for making them, and
Parbold shook his head very decidedly, and said that
he should very much like to see a young man "go
out" from the Bramwell circuit, but mentioned the
names of two or three others, who were, in his judgment, more likely than John. The super. was inclined
to regard this as decisive, but just as he was crossing
the market-place on his way back to the paint shop,
he ran across his colleague, who was in his third
year, and therefore knew more of such matters than
he could possibly do himself, as he was only about
half-way through his first year. The Rev. T. Burcliffe
was warm in John's praises, and described him as a
studious, painstaking young fellow, who made up for

the lack of showy gifts by assiduous application; but when the object of the super.'s enquiries was named to him, he hesitated, and ventured the opinion that such a thing had never entered the Minder's head. Well, then, if John had never thought of it, and the people who would have to vote on the subject had never thought of it, what was the use of the super. bothering his head about the notions of such irresponsible and scatterbrain fellows as the frequenters of the paint shop. Besides, he was in his first year, and did not know enough to justify his undertaking so serious a task as that of piloting a candidate through the examinations and tests required. Of course, he could get John to preach for him some week-night in the circuit chapel; but why should he give himself the trouble about so very dubious a case? No! he would not absolutely shelve the question, but he could at any rate defer it for a year.

But that same afternoon, whilst doing a little pastoral work, he received two spontaneous testimonies about a sermon young Ledger had preached recently at the mission-room, both accounts being given in a manner which showed that the speakers had no idea whatever of the suggestions which had, that morning, been made to him. He was the last man in the world to be superstitious about coincidences, but certainly he thought this a little remarkable; and when, after the Monday night prayer meeting, Nash, the fishmonger, as they walked home together, unconsciously revealed to the minister the genesis of the whole project, he was more impressed than ever. It appeared that the week previous, Nash, old Zeph Wood, and two or three others, had been conversing together at Nash's stall in the market, when some one alluded to the very sermon the minister had heard of twice before that day; and old Job White, a shrewd but cautious and fastidious sermon critic, had predicted that John Ledger would go into the ministry, "where his father ought to have been before him."

This, then, was the origin of the whole thing, and old Zeph Wood had evidently taken it up and introduced it at the paint shop. The super. was perplexed. Coming from such sources the suggestion certainly need not be taken too seriously, and he still saw no reason for proceeding further at present. But, on the other hand, he did not want to stand in any man's way, neither did he care unnecessarily to provoke the opposition of the paint shop, of whose fighting qualities he had heard so much. Then another idea occurred to him; he would send for John himself, and sound him, and if what his colleague had said was true, he would either stop the thing himself or give some more substantial reason for proceeding. He was a cautious man, and so dallied until Thursday before he made up his mind, but on that day he sent a note to Shed Lane, asking John to call upon him on the following evening.

Meanwhile, in blissful unconsciousness of what was preparing for him, John was prosecuting his courtship with delightful success. Sallie, with a charming air of spoilt-childishness allowable always in invalids, had quietly taken possession of him, and assumed towards him the rights of a fiancé, and the bewitched minder, regarding this as a gentle womanly consideration for his shyness, added intense gratitude to all his other emotions, and was in the seventh heaven of lover-like bliss.

But it was time he told his mother about it. He and she had no secrets from each other, and though it was not deemed strictly necessary for people in their position of life to observe the formalities required in other circles, he wanted to talk to somebody about his happiness, and he knew perfectly well that his mother would be suspecting something, and would be wondering why he did not speak. He got back from the farm a little earlier than usual on Thursday night, and found his father still out, and the rest in bed. Now was his opportunity.

Mrs. Ledger was one of those meek, silent women, to whom words seemed fearful things, to be used sparingly, and so whilst John absently consumed his supper, she moved softly about the house preparing the breakfast he would take with him to the mill next morning.

"Sallie's a lot better, mother; she'll be out by the week-end."

Mrs. Ledger was seeking something in the little side-cupboard near the window, and seemed to have difficulty in finding it; but John, if he could have seen the quiet face, would have been alarmed at the cloud which suddenly spread over it. She did not speak, however, and John, occupied with his own happy thoughts, and looking smilingly sideways into the fire, went on with a glad little laugh—

"Hey! I thought she would have been hard to catch, but she wasn't."

Mother had found what she wanted in the cupboard, and, returning to the table, commenced sprinkling salt upon the little cold meat sandwich she was preparing. In anybody else the silence would have been noticeable, but John was used to her speechless ways.

"I've thought of her for a long time, but I couldn't pluck up. I can hardly believe it yet; it is so sudden."

He glanced up at her face as he said this, but she turned her head away; and just when he had concluded that she was not going to reply, she bowed her head over the little bundle of victuals, and said in low tones—

"Ay, lad, *too* suddin."

" Mother ! "

" An' too easy, too."

" Mother ! "

He was looking at her with amazed and distressful looks. He had always been so sure of her, and as he stared she put out her hand as though warding off some attack, and went on protestingly—

" I dunna' like it! I canna' help it, John, but I dunna' like it ! "

" Why, mother, I thought you liked Sallie !   You never said anything ! "

But she only dropped into her own iron-rockered chair with a weary, perplexed shake of the head.

" I dunna' like it ! "

" But I've thought about her a long time. Couldn't you see that ? "

" Ay, an' so could she."

John sprang to his feet in utter distraction.

" But, mother ! I couldn't ask her till I'd got my wheels ! "

And the agitated woman looked long and dreely into the fire, and then, turning her eyes full upon him so that he was compelled to meet them, she asked—

" *Did* you ask her, lad ? "

" Yes, mother ! That is—I mean—I did what was the same thing. But whatever does all this mean ? What's got into your head, mother ? "

But the slow-speaking woman had resumed her musing contemplation of the fire, and presently she gave herself a sudden shake and rose to her feet.

" God forgi' me ! " she cried. " I believe I'm jealous o' t' lass. Heaven bless you both, lad ! " and then her eyes filled with tears. " I'se be number two now, I reacon ! " And as John was opening his mouth to protest, a light broke through the tears, and she went on in tremulous tones—" But I'd rather be number two wi' thee than number one wi' anybody else."

It was perfectly clear to John that this sudden turn of topic was intended to be a shelving of the matter for the present, and though it did not in the least accord with his own views, he knew it was no use trying just now to get anything further out of his mother; however tantalising to himself and unjust to Sallie, he must wait. He hastened to bed, therefore, and spent weary hours in trying to fathom the mystery of her opposition. That it was not mere jealousy he knew well enough; but what there was lying behind his mother's words he could not for the life of him divine. It occupied his thoughts all next day, and was only temporarily displaced by curiosity when, on his return home in the evening, his mother handed to him the super.'s note. It was a brief request that he would call some time that evening at the Manse, and his first surmise was that it meant a request to take somebody else's appointment on the approaching Sabbath. A few minutes before eight, washed, and dressed in his Sunday best—for a visit to the Manse was a ceremonious occasion—he presented himself at the minister's residence, and was ushered into the study.

"Oh! come in, Mr. John. Glad to see you!"

"You want to see me, sir."

"Yes! I want to have a bit of talk to you. Sit down, and draw near the fire." And the minister fell upon an obdurate piece of coal in the grate, and having satisfactorily demolished it, still retained the poker in his hand, and twirling it rapidly round, he asked—"How do you get on with your preaching, Mr. John?"

John's heart sank. The super. had heard complaints, and was going to lecture him.

"Not very well, sir, I'm afraid."

The super., still toying with the little poker, eyed him over hesitantly; the youth was either very modest or very sly.

" Do you enjoy preaching ? Now, don't be afraid. I've a reason for asking."

" Reason enough," thought John. Well, if he *was* going to be invited to give up preaching, it would, on the whole, be a relief.

"I can't say that I do, sir—not yet," and he seemed to sink back further and further into the arm-chair on which he sat so stiffly as though he would like to have disappeared altogether.

The super. eyed him over sideway, and could not help thinking what sallow weedy youths these factory lads were.

" H'm. Ah—what educational advantages have you had ? Only the Board school, I suppose ? "

" That's all, sir, and a few evening classes." And John felt rather glad to have this chance of saying so. It would be some sort of excuse for his poor preaching.

" Evening classes ? What subjects did you take ? "

" Mechanical and technical."

" Oh ! to help you in your work, I suppose ? "

" Yes, sir."

Mr. Haley was puzzled. This young fellow was ingenuosity itself ; there seemed no presumptuous ambition here. But John was thinking too. The super. evidently had something unpleasant to say, but was too kind-hearted to say it. Well, he would help him, and get it over at once.

" I'm sorry I don't do better in preaching, sir ; but I'll give it up willingly if you think it would be better."

The super. knit his brow and looked at John as though he would have read his soul. Was this fellow what he seemed, or was he only an unusually sly dog. The scowling gaze embarrassed John, and he moved his eyes about nervously. Oh, why didn't he get it over?

"Then you really don't enjoy preaching?"

"No, sir, I don't; and a—a—I think I'd better give in my plan at once," and the disheartened fellow began fumbling in his pocket.

"Wait a moment. Have you ever thought of becoming a candidate for the ministry?" And as he asked the question the minister shot at his visitor a keen glance, and put the poker carefully in its place.

The glance told him all he wanted to know. Yes, he had hit the bull's eye at last, and surprised his secret out of him. John's eyes, which had for the moment opened with amazement, all at once became dim. He felt that his sallow face was burning, and all at once he fell forward, and burying his face in his hands, uttered a smothered sob.

The super. pulled himself together. Yes, he had this ambitious lad's deepest secret—that tell-tale look was eloquent of much. Well, he must put him right and make him understand what this wild dream of his meant.

"Well, John! you don't answer me?"

There was a momentary silence, and then the young local preacher rose to his feet, his face white and stern, his lips quivering, and his eyes blazing.

"There's my plan," he cried, in choking tones; "and the next time you want a young fellow to resign, please remember that even factory lads have feelings, and do your work less cruelly."

"Cruel, sir?"

"Yes, cruel! cruel in anybody. But doubly cruel in you—God forgive me for speaking to my minister like this."

The super. was dumbfounded.

"John, whatever have you got in your head? What *do* you mean?"

" I mean this, sir. You seem to think that because I'm poor and ignorant I'm not capable of the desire to do Christ's work for Christ's sake, but must of necessity be casting my eyes on the holy office you hold. It's cruel, sir! it's unchristian!"

The minister stepped over the hearthrug and drew John back into his chair.

" My dear fellow," he said, huskily, " sit down. I'm afraid we have been talking at cross purposes. Now, the fact is, I've heard some excellent things lately about your preaching, and the other day it was suggested to me that you might make a minister, and I've sent for you here to-night to talk about it."

John listened to his pastor with suspicious, incredulous eyes.

" Then you hav'n't any fault to find with me, sir?"

" Fault? not at all! Who put that notion into your head? Look here "—and the minister felt that he was making a plunge now, but had grown a little reckless from what he had seen and heard—" if you feel inclined to offer yourself for the ministry, I'll bring you forward."

" Oh, sir!" and John showed such signs of returning distress that the minister hastened to pacify him.

" Well, well, you are taken unawares! Go home and think about it, and come and see me again."

" Sir!" cried John, vehemently. " As God is my witness, I have never thought of such a thing. It's preposterous! I'm a factory lad, sir."

The minister paused and reflected.

" Well, but, now that it has been suggested to you, the call of the——"

" Don't, sir! Don't! I cannot! I will not hear of it. It would be sinful presumption; it would be the sin of Korah."

" Oh, take a little time "—the minister was amazed to find himself actually pressing this factory lad, but he was not quite responsible for himself just then—" Take a little time, and see me again."

John rose to his feet, and modestly put out his hand.

" No, sir! it was hard to believe you at first, and it gets harder as I think of it. I'll try and do my duty in the position in which God has placed me, but I hope neither you nor anyone else will ever mock me by suggesting it again."

These were daring, almost rude, words, but when his visitor had gone, the super. still stood on the hearthrug, musing on the strange interview which had just closed.

" But I *shall* think of it, my young friend, and watch you too, and if your head turns out to be as good as your heart, it shall go hard with William Haley if he does not make a minister of you after all."

And next day every Methodist almost in Bramwell heard the amazing intelligence that John Ledger, the factory lad, had had a chance of going into the ministry, and had refused.

CHAPTER V

JOHN FINDS THERE ARE MORE WAYS OF LOOKING AT A THING THAN ONE

WHEN John left the minister's house that night he was still smarting under a sense of humiliation; the super's words had touched him upon one of his tenderest points. Lancashire people have an idiosyncrasy which seems to a stranger a contradiction. They are free-spoken, self-reliant, and independent in the extreme, and insist tenaciously that " Jack is as good as his master," and yet amongst themselves they have an intense, almost morbid, horror of anything approaching to pretentiousness, any attempt to appear other than they are being keenly resented upon the offenders. And John was thoroughly Lancashire, and took a pride in knowing his place and keeping it. He had listened again and again to conversations between young fellow-preachers, and had detected their ill-concealed aspirations to the ministerial office with surprise and contempt; and here the very first time he gets a peep into the mind of his ecclesiastical chief, he makes the humiliating discovery that he is supposed to entertain these ignorant and vulgar ambitions himself. Of course he was greatly exaggerating the thing; he was morbidly sensitive, and possessed quite his share of that poor person's pride which is as real and unreasonable as the kind he so fiercely hated in others. He paused when he got a few yards from the Manse, and looked absently up at the murky, moonless sky. The minister's proposal had been seriously made, that was clear, but that only meant that people had been talking, and had in their minds credited him with the wicked ambition he so much despised. Oh! why couldn't people let him alone! If he had done anything remarkable, or had made any uncommon impression as a preacher, there might have been some justification for the proposal, but to make it to *him*, the feeblest of the feeble, was only to show how ingrained was the belief that all his work had been done from more or less ulterior motives. Thinking thus, he began to move homewards, and as he did so, he recalled the minister's encouraging reports of his preaching, and whilst it made him resolve to work harder than ever, it galled him to think how he was being misunderstood. The fact was he had suffered so long from overwork and insufficient food and premature earthly anxieties that he had little of the buoyancy of his age, and was most painfully prone to pensive and self-depreciatory views of things. It was too late by this time to think of visiting Sallie that night, but the thought of her brought comfort to his mind; she at any rate would understand him, and so he turned in home and got to bed. Next day, as he mused over the transactions of the previous evening, he saw more and more reason to justify the course he had taken, and came as near to self-complacency as he ever allowed himself to get. Alas! poor fellow, he had little idea of what was in store for him.

As he sat over his dinner, and was just about to tell his mother of his interview with the super., he caught sight of his father, with long hair, coat-tails, and whiskers, all flying behind, darting past the window, and a moment later the painter burst into the house, and standing with his hand on the door, he cried, "Thou mun come, lad! Pickles will be here at five o'clock for yond window-sashes. Come an' help me to glaze 'em!" and without waiting for any reply, he banged the door and was off again.

John sighed, and glanced at his mother, whose face wore an apologetic deprecating expression. It was a very common thing for this erratic inconsiderate parent of his to do, and John had grown accustomed to having his one weekly half-holiday thus filched away from him, but to-day he was unusually disappointed, for he had been hoping to spend the whole time with Sallie. He ate on, however, in silence, glancing every now and then at his mother, whose manner seemed extremely restrained, even for her. She had evidently not forgotten their conversation of the night before, and it struck John that with her well-known pride in her only son she would be glad to hear what the minister had suggested.

"Do you know what the minister wanted me for last night, mother?"

And to his surprise her face fell, the light faded out of her eyes, and looking unsteadily out of the window, she uttered a single muffled monosyllable, "Ay!"

John had sudden misgivings, but choking them back, and trying to speak as easily as he could, he went on—

"Did you ever hear of such a thing!"

Mrs. Ledger dropped heavily into a chair on the other side of the table, and picking up her apron began to pull nervously at the edges, but not a word did she speak.

"It's a bit encouraging after all, isn't it?"

And then the troubled mother dropped her elbow on the table, and shading her eyes with her hand, faltered out—

"It's broken my life-long dream."

" Mother ! "

" I've telled the Lord for twenty year He could put what He liked on me, if nobbut—if nobbut——"

" If only what, mother ? "

" If nobbut I could see my lad a minister."

John had been his mother's chief confidant as long as he could remember anything, but though she had always eagerly encouraged all his inclination towards religion, and broken the silence of a lifetime by crying out in tearful ecstasy when he went to the penitent form, she had never given him the slightest idea of the thought she had just expressed. It was highly characteristic, however, and he understood that she would have regarded any hints of hers as interferences with the Divine will. All the same the discovery greatly distressed him, and all the more so as he realised how small hope there was of it ever being fulfilled. There was a painful pause whilst he struggled with these thoughts, and then he cried in blank dismay—

"But, mother! I'm ignorant, and unqualified, and—and—and we're poor ! "

" That's it ! that's it ! " she cried, setting her teeth and clenching her hands in a passion of resentful grief. " T' ministers talks about poverty being a refiner. Oh, if they'd had it stoppin' their way an' spoilin' their plans an' freezin' their love and wreckin' their lives as I have, they wouldn't talk like that ! "

John listened with something approaching to horror to this distressing outburst. He was burning with desire to comfort ; the words would not come, and so he slipped his hand across the table and began to timidly stroke the back of his mother's. She seemed to feel it, and a sort of shiver went through her frame, and suddenly snatching at the hand that touched hers she leaned forward, and with hot pain-drawn face, she asked—

" Thou said ' No,' because thou knew we couldn't
do without thy wages ? "

" No! mother. No! it was because I knew I
wasn't fit. I hav'n't the gifts, you know."

Mother lifted her head with an irritated, impatient
gesture, evidently resenting this constant harping on
his lack of qualifications. She did not speak, however, but hung down her head, and sat looking
sorrowfully at her apron. Then she rocked herself
gently, and clearing her throat with an effort, she
moaned—

" I was feared as when t' time came I shouldn't
be counted worthy—Well! His will be done."

And John, with a bursting sob, jumped up and
put his arms around her, and stroked her face and
crooned over her, and poured into her ears words
such as impassioned swain never uttered to fair
woman, and she leaned her head against the back of
her chair, and sighed, and smiled, and then shyly
kissed his oily hand, and when on sudden remembrance of his father's summons he hastened away,
she still sat musing and softly crying, and at last she
murmured—

" Forgive me, Lord. There's nowt i' all heaven
Thou could gi' me after Thou'd gi'en me him—a—
a—nobbut Thyself."

It took John all his time to recover his composure
on his way to the paint shop, and his effort was not
made easier when on his arrival he discovered that
the summons had been more or less of a pretence ;
for the work was already nearly finished, and he
guessed at once that he had been called in order to
be " carpeted " by the authorities about his refusal
to become a candidate for the ministry. He spoke
to his father on entering, but was received with
portentous silence, the painter, with a painfully
elongated face, looking at him fixedly for a moment,

and then turning to his work again with a dismal groan.

Sam Kepple sat upon the side bench, unable to conceal how deeply the prospect opening before his rival was affecting him. If John entered the ministry he would, in Sam's view, cease to be a competitor for Sallie's hand.

Wilky had relinquished his usual long clay for a short briar, and as it was Saturday afternoon, he hovered about the doorway, keeping a reluctant eye upon the sundry articles of furniture displayed on the pavement outside his place of business.

Sampson sighed again, and gave his long queer head a melancholy shake, and Wilky emitted a scornful snort and waddled to the door.

John had already possessed himself of putty and a pane of glass, and had stooped down upon his toes whilst he inserted the glass, when his father groaned again, and muttered, as he ruefully shook his head, " I have nourished and brought up children "—but apparently his feelings were too deep for words, so he left the quotation unfinished, and merely wagged his head in weary despair.

Wilky was evidently swelling with suppressed indignation.

" *Thou* nourished ! *thou* brought up ! " he rapped out, and then he broke off with a smothered exclamation of impatience, and hastening to the kerbstone, he shouted across the street to a man examining a second-hand perambulator of antique but sturdy make, " Six shillin', wo'th more nor that for old iron." And then he wheeled round, and standing sideways in the doorway, prepared to keep up a double-barrelled conversation, one in shouts across the street, and the other in rasping snarls in the shop.

The little broker's ideas of business were somewhat

peculiar. He was so uncompromisingly honest that townspeople would gladly have done more business with him than they did, but as the cardinal principle guiding his professional conduct was that business was an advanced form of philanthropy conducted by himself and his fellow-tradesmen for the public good, and out of pity for the ignorance and helplessness of the average purchaser, he thought he had gone far enough in the way of concession when he had provided articles they might need, and not only saw no necessity for those little courtesies commonly practised by the seller towards the buyer, but regarded them as weak and cowardly panderings to depraved tastes, and certain indications of ultimate fraudulent intentions.

The painter was thrusting putty into a square, groaning and shaking his head in a manner that excited most savage feelings in the mind of Wilky, who was watching him resentfully. Presently Sampson drew down the corners of his mouth, gave a twist and a sniff to his nose, and glancing sorrowfully over John's head, he remarked solemnly—

" And Jonah fled to Tarshish."

" Tarshish ! " Wilky fired off. " Ay, an' it's a pity we hev no Tarshish now. I'd pay t' passage o' some o' t' modern prophets if we could nobbut get rid on 'em. First-class cabin fa——" and then he broke off, and rushing to the kerbstone, he bawled out, " Ay, American cloth ! common American cloth ! an' flocks ! Thou ought to hev live horse-hair an' Rooshian Morocco for six shillin', oughtn't thou ? "

Wilky's over-candid depreciation of the goods he had for sale was in strict harmony with his whole plan of business operations, and people took it as they usually took the ordinary tradesman's special recommendations.

The customer turned round, therefore, and began to re-examine the vehicle, whilst Wilky, with a grunt of disgust, strolled back into the paint shop.

Sampson, who during the interruption had removed the window-sash upon which he was engaged, now commenced upon the one John had in hand. He groaned again and again whilst the broker was busy, but when he came back into the doorway he looked sheepishly round, and then, with a sigh of awful significance, he murmured something about those who, "having put their hands to the plough, looked back."

"Best thing as they could do," roared Wilky, "if they are not ploughmen, but only tinkers an' tailors an'—an'—Mollycots. Some on 'em neither looks back'ard nor forrad, bud maks furrows all in and out like a dog's hind leg. Every man to his tra——" but here he broke off again, and made another rush to the kerb. "Five shillin'!" he shouted. "No! nor five-and-six, nor five and 'levenpence halfpenny! Six shillin'! Hess, hi, hex—six, and bring' t' brass here."

There was a little counter which stood lengthways out from the window, and when Wilky had finished with the customer, and had returned, he found Sampson waiting for him behind the counter.

"Wilkinson," he demanded solemnly, as he pointed a paintless dust-brush at the defiant broker, "wot did t' apostle say about young Mark when he turned back?"

"T' apostle?" and Wilky looked a little blank for a moment, for he was very fond of flinging St. Paul at his opponents, and was now about to be hoist with his own petard. But suddenly a flash of recollection lighted his face, and drawing down his thick eyebrows scowlingly, he demanded, "Which apostle?"

" Which apostle ? " cried Sampson, stepping back and surveying his friend with reproachful sorrow at his evidently wilful ignorance and evasion. " Why *the* apostle—the great apostle of the Gentiles."

This was what Wilky was waiting for.

" An' this is t' sort o' man as stan's up i' pulpits ! This is him as sets up as a hinstructor of the public ! " he cried, apostrophising space, and then, pulling up suddenly with a plunge against the counter, he cried, " Has thou nivver heard of a man called Barnabus ? "

" Barnabus ! What by him ? " asked Sampson, with an uneasy sense that there was something he ought to have remembered and didn't.

" Here's hignorance ! Here's blockheaded hignorance ! " and Wilky stepped back, and flourishing his left arm oratorically, " This Barnabus was an apostle an' he backed Mark up an' trotted him out an' made a man on him. That's wot Barnabus did."

But John had by this time finished his glazing, and knowing that sooner or later he must go through the ordeal, he rose from his stooping position, and looking steadily at the last of the window-frames, he cried—

" What's the use o' talking ? I hav'n't the gifts, and you know I hav'n't."

Sampson sighed heavily, turned and looked long and musingly out of the window, and then, punctuating every word with a solemn wag of the head, he said—

" That's just what Moses said, an' Joshua, an' Jonah, an' Isaiah."

" Yes," jerked out Wilky, and the words followed each other like pellets from a badly-working pop-gun. " Bud numskulls never says it ! Thickheads an' scatterbrains never says it ! They hav'n't sense to know as they hav'n't ! T' fost sign o' brains is to feel t' want on 'em."

"Whom the Lord calls, He qualifies," quoted Sampson unctuously.

"Does he?" and Wilky, ignoring altogether John's right to a share in the discussion, plunged off again more recklessly than ever. "Then t' biggest part o' t' names upon our plan has nivver been called—that's sartin. A hempty head's like a hempty pot an' rattles all over, but a full head's like a full 'un —silent."

John was laughing in spite of himself at this characteristic outburst, and before he could straighten his face, his father had turned upon him—

"Woe is me if I preach not the Gospel."

"But I *will* preach the Gospel, father, in my own way, and to people of my own sort. To attempt the other would be to bring the ministry into contempt."

Sampson turned away with a sigh, and Wilky was just about to make some reply, when he spied a woman examining a peggy tub and stick. She was dumping the stick down upon the tub bottom, to make sure that the wood was sound, and as this was a sort of reflection on his character, and the woman made her experiments none too gently, he stood staring at her in speechless indignation for a moment, and then, rushing out, he cried angrily—

"It's wood, woman!—common English wood! It's not nine-inch armour-plate, it's wood!"

For a moment or two John watched Wilky's peculiar business methods with amusement, and then, as his father seemed to be deprived of the courage of his convictions in the absence of his opponent, he moved quietly towards the door, and was making off when Wilky spied him. The little broker was giving change to his customer, but as he observed John slipping away, he took the two half-crowns, which he had placed temporarily in his mouth, into his hands again, and leaving the female standing where she was, he darted after the young minder, crying—

"Here, here!" And then rushing at him and shaking his fists fiercely, he cried, "Thou's gotten ower him, bud thou hesn't gotten ower me yet." And with a nod of portentous warning, he turned his back and went away to his business.

John, glad to have escaped his father and his father's friends so easily, and eager to join his sweetheart, returned home in haste, and washed and dressed himself. By this time his sister had prepared tea, Mrs. Ledger being busy with customers; and though the young minder had hoped to take his afternoon meal at the farm, he soon saw what was expected of him, and sat down at the table. Lucy then volunteered to attend to the shop, so that "mother" could have her refreshment in peace. John, who from long practice had come to be able to read his mother like a book, was comforted to observe that she had resumed her ordinary placidity of manner, and chatted more freely than usual about domestic and chapel matters. This was her world. She was interested in little beyond.

Lucy, bright and merry, and dressed in a curious mixture of working and holiday garments, took her meal in the intervals of business, and slyly chaffed John about his evident impatience to get through what was usually the most leisurely meal of the week; and as mother seemed rather to enjoy this banter, he lingered reluctantly at the table, reflecting how soon he would be enjoying himself to the full. Presently, however, he was able to make his escape, and left the house to a running fire of roguish cautions from his sister.

Well, he was done with this troublesome and ridiculous ministry question, at any rate, and with his own improving worldly prospects, and his remarkable and unexpected success in wooing Sallie, life seemed less dull to him than it had appeared for a very long time. He met old Zeph in the lane, and his pleasure at the prospect of finding Sallie alone was dashed by the curtness of the old man's salutation. An uneasy pang smote his heart as he hurried on, but remembering his own foolish proneness to believe evil of his own affairs, he laughed a little forcedly, and refused to be discouraged.

Yes, Sallie was alone, except that he could hear someone—probably Robina, the day-girl—washing up in the back kitchen. But Sallie was not dressed. She still wore her ordinary working clothes, and her face had a clouded, weary sort of look when he entered. When he inquired somewhat anxiously how she was she replied with cold indifference that she was " Right enough," and looked anywhere and everywhere except at him. He had dropped into a chair beside her, and was looking eagerly into her face; but she averted her eyes and pushed back her chair. Poor girl! This was reaction and weakness after her illness—these high-spirited people were all subject to these trying fluctuations—so he sighed sympathetically, looked dreely into the fire, and waited.

" I met your father in the lane. He seemed put out a bit," he ventured at last.

" He might well," she responded, jerking her head away, and looking cloudily at the circuit plan hanging by the side of the fireplace.

" Why, what has happened ? There's nothing wrong, is there ? "

" Oh, no, of course not ! " and she tossed her head with angry scorn.

" Sallie, what's matter ? Whatever's to do ? "

She did not answer at first, but after a long pause she turned and looked at him, and then, with resentful contempt, she demanded—

" What have you been saying to Mr. Haley ? "

" Mr. Haley ? What about—the ministry, do you mean ? But Sallie, it is ridiculous ! "

" What's ridiculous ? "

" Me setting up for a preacher. It's presumptuous. I couldn't think of it."

" And what about me ?"

" You ? "

" Yes, me ! Do you think I should ever have listened to you if I had thought you were going to be nothing but a self-actor minder ? "

" Sallie ! "

And the look of utter amazement and horror on John's face impressed even her; but she stuck to her point.

" Don't ' Sallie ' me ! If a man's no push and ambition before he's married, what is he going to be after ? That's how lots of girls spoil their lives."

John gave a gasp of utter helplessness. A girl with these views, he realized, would be utterly unable to comprehend his position.

" Oh, Sallie, Sallie ! " he moaned ; and then, leaning foward, he propped his elbows on his knees, and hiding his face in his hands, uttered something very like a sob.

Sallie had risen to her feet, and stood leaning with one arm against the mantelpiece, watching him intently, but with troubled though resolute face. Presently, with an impatient little gesture, she cried—

" Sit up with you, and be a man. A woman wants somebody she can look up to—somebody that will climb the ladder and pull her with him, someone to live for and strive after."

" And I will ! " burst out John, and lifting a haggard but eager face. " I will ! I'll work for you, slave for you, do anything for you, but not that way, Sallie, oh, not that way."

Sallie could scarcely contain herself with impatience, but checking herself under the influence of some fresh idea she leaned heavily against the mantelpiece and drew her hand across her brow with an evident effort at self-control. There was silence for a few moments, and then as she looked meditatively at him, as if debating some further question, she moved softly towards him sideways, raised her hand to his forehead, gently stroked back his dark hair, and said—

"I wonder how it is that the best men have the least ambition! You were made for something better than a minder, Johnny."

Her presence so near to him, her light, cool hand on his brow, the soft coaxing sympathy in her voice, and the caressing tone she threw into her pronunciation of "Johnny" thrilled him through and through, and as a new hope began to rise within him he cried—

"Oh, Sallie, you don't understand; let me explain it all to you."

But she drew her hand down over his face, and placed it upon his mouth.

"It's *thee* that doesn't understand, lad, but *I* do; I know what folk are saying about thee, and what thou can do if thou likes. I'm ambitious, because I'm proud of thee and—and—and—like thee. Thou'll have to go on with this, for my sake and—and thy mother's."

The humble, caressing tone in which all this was said, the loving significance of her use of the familiar dialect, the subtle flattery interblended in the words, and the touching and altogether unexpected allusion to his mother, came rolling like so many inbreaking waves over John's heart; the pleasantness, the worldly advantage, the popularity of the course she was urging upon him, seemed to have taken all the stiffening out of his resolution, and for a moment or two he felt himself being swept along helplessly towards surrender. But the very strength of the rushing current saved him; its force was the measure, to him, of its dangerousness; if he yielded now he was undone for ever. All men have their testing times, and his was come, and come in the most dangerous of all possible forms.

"Sallie," he cried, "I cannot! If it were a worldly calling, an ordinary matter of life, I would do anything to please you, but this is a holy calling. No man taketh this office upon himself; it comes by what I've never had—a call from God. You wouldn't bring the curse of Korah on me, Sallie?"

Sallie allowed his emotion to subside somewhat, and then returned to the charge; softly, coaxingly, with pretty poutings one moment and subtle hints of love the next, now patting his cheek and using such terms of endearment as were rare and precious amongst the reticent folk of her county and class, and then putting her own soft lips to his and whispering words that would have melted a Cybarite. She did everything that woman's wit could think of, and at last flung herself down into a chair, and fell back on woman's last and mightiest argument—tears.

Love, pity, self-reproach, and a miserable sense that he was narrow, hard and pharasaical, struggled for a while against these blandishments, and when at last he heard her soft low sobs, and the hissing of her tears as they fell on the hot fender, all power of resistance was gone, and had she returned to the attack at that moment it seems certain that she would have carried her point. But she simply sat where she was and cried, and John, sick with embarrassment and penitence, held his tongue from sheer cowardice, until presently she rose from her seat, made a dart for the staircase, and a moment later, in spite of his attempt to stop her, had gained her bedroom above.

John waited in sore distress for a few moments, and then went to the bottom of the staircase, and called—

" Sallie ! "

No answer.

" I'll come again to-morrow, Sallie."

Still no answer.

At that moment Robina the maid came into the parlour, and John, partly to conceal his agitated looks and partly to get time to think, opened the front door and slipped out of the fold yard into the lane.

CHAPTER VI

SHOWS HOW SALLIE "WILL BE OF THE SAME OPINION STILL"

IT was twilight, and the stars were just appearing when the young minder got into the open air, but he noticed nothing. With head down and heart sinking within him, he plunged along homeward without any thought as to where he went or what became of him. Suddenly he remembered that if he returned so soon it would awaken his mother's suspicions and lead to more anxiety on her part, and perhaps to awkward questions. He stopped, therefore, stood trying to collect his thoughts for a moment, and then, turning back, got over a stile and gained a footpath that led through Brinksway Woods and over the hill into the Rushton and Manchester turnpike. Crossing the fields, now almost running in the agitation and impetuosity of his thoughts, and now stopping to look distractedly around, he presently crossed a little footbridge, passed through a narrow wicket-gate into the wood, and flung himself down under a great tree, and burying his hot face in the new-springing bracken, he groaned out a spasmodic prayer for help and tried to collect himself.

It was a very difficult work, and for the first ten minutes he simply rolled about on the ground and moaned. Then he sat up, leaned his back against the trunk of a tree and tried to clear his mind.

Where was he? What was his position now? And immediately such a flood of bitter memories came rushing upon him that he seemed completely over-whelmed. Circumstances were all against him, and wherever he turned for comfort he only met some new phase of trouble. But life had taught John Ledger the uselessness of mere repining, and so with gathered brow and clenched hands he tried to look the situation in the face. It seemed as though he were resisting something which God and man were combining to force upon him. *Was* he a cowardly Jonah? Was this his "watery deep" and "whale's belly"? and for the moment a wild, mad hope, which he had been treading ruthlessly down in his heart ever since this idea of becoming a minister had been suggested, seemed to elude his grasp and get the mastery. But it was only for a moment; that wicked worldly ambition which he had seen, and been so keenly ashamed of in others, must never get a foothold in his mind, its very presence so close to him seemed to cheapen and vulgarise him; and as the easiest thing in the world to him was to convict himself of some delinquency, he was soon concluding that God had detected the risings of ungodly pride in him, and was resorting to this severe discipline in order to effectually exorcise the evil spirit. And it was an added misery to him that at the moment when everybody he cared for was pushing him forward towards this great decision, he was more absolutely certain than he had ever been that to indulge the idea even for a moment would be to dishonour himself, insult the great calling, and sin against his Maker.

So clear indeed was all this to him, that he wondered with new dismay how it was that none of his friends seemed able or willing to see the matter as he did. He ought not to blame them; in fact, he felt

another pang of self-reproach at the very thought.
What they had said and done were so many signs of
interest in him, and interest for which he could never
be sufficiently grateful.   Even Sallie's attitude, which
affected him most of all, was only the manifestation
of an ambition for him for which his lover's heart
ought to be both proud and thankful.   It was only
that her standpoint was different, and that was not
very remarkable, seeing everybody agreed with her
and nobody with him.   And then, as usual, it all
came back upon himself.   He was odd, he was
different from anybody else.   Was it not at bottom
a piece of mere pharisaism and self-righteousness?
All this will seem very morbid to the healthy-minded
reader, but John Ledger was highly sensitive and
conscientious; he had been trained in a narrow but
intense and introspective school of faith, and was
overworked and underfed, and just now, at any rate,
insufficiently vitalized, whilst the experiences of the
past few days had severely drained his already scanty
nervous resources, and so he dwelt long upon this
process of injurious self-condemnation.   When he
came to ask himself, however, whether he or they
were right, the answer in his own heart was as
emphatic as ever; he had no such gifts as this great
work required; he had not sufficient education, and,
above all, he had no real call.   He had risen to his
feet again by this time, for the ground was striking
the damp through his clothes.   It was very still and
dark about him, and the sense of solitude which at first
had soothed now began to depress, and for a moment
he had to check a feeling that he wished his life's
battle were over, and his fretted heart for ever at rest.
    Naturally, he thought most of the interview he
had just had with Sallie.   The rest he could have
borne easily, but her attitude was not only serious in
itself, but derived an added significance from its

agreement with the opinions of all the rest of his friends. Then some of her words came back to him, and with them the remembrance that they had sounded hard and mercenary, but as this seemed disloyal to her, he tried to dismiss it, and found more difficulty than he had expected. He shook himself to cast away unworthy suspicions, and resumed his walk. Do what he might, however, he could not get away from the feeling that Sallie cared more for his prospects than she did for him, and he found himself fighting, not altogether successfully, the fear that her sudden complacency towards him on the night of the fateful kiss might have had its origin in some wandering rumour that he was a probable candidate for the ministry. But this only led to a further self-castigation. What a small, mean mind he must have to be capable of such unworthy suspicions. It was mere coincidence. Sallie was a true, honourable, open-minded girl, and though she did not see this important matter as he would have expected a Methodist of the third generation to do, she was, at any rate, no worse than others, and, in fact, her ambition might very well be the very strongest proofs of her love. By this time he had reached the highway, and was able to come to at least a temporary decision. He would wait until Sallie's evident anger had subsided, and then explain things to her at length. He would show her the difference between a profession and a holy calling. Probably, he told himself, she would see it, and if she did not—well, he must leave that for the present. He had grown calmer by this, but whether from peace of mind or emotional exhaustion is an open question. So he strolled slowly along, muttering now and again a prayer for guidance, and presently he entered the town, and made his way home. Arrived there, the ruffled, though rather abashed, look of his father, and the forced calm of his mother, indicated but too clearly that there had been a domestic wrangle of which he had been the subject. For though of late the elder Ledger had shown a sort of fear for his son, John knew only too well that what would once have been said to him was now poured out unmercifully upon the head of the patient mother he adored. He got to bed earlier than usual, and though his first hour was spent in going over the whole weary ground of his conflict once more, his very exhaustion and the crisp spring air in which he had spent so much time came to his rescue, and he slept better even than usual. John was a Sunday school teacher, and as he was passing with his class from the school to the chapel next morning, Robina, the day girl at the farm, called him aside, and told him that Sallie wished him to go down to tea. This was better than he expected, and had the effect of considerably raising his spirits. If only he could get Sallie to see matters as he did all might yet be well. As soon, therefore, as afternoon school was over he started for the farm, and was not too well pleased to discover when he turned into the lane that he was overtaking old Zeph. Somehow John had never liked his future father-in-law; he was a hard sort of man who barely concealed a grasping spirit under a bluff and jocular manner. Report credited him with remorseless bargain-driving, and all the Woods for generations back had borne similar characters, and John did not like to feel that the girl he loved had been brought up— and in these times so critical for him—was still living under such influences.

"What, already!" cried Zeph, as John came up. "Hey, young folk! young folk!" and he shook his head with waggish depreciation.

"How's Sallie?" asked John, pulling up and dropping into the old man's step.

"Right! all right! conva*l*escent, as yo' fine talkers say. Hey, John, she's ta'en some rearin' hez that wench! Cost!" and here he pulled up and dropped into a solemn tone, "that slip of a lass has cost me many a hundeerd pound!"

"And she's worth it," cried John with a burst of sweet, lover-like feeling. "She's worth it all, and a fine sight more, isn't she?"

They were still standing in the lane, and Zeph followed each word John uttered with a little nod, as though he were counting, and then puckering his brows and pursing out his lips, he stuck out an argumentative forefinger, and shaking it at John, he cried—

"Ay, bud t'question is, shall I ever get it back? That's t'point."

John opened his eyes.

"Why, Mr. Wood, you are getting it back every day, and you will do, I hope, as long as you live."

This was not quite the answer Zeph had expected, and so with a little wave of the hand to dismiss it, he pointed his finger once more at John, and demanded—

"What I want to know is this. Would it be right after all t'hedication I've gi'en her, an' all I've spent on her, and t'snug little bit she'll hev when I've done wi' it, would it be right for her to throw hersel' away? Now that's t'point."

Zeph put this query as though he were merely raising a purely hypothetic case, but it was palpable enough to John. It came so unexpectedly that he was taken somewhat by surprise. His heart sank, and he was collecting himself to reply, when the old man, who was evidently very intent on making his point, resumed—

"I'm her father, am not I? Isn't it my duty to see as she doesna throw herself away?"

John dropped his head upon his chest and uttered a reluctant and husky—

" Yes."

Zeph's thoughts, like his words, were jerky and disconnected, and so instead of taking up John's reluctant admission, he burst out—

" Our Sallie's a Wood ! ivvery inch on her! She means to ger on and ger hup i' t'world, an' why shouldn't she?"

" Mr. Wood," said John slowly, " I understand what you mean, and I cannot complain. Sallie said much the same thing herself last night, but she has sent for me, and if it is all the same to you, I prefer to take it from her, if I am to be dismissed."

" Oh, well ! do as thou likes. Young folks allus is pig-headed. But mind thee, what I thinks Sallie thinks, an' what Sallie thinks I thinks ;" and with a gesture of dismissal, the old man fell back and allowed John to proceed on his journey.

The young minder felt sick at heart, and strongly inclined to give up the matter and go home, and perhaps write to Sallie. But he was not a coward, though his courage took the shape of quiet tenacity rather than demonstration, and so, with a desire to see his sweetheart and a dogged Dutch sort of pluck, he preceded Zeph down the lane.

Sallie herself opened the door when he reached the farm, and her reception at once reassured him. She was tastefully dressed, and the little blush that rose to her cheeks as she greeted him made her look, in his eyes at least, prettier than ever. She did her best, certainly, to make him feel at home, and showed him many little attentions, which touched him the more as he was haunted with the feeling that this might be a sort of valedictory meeting. The tea was co mplimentarily pretentious, and though both the lovers and old Zeph had a little constraint

upon them, the meal passed off better than might
have been expected. When it was over and old
Wood had settled down to a pipe in the chimney
corner, Sallie, after carrying the tea-things into the
kitchen, strolled towards the parlour on the other
side of the house, and, turning her head as she
entered, beckoned John to follow her. She was
sitting at an old-fashioned piano when he reached
the room, and she continued strumming lightly on
the keys whilst he wandered awkwardly to a seat
near the fire. The chair upon which he sat was
almost filled with decorative rather than useful
cushions, and Sallie, with a not quite natural little
laugh, got up, took one away, made the other comfortable for him, and then, with a playful little tap
on the cheek, bade him sit back and look as if he
were at home.

John sighed and looked at her, and did as he was
told, and then she dropped on her knees upon the
white imitation skin hearth-rug, and sat looking into
the fire with her right shoulder touching his knee.

John glanced at the bright room and fire, and then
down upon the dark hair and delicate pink cheeks,
and felt how happy he would have been but for
something. He had plenty of that sort of courage
which can go straight to an unpleasant subject, and
so without waiting he plunged off at once into the
question that was between them. Slowly, carefully,
and with a seriousness that was almost solemn, he
explained his position and convictions, and the
nature and absolute necessity for the call to preach.
And as he talked she listened attentively, looking
steadily into the fire all the time, and nodding now
and then in sympathetic comprehension. The firelight played upon her face and white neck, and made
her appear something wonderfully beautiful, so much
so in fact that he once or twice lost the thread of his

argument, and was pulled up and brought back by a quick, inquiring glance from her deep eyes. He was greatly encouraged; he was evidently making an impression. After all, he had once more been making mountains out of mole-hills, and Sallie was proving to him that she was the true-hearted girl he had always supposed. He warmed, therefore, as he proceeded, and grew almost eloquent for him. In the earnestness of his argument, he had unconsciously sat further and further forward, and was now bending slightly over her. She looked so serious and interested that hope was high within him, and in the anticipation of his victory he began to smile.

Sallie was still gazing musingly into the fire, and apparently weighing his last words; and just when he began to wonder why she didn't speak, she turned her face quickly towards his, and looking right into his pleading eyes, she cried, arching her brows and speaking in tones of conscious triumph—

"And that's you that says you can't talk! For shame, John!"

And the mingled elation and flattery in her tones only revealed to John how completely he had failed to make any real impression. He was not, however, nearly so disappointed as he ought to have been; there was something very seductive in his surroundings, and he found a subtle delight in talking to one who listened with such stimulating interest and innocent, unconscious beauty; and so he commenced again, and still further elaborated his arguments. She listened as earnestly as before, and seemed almost anxious to be convinced. She lifted a little sigh when he had done, and looking steadfastly at the fire, she murmured—

"Oh, John, you're *too* good! you are indeed."

John sighed helplessly; what could he say more?

And yet it was only too clear that he had made no real progress. And there he sat looking down in admiration at her, whilst his heart sank within him, and became heavy again.

And then Sallie took up the tale, and with a sweet reasonableness and insidious speciousness that almost blinded him to its danger, she touched point after point in his arguments until he saw them—he knew not how—disintegrating and crumbling to pieces before her soft pleas. Then she put her own side of the case, but with the same soft touch and the same subtle flattering deference as before. He grew alarmed and interrupted her. She was wonderfully patient, and seemed pleased to hear him re-state his position, but she talked on, and John grew more and more uneasy. The witchery of the firelight in the gathering twilight, the soft stillness that seemed to pervade the house, and the rise and fall of her coaxing voice had a sort of enchantment in them, and he felt as if he were being snared in some wizard spell or other. He grew afraid of her and the influence she was having over him, and most of all afraid of himself. He tried to say something definite and decisive as gently as he could, but the right words would not come, and he sighed and looked helplessly around. The silence grew long and oppressive. Sallie had leaned a little towards him and placed her cheek against his knee, then looking into the fire, and speaking in low, musing tones, she told him how often she had sympathised with him and his mother in their struggles, and in a half whisper slipped out low, apparently unintentional words of admiration of him, and then in stronger tones expressed her confidence that he would make his way in the world.

John hastily assured her that if hard work and severe self-sacrifice could do it he would get on, and then in impassioned words declared that for her he could do anything.

And with a long, soft sigh, she answered—

" Anything but the one thing. Oh! I should be proud and happy, John, if you would do *that* for me."

And John, choking and husky, snatched her hands, and holding them tightly told her that she did not know what she asked, and that he was sure she did not want him to sell his soul. She pulled her hands away in silence and turned from him, and then after a few moments more of painful stillness, got up and went to the piano. He joined her there presently and turned over the music for her, and asked her to sing, and with a pretty resigned and pensive air she obliged. Then they began to talk again, and he attempted to return to the painful subject, but she always evaded it, and grew more and more constrained as the evening wore on. John, though he scarcely knew what to do, stopped to supper. He was by this time exceedingly uneasy, and looked at Sallie anxiously again and again, but she always turned her eyes away. A flush of relief and hope passed over his heart when, upon his leaving, she came with him as on that first night to the gate.

" Then you can't do that—a—even for me, John," she said, as they joined hands in parting.

" Oh, Sallie, I will do anything—anything but that."

She paused a moment, and then letting slip his clinging fingers she said slowly, but with hardening accent—

" Then you need not come any more, John!" And before he could stop her or reply she had retired to the house, and was closing the door behind her.

CHAPTER VII

A RACE FOR A PULPIT

JOHN could not have either said or done anything
to stop his sweetheart's flight if his life had depended
on it. With open mouth and dropped jaw he
watched her vanish absolutely tongue-tied, and then
stood staring at the door as though he could not
believe his eyes. Sallie's manner during the evening
had seemed to indicate that, though she loved him
very much, she was not going to give way on a point
in which his best interests were so much involved
without a struggle, and he confessed to himself that
he would never again be so near surrender and
escape. But this sudden change astounded·him,
and made it clear that he could have no hope of
winning her so long as he remained a mere mill-
hand. She did not, therefore, care for him for his
own sake, and his mother's doubts, now made painfully clear to him, had at least something to justify
them. A chill crept over his heart, and with a last
regretful glance at the inexorable door he turned
away, and walked slowly down the lane. As he
went along he was conscious of a change in his own
feelings, a dull, dogged stubbornness rose up within
him ; he loved this bewitching girl he told himself
again and again, but he knew her better. She was
smaller-minded than he had feared, and narrow and
earthly ; so far from being able to appreciate his
motives she could not even understand them, and

if she did not and could not be brought to see as he saw there could never be anything in common between them, and, painful though it was to contemplate, she had done the very best thing, both for herself and for him. All this and more his reason told him, but his heart still clung to the old hope, and he understood himself well enough to know that it would be useless to try and stifle the feeling all at once; he must wait and gradually school himself to resignation, but he did not disguise from himself for a moment that the process would be a long and weary one. It was a relief to him, therefore, when he reached home to find round the hearthstone several of the chapel people, kindred spirits of his father's, and he gathered at once from their solemn, half-reproachful looks that his father was holding forth in his own voluble style about his son's stubbornness. As he entered Sampson was comparing himself to Isaac deceived in Jacob, and David disappointed in Absalom. He broke down somewhat confusedly on catching sight of his son, and wandered off into vague and mysterious hints about the similarity of his trials to those of the patriarch Job, finishing up with a pathetic and lachrymose picture of himself sitting on some metaphorical dung hill, deserted alike by God and man. So carried away, in fact, was he by this melting picture of his own imaginary sufferings that his voice broke, and tears ran off the end of his nose, whilst the rest of the company sighed again, solemnly wagged their heads, poked the ends of their fingers into the corners of their eyes, and groaned under the influence of this moving discourse.

John was accustomed to these manifestations, and inwardly despised them; to-night also he felt they were irritating and even humiliating, and so he beat a hasty retreat and stole off to bed.

Next day was the Quarterly meeting, the chief official

gathering of the circuit, and John had expected to take his seat there for the first time. But recent occurrences had changed all that, and not knowing what rash thing his father or Wilky might do, he went off as soon as tea was over for a long walk, that he might be out of the way if any attempt should be made to force the super.'s hand. He entered the town by the lane leading along the back of the chapel on his return, and was a little alarmed to observe that the band-room was still lighted up, and presumably the meeting was still sitting. He made his way home, therefore, as fast as he could, hoping to get away to rest before his father returned.

Just as he was finishing supper, however, in came Sampson and Wilky, wrangling in high tones about something. Ah! it was the old story, but Wilky was in unusual force, and gradually beat his opponent down, maintaining with all the strength of his strident, raspy voice that the men who preached for nothing were far more valuable and important to the Church than those who were paid. This was in direct and flagrant contradiction to Wilky's usual sentiments, but as nobody ever expected consistency from the little broker John smiled quietly to himself, nodded in token of gratitude to his defender, and stole away upstairs. Well, the matter was settled now, and could not be revived again for at least twelve months, and he comforted himself with the reflection that the whole thing would probably be forgotten in that time. He was a little surprised and humbled to discover that, now that the question was disposed of, there was something approaching to disappointment in his mind, and he reflected a little sadly that this was only another evidence of how little we know ourselves, and how necessary it is to be constantly on the alert against the "old Adam." Then of course his mind reverted to the old sorrow, and, recalling how recently he had pitied poor Sam Kepple, he realised that he was now relegated to the same company of rejected suitors.

He felt for a moment or two a little bitter, but very soon his love for Sallie extinguished all that, and he found himself wondering at the extreme reasonableness of the course she had adopted, from her standpoint. A fortnight passed away, and though during that period he had met Sallie several times he found that she had returned to her usual manner, and was evidently not too much distressed about what had taken place. Then something happened which, though altogether unconnected with John's troubles, added considerably to them, and had important and far-reaching results. On the first Sunday in April he was appointed to preach at Trundle-gate, a pretty village about three miles from Bram-well. He had never been "planned" there before, for the village was inhabited by substantial farmers and well-to-do retired tradespeople from the circuit town. The congregation at the ornate little Gothic chapel was therefore highly respectable ; the ministers preached there every other Sunday, and only the best of the local preachers were allowed to occupy the pulpit. John was taking the least important of the services, the afternoon one, and a popular layman from an adjoining circuit was to preach at night. It was a lovely spring day, and John would have enjoyed the walk but for his nervous apprehensions. He got through his work, however, fairly well, he admitted, for him, but was not particularly reassured when he was invited to take tea with old Mr. Pashley, who was a comparatively rich man, and lived in the most pretentious house in the place. Pashley was an old-fashioned Methodist, who thought it a most improper thing to puff up young preachers, and so, to John's relief, he made not even the most distant allusion to the sermon. Mrs. Pashley, a much younger person, had, however, no such scruples, but paid John so many kindly little compliments that he became fearful lest her kindness should trench upon veracity.

The old gentleman did not, however, seem very disturbed about his wife's politeness, but detained John as long as he could after tea, and then, the day being so very inviting, he offered to walk a little on the way with him. They had turned out of the village street into the lane, and Pashley had already paused to take leave, when lifting his eyes and looking down the road, he said—

"Who's this coming? It looks like a preacher; I hope Mr. Craven is not sending a substitute again."

John raised his eyes and examined the approaching figure. The man looked rather too grand for an ordinary local preacher, and John was just turning to reassure his host when something about the stranger's gait attracted his notice, and darting a quick glance backward, he said—

"Why, it's Mr. Ferridge!"

"Ferridge? He who was put off the plan last harvest?"

"I think so—yes," replied John. "It is he, certainly. I daresay he is coming to hear Mr. Craven. They used to be old friends, you know."

The old gentleman made a sudden start forward, and taking John's arm and beginning to walk rapidly forward, he cried—

"Go on! I must let him get past. I wouldn't walk down the village with him for anything."

But the approaching man had seen them, and was already waving a stylish umbrella by way of salutation.

"Oh dear, oh dear! What shall I do? I'm sick with shame."

M.

And the agitated old gentleman put a hand that was shaking with indignation and fear upon John's arm, and went on—

"Don't leave me, whatever you do."

The man they were meeting was tall and burly. He was dressed in a new suit of shiny black, with a large open shirt front upon which gleamed a big star-shaped stud, whilst a loud, thick gold chain stretched from his vest pocket to his button-hole, and from that to the opposite pocket. A glossy new silk hat was tipped a little back on his head, exposing a perspiring forehead and hot, red, somewhat bloated face. He had gloves, also, of painful newness, on his fleshy hands, and whilst still some yards away he began to speak.

"Well, I never! My old friend Pashley! This *is* nice. How are you, my dear brother; how are you?" and entirely ignoring John, he seized Pashley's hand and began to shake it with eager enthusiasm.

"And how's Mrs. Pashley, sir? Well? I'm delighted to hear it. Take care of her, my friend; such people as her are scarce."

He still held Pashley's limp and reluctant hand, and thrust his face close to the old man's in apparently eager interest in the old gentleman's affairs.

"We're both pretty well, thank you, Mr. Ferridge," said Pashley, with nervous restraint. "I'm walking along the road with our young friend here. Good-day."

And he began to push John before him.

"Ah, good!" cried Ferridge with a forced heartiness, and taking out his watch he continued, "Yes, there's plenty of time. I'll go along with you, and then we can return together. The service is still at the old time, I suppose?"

"Oh, have you come over to the service? I heard

yesterday that Mr. Craven was not well; he may be
sending a substitute——"

"Yes, he's sending me. He wrote on Friday.
Poor fellow, he's been in bed a week. What a
lovely afternoon it is! Ah, I always say there's no
place like Trundlegate in spring time."

John began to fear there was going to be a scene,
for Pashley was evidently much excited, though he
tried hard to conceal it, and so he dropped the old
man's arm and was preparing to move off when his
host snatched at it hastily, and turning to Ferridge
he cried, in scandalised tones—

"But you are not going to preach, Mr. Ferridge?"

"Oh yes, sir; certainly. Brother Craven wrote
asking me. We've helped each other many a time.
It's all right, sir."

Pashley was pinching John's arm until he
winced.

"But, Mr. Ferridge, you cannot preach after—
after what has happened!"

"Happened! Oh, ay! But that's six months
since, you know, and I'm a new man. I certainly
was a little overtaken, but I've passed through the
fire, brother, and I'm all right now."

Pashley looked at the canting, fleshy face before
him, and tightening his grip on John's arm, whilst his
venerable face grew stern and white, he said—

"But you cannot preach at Trundlegate to-night,
sir."

"Mr. Pashley! Mr. Pashley! Have you become
a hard-hearted Pharisee? What did the dear
Lord do to Peter and Thomas when they made
their little slips? I didn't expect it from you,
sir. I never thought my old friend Pashley would
cast the first stone," and in cleverly simulated
emotion he turned his face away and buried it in
a gorgeously-flowered pocket-handkerchief, and

sniffed and snuffled as though struggling with tears.

John felt touched for the moment, and noticing that Pashley seemed similarly affected he said, with a view to helping Ferridge—

"If the super. has consented, you know, Mr. Pashley——"

Ferridge turned sharply towards John with an angry gesture, but another thought striking him, he changed his manner.

"Exactly; that's it, you know. Leave these things to the super., Brother Pashley."

"But does the super. know you have come here?" asked the old gentleman, with returning alarm and not a little indignation.

"I saw him only yesterday, sir. Ah, he's been a true friend to me in my—a-a-a-affliction."

Pashley, puzzled and grieved, was evidently inclined to give way, but it had struck John that Ferridge's last words were vague, and that his host was being deceived, and so he said quietly—

"Does the super. know you are taking this service, Mr. Ferridge?"

Ferridge jumped round with a snarl that amply justified John's suspicions, and shouted—

"Don't I tell you that I saw him yesterday?"

Pashley was carefully scrutinising Ferridge's face and manner, and it was evident that he was more suspicious and alarmed than ever. Perceiving this, and indignant that the old man should be subject to this excitement, and absolutely certain now as to the truth of the matter, John said, looking steadily and fearlessly into Ferridge's flaming face—

"Mr. Ferridge, have you told the super. that Mr. Craven has asked you to take this appointment, and has he given his consent?"

Ferridge's face was almost livid.

" What's that to you, cock-chin ? I'm responsible to the super. and not to factory lads ! "

" Mr. Ferridge," broke in Pashley, " let me beg you to return. I'm sure that Mr. Craven cannot have known that you are not now on the plan. This young man will take the service."

John gave a little start and an exclamation. It was no joke to be called upon to preach at a few moments' notice, but before he could speak Ferridge burst out—

" Will he ! Don't get your rag out, Mr. Pashley ! I've come to take this service, and I shall do, for you, or anybody else ! " and he turned away with the evident intention of making for the village.

" Oh, man, you'll not !—you'll not desecrate——"

" Won't I ? I'll show you ! " and with a rude push which sent the old man staggering into the hedge he started towards Trundlegate.

But for the moment he had overlooked John, who, when Pashley gave a shocked cry, sprang forward and planted himself on the narrow flags in front of the bully.

" Mr. Ferridge," he cried, with quiet but unmistakable decision, "you will not enter that pulpit to-night."

" Let him go ! let him go ! " cried Pashley, now thoroughly scared, but John stood his ground.

" Out of the way ! " shouted Ferridge, who had now lost all self-control, and as he sprang forward he raised his clenched fist, and would doubtless have felled the young minder. But he did not flinch, and as he still looked steadily into the gray-green blazing eyes of his opponent, the uplifted hand fell harmlessly to his side, and with an afterthought and a sudden chuckle, half scorn and half triumph, he sprang from the high-banked footpath and dashed past his resister.

" Let him go! God will judge him!" cried Pashley, now in a state of pathetic fear; but John's blood was up. A man like that to get into a pulpit, and no voice to be raised in protest! The thing was not to be thought of for a moment. And so, disregarding his frightened and now horrified companion, he turned on his heels and darted off after the transgressor. Hearing his footsteps, Ferridge looked round, and perceiving instantly that John was intent on passing him and reaching the chapel before him, he darted sideways, and spreading out his great arms to stop him, bellowed out all sorts of coarse threats. But though he was big and strong, he was also heavy, and the young preacher easily dodged past him, and for some yards there was seen on that quiet spring evening the strange spectacle of two men racing for the possession of one pulpit. It did not last long, however, for, after running about eighty yards, the heavier man pulled up, and began wiping the perspiration from his face, bawling all sorts of coarse epithets after his opponent.

When John reached the chapel, panting and out of breath, the caretaker, a woman, was just unlocking the doors. In a few breathless words he explained what had happened and who was coming. To his perplexity, she stared blankly at him for a moment or two, and then, dropping a red handkerchief containing a gorgeously-bound book, precipitously fled. By this time Ferridge had entered the village, and was approaching. John's blood boiled within him; this blatant, coarse-minded fellow should not preach there that night whatever happened; and so, on sudden thought, he dashed into the chapel, closed and locked the door, and then setting his heels in a crevice of the tiled floor and his back against the door, he prepared to resist any attempt to enter by force.

But the door was a two-leaved one, and John had forgotten that there was a bolt at the top as well at the bottom, and just as he realised his mistake, the form of the burly Ferridge was flung against the outside, and the young minder with a gasp felt that he was being overmatched. With all the strength he possessed, however, he pushed, and the door went back into its place, and then bent inwards upon him again. For a minute or two the discreditable struggle was continued, and then it ceased suddenly, as though Ferridge had given up. It was only for an instant, however, for before John had properly realised what was happening, the man outside, now perfectly wild with rage, flung himself against the doors and sent John flying into the aisle. Just at this point, when victory seemed to be within the grasp of the big man, other voices were heard, and when John rose to his feet he discovered that the chapel-keeper had thought of something he had forgotten, and had fetched the constable, who, as it happened, was a Methodist. The presence of the representative of the law cooled the big man suddenly, and as the worshippers now began to gather, he deemed it prudent to beat a retreat. Then old Pashley turned up, still very much alarmed, and when he had told his tale John was soon surrounded by a knot of grateful admirers, who greatly commended his conduct. They insisted of course that he should occupy the vacant pulpit, but he was so agitated that he doubted whether he could sufficiently collect his thoughts. Bynton, the leader, offered to open the service for him, and by the time that had been done John had obtained some sort of command of himself, and did his best. The chapel filled as the service proceeded, curiosity evidently bringing many unwonted hearers, and John had the largest congregation that had been seen in the building since the last anniversary. The delighted

officials made much of the preacher when he had
done, and thanked him heartily, as well for his sermons as his valiant defence of the pulpit, and it was
somewhat late when he got away. Alone now for
the first time, he began to run over all the disagree-
able circumstances of the evening, and realised that
he had probably made an enemy. He saw no reason,
all the same, to regret what he had done, though
he would have preferred that some older and
more important individual should have had the
onus of it. It was always the easiest of all things
to find some reason for self-reproach, and he was just
sighing a little regretfully over the matter, when he
thought he heard a single footstep behind him, as of
some person walking on the grassy edge of the footpath, who had unintentionally stepped upon the flags
for once. He was nervous, and did not look round
for the moment, but when he did so there was no
one to be seen. A little later he thought he caught
the step again, and a little nearer, and turned at once,
but nothing was to be seen. Then he smiled at his
own nervousness, but quickened his pace, and had
already reached the turn where the Bramwell lights
could be seen when there came behind him a sudden
rush and then a crash, and he staggered forward into
the gutter and all was blank.

CHAPTER VIII

HOW WILKY BECAME A CONSPIRATOR

SAMPSON LEDGER opened the paint shop on the morning after the events narrated in the last chapter in an absent, preoccupied, but solemnly uplifted frame of mind. It was ten o'clock before he reached the premises, and nearly half-past before he deigned to take down the shutters. He was, of course, greatly distressed at what had overtaken his son; but no less than seven of the principal people of the chapel had sent to the little cake shop in Shed Lane to make inquiries, and he had been stopped at least half-a-dozen times on his way to business to give particulars of the shocking occurrence; consequently, though he wore the manner of one who was suffering under some grievous visitation, yet underneath it all was the supporting consciousness that he and his family were, temporarily at any rate, the objects of most flattering sympathy. He was not the principal sufferer perhaps, but mental pain is after all the most acute and terrible, and he lost sight somewhat of his son's condition as he dwelt in keen self-pity on his feelings as a father, and the harrowing effects of those emotions on his spirits. It would have been disrespectful to his son, a sort of sacrilege, in fact, to have given any attention to mundane matters under present painful circumstances, and so he opened the shop with a resigned, almost stoical aspect, and immediately settled himself on the log near the newly-lighted stove and commenced to smoke. There was an air of mystery about the matter that greatly inflated his self-consciousness, and he shook his head with solemn deliberateness, and fetched long, appealing sighs.

John, rendered unconscious by the blow he had received, must have lain by the side of the footpath for some time, for it was after nine o'clock when he was discovered by a pair of lovers. With the aid of the post gig, which passed along whilst they were trying to bring him round, they had got him home, and the doctor, when summoned, had declared that it was a very serious wound, which could not have been caused by a fall. And there the matter rested. Why had John not returned earlier? and what had taken place to bring about this brutal assault? And, most perplexing of all, who was the mysterious assailant?

Old Zeph strolled into the shop as Sampson lighted his pipe, but as the two had met before that morning, he simply wandered to his seat on the side bench and sat down, accompanying his actions with the remark—

" Well, this is a licker, this is!"

" Many are the afflictions of the righteous," moaned Sampson, with solemn shakings of the head.

" It might 'a' killed him, a clout like that," said Zeph, glancing round as the little broker waddled into the shop.

" Joseph is not! Simeon is not! and now ye'll take Benjamin also," whined the painter with a wheezy snuffle and an excited blinking of the eyes, and then he went on, " O Absalom! my son, my son!"

It was doubtless the pathos of these quotations that commended them to Sampson rather than their relevancy, but it was the striking inappropriateness of them, and the fact that the latter of them contained an implied reflection on John that struck the dwarf, and so firing up, partly out of contempt for a sorrow in which he did not altogether believe, and partly out of natural contradictiousness and a sense of the necessity of defending John, he rapped out—

"Bosh! blather! t' boot's on t' other leg, by jings."

Sampson took a long breath, and then with a pulpit flourish of the hand and a weary wag of the head, he cried—

"Rail on, Eliphaz! rail, you—you other Job's comforters. I must take up my cross! None but a father knows a father's feelings."

This kind of lachrymose nonsense was the most irritating of all things to Wilky, and he was just about to make a scathing reply when Zeph chimed in.

"Come! come, lad! He'll be all right in a day or two."

"He will, if he's owt like his father," cried Wilky, savagely. "It 'ud take a steam hammer to do any damage to *his* skull."

"Friends!" cried the painter solemnly, "you don't know! If you did you'd have some feelin', but you don't know all, you don't know all."

There was evidently something behind this doleful whine, and Zeph lifted his head inquiringly, whilst Wilky, taking his pipe out of his mouth and holding it in a waiting attitude, demanded snarlingly—

"Wot don't we know?"

"It's not the blow as t' doctor's feared on, it's summat worse! summat w-o-r-s-e!"

The men on the bench exchanged glances, and a look of impending penitence came upon Wilky's scowling face. He was not going to admit anything, however, too hastily, and so he demanded shortly—

"Wot is it, then? What's t' owd jolloper say?"

Sampson looked as though he were not going to reply, but covetous of his full meed of pity, and proud of having acquired a brand-new scientific term, he leaned forward suddenly, tapped the broker's foot, which projected from the bench on the level of the ordinary man's knee, and dropping into a tragic whisper, he said—

" It's mental gitis."

The painter was perfectly satisfied with the effect of his announcement upon his friends ; they had never, either of them, heard of the disease, at any rate under this staggering name, and were therefore duly impressed, for to have been sceptical of a man's need of sympathy when his son was in danger of disease with such an awful title, and which they both concluded was some new and terrible form of insanity, would have seemed hard-hearted indeed, and Wilky was just asking in a much softer tone what " gitis " meant, when the super. appeared in the doorway. Instead, however, of saluting them, he carefully closed the door, which was usually left open for Wilky's convenience, and then stepped up to the debaters.

It was evident at once that there was something in the wind, and the friends looked first at him and then at each other.

" Well, Brother Ledger, I've got to the bottom of it. Ah, it's a bad business—the scoundrel ! "

" Sir, my John a scoundrel ! " cried Sampson, ready for another bath of the martyr spirit, but the super. broke in upon him—

" No, no ! John's a hero ; he's a brick, poor lad. He's got this by standing up for the cause, but let me tell you "—and then he plunged off into the whole story. Old Pashley had come in from Trundlegate to report on Ferridge's outrageous conduct entirely ignorant of what had happened to John. The super. had put the two things together instantly, and when he told his visitor the sad sequel he was white with sorrow and indignation. Pashley was for going to the police station at once, but the super., who was a great believer in the virtues of second thoughts, asked him to wait a while.   But Pashley had insisted, and they had seen the superintendent of police, who, whilst he agreed with them that there was only one conclusion to be drawn, asked them to leave the matter in his hands, as, of course, nothing could be done without direct evidence of the assault.   This, and much more, the minister told the amazed and outraged friends, but whilst begging them to keep eyes and ears open, he cautioned them against circulating the information until the required proofs should be obtained.

Sampson was now most genuinely distressed; but as the little broker watched him, he was not quite satisfied; there was something in the haggard look and frightened eyes that excited his most uneasy suspicions.   But everything else was forgotten in the presence of this dastardly outrage.   Before the super. had got halfway through his tale Wilky had shuffled off the bench and was walking backwards and forwards, stamping his puny feet and threatening direst consequences to the "wastril" Ferridge.   He stretched up his four feet something, and shook his fat little fist and vowed he would break every bone in the mighty Ferridge's body; he would horsewhip him, he would shoot him dead as a herring, and finally, he would spend his last shilling in "lawing" him.

"Mr. Drax, there's somebody wants you," cried a little girl, cautiously opening the door just as Wilky reached the climax of his threats, but the enraged broker chased her away with a roar, and banging the door and returning, poured out a fresh volley of denunciations of John's enemy.   As he talked he glanced now and then at Sampson, but that worthy still preserved a most unusual and ominous silence, and avoided the other's eye.

The super. listened a little absently to Wilky's tirade, and was moving towards the door, when it was opened by a stranger, who, putting his head inside and dodging it first to one side and then to the other in a vain effort to see past the minister, called out—

"Is Wilky here? Now then, what do you want for yond' owd rocking-chair?"

"Old! old!" cried Wilky, whisking round and bristling all over with pugnacity. "It 'ull be a fine sight older afoor thou gets it, man. It's hantique! hantique hoak, stupid."

"What's t' price?" demanded the customer, impatiently.

"T' price?" and Wilky threw his great head back with a sarcastic laugh. "T' price is sixpence hawpenny an' a set of mahogany drawers thrown in, that's about thy figure, isn't it?"

"How will ten shillin' do?" and with a patience born of much experience the buyer held the door in his hand and waited for Wilky's return to reasonableness.

"Ten shillin'!" and Wilky looked unutterably indignant, but all the same he strolled leisurely towards the door and followed his customer across the street, snarling and sniffing as he went.

The bargain, however, was soon struck, and the little broker started to return to the paint shop; but as he noticed that the super. was leaving, he stopped in the middle of the road, surveyed meditatively his own place of business, turned slowly back and glanced over the various articles in front of his shop with a sort of weary contempt. Then he entered the shop itself; it was crammed from floor to ceiling with new and second-hand goods, the only signs of orderly arrangement being in the neighbourhood of the window. Glancing still more discontentedly at the inside stock, he passed on and entered the back room. This was smaller than the other by the width of a staircase, but was in the same disorderly and overcrowded condition, and it was not without difficulty that he wriggled his way to an oversized armchair upholstered in an undecipherable pattern of print. A pouch-like box hung on the outside arm of the chair, and it was full of old newspapers, letters, Circuit and prayer-leaders' plans, a choice selection of pipes in various stages of blackness and disrepair, half-used packets of tobacco, and a heterogeneous collection of indescribable odds and ends. A fire, half-choked with ashes, was maintaining a sulky sort of struggle in the grate, and the mantelpiece, besides a bewildering variety of odds and ends of ornaments, supported three mirrors, leaning one against the other. Wilky kicked a footstool which had a spittoon let into the top of it towards the chair, and hastily mounting to the seat settled down with his pipe.

From where he sat he could see his own face and head in the far corner of the front mirror, and as he turned his thoughts about in his mind he glanced at the reflection of himself in the dusty glass, much as a man looks at a friend with whom he is holding a conversation.

Wilky's face was puckered in serious cogitation and the smoke came through his lips in short rapid puffs. At last he raised his eyes, and looking at the mirror, shook his head like a person who is having foisted upon him an insufficient explanation, and jerked out—

" I don't like it, Wilkinson, I don't."

Then he puffed away furiously at his pipe with renewed glances at the mirror, and presently leaning forward and scowling at himself in the glass, he demanded fiercely—

" Ferridge is a club collector an' rent an' debt collector an' money lender, isn't he ? "

The Wilky in the mirror must have made some sort of reluctant but inaudible concession, for after a moment's pause the Wilky in the chair leaned forward and went on—

"An' yond' owd muddle-head's allus up to t' eyes i' money messes, isn't he?"

The significant glare with which the broker in the chair transfixed the broker in the glass ought to have driven comprehension even into quicksilver, but as there was still some evidence of doubt on the point, Wilky, with a snarl of impatience, went on—

"Well, what did he say? What did he look like when Ferridge was mentioned?"

The obtuse man in the mirror was seemingly not even yet quite convinced, but to Wilky it appeared so perfectly clear, that he dropped back into his chair with a sigh.

"It's there, Wilky, it's there, lad! and that rapscallion 'ull slip through our fingers." And then, as the thought seemed to cut him to the quick, he kicked the footstool away and sprang to his feet. "Will he? confound him! I'll show him! I'll show him, if I swing for it."

But at this moment there was a cry of "Paper!" in the shop. Wilky, still boiling with indignation, toddled into the front place, picked up the copy of the *Bramwell Mercury*, and was soon ensconced in his chair again, and reading with wrathful maledictions an account of a "dastardly outrage on a local preacher."

There was nothing else in the paper that interested him, and so after reading the half column for a second time, he let the paper drop upon his knees and was soon in a brown study. A few minutes later he was roused from his reverie by a summons into the shop, and after a characteristic wrangle with a woman who thought she knew what sort of furniture paste she wanted, he suddenly popped the article he was offering back upon the shelf, and turning his back upon the customer, left her standing in the shop. He fell back so deep into his chair that his diminutive legs stuck straight out like railway signal arms. He remained in this condition until another idea came, and he got down upon the floor again. He stood staring broodingly into the fire for a little while, and then laid his pipe carefully down, brushed the tobacco ashes from his waistcoat, looked himself over from head to foot, and finished by dolefully scrutinising his hands. Then he stood upon the stool to get the full benefit of the mirror, pulled the knot of his dingy scarf back into its place, took his hat off, and hastily smoothed down his still abundant hair, picked up the paper, and assuming an amiable and even affectionate expression that made his pugnacious face look almost handsome, he stepped to the staircase, toiled softly and painfully up, and just as he reached the top, commenced in the tenderest of tones—

" Well, how's my little love this morning?"

The little love turned out to be a woman, tall beyond the wont of women, but so finely proportioned that her height was not particularly noticeable. She had an abundance of wavy brown hair, a broad white forehead, soft violet eyes, and a complexion so delicately pink and white as to suggest, along with the puffy flesh of her fingers, the invalid. She was reclining on a low wide couch, and wore a rather faded, but neatly fitting, blue dressing-gown of some soft material. The room, which was large and airy, though rather low, was almost luxuriously furnished, and gave evidence everywhere of a refinement rather unexpected under the roof of the little broker. Mrs. Drax was suffering from some obscure and chronic spinal complaint, which kept her in her room for months together, but the smooth, unwrinkled face, the baby dimples, and the gentle, pensive expression gave little indication of suffering, and none at all of complaint. Everybody had marvelled when this handsome popular woman married the cross-grained and misshapen little broker, and put it down to woman's incomprehensible whim; and nobody, not even the smiling bride herself, knew that Wilky, her father's executor, had sacrificed all his little savings to cover her father's name from dishonour when he died and left nothing but debts; and the staggering stock of new goods which the little broker crowded into his shop immediately after his marriage was taken, as he intended it should be, as an indication that her money had set him up. That this ill-assorted couple loved each other passionately was evident the moment Wilky entered the room. There was a welcoming smile on the invalid's face, and the crusty husband looked almost ridiculous with his lover-like smirks and grins. It is not for us to pry too closely into the little billings and cooings of this couple of everlasting lovers; suffice it to say, that in a few moments Wilky brought gravity into the fair face on the sofa as he cautiously broke the news of John's misfortune. She was secretly one of John's champions, and had kept her husband from disliking the shy, reserved lad she did not understand. Presently Wilky squatted down on a hassock by the side of the couch, and carefully unfolding the paper, read in an emphatic, official sort of tone the paragraph relating to the outrage. There was a tear of soft sympathy in Mrs. Drax's eye when her husband had finished, but when he noticed it he crushed the paper between his hand, and flinging it away from him, burst out with a return to his old manner—

" Now then, silly old stupid, I'll never tell you anything again. Look at me, I don't go snivelling about every little thing," and in confirmation of this statement the little man, whose voice had already broken suspiciously, walked to the front window and demonstratively blew his nose. And whilst Wilky was trying to convince himself that his quick sympathy with his wife's pitifulness had not compromised his manhood, she was leaning back upon the couch meditating.

"Wilky," she said at last, "come here, my man."

With reluctant, aggrieved look on his face, as though he already guessed what she was going to say, he drew near the sofa, and resumed his place on the hassock. Mrs. Drax looked musingly at him for a moment, and then softly stroking his hair, she said—

"Can't we help them, Wilky?"

"Us? How can we? The old chap's a muddler, goes staring at t' stars and tumbling in t' gutter; an' t' others is as proud as pouters."

"John is a good lad, Wilky."

"Ay, good for gettin' into hobbles an' making silly women cry."

Mrs. Drax waited a little, and toyed with a stray tag of her husband's hair, and then she said, gently—

"I know somebody who would have cried—she—she—thought the world of poor John."

Wilky made an exclamation, and his face grew suddenly pathetic, whilst he shot a frightened sort of look at a large photo in an elaborate frame which stood on the table, at the head of the sofa. It was the picture of their only child, who had been dead some time, and who had been John's child sweetheart.

Wilky was not equal to contending with such pleas and such a pleader, and so he gave an inarticulate grunt, and catching the sound of knocking downstairs, he made haste to escape, and when he had disposed of the customer he did not return, but took refuge in his arm-chair, and charged his pipe. For some minutes he sat in abstracted silence, then he began to intersperse his puffs with surly grunts and little "Tchats!" and "Boshes!" mingled with sarcastic little laughs. Then he grew silent, and began to rub the stem of his pipe in his hair. This action was followed by a fit of open-eyed astonishment, and a great self-satisfied grin spread itself over his face. He followed this up by leaning back in his chair and treating himself to a series of triumphant chuckles, and at last he got up, winked wickedly at himself in the mirror, and waddled off to his old rendezvous at the paint shop.

CHAPTER IX

THE next day or two brought little or no light on the mysterious attack which had been made upon young Ledger. The superintendent of police reported after careful search that he could find no clue as to the offender. Pashley had openly charged Ferridge with the assault, and had been ordered off the premises, and on Wednesday it was known that the suspected man had left the town, but had been insulted and hustled by indignant townspeople at the station. John had by this time recovered consciousness, but could give no information, and protested as energetically as he was able against any action being taken against a man they only suspected.

On Thursday Wilky was thrown into a state of excitement by the receipt of a lawyer's letter charging him with slandering "our client Mr. T. Ferridge," and threatening legal proceedings. It was a sight to see the little broker. He kicked his favourite footstool as far as the crowded condition of the little back room would allow; he strutted before the fire and threatened Ferridge and his "swindling lawyer" with "Court of Queen's Bench" and every other legal bogie he could think of. For timidly inquiring if he would have some more coffee (he received the missive during breakfast) he rushed at Julia Ann, the little rough, cross-eyed servant, and drove her in terror into the kitchen, and then strode across the road and poured out the vials of his wrath on the melancholy Sampson. It was well into the forenoon before he was calm enough to venture into his wife's presence, and when he had told her his tale she reminded him that the money he proposed to spend in fighting the case would be needed for a little project they had hatched together, and on the accomplishment of which she had set her heart. Wilky allowed himself to be persuaded, of course, but that did not prevent him denouncing Ferridge whenever he had the opportunity, and hinting with darkened face at mysterious but exemplary vengeance.

A week passed away, and John began to show decided signs of recovery, but even then could add nothing to what was already known about the causes of his sufferings, and protested, in a way that disgusted Wilky, that it was not right to condemn any man on mere suspicion. The fact was, John was already occupied with domestic anxieties that put himself and his calamities out of his mind. Sallie had shown him just such attentions as were neighbourly, and no more, and though she called several times she always contrived to keep his mother in conversation, and went away leaving him disappointed and perplexed. And then the mill went on short time, and was only running four days a week, which meant that his wages when he returned to work would be little more than they had been before his promotion, and the old struggle with poverty would have to be renewed.

Whilst John and his people were occupied with these anxieties Wilky had concerns of his own, which evidently took up much of his time and thought. He was known to have a strong prejudice against medical men, but for some inscrutable reason or other he suddenly struck up a violent friendship with old Deevers the doctor, who had attended John, and one day the medico greatly surprised the Ledgers and increased their distress by announcing that John must on no account go back to the mill at present, but that, for some months at least, he must have light outdoor occupation, which would not be too great a strain upon his constitution.

Sampson's face was long and woeful when he reported these things to Wilky, but it grew positively frightful as the little broker confirmed the medical verdict, and declared he could have told them that John was sickening months before the assault.

" Many are the afflictions of the righteous," sighed Sampson, rolling his eyes upward.

" It's more nor we can say for their brains," snapped Wilky. " Some folks goes whining about taking up their cross when they ought to be walloped wi' it ! Resignation ! " he broke in, as Sampson sighed out the word. " Resignation be blowed ! It's common sense as we want. There's lots o' folk resignated into their graves wi' their do-less relations."

It was quite a different tune, however, which he sang to John's mother. He usually treated that suffering soul much as he treated his own wife, and when, after two fruitless visits, he found her alone, he affected both surprise and delight at the information she had to impart.

" Sarve him right ! " he grunted, with a not quite successful attempt at the usual gruffness. " It's t' best thing as could a' come to him. There's some silly folk i' this world as hez to be wolloped to bring 'em out. He's no more made to be a sal-fac (self-acting) minder nor I'm fit for a harkangil."

And then he suddenly stopped, poised himself on tip-toe, made a grab at the anxious mother's neck as though about to kiss her, and pulling her head down and placing his mouth at her ear, he whispered huskily—

" The bud may have a bitter taste, but sweet will be the flower."

Ten minutes later he was standing in his own back room and grinning from ear to ear. He nodded and chuckled at himself in the mirror, and cried delightedly—

" It's working, Wilky lad, it's working ! "

That week-end the *Bramwell Mercury* contained the following advertisement:—

WANTED.—A Young Man as Assistant, and to make himself generally useful. One accustomed to plain painting and polishing preferred. Apply to Wilkinson Drax, Broker, Station Road.

The little man, who pretended to a supreme contempt for all newspapers, could not wait for the boy to bring his *Mercury* along with the other weekly publications he patronised, but was at the office a few minutes before the time of publication, and gave the shop girl a most uncomfortable time of it as he strutted about the place and fumed and snapped about the unpunctuality of tradespeople, especially printers; and when at length he got possession of a damp copy he hurried off home, and sitting in his chair, read it over and over again with great delight, and then took it upstairs to show to his wife. Some half-dozen applicants presented themselves during Friday evening, and three more on Saturday, but Wilky seemed to know they would not do almost before he had seen them, and dismissed each and all with sarcastic jibes, that sent them away crestfallen and indignant. About six on Saturday evening he observed Sampson closing the paint shop, and as this seemed in some strange way to be a new grievance to him, he walked across the road and poured out a string of vague but stinging denunciations on the young men of the period. He evidently expected Sampson to ask questions which would give him the opportunity of introducing the subject of the advertisement, but that worthy was so preoccupied with his own dismal forebodings as to what would become of the family now that the chief bread-winner was out of work, that the palpable " leads " were none of them taken up, and Wilky, as the painter locked up, went back to his own premises in an irritable and explosive frame of mind. During Sunday, however, he hit upon another expedient for providing himself with a manservant, and on Monday morning a large furniture paste advertisement card was hung up in the shop window, but the printed side faced inside the shop, and on the back, facing the window, was written in a large, sprawling hand, eked out by numerous capitals, an abbreviated version of the advertisement in the *Mercury*. For three whole days the card hung in its place, and though it brought several new applicants, they seemed even less satisfactory than the others, and Wilky seemed doomed to final disappointment. During these days, also, he made several clumsy excuses for bringing the card under the notice of the painter, but Sampson either could not or would not understand, and at last he told a wonderful story of a wholesale man who had sent him some rascally apology for varnish, which he declared was nothing but black treacle. So outrageous a case naturally appealed to Sampson's professional sympathies, and at last he strolled across the road with his companion to inspect the offending preparation. The chairs upon which the varnish had been tried had been placed immediately under the advertisement, and when Sampson had decided that the varnish in question, though poor, *was* varnish, he raised his eyes and caught sight of the notice. Wilky began to hum " Rock of Ages," and, turning his back to the window, became much interested in the proceedings of a young butcher who was trying to get a bullock down a passage. Sampson had now finished his inspection of the advertisement, and become suddenly very thoughtful, whilst the broker still hummed away at his tune. Wilky could get nothing further out of his friend, who seemed to be in a most unusual hurry to get home, but as soon as he had gone Wilky hurried back into the shop and up the stairs, and burst in upon his smiling wife with a triumphant " It's workin', love; he's limed, he is by jings ! "

Wilky was in such uncommon spirits that he invited himself to take tea with his wife, and kept up a brisk prophecy all through the meal as to the results of the little plot he was working out, whatever that might be. Between seven and eight that night the broker, having brought in the goods that usually stood on the pavement, and piled them higgledy-piggledy in the shop, put down the door latch and planted himself in his chair in evident expectation of a visitor. He was impatient and fidgety, and looked uneasily at his watch every minute or two. No one appearing, however, he was just resolving to lock up and retire when the door-bell rang. Wilky immediately fell back in his chair, assumed an air of weary indifference, and bawled out to the invisible visitor—

" Well, what is it ? "

" It is I, John Ledger, Mr. Drax."

" Well, what are you standing there for ? Come in, man."

When John reached the back room Wilky had taken on the expression of one utterly weary of life and who could not be interested in anything.

" I came to see——"

" You came! An' what business has a pale-faced invalid as is on his club to be out at this time and i' this wind?"

But though the tone was rasping, the manner was indifference itself.

" I'm all right, Mr. Drax. I'm ready for work again, and I've come to see you about this advertisement."

" Thee!"

And Wilky's wondering amazement might have deceived even a sharper fellow than John Ledger.

" Yes, the doctor says I'm to have some employment that is less confining for a time."

Wilky rolled his big ruffled head about against the back of the chair with long and apparently very decided shakes.

" Did anybody ever hear of such a thing? Why, man, what does thou know about furniture?"

" Not much; but I'm a painter's son, you know, and used to plain painting and polishing."

Wilky's head-shakes were longer and more decided than ever.

" What's t' use o' talkin', man? I want somebody as is as strong as a elephant. Look at all this ruck of lumber!"

The little man had the air of one who was being pressed into a thing that was plainly impossible, and seemed in danger of losing his temper.

" John, it's ridiculous. What's t' use of harguing? What does thou know about furniture? And then look at t' hours. Seven i' t' morning to eight at night, half-past nine o' Fridays, an' ten-thirty o' Saturdays."

" I don't mind the hours. Will you try me for a short time?"

" Try thee! Oh, for goodness sake, shut up, man! I cannot pay minder's wages, man; t' furniture trade isn't a gold mine!"

"What were you thinking of paying, Mr. Drax?"

"Oh, hush man! it won't do at all, it really won't," and Wilky looked exasperated almost to the explosive point. But he had not answered John's question, and as the young fellow was still waiting for a reply Wilky went on, as a painfully reluctant concession to John's aggravating persistence, "Five an' twenty shillin' a week's my figger, that's all."

"I'll be glad to come for that, and even less if you'll try me."

"Confound it!" and Wilky rose and stood one leg on the footstool and one on the floor. "Don't aggravate me, man! it won't do at all!"

John sighed, and looked disappointed; and Wilky, studying his face by slyly squinting into the mirror, saw that for the first time he was giving up the contest.

"If I thought thou"—the broker began with the first sign of wavering in his face, but then, after looking hard at his visitor for a moment, he continued, "I want a helper bad enough, but it won't do! it won't do!" And he settled himself in his chair as though he had settled the question, and wouldn't allow of its being reopened.

John turned reluctantly to the door, keen disappointment in every line of his face; but as he began to move off the broker resumed—

"Look here," and he pulled him into the shop, and showed him all the topsy-turvy, dusty, greasy piles of furniture, and John, as he glanced from one to the other, was fain to admit that there would be work enough for a time, but he still declared he would only like the job of bringing order into this confusion.

Wilky "pish"-ed and "pshaw"-ed, and prophesied that he would not stick to it a week.

"If only you'll give me the chance, Mr. Drax!"

"Chance! chance!" and the broker was apparently quite exasperated, "if thou *will* break thy back thou shall do it! Come on Monday mornin', and if thou doesn't repent afoor t' first day's out I'll—I'll eat my hat!"

And when John, joyful and a little surprised, left him a minute or two later at the shop door, Wilky returned hastily to the back room, and mounting upon his footstool, made a series of indescribably grotesque grimaces at himself in the mirror, finishing with a grand comprehensive wink that involved his whole face.

Wilky saw John every day between the interview just described and the commencement of his new employment, and on each occasion he had some fresh objection to the arrangement, and several strong reasons why John would not do at all, and the young minder was thus kept in a tantalising condition of uncertainty.

During the same period also Wilky was engaged upon some rather mysterious operations of his own. He removed some of the stock accumulated round the big chair in his room, and though it produced much perspiration and many unparliamentary objur- gations, he at last succeeded in his purpose, and havin gmade room for it, brought a dingy old book- case and fixed it up in the corner next to the fire, and between that and the back window; being careful, for some strange reason or another, not to disturb the dust. Then he ferreted out a rickety old stationery case, which he stocked with writing materials, and placed on the bottom shelf of the bookcase. To these he added a couple of dog-eared ledgers, and several greasy account books. Then he raked together from different parts of the premises a number of books—odd volumes of commentaries, several more or less venerable theological treatises, the "Lives of the Early Methodist Preachers" (complete), with a miscellaneous stock of literature, all more or less theological and Methodistic. Many people in Wilky's place would have dusted the shelves and knocked the books together, but the broker, for some hidden reason that gave him secret amusement, took particular pains not to disturb the dust. A few of the books were modern, and their owner regarded their comparative newness with dissatisfaction, and taking them down, doubled over the leaves here and there, and ran a dirty thumb down the creases to make them look old.

On the Friday morning the shop was closed, for Wilky had gone to Manchester, and when he returned, for a late dinner, he brought with him another parcel of books, all new. They were works on modern theology, with a couple on preaching, and a one-volume history of Methodism. When he placed these additions by the side of the others the result made him shake his head. Then he rearranged them, sandwiching the new ones between older volumes, but the result was not even then satisfactory. He was getting a little impatient by this time, and after standing back and critically surveying the little library, he dashed recklessly at one of the most staringly new of the books and rubbed it vigorously, back and sides, in the dust lying thickly about on the furniture. He did the same with each of the new volumes, and was just beginning to look more satisfied with the result, when he discovered that most of them were uncut; and so, when the shop was closed that night, he went ruthlessly through them all—doubling down leaves here, marking paragraphs with a joiner's lead pencil there, and, in fact, doing everything he could think of to give the books the appearance of having been purchassd some time before, and at least partly read. There was one tome that particularly provoked him; do what he would it still persisted in presenting a glaringly new appearance, and so at last he took off the much-thumbed cover from one of his wife's story books and cased the offending volume in it; completing the whole thing by going through the book on Sunday afternoon and marking it here and there, and even going to the length, now and again, of adding sarcastic marginal annotations. This was a new compendium of theology, then very popular in Methodism, and when he had sufficiently disfigured it, and subdued its scandalous newness, he took it downstairs and threw it on the lowest shelf of the bookcase, and then began to beat the dust out of the surrounding upholstery so that some of it would settle on the book.

He received John on Monday morning in his very crustiest manner, and as he consumed his own breakfast he held out once more on the enormous quantity of work to be done. First of all he wanted his own room made tidy, and instructed him to clear out some of the rubbish and "titivate" things up a bit; dwelling with anxious particularity upon the fact that the bookcase was not to be disturbed any more than was absolutely necessary. John, whose mouth watered as he glanced over the volumes, felt a momentary surprise that he had never noticed them before; but as they had the appearance of having been there for a long time he put it down to his lack of observation, and secretly hoped to get a peep now and then at the insides of the works.

For several weeks the young assistant worked hard, gradually introducing some sort of order and cleanliness into the business, and trying to get rid of his own disappointment concerning Sallie by putting all his energies into his work. Everything both in the back room and the front shop was soon as straight as a new pin, and then that inextricable medley in the back warehouse behind the kitchen was attacked and finally subjugated. Between-whiles, John was taking peeps at Wilky's books, and though a little surprised to see his master in possession of so much modern theology, as he was not naturally very curious he never pursued the thought, and was hoodwinked by the fact that Wilky made frequent and ostentatious use of the volumes, and would even occasionally read extracts to him and engage him in discussion as to the points raised. The work began to slacken; little by little the articles requiring to be painted or repolished got finished, and John began to wonder what his master would find for him to do next.

The accounts were in a shocking state, however, and these occupied several more weeks, especially as he soon discovered that it was not possible to comprehend them except when his master was at hand to explain the cryptic entries. But Wilky with somebody in charge was rapidly developing roving propensities; sales seemed to come with amazing frequency, and he often absented himself for hours together when there was no such things to attend to. The little broker, moreover, developed peculiar views of business, and after the shop had once been made something like decent he laid it down as an inflexible rule that when he was away, and John was in sole charge, he must do nothing else but attend to the shop. He might read a newspaper or even a book, the master conceded, but he must be at liberty to attend to the shop with the utmost promptitude immediately a customer appeared. Which goes to prove that precept and practice are not always the same things even with furniture brokers. Left thus to himself and with much time on his hands, John was drawn more and more to Wilky's book-shelves, and gradually began to realise that when the time came to leave his present employment and return to the mill, the hardest things to part with would be these same precious volumes. All the same the long hours he spent in reading made him increasingly uneasy, for it was as plain to him as anything could be that now, at any rate, he was not earning the money Wilky paid him. It was summer by this time, and one Saturday evening, as he was returning from delivering a repaired chair, he was attracted by a small crowd standing round what was still called the market cross and listening to a speaker. He was evidently some sort of Socialist, and the jibes he was throwing out about the Government and the aristocracy were stale enough, and John was just moving on when he was arrested by a few cheap sneers at religion. The crowd laughed and seemed to relish the sneers, and so the speaker went further and began to hold forth on the discrepancies of Scripture and its many and flagrant self-contradictions. John was piqued, but interested; and the crowd showed its concern by dropping into silence. Elated at the attention he had awakened, the speaker, who had a ready tongue and sharp wits, went further, and was just holding up to ridicule certain passages of Scripture when John, as much to his own astonishment as to anybody else's, cried out indignantly, " Fair play ! "

" What? What's that young ranter say?" cried the orator. " Nay, don't duck your soft head, my budding theologian ; come up here and don't be afraid to back your opinion."

" I'm not afraid," cried John, and in a moment he was at the speaker's side.

The Socialist obsequiously made room and flung out certain witty remarks about John's personal appearance which mightily tickled the audience ; and then turning blandly to the young minder, he cried—

"Now, my young Boanerges, speak up, and let us hear what you have to say."

"I've nothing to say," said John, "except that you are using one of the favourite tricks of your class and not quoting Scripture, but *mis*-quoting it."

"Ah! who'd have thought it? He doesn't look much like a Regius Professor of Divinity, ladies and gentlemen, does he? Looks rather like a Salvation Army soldier that's been drummed out. Now, General Booth, tell us what it is I've misquoted. Order! ladies and gentlemen; listen to this compressed philosophy."

John's spirit was stirred. He felt that this man was trying to make him lose his temper, but he felt cool, astonishingly cool, he reflected afterwards. And so, turning to the crowd, he said—

"Ladies and gentlemen, I'm not criticising this gentleman's arguments, nor you for listening to him, but you'll all agree that if a man quotes he ought to quote correctly."

"Hear! hear!" said one or two, and the orator drew himself up, turned up the collar of his coat, and pulling a long, sanctimonious face, whined out, "A-m-e-n!"

John waited, and observed that whilst a few laughed at the mountebank's jeers, others looked a little disgusted.

"I think the gentleman mentioned St. John's gospel; well, there is no such passage in St. John at all."

The lecturer began to fumble hastily in the inside pocket of his coat, evidently seeking some pamphlet.

"He quoted it as a saying of Jesus Christ's. It is nothing of the sort! It is a saying of the Pharisees, his opponents, and you will find it in the gospel by St. Mark. As for that last phrase of his, I should like to ask him where, in the Bible, he found that?"

"The walking dictionary! The infant prodigy!" began the orator.

"Answer him! no shuffling! Answer him!" cried several delighted ones in the crowd.

"Gentlemen, we have got here the infant Spurgeon, the——"

"Answer him! answer him!"

"Gentlemen," said John quietly, "I'll answer myself. The passage is not in the Bible at all; it is a bit of Young's 'Night Thoughts.'"

The crowd cheered and commenced to laugh, and John, elated and valiant, plunged off into a description of some of the social and political blessings Christianity had brought, and then reminded them that he was their townsman and had nothing to gain by deceiving them; and then he tumbled out confusedly a bit of his own religious experience, and when at the end of ten minutes he paused, out of breath, his antagonist was just disappearing behind him. Some of the crowd began to hustle the retiring and vanquished agitator, and others shouted to John to go on.

"Friends," he gasped, "I'm a bit out of breath," and then, as a great daring idea flashed across his mind, he went on, "but I'll come here next Saturday night and say something more if you like."

The crowd cheered, and John, now beginning to feel reaction, got down and speedily made for the furniture shop. He had many misgivings during the next week and blamed himself not a little for his impulsive offer, but faithfully next Saturday he turned up at his post and preached. One or two interrupted, but he found their quibbles very easy to dispose of, and soon began to look for them; for his quick replies were the things' the audience most enjoyed. He found no lack of assistants, however, and in a short time the service at the market cross became a regular part of the Saturday evening's proceedings, and began to make its influence felt on some of the working men of the town.

As time wore on, however, John became more and more uneasy about his position in Wilky's business; the books were now in order and the business had actually increased a little, the people finding John so much easier to deal with than his master; but John knew enough by now to realise that his employer could not afford to pay him, as he was doing, out of the profits of the concern, and, most alarming consideration of all, he had so much time on his hands that he was growing dangerously fond of Wilky's books. He was, moreover, stronger and healthier than he ever remembered to have been in his life, having broadened out somewhat and got a more wholesome look about him. There was no reason therefore why he should not go back to the mill, especially as it had " gone on full time," and just then something happened that precipitated his decision.

It was the holiday season; the super. was away at Conference, the second minister was busy preaching anniversary sermons in the villages, and so, as usual, local preachers were given the rare distinction of appointments in the circuit chapel. On the first Sunday in August, Wilky Drax was " planned " for the evening service. The fixture was a perfectly safe one, for the little broker, grotesque in appearance and brusque of manner, had a very decided gift, and was as popular with the quality for his incisive proverbial philosophy as he was with the rest for his other gifts. All the same the appointment only came at rare intervals, and all the week previous Wilky was apparently passing through all the struggles of mental production. First one and then another of his books was consulted and then flung with a petulant " Bosh !" upon the book shelves, and woe to the misguided customer who presumed to "haggle" that week. Two things, however, puzzled John, one was that his master never seemed to write anything and the other that Wilky never opened the newer volumes which he had so often and so pointedly commended to his assistant. In the quiet hours of Friday forenoon, the slackest part of the week, Wilky condescended to consult his young employée about a text. "But Mordecai (pronounced by the furniture man Mor-de-*cay*-i) bowed not nor did him reverence." John laughed at the text, but his master seemed no little proud of it and invited his assistant's ideas, and so they slipped off into a long discussion which had no result save a withering condemnation of John's "one-eyed" notions and a sweepingly scornful denunciation of modern commentators. The discussion piqued John's curiosity and he looked forward to the Sunday evening service with considerable interest. But why did his master spend so very much time in examining the plan and in whispered discussions with resident local preachers? Sunday night came and John was in his place under the gallery in good time. The congregation, as he expected, was small, but better than usual for the time of the year. The preacher had a reputation for fastidious punctuality, but to-night he was behind time, and when the chapel clock struck six the chapel-keeper had not brought the books into the pulpit. John consulted his watch and ascertained that the clock was not fast; what had become of Wilky? Three or four minutes passed and then Barlby, the Society steward, opened the vestry door a few inches, peeped here and there over the chapel; and still no Wilky. Then the vestry door was opened slightly again, and Barlby looked straight across at John's pew. John's heart came into his mouth, and he was just wondering for the twentieth time what had happened to detain his master when the folding entrance door behind him creaked softly, and a hand was placed on his shoulder.

"Come and open the service," whispered Carr, the junior steward. "Barlby's gone to seek Wilky."

John turned round with a suddenly whitened face and gasped, "I cannot. Get some of the others."

"You are the only local here. Come on!"

John's mother, who was sitting next to him, gave him a gentle nudge, and, scarcely knowing what he did, he got up and followed the steward into the vestry. It took five minutes to get his consent, but as Carr had now been joined by three other alarmed officials, and they all insisted upon it, he at length consented to commence the service, but only when he was assured that Barlby had actually gone to seek Wilky. His master had sent in the hymns the day before, but, though that seemed reassuring, John could not help fearing that his employer had found Mordecai too much for him. There were astonished and inquiring looks as John, with shaking legs, ascended the stairs into the tall pulpit, and his voice shook so that his trembling mother bowed her head and prayed. The hymn over and the prayer concluded John announced the chant, and looked round anxiously towards the vestry door. It opened sure enough, but only Barlby, red and perspiring, emerged.

"I've knocked and knocked but I cannot get in," said the steward, standing on the pulpit steps whilst the singing proceeded. "He must have gone away; you'll have to go on."

"I can't go on, I really can't," gasped John.

"There's nothing else for it. Go on, lad, and God help thee," and Barlby descended the stairs and walked off to his pew.

John broke out into a cold sweat, and then raising his eyes for the first time he glanced round the chapel in search of some other preacher. They were not there, but the deep steep gallery half full of worshippers was there, and he felt as if it was coming over upon him to crush him. But the singing stopped and he had to get up hastily and read. Then more singing, and the poor preacher realised that the sermon came next. He put his hand into his pocket and discovered to his relief the notes of an old discourse ; he tried to read them, but the writing ran together and danced before his eyes. He felt as though he were choking. One more glance at that awful gallery, one more appealing look at that inexorable red baize vestry door, and then the singing ceased, and he was face to face with his fearful ordeal. He tried to commence, but the insides of his lips seemed to have upon them a thick coating of glue and cracked as he parted them. The chapter and verse of the text could only be heard by a few ; the words seemed muffled, and a passionate impulse to burst into tears came to John, and he lifted his eyes helplessly towards the gallery. And that look saved him ; that overpowering collection of men and women all at once became a powerful magnet ; the sight of those faces woke the preacher in him, his brain cleared ; suddenly an unnatural collectedness came upon him, and in a full, clear voice he began to speak. A Methodist congregation is always interested and sympathetic towards a case of this kind, and the attention which the Bramwell worshippers gave to the preacher cured him for the time of all undue nervousness. It was seen at once that he would never be the man his father had been ; words, instead of rolling and tumbling one over each other as they did when the elder Ledger occupied the pulpit, now came one by one, slowly and with sparing economy ; picked words evidently, and short but "grippy" sentences ; instead of the bubbling, sparkling headlong rush, such as the older Methodist loved, there

came a quiet deep stream. Presently some of the
men began to look round at each other and nod, but
the preacher did not see them, he was now wholly a
messenger of the skies, not a factory lad and the son
of a working man; all that was lost sight of, his
message was everything.

It filled him, it mastered him, and took absolute
possession. He was confident enough now, but it
was confidence in the truth he uttered, and its fitness
for the needs of his hearers; self was absolutely
forgotten. Coolly, quietly, with simple epigrammatic
terseness, and with phrases that were half pictures,
he argued his case, and when finally, after a three
minutes' strong appeal, he finished, the congregation
looked round in astonishment to discover that he
had been preaching a full half-hour. As wine leaves
its flavour in the cup, so the inflation of the moment
clung to John and kept him up during the concluding
part of the service. It was fast passing away, however, and by the time he came to the benediction
self-consciousness had returned, and he crept down
the pulpit stairs with a sickening sense of failure.

"John! John!" whispered Barlby, meeting him
at the foot of the stairs. " Thou's forgotten the
prayer-meeting."

With another pang of shame John hurried back
and gave out a hymn, and as he timidly found his
way down into the communion the congregation
dismissed, a few only remaining for the after-service.
The people from the gallery, however, came in, in
some numbers, and when the prayers commenced
John bowed his head on the communion table and
gave way to acute mental distress.

" Another prayer, please," he said in absent, per-
functory manner, at the first pause, and a great gush
of emotion swelled up within him as he heard
suddenly a voice he had never listened to before in

that building—the voice of his silent, suffering mother. She seemed inspired, her face shone, though her voice shook; she made no reference to the service, she was praying for the ungodly, the careless, the lukewarm, and in the midst of her low, intense pleadings John heard a sound of pew doors being opened and a scrambling of feet, and raising his head, lo! there were three of the rough fellows he had harangued on succeeding Saturday nights at the market-cross being now led up to the penitent form, and as he choked back the rush of emotion, it welled up afresh in irresistible gushes, as, looking round, he saw his favourite sister Lucy rise from her place, step past the still pleading mother, and kneel down by the side of the men. This is the sort of scene that appeals to all Methodists, and when at length the after-meeting closed the elders present crowded round John and made his heart burn with gratitude, and a sort of joy to which he was a stranger, as they congratulated him on the " good time " he had had. John, shyly happy, wanted to get away, but just as he was turning into the vestry a woman from the free seats suddenly pushed her way to him, and seizing his hand cried, " God bless thee ! thou'rt but a lad, but thou's found me a lost husband to-night;" and behind her a shaking old body raised her chin over a bystander's shoulder and said, " I'd sooner be thy mother than Queen of England." Then there was a cry in a distant pew, and John's mother was seen hugging her newly-converted daughter, and John, abashed but happy, was glad to escape. He did not get clear away though, without several other congratulations, and when he did so his first thought was what had happened to Wilky. He hurried off to see, and found, in spite of Barlby's positive statements, the furniture shop door wide open. He could hear many voices all talking together as he entered, and when he reached the back-room there were three local preachers, his father and old Butterworth the exhorter; whilst sitting in the big chair, muffled up and bewrapped as if it had been winter, and he had taken a severe cold, was Wilky, who, as soon as he caught sight of John, pulled a long face, rolled up the whites of his eyes, and groaning out, " I've gotten t'mental gitis," burst into a loud triumphant guffaw.

CHAPTER X

"Master, I want to speak to you; I want to give you a week's notice."

"Eh? what? Don't bother me, I'm reading," and Wilky became absorbed again in his newspaper, only John observed that it was the sporting page and was therefore not deceived.

"I want to leave you next Saturday night."

"That's it! That's it," and Wilky threw the newspaper from him, gave the footstool a savage kick, and sprang down from his chair. "Another blown-up bladder! Another young jackass as canna carry corn. He takes his wages in a second-hand shop o' Saturday night an' says, 'Thank you,' but canna look at nowd less nor a harchbishop or a president o' t' Conference 'cause he preached i' t' circuit chapil o' t' Sunday."

John listened patiently to this outburst, and then shook his head with a quiet smile and said—

"Ah, master, I've found you out."

"Eh? Me! Well, that's a walloper! What next?" and Wilky put on an excellent pretence of injured innocence, but laughter and triumphant recollection gleamed in his eyes, and his mouth twitched mischievously at the corner.

"You never wanted an assistant at all, Mr. Drax, you only wanted to help me.'

"He's off it! He's fair off his chump! That owd

woman's blather and soft sawder last night has turned his silly head."

John waited until the tirade was finished and then went on—

"And I've found out what those books in the corner mean, too."

"Books! Has thou been reading my books? I don't allow nobody to touch them;" but as Wilky had seen him reading the volumes times without number, this last response only went to show how hard put to it he was for a reply of any kind.

"Master," and John's face became grave and his voice thick, "I shall never forget your kindness to me—and—mine—but I cannot let it go on——"

Wilky jerked his head back with a contemptuous snort, and then with sudden change of thought he dashed at his assistant, grabbed him fiercely by the coat, and looking hard into his face he demanded—

"An' what about t' ministry?"

A light came into John's eye. He drew down the lids to hide it, and answered hesitantly—

"That we must leave to God, master."

"That's it!" and Wilky let go his hold and twisted round with a scornful gesture. "It's goin' to be shoved on God now! We goes clashin' and mashin' till we're stuck, an' then we turn pious and leaves it to t' Almighty. We calls it resignation, by jings! when it's nowt but duffin' cowardliness! Leave it to t'Almighty! two-thirds of all t' resignation i' t' world is simply lazy lack-o'-pluck. God helps them as helps thersels, that's my motty."

"But I don't want to be a minister!"

"Well, did Moses? an' Isaiah? Did Paul? Them as wants, isn't wanted; it's them as *doesn't* want as get called."

For a quarter of an hour longer the discussion went on, and as John had gone further this time than he had ever done before, Wilky was afraid to push him more and finally broke off the interview and toddled across to the paint shop.

Left to himself in the little back room John became the prey of conflicting and anxious thoughts. His success of the night before had reopened the question of his future, and he did not hide from himself that he would have to face the matter once more. One thing that had helped him hitherto had been that he lacked that indubitable sign of the call—fruit, but he could now fall back upon that no longer. The call of the Church, too, now became unmistakable, only the very extravagance of the language used by his new admirers frightened him. This uneasiness was deepened by the discovery that at the bottom of his heart, kept down by self-mistrust, he now found a new and alarming eagerness which awakened his strongest suspicions. He had been brought up in a circle in which certain standards of pulpit ability were recognised, and he knew that he did not possess a single one of the qualifications which were regarded as essential. He had not what was commonly known as the " gift of the gab ; " he knew that he could not speak unless he had something to say. But he did not know *then* that that was one of the surest guarantees of success, and that one of the most dangerous gifts that a minister can possess is a " fatal facility of speech."

The compliments he had received the night before had frightened him, but the consciousness that a mysterious change had taken place in his own feelings was more alarming still. Well, at any rate, he could " sit tight," and in spite of Wilky that was what he would do. But the question refused to be thus disposed of, and returned again and again. The improvement in his health had restored to him some of the natural buoyancy of youth, and his contact with Wilky's hastily collected but seductive library had quickened his natural taste for study, and he was compelled to admit that preaching had become a pleasure to him, though a somewhat fearful one. If the Church thought he had gifts and insisted upon calling him, it was a serious thing to refuse. Were there not men he knew, his own father for instance, who had according to local Methodist opinion been unfortunate in all their undertakings because they had, at his age, resisted the call of God? If he could be sure, if God would condescend to give him some definite sign; if, best of all, God would so order events that he was left without option, he could accept the position with something more than resignation. But that was the very point; whatever others might say, however constraining the nature of events, he could not for a moment allow himself to suppose that the burden of choice would lie anywhere but upon his own conscience, and if it rested there he had no confidence whatever which justified him in allowing matters to take their own course. And supposing he did go forward as a candidate and was accepted, what about the financial considerations involved? He had during his service with Wilky saved about four pounds, the largest sum he had ever had of his own; his education and maintenance at college would, of course, cost nothing, but he would want some sort of outfit, and several pounds at least would be required for that. But most serious consideration of all, what would become of his family if his support were withdrawn? Could they do without him? They never had done since he could remember, or, at any rate, since he began to work; his father's contributions were never a full man's wages, and every year or two those dreadful crises, which always aged his mother and left a sickening scare on his own mind, came—crises arising from legal proceedings taken by the painter's creditors to recover overdue accounts. In these matters his father was always secretive, and whilst it was easy to read his mind on most questions, they generally knew nothing of the difficulty until the sheriff's officer walked into the house. John had been brought up in circles in which such texts as "Whoso loveth father or mother more than Me is not worthy of Me," were interpreted with the baldest literality, and he knew that if he got an indubitable call, mother or no mother, cash or no cash, he would have nothing to do but obey; but as yet there was no such peremptory summons, and he was at liberty to debate these things; and as he did so his heart and even his eyes filled, and he declared again and again to himself that he could not and would not leave his mother to struggle on with the burdens that had crushed all her married life. His mother had made a sacrifice of position and friends when she married his father, and had instilled into him a feeling of almost awe for his parent, but as he had grown up and come to look at things for himself, he had separated the preacher from the man and had gradually grown to regard himself as his mother's protector. How could he leave her to fight this endless, hopeless battle of hers alone! He would not do it; it would be cowardly and selfish! Nobody should ever worm out of him the real reason, but the patient, heroic woman he loved should not be left to struggle by herself. And from one woman his thoughts moved easily to another. He still loved Sallie; she had dismissed him from motives which, if he could not sympathise with, he could perfectly understand. From the ordinary standpoints of life she was not to blame for being ambitious, and surely not for being ambitious for her lover. It looked very much as though she had only encouraged him when she thought there was a chance of becoming a minister's wife, but his own pride and the faith born of his love for her, rebuked such a suggestion and he fought it down. She was a clear-headed girl, and belonged to a shrewd, if rather worldly family; she loved him, but would not show her affection because there seemed no chance of it ever coming to anything, as long as he was only a minder. When there had appeared to be better prospects for him she had not been able to conceal her joy, but had betrayed her real feelings. That was the view he took of it. Once or twice the facts took on a quite ugly appearance as he looked at them, and seem to say that she did not care at all for him for his own sake, and the thought, though he rebuked it as unworthy and unjust to Sallie, somehow would not be altogether silenced. He had not seen very much of her since the day of his dismissal. He had felt humiliated and somewhat embittered when he found himself relegated to that company of snubbed admirers of which Sam Kepple was the most conspicuous member. There was really no cause for him to complain. Sallie had been painfully open through it all; she liked him, but she would not marry a mill-hand; and he had every reason to believe that if he did become a candidate for the ministry she would receive him eagerly. Ah! where was he drifting to? The whispering syren was suggesting so very pleasant a course that, as usual, the attractiveness of it alarmed him; a thing so delightful to flesh and blood must be bad. No! the questions must be kept entirely separate. If he allowed his circumstances on the one hand, or his chance of gaining Sallie on the other, to come into the discussion, he was compromised at once; the question of the ministry must stand absolutely by itself; to allow any of these things to influence him would be to betray his trust.

And whilst John was engaged in these reflections, the left wing of the Bramwell Methodists was holding solemn conclave at the paint shop. Four or five of the lay preachers and minor officials had assembled for the purpose of congratulating Sampson on his son's success, and the little broker on the strategic brilliance of the scheme he had so cleverly carried out.

Jacob Ramsden, the leader, who was an ardent admirer of the declamatory and picturesque oratory of the older school, was declaring, as Wilky joined the company—

" He'll nivver be t' man his father's been—for hunction."

" Thank goodness for that ! " grunted the little broker, strutting to the bench and screwing himself upon the seat.

" He's gotten an old head on his shoulders, too," said Zeph Wood, staring before him with a look of profound conviction.

" It's nivver his own head, that isn't ; he picked it up i' some old churchyard, that's what he did," assented Gridge, the water-rate collector, hitching his book tighter under his arm and looking round on the company as though defying contradiction.

Wilky snorted with an air of superior contempt, and the rapid motion of his little legs created the expectation of speech, but before he could get started, old Zeph, cocking his head on one side calculatingly, broke in—

" It costs summat, I reacon, to send 'em to college ? "

" An' riggin' 'em out," added Ramsden.

" Yes, brethren," said Sampson with a sigh of martyr-like resignation, " it's a serious question, is that, what that lad's cost me i' heddication "—and then breaking off in the triumph of sudden but gigantic self-sacrifice—" but it shall be done, if it cosses me my last penny ! The Lord gave, an' the Lord taketh away."

M.   K

Wilky glared at the painter with indignation, knowing as he did that John had been for years the mainstay of the family, and had brought in more pounds than he had ever cost shillings. In another moment he would have withered his friend with an unusually scorching reply, but just then Ramsden broke in—

" Ay, it 'ull be a great sacrifice for thee, Sampson ! "

" Sacrifice ! " and Sampson rolling his eyes upward and tossing back his long hair, went on : " Every heart knoweth its own bitterness, but this shall be my box of ointment, brethren. Have we received good at the hand of the Lord, and shall we not receive evil ? "

" Evil ! " roared Wilky, and switching off his seat and stepping where he could take a professional glance at the shop opposite : " Evil ! He has a son as is called to be a minister, an' he calls it evil ! He gets a chance of paying back all the Lord's lost by him, and he calls it evil ! Bosh ! Blather ! " —but here he broke off, and rushing to the door he shouted to John, who was arguing with an evidently awkward customer : " Don't let her have it at any price, lad ! " and then shaking his head and nodding consequentially he waddled, with a disgusted you-can't-come-over-me sort of look, to his place on the bench.

Zeph Wood was rubbing his rough chin in a painful cogitation. When it came to parting with money he generally had to do considerable screwing up of himself.

" There was a subscription gotten up for Bob Clumberson, wasn't there ? " he said at last, forcing the words out with difficulty and hesitating between each one.

" Ranter folk hez ranter ways," objected Wilky shortly.

Sampson had pricked up his ears at the mention of a subscription, but as he caught Wilky's stern eye fixed upon him he raised his brush, and holding it between his face and the light he screwed up one eye and squinting at his stumpy tool, he said resignedly—

" Him as sends t' prophet 'ull send t' ravens to feed him."

Gridge, the collector, began to move towards the door.

" Well, if there's anythin' done, I'll stand my corner," he said.

" Same here," said Ramsden, puffing grimly at a pipe.

" Put me down for a fi' pun note," added Zeph with a reluctant sigh.

This was the largest subscription that the old fellow had ever been known to give, and he had offered it spontaneously ; and every man there stole a sidelong inquiring glance at him, for, with the possible exception of Wilky, none of them knew anything of John's relationship with Sallie.

" T' brass is nowt," cried Wilky, with a petulant jerk of the head, " it's t' chap as stan's i' t' road."

Sampson heaved a sigh, so long and appealing that the irascible little broker could not allow it to pass.

" Wot's up now ? " he demanded crossly.

" The whale ! I see the whale," and Sampson, striking a sort of prophetic attitude, and using the brush as a wand, went on in funereal tones, " the way of duty is oft through the vasty deep ; the way to Nineveh is through the whale's belly."

" An' the way to crazy Bedlam's through a bloomin' paint shop," and Wilky, who had slipped off the bench, assumed an attitude in imitation of Sampson's mock heroics, and whined out the " bloomin' " in a manner that set the others off in explosions of laughter.

K 2

"Good morning, gentlemen! Good morning! Well, Brother Ledger, your son had a grand time last night," said the second minister, stepping in his brisk way into the shop.

"There's been nowt like it i' that chapel this ten year," cried Wilky, characteristically ignoring both that he had not heard the sermon, and that he was speaking to one who might take it as a personal reflection.

But the minister seemed to be thinking of something else, and so, accepting the stump near the stove, he sat down, and with an absent glance round the shop he said—

"I suppose your son has an excellent memory, Mr. Ledger?"

"Moderate sir, moderate!—for him."

Sampson evidently wished to convey that his son's memory was about equal to his other gifts, but that neither in that nor in other things could he be expected to be equal to some others—himself, for instance.

"He doesn't get his sermons off by heart, if that's wot you mean," cried Wilky, eyeing the minister with surly suspicion.

"H'm, do you happen to know how he prepares his sermons, Brother Ledger?"

Every one present was watching the minister now with strained attention.

"Me, sir! No, sir; he takes counsel happen wi' the stranger, but never with his own parent."

As this was a fling at both John and his employer, Ramsden and Zeph winced in expectation of an explosion, but the little broker was evidently thinking hard upon some problem in the presence of which Sampson's little slur was as nothing. He took his pipe out of his mouth, and absently dropped it into the pocket of his over-sized coat; then he cleared his throat, as if he was about to speak, but contented himself with watching the minister like a terrier at a rat-hole.

"Does he read much sermon literature, should you think?" was the next question.

"I fear not, sir; he doesn't even look at that blessed paper, the *Christian Prophet*."

"Christian humbug," interjected Wilky, with ineffable contempt.

The minister seemed hesitant and perplexed.

"He doesn't take in any preacher's publications—the *Christian World Pulpit*, for instance?"

"He may do, sir, he takes in a lot; but he keeps 'em locked up in his desk upstairs."

"Ah!"

After a moment's rather awkward pause the minister rose, and began to move slowly doorwards; but Wilky was before him. Planting his stumpy form in the way, he cried peremptorily—

"Hold, sir! Tit for tat. You've been axin' a lot o' questions, happen you won't mind answerin' one or two."

"Well, Brother Drax?" and the cleric's face expressed more amusement than concern.

"We want to know what there is behind these here questions o' yours, sir."

"Oh, nothing, sir, nothing—at present," and the reverend gentleman tried to pass his interrogator.

"It won't do, sir," and Wilky shook his head with defiant resoluteness. "I'm not the father of this here lad, thank the Lord, I—I wish I was, but I'm his gaffer just now, an' I'm goin' to stick up for him, b-b-less him," and the little man suddenly became husky and rather incoherent.

The minister smiled again at Wilky's self-contradictions, but seemed touched by his evident emotion, and so he said—

"Well, the fact is, I have heard three times this morning that John preached somebody else's sermon, and Flintop has been to me to say he'll have the thing bottomed."

Wilky stood glaring at the minister thunderstruck, then he turned with blended amazement and appeal in his eyes from one to the other of his friends, and suddenly whisking round he made a dart towards the street with the evident intention of fetching John. But the minister was too quick for him; snatching at his coat collar he pulled him back into the shop and then begged him to listen to reason.

" Reason ! It's slander ! It's spite an' malice. Let me go——oh !—oh, by jings, my coat's afire ! " and the excited little fellow jumped round, and, taught by past experiences, jammed his coat against the wall and began to crush out the smouldering in the cloth ; the fact being, of course, that his forgotten, but still lighted pipe, had burnt its way through the pocket and set fire to his clothing.

When Wilky had extinguished the burning, and flung the offending pipe into the street, Sampson, who had taken very little notice of an incident that was not very uncommon, stood staring through the dusty window, and as soon as there was silence he brought back the conversation by saying in lame, apologetic tones—

" The poor lad was taken unawares, you know, sir."

The minister looked at the painter curiously. It was odd, even suspicious, he thought, that the father of the supposed culprit should be the only one to think that the charge might possibly be true. But whilst he was occupied with these thoughts, Wilky, whose left trousers leg now bulged out and stuck in the top of his Wellington boot, had dodged past his pastor and now appeared dragging John fiercely by the collar across the street, and then pushing him before him he cried—

" Come on ! Come on ! Own up wi' thee! thou'rt a hypocrite, thou'rt a sneaking thief, thou'rt a swindling playgerist ! "

" No, no ! Brother Drax, don't be so violent ! " cried the minister in distress, but as there was now no way out of it he looked at the bewildered John and went on. " The people are so surprised with your sermon last night, Mr. John, that they wonder whether it was your own ? "

John opened his eyes widely, and then with smiling incredulity he answered—

" Nobody who heard it has any doubts, sir."

" No ! Why ? "

" If ever I do steal a sermon, sir, it shall be one worth stealing," and John, in the easiness of innocence, smiled again.

" Then this sermon was your own—absolutely and entirely your own ? "

" Of course, sir ; those who heard it know that."

" But you quoted somebody pretty freely, perhaps? "

John thought for a moment.

" No, sir. I don't remember to have quoted any-thing but Scripture."

" But you have seen somebody else's sermon on the text and have, unconsciously, I daresay, adopted the thoughts."

So far John had been more amused than anything else, but now he began to think it must be serious.

" Oh no, sir ; I've never even heard a sermon on the text."

" And you haven't borrowed the thoughts from any published sermon on any other text ? "

" Oh, sir, if you had heard the sermon you would know that ; the fact is I only had a few notes, but I'll show them to you, sir."

"Thank you; the very thing, if you would!" and then pausing and looking at him steadily he said: "John, I believe you absolutely, but this is more serious than you, perhaps, think. Flintop says he is certain he has seen the discourse in print and can produce it, and if he does—but you had better give me your notes, here and now, in the presence of witnesses. Flintop is not easily shaken off, you know, and if he should make a clique, well——" and he shrugged his shoulders expressively.

John hurried off to fetch the notes, and when he had gone the minister turned to the others and said: "You see, gentlemen, the super. and I have set our hearts on John being a candidate, apart altogether from what took place last night; but if Flintop thinks a thing he sticks to it, and if he and his friends, even a few of them, voted against John it would be serious, for the exact numbers, for and against and even neutral, have to be returned on the schedule."

As the preacher finished his explanation Ramsden leaned forward, and glancing across, called Wilky's attention to the fact that a customer wanted him.

"Ler 'em want," snapped the broker, and deliberately turned his back upon the door. "Who's owd Flintop? Who cares for him? Doesn't he oppose everything?"

"Perhaps so! But, you see, in this case he could make it very awkward for John—and for us."

"He can make it very awkerd for hisself. Ler him do it! just ler him do it! an' then ler him look out for Robert Wilkinson Drax, that's all," and banging his fist on the dusty counter Wilky glared defiance at the whole universe.

"Many are the afflictions of the righteous," groaned Sampson with a sniff, but as the broker's nerves were just then screwed up to their highest tension he

whipped round, and flashing a look of annihilation
at the painter, he snarled—

"Ay! but them as lives wi' 'em 'as a fine sight
more."

But at this moment John returned, and handed a
closely written sheet of paper to the minister, who,
after examining it, said—

"I'll take this, John, and keep it for a while—
a—a—don't worry yourself. I think we shall be
all right now. Good morning!" and with a glance
round and a nod he hastened away.

John went back to the little inner room at the
shop feeling weary and out of heart. The charge
of plagiarism did not of itself trouble him, but he
realised that, though it would have been talked about
in any case, it drew most of its seriousness from his
supposed candidature, and he half wished that the
delusion might be believed, and thus extinguish all
idea of his being brought forward. Then he wondered
what he could do, short of openly refusing, in order
to set the matter for ever at rest, and in this connection, as in all others, his mind went back to Sallie.
Why not get her and marry her, and thus end all
this bother? But he had never seriously tried; he
had accepted his dismissal in the tamest possible way.
"Faint heart never won fair lady;" why shouldn't
he try, and keep on trying until he succeeded? She
was a woman after all, and as amenable to impor-
tunity as other women; she *did* love him, she had
shown she did. What a poor sort of a fellow she
must have thought him when he accepted his dismissal in that chicken-hearted way! He was not
worthy of her if he gave her up like that; he would
try again.

"You're in a brown study, John."

John started guiltily and looked round, and there
stood Mrs. Drax on one of her rare visits downstairs.

He jumped to his feet and offered her the big chair, and as she smilingly accepted it she raised her eyes, and said—

" Well, John, you have become quite famous all at once. I'm almost as pleased as Drax and the others."

" Thank you, ma'am ; but I wish they would let me alone."

Mrs. Drax smiled complacently; she held firmly the old Methodist belief that reluctance to " go out " was a sign of special grace, and that only those who felt like that were really fit and called. John's answer, therefore, was the most satisfactory possible. Looking at him affectionately, she said—

" It's a serious thing to refuse the call, John."

" It's much more serious to *mistake* it, ma'am."

" But if the Church calls you, they are responsible, not you."

" No, ma'am ; God's given me reason and will and conscience. I am responsible."

The large, sweet woman's heart was glowing with thankful pride ; this attitude of John's was almost ideal to her. Presently she leaned forward, and touching him gently with her soft hand and dropping her voice into a confidential tone, she asked—

"Wouldn't you *like* to be a minister, John ? "

A warm gush of feeling flooded John's heart, and he answered, with shaking voice and shining eyes—

" Oh, ma'am, I should glory in it—if I were fit."

" Is that your only objection, my dear ? "

Terms of endearment were rare amongst the class to which these two belonged, and the tender words thrilled John through and through ; his head dropped a little, and he turned his face away, but he did not answer.

Mrs. Drax sat watching him with sympathetic intentness for a few moments, and then she said, in tones that were soft to commence with, but that grew in intensity as she spoke—

"Laddy, thy mother and I were girls together; she was the proudest girl in Bramwell and the prettiest: she's borne her long struggle with poverty like a saint, but if she thought that poverty was going to spoil the life of her idol, I verily believe she would curse her Maker."

As John covered his face with his hands and sighed she saw that her suspicions were justified, and that this dread difficulty had a prominent place in his thoughts. She watched his distress with tears gathering under her own lashes, and presently she said gravely—

"If you are sure you ought not to offer, laddy—but, oh, be sure of it—then we must find some other reason than poverty; it would break her heart."

Even yet John did not speak, and so thinking, woman-like, of the only argument that appeared applicable, she went on—

"Wouldn't you like to see her proud and happy, John? It's time she had something to comfort her, she's had trouble enough."

And then John lifted his head and looked at her; he seemed to hesitate for an instant, and then commenced, and told her all his fears and struggles, and showed her with ample detail how that it was not a question of like or dislike nor even of lack of means, though he saw not how that was to be overcome; it was solely that he could not be sure that he had either the gifts or the call of God. He was sure of her sympathy and had great confidence in her judgment, and so he talked freely, and she nodded and smiled, and looked grave again, as he went over the case point by point.

"Well, laddy," she said, with a sweet, motherly smile, "there's one remedy left, and we must try that. It's borne in upon me that you are to be a minister, and if God sends the call, He'll find the way," and John did not know that she had sacrificed her summer's holiday and her husband a new suit of clothes in order to find employment, and give opportunity for study, to their unnecessary assistant.

John realised that he was approaching a crisis; all that afternoon he went about with burning head and lips that moved in silent prayer, and when his duties were finished, instead of going home, he turned into Station Road, and then into the fields beyond. It was a balmy August evening, and as dark as it would ever be that night, and he crossed Ringham's pasture and worked round towards Shed Lane. Just as he reached the footpath he heard a soft laugh that went through him, and lifting his head and looking over the hedge he saw a couple of courters on the other side of the lane. The man had his arm in the girl's, and the girl was Sallie Wood.

CHAPTER XI

An exclamation, smothered e'er it could escape, rose to John's lips, and he stood staring in a perfect rage of sudden jealousy after the retreating figures. His first impulse was to dash after them, and pour out his reproaches upon the shallow-minded girl who could so easily abandon him; but, standing there in the twilight, he checked himself. He was not mistaken either in the voice or the trim, easily recognisable figure, and he watched them go round the bend of the lane and pass out of sight, with a heart full of hot, raging passion. Then a faint feeling crept over him; he felt he had lost something, and lost it for ever. It was some time before he could think clearly, and then he was glad he had not obeyed his first impulse. Sallie was perfectly free; it was five months at least since she had given him his *congé*, so that he could not charge her with indecent haste. There had never been the least indefiniteness in her attitude, he knew from her own lips why she could no longer entertain his suit, and there was no reason whatever why she should not console herself with some more tractable aspirant. These things were easy to see; but there was something behind them all, something deeper and more significant, something which he had not the courage to put into words all at once. She did not love him, she never had loved him, as he understood the word. He saw now that he had been nursing a delusion; he had resigned her, given her up, and accepted his position; but now he knew that he never really had resigned her, and that underneath all this fear and sorrow of his there had always been the hope—the belief, in fact—that she *did* care for him, and that even her worldly-minded attitude towards his future was only a left-handed sort of manifestation of that love. How much that hope had been to him he only now knew, and the cowardice, the self-deceit, the madness of longer clinging to it, he also knew. In that bitter moment his love did not die; it became a forbidden thing. He felt like a judge called in the course of his duty to pass the extreme sentence on some dear friend, certain of his duty, but paralysed by his affection. If Sallie had turned back in the lane just then, he was not so sure that he would not have taken her to his heart; but he knew that in so doing he would have been outraging his conscience and degrading his manhood. He turned now, and began to move slowly homewards. All that night and the next day he wrestled with his perplexities. Sometimes it seemed to him that he was making an unnecessary trouble of it, the situation was not after all much changed, and where it was, it was clearly a change for the better, and ought to assist his resignation; but whenever he got to that point, and was deciding to let things slide, an imperious protest rose within him. He was once more seeking to evade the responsibility of personal decision, and an accusing voice called him traitor.

"John," said Mrs. Drax, to whom at last he imparted his aching secret, and whose gentle face became grave and almost stern as he told his tale,

John, Sallie is a clever lass and a bonnie one.

She's just the girl to help a man to get on, and she will—if she loves him; but God help the man who gets her without her love."

He thanked the good woman for her words, but he didn't like them. It was just what he felt himself—just the sort of fear he knew his mother had; and this strong confirmation, he was distressed to find, annoyed him. All the help he got came to the support of his judgment; but oh, he wanted somebody to say a word for his clinging, reluctant heart.

All that week John and Wilky kept up a succession of skirmishes about the notice he had given to leave, and when Friday afternoon came and he asked "off" for an hour to apply for work at Carkham & Horrocks' factory, Wilky flatly refused, and treated him to a string of his most energetic English. It increased his embarrassment to note also that his master and the rest of the paint-shop fraternity were taking the charge of sermon stealing very seriously, and assuming in all their debatings that the question of his candidature was settled. Altogether he spent a very painful week, and when on Saturday evening, after a final "flare up" with Wilky, he returned home he was a weary, life-sick fellow.

As he approached his own dwelling, a bright, fluffy head of hair, belonging, he well knew, to his sister Lucy, appeared for a moment at the door and then suddenly vanished, and John smiled to himself, for it was clear she was on the look-out for him.

"Halt, sir!" cried a voice, trying to speak in tones of strong masculine command, but betrayed by treacherous laughter-like waverings, as he opened the door, and there on the hearth-rug stood his sister in the traditional attitude of a tragedy queen, right foot forward, long trailing dress (mother's), a coronet made by twisting a feathery boa round her brows, and a toasting-fork for sceptre.

"What ho, varlet!" she cried, threatening him with her wand. "Where's thy hat?"

John humorously uncovered, and bowed a little.

"Out, knave! Dost bring thy mill manners here? 'Tis the priest we want, and not the minder!"

Smiling in spite of his heavy heart, John raised his hat again, and made a profound reverence.

"'Tis well! Advance, and bend thy haughty knee!"

John did as he was commanded, and with an air, half disdain and half condescension, whilst her bright eyes danced with fun, she laid her toasting-fork on his head and bade him rise.

"Lucy, Lucy! don't be giddy," said Mrs. Ledger; but John could see that she also had some secret source of gratification that was making her eyes shine; whilst Annie near the window was looking on with something more than complacency.

"Your majesty has received tidings?" said John, falling smilingly into the vein, and bowing once more.

"Tidings, my lord, the best!" and striking a fresh attitude, she went on with almost the only Shakespearian quotation she knew—

"Now is the winter of our discontent
Made glorious summer by this—this daughter of Lancashire."

John shot at her a quick, inquiring glance, but he would not spoil her little play. With another smile and another bow, he said—

"Your majesty's liege subjects grow impatient. 'Good news is bettered by being shared.'"

"The queen" had some very unmajestic emotions evidently, but checking herself and waving her toasting-fork, she cried—

"Tell him, my Lady Annie; tell him, proud dowager," and then breaking down and flinging the sceptre unceremoniously away, she rushed at him, and throwing her arms round his neck, she kissed him impulsively, and burst out, "Oh, John John, I've got a situation!"

John gave a start of delight. She was seventeen and pretty, and in some ways clever, and at great sacrifice the family had conspired together to keep her out of the mill. John wished her to be a teacher, but she had proved helpless at figures and mathematics, and that idea had to be abandoned, whilst no other opening had as yet presented itself. She was musical, but it would be a long time before she could earn much, and they had no piano, and not even a harmonium. Their father, in one of his fits of pride and generosity, had obtained an instrument on the hire system, but, as they saw no means of paying for it, John and his mother had sent it back, and neither father nor Lucy raised serious objection.

Lucy dragged her brother down into a chair, and then, though she was nearly as tall as he, mounted on his knee, and put her arms round his neck again.

"Now, who says that shorthand is no good for girls?" she cried triumphantly, as she slid her slim fingers between his neck and his collar and began to tickle him.

"But you are not going to be a shorthand writer," he said, catching at her hands.

"I'm going to be a shorthand writer, and I'm going to have—guess how much, old never-hope?"

"How much? Oh, half-a-crown a week," said John teasingly.

"Fifteen shillings per week, and I commence on Monday morning at Hays & Vickers';" and then taking his hands in hers and looking earnestly down into his deep eyes, she went on, "And guess who's got me the place."

"Oh, Ferridge, or happen Flintop." John mentioned the two names that were most unpopular with his women folk just then.

M.   L

"John, you're horrid! Guess again!" and she made a grab at his very youthful moustache.

John did as he was bidden, always selecting the very unlikeliest names he could think of; but at last, with almost absolute confidence, he named the little broker and his wife.

"No, no!" cried Lucy, with increasing delight. "You couldn't guess if you tried all night and all day to-morrow."

"Well, who is it, then?"

"You'd never, never guess."

"Tell him! tell him!" cried "Mother," as eager to see the effect upon John as he was to know.

"Sallie Wood!" and she drew herself back to watch his face.

She was more than satisfied with the effect produced, and too excited to note its exact character. John gasped, the blood mounted into his face, he let his eyes drop lest the tell-tale light should betray him, and then began to secretly reproach himself for thinking hard of Sallie.

Then Lucy poured out a torrent of delighted explanations and details, and from these went off to rosy prognostications of what they would do with all their wealth when she got into full wages, for she was only to have half-pay until she was thoroughly proficient with the typewriter. The others joined her, and John soon perceived that they regarded this stroke of good luck all the more favourably because it would remove one of the stumbling-blocks out of his path.

Her wages would not be equal to his, but it was evident that in their judgment they would be able to live, even though he should leave them. It seemed to John, however, that just when he was bringing himself to look resignedly upon the dead body of his love for Sallie, something had happened to give new life to the corpse, and the occurrences of the next day very greatly strengthened this feeling.

On the following night he was appointed to preach at Whittle Green, about a mile and a half from Bramwell, and half that distance beyond the residence of the Woods. His heart beat a little quicker as he passed the farm, but he kept his head down and trudged doggedly on with a sore heart.

"You don't object to a solo, do you, Mr. John?" said the leading singer as they were consulting together in the little vestry.

"Oh no; I like them if they are appropriate."

"Thank you," and handing John the service sheet, the leader took up his tune book and went into the chapel, and the preacher, glancing absently at the sheet, read, "Solo, Miss Sarah Wood."

Whittle Green was a sort of outpost of the Bramwell Church, and was worked on mission lines. John was not surprised, therefore, at the arrangement for special singing; but it was certainly a new thing for Sallie to come out as a soloist. He announced her all the same when the time came, and she stood up there, supported by two fiddles and the harmonium, and began to sing one of Sankey's less known hymns. The choir sat immediately under the pulpit. Sallie was on one side, and so John, who could not have prevented himself watching her whatever had been the consequence, only got her face in profile. Everything she did pleased him. He liked the evident effort it was costing her, he liked the song she had selected; but most of all he was pleased to note that she was not regarding the thing as a performance, and trying to sing as well as she could, but was throwing herself into the spirit of the service, and trying to make her little effort an appeal in song. For the moment she was a pleader, using the simple melody and her own fine voice to bring the Gospel message more closely home to the hearts of her hearers, and as his smothered love, thus helped, forced its way up through suspicions and misgivings, she sank back into her seat with a sudden return to self-consciousness and modesty that drove the blood into her face and a warm glow into John's heart. He couldn't have believed it of her; there was evidently a side to her nature he did not understand. How little people really understood each other, and how narrow it was to expect everybody to show their religion in the same way!

There was an unusually large congregation that night, and some sort of " spirit of expectation " had possession of the people. The news of what had taken place on the previous Sunday had reached the place and created the hope of similar results. John noticed also that two or three of his last Sunday's converts were present, and so he was not surprised that, when the prayer-meeting came, there was what Methodists call " another breakdown." In the joy of his reward he forgot all about Sallie, and gave a little start of surprise when, on entering the steward's house, he found her seated at the table with a glass of home-made lemonade in her hand. She had a grave, spiritual sort of look, as though the quickening influences of the service just concluded had raised her altogether above ordinary affairs, and she listened to a story the hostess was telling about one of the converts with ardent attention. John had a glass of milk, and as he sat with his hat on, ready to depart, he began to feel that it was rather hard to have to fight a battle with himself and force himself to stern duty just when he felt most tender and sympathetic toward all the world. Sallie and he would, of course, go home together. It would be pleasant to have to thank her for her kind interest in his sister, but he had resolved that upon the very first opportunity he would let her know that he was aware she had another lover, and thus break the last link between them. It was hard to have it to do at all, but it was harder after the uplifting experiences of the night.

Sallie lingered over her lemonade, and even when John rose to go she did not move.

"We go the same way, don't we, Miss Wood? May I have the pleasure?" he said, at length, fumbling nervously with his umbrella handle.

Sallie, still apparently engaged in conversation with the hostess, turned quickly round with a look of surprise and seeming reluctance.

"Oh, no, Mr. Ledger, don't wait for me. I'm near home, you know."

John was surprised and a little self-rebuked. He had not been able altogether to keep down the suspicion that for some reason she had thrown herself in his way that night; but her words, and her manner even more than her words, seemed to show that he had once more been guilty of unworthy thoughts about her. She might have given him up definitely, and if so, she was acting in simplest consistency with that fact. He hesitated. Flesh and blood clamoured within him for a postponement of the ordeal, but an inexorable instinct urged him on. The more difficult the task the less reason for deferring it. And as he stood there wavering, Sallie looked at him again, and seemed reluctantly to give way.

"Wilful *man* must have his way," she said with playful resignation, and then she moved towards John and the door.

The young preacher held open the garden gate for her, and then stepped stiffly to her side, nerving himself to his difficult task. They had scarcely passed the mission room, however, when Sallie snatched impulsively at his arm, and clinging confidingly to it, lifted an anxious little sigh, and began to talk with nervous rapidity.

" Oh, John, I *do* wish I was a man and could preach like you."

" You! Why you preached better than I, to-night."

" For shame, John!" And she gave his arm a hasty shake, and then with a sudden plaintive cry she went on, " Oh, I should like to do something to make the world better!"

John had several sharp stabs of self-reproach.

" Why, Sallie, you've done something to-night, and you did something when you got Lucy that——"

" John!" she interrupted, " do be serious. You vex me, talking of such trumpery things, and all the time you know I am bad."

" Bad, Sallie?"

" Yes, bad! I'm a mean, mercenary, worldly girl, John, and you know it," and she looked up into his face with such innocent distress that John's heart softened. The scene he had witnessed so recently in that very lane came back to him, however, and he did not know whether he ought to harden his heart against her or rebuke himself for unjust suspicions. As he hesitated, Sallie, who glanced searchingly up at him once or twice, suddenly pulled up—

" John, now you're a preacher, how is it that I sometimes feel more sinful than I did before I was converted? I feel sometimes full of desires to be good and useful and devote myself to good things, and then sometimes I'm so mean and selfish, and do such hard, cruel things, that afterwards I can't bear myself. How is it?"

She was standing there on the footpath before him, and looking up so seriously into his face whilst her dark eyes shone with eager concern that John was momentarily disarmed; but the unspoken confession in the last few words struck on his ear with an uncertain ring, and he held his breath and stood gazing down upon her. She did not flinch. She knew where her power lay, and John was so strangely affected that he could do nothing but look into those deep eyes. The impulse to snatch her in his arms was well-nigh irresistible. But its strength was his salvation. He instinctively suspected anything he found his whole nature clamouring for, and so he checked himself, sighed, and then hedged off into a theological explanation of the condition she had described. She listened with the same serious attention, looking steadily into his face and nodding comprehendingly, as he passed from point to point ; but a more suspicious person might have noticed that her eyes wandered a little, and she seemed to be studying him rather than his words.

" I see, I see," she murmured musingly as he finished, and then she took his arm again, and they began to move along the lane once more. They walked in silence for a minute or two, and he was just choosing his words for the question that lay nearest his heart, when she resumed : " John, do you think I should ever be good enough to be a sister ? "

" A sister ? "

" Yes, to work amongst the poor. There's only father and I, you know, and when he's gone I should like to do something of that sort, only—only I'm not good enough."

" But, Sallie——"

" Yes, I know. You think I'm not good enough, too," and it was not resentment he found in her tones, but humble, regretful tears.

" But, Sallie, I thought you were of the marrying sort ? "

" John ! How can you—after to-night ? "

John had the feeling that he was the worldly one

now. It was no matter, though. He had one thought in his mind, and one only. He had felt much of the spiritual upliftedness that was evidently governing Sallie's words; but everything disappeared before the struggles and suspenses of tortured love. He could not live in that state; he must end it one way or the other; and so, conscious that he was doing an almost brutal thing, he blurted out—

"Sallie, who is your lover now?"

"John!" She seemed angry, and hastily withdrew her hand, though her quick eyes narrowly scanned his face. "Oh, John, I've done with those things now. They seemed sinful since—since—you know when."

They had reached the gate of the farm by this time, and she turned her head away to hide her emotions.

"But, Sallie, I——"

"No, John, no! I'm going to live for better things. Pray for me, John!" and she held her hand up to keep him away, and leaned sorrowfully on the gate.

John was still fighting down his suspicions, and her last words did not help him. He drew nearer to her; but before he could speak she pushed him gently away.

"The world is so full of suffering and sorrow. Those who ought to go and help will not, so somebody must do it."

He saw exactly what she meant. Oh, if only he could have believed her capable of sentiments such as these, but the other thought was still tormenting him, and he must get to the bottom of it.

"How long have you felt like that, Sallie?"

"Often, lately, especially since I—since you—but I'm fully determined, after to-night," and then, as if by a sudden irresistible impulse, she stepped up to him again, and lifting her eyes, soft with tears, to his, she said—

" You'll pray for me, John, won't you ? "

It was too much.   Suspicion, fear, pride, curiosity as to her real feeling, all melted away.   The love that was in him, increased by stern repression, rose with a sudden overwhelming flood, his arms were thrown around her, and in another moment he was raining kisses upon her teary face.

CHAPTER XII

THE CASTING OF THE LOT

" Jack ! Heigh, Jack ! here ! "

John, who was returning from the mill one blustery October evening, turned round and saw Jim Flintop, an old schoolmate, hurrying after him. Jim was the son of the man who had started the charge of plagiarism against him, and who, in spite of the second minister's persistent efforts, still stuck to his text.

" Hello, Jim ! what's up ? "

Jim was a big, red-haired, red-cheeked fellow, of fiery disposition, and he now came fiercely up to John, and grabbing at the lappel of his greasy mill jacket, demanded—

" Is it true as thou'rt on wi' Sallie Wood again ? "

" Ay, what by that ? "

" An' would thou tackle her again after she'd squashed thee once afore ? "

" Who says she did squash me ? " and John's choler began to rise.

" Who ! she told me so herself."

" What ! "

" She—told—me—so—herself, she took me on—softy as I was—when she squelched thee, an' she told me all about it, an' now she thinks thou'rt goin' to be a parson, she chucks me, and takes up wi' thee again, Jack ! she's a——" but Jim could find no name strong enough.

John was very angry, and also uneasy.

" Jim, thou'rt mad ! I know that girl, and nobody shall speak of her like that."

" But, man ! it's true ! She daddled me about for months ; she was keener on it than I was myself, but after thou'd preached at t' chapel she chucked me away like a sucked orange."

John was dumb with confusion and resentment ; all his heart rose in defence of Sallie ; everybody was against her, surely he must defend her. If only he could stifle—but he would ! He would stand by her against them all.

" Jim," he said, speaking almost as fiercely as the other, " Sallie Wood is mine, and neither you nor anybody else shall say a word against her."

" Sha'n't I ? Well, I'll show thee ! Look ! I'll have her. I'll have her to spite thee, and when I *do* get her, by the Lord I'll make her smart for it."

Jim was foaming at the mouth with fury, and did not perceive that he was betraying himself and easing John's mind.

" Thee ! " he went on, " thee take her from me ! Try it on, and I'll knock thee into sausage-meat."

But John saw that Jim's language was too strong to be taken seriously, and that he need care no more for his information than he did for his threats, and so got away as soon as he could, although it was some time before he recovered his self-possession. It was Jim, then, with whom he had seen Sallie on that sad Friday night ; well, she had evidently never cared much about him, so he fought down this con- firmation of his own misgivings, and resolved to trust his sweetheart. He kept in that mind all night, and did not even mention the circumstance to Sallie when he saw her later ; but next day at his work his doubts and fears back came with most distressing persistence, and so, for some time, he was torn with conflicting hopes and fears. His visits to the farm were times of unalloyed delight, but his days, as he paced barefooted after his wheels, were periods of racking misgivings. And so the days slipped by, Christmas drew near, household prospects looked brighter than he had ever known them, his mother had a wistful sort of hopefulness about her which gave him the keenest satisfaction, and but that the question of all questions remained unsettled he would have been contented. He had never named Jim Flintop to Sallie, and as he knew that his rival was still pursuing her with his attentions, he was perplexed to know why she never alluded to the matter. But he was weary of harassing suspicions, and ashamed to pay court to a girl and think evil of her. He ought to trust her, and as he had a considerable fund of trustfulness he did not find it very difficult. And so the time sped along, and from hints he received John began to be in daily fear of a summons to see the super., his uneasiness being considerably increased by the knowledge that if he had to offer for the ministry it was high time he made definite preparations.

The super. had told Wilky that he intended to give John an appointment at the town chapel on the new plan, so that those who would have to vote at the Quarterly meeting might know what they were doing. This set the little broker on pins, and he fell upon John so fiercely whenever they met that he began to avoid him, and dropped his frequent visits to the furniture shop. On the Sunday of Christmas week John was appointed at Sneldridge for the afternoon service, and Wilky at night; and John's father brought word that the broker would like John to stay for the evening service and walk home with him.

John did not like the prospect; he guessed that it

would mean an unusually prolonged and, perhaps, heated discussion on the ever-present topic of his call, and it would also interfere with courting arrangements, but as he could not easily refuse his old master, he waited and heard him preach. To John's amazement Wilky commenced what turned out to be a strikingly original sermon on the parable of the sower. Ignoring all rules of interpretation, and looking as far away from his young friend as he could, the preacher opened with the startling question, " What would have happened if the sower had ' funked' the job, or gone to sleep, or sat down and read the newspaper, or gone courting, or spent his time making dolls and tin trumpets for the children ? There were people like that ; they looked after themselves, or their wives, or their sweethearts, whilst the work of the Lord was spoiling ; they sat there "—and here Wilky had a great inspiration—" sqawkin' on a fiddle whilst Rome was burning ; the fields were white unto the harvest, but the labourers were few."

But this was only the exordium. Carefully avoiding John's eye, Wilky discussed the seed, which was all it should be, and the ground, which was of different kinds—and here he gave astonishingly clear descriptions of the soil and the truths embodied in the figure—" But what was seed or soil or anything else if there was no sower ? Pray ye the Lord of the harvest," &c.

John listened to this amazing distortion of the Scriptures with mingled feelings ; he saw, of course, the all too palpable moral, and was shocked and a little grieved at the whole affair. To his relief Wilky never alluded to the sermon on their way home ; but as they were parting, he looked with a comical seriousness at his young companion, and said, sententiously, " Faithful are the wounds of a friend," and then he turned and dashed off homewards in a most violent hurry.

But even these extraordinary efforts, Wilky discovered, produced no effect upon the obdurate John, and as he now avoided him more than ever he adopted other means of reaching him. Whenever he thought it probable that the young minder would be at home he would trot off down to the little cake shop, open the door hastily, bawl out, " Whom shall I send, and who will go for us ? " or " Woe is me if I preach not the gospel," or " Demas hath forsaken me, having loved this present world," or some such passage ; bang the door, and hurry away as fast as his diminutive legs would carry him.

As this produced no effect, he changed his tactics, and when John came home one night from his work, he found a letter waiting for him. He did not recognise the handwriting, but opening the envelope he discovered a packet that looked like a long, carefully folded epistle. He removed the outer cover, and found a sheet of blank paper, then an inside sheet, then another, and at last he came to a bit of not too clean cardboard, upon which was written in drunken Roman capitals—

ISAIAH vi. 8.

This was followed two days later by a similar consignment, containing

LUKE ix. 62 ;

and a week later it was a gentler but still urgent sentence—

JOSHUA vii. 10,

followed the very next post by

MATTHEW xxviii. 19.

John smiled again and again as he received these messages, but his mother took them seriously, and arranged them in a row on the mantel piece of his little bedroom. Then the mysterious missives suddenly ceased, but one evening, when John reached home, he found a message awaiting him to the effect that Mrs. Drax wanted to see him. She was such a dainty person that John always thought it necessary to change his clothes before he went into her room, so that it was seven o'clock before he answered the summons.

" Come in, John, I'm glad to see you—— Wilky, you mustn't go. Come here ! "

The broker gave a surly grunt as John entered, and was making for the door, but at his wife's command he waddled back to a chair, and sat down in a tentative ready-to-go sort of attitude. John uttered the usual civilities, and then there was an awkward pause.

" John," said Mrs. Drax, gently, " what am I to do with this awkward man of mine ? He's nearly worrying my life out about you."

" Me, ma'am ? "

" Me ? Me ? " cried Wilky. " Well, that's a corker ? What next ? Me bother about *him;* he can go to t' land o' green ginger for me."

Mrs. Drax and John smiled at each other, as the little man blew off steam, and then closing her eyes to think, the good woman went on, with a grave look—

" We are all hoping about you, John—and—praying."

Wilky snorted to signify that he particularly insisted on not being included in this statement.

" You are very kind, ma'am, but I wish you wouldn't."

" Not pray, John ? "

"Course not! What's prayer? We don't need nobody to pray for us! We're hinfallible, we are," and the broker laughed a cynical, contemptuous laugh.

"I hope you will always pray for me, ma'am, but I do wish you would not think about the other."

"But that's what we pray about, John."

John sighed, and shook his head slowly; presently Mrs. Drax asked—

"Is it still the old difficulty, John?"

"Yes, ma'am, I get no nearer; I have no call."

"But the Church is calling you, and the fruit you have had is surely a call?"

"But I want the call of God, ma'am."

"T-h-a-t-'s i-t!" and Wilky snatched at one of his wife's antimacassars, which had caught on his coat buttons, and sending it flying across the room, he ripped out, "He's a nonsuch, he's not goin' to be called like the common riff-raff. He mun have a miracle! He wants a depytation o' cherybims to call him! T' Almighty mun get down off His throne an' come an' ax him if he'll kindly oblige—that's wot he wants."

Mrs. Drax waited with closed eyes until Wilky's scornful wrath had spent itself, and then went on—

"But you *would* go, John, if the Church called you?"

"Mrs. Drax," cried John, with tremulous vehemence, "if there was only one poor sinner left in the world, I'd go to the deadliest climate or the foulest fever den on earth to reach that soul, if only my Master said one little word."

Something very like a smothered sob came from the direction of Wilky's chair, but it was covered under a violent succession of snorts and grunts and scrapings of throat. Mrs. Drax waited a moment, evidently not very sure of her voice, and then just

as she was commencing to speak, Wilky's chair flew
back, and they heard him say, in husky tones—

" Let us pray ! "

John dropped upon his knees with a full heart,
and was just murmuring, " Lord help," when Wilky
said in low tones—

" Sister Drax, will you pray ? "

She was lying on the sofa as usual, but she took
her hands from her face, and in low pleading tones
that vibrated through John's soul she commenced to
pray.   Tenderly, humbly, she pleaded that their dear
friend might be guided and strengthened and re-
warded for all he had done for his dear mother.   A
perfect woman's prayer it was, and John shook with
emotion.   She finished at last, and he was just rising
to his feet when the rough little broker commenced
in strangely tender tones—

" O, Lord, Thou 's given us everything ; Thou
's given us Thy Son, an' we've nowt we can give
Thee ; but we want to give Thee this dear lad of ours.
He's a lot to—to sister Drax an' me, an' more to his
mother, an' that's why we want to give him to Thee.
Take him, Lord !   Call him, Lord !   Make him a
good soul-winner.   An' oh, Lord, above all things
make him a good lad.   He doesn't want no glory,
no popperlarity.   He wants to hear Thy voice behind
him.   Speak, Lord !   Speak soon !   Speak now ! for
Thy name's sake, Amen."

Wilky looked very abashed and confused as he
rose to his feet, and as John, overcome with emotion,
remained as he was, Wilky was glad to respond to the
knocking which had been going on for some time in
the shop below ; and when a few minutes later, after
having promised Mrs. Drax that he would do nothing
hastily, John went downstairs, he found the little
broker stormily thrusting a woman out of the shop,
and trying to cover up the fact that he was taking

M.   M no payment for the brush she wanted, under volleys of his shot-like raillery.

A few days later, when John returned from his class-meeting, he found a note from the super. awaiting him. It was the long dreaded summons to an interview on the following Friday evening, and as he shyly slipped it into his pocket, Lucy challenged him to tell them the contents.

When he smiled and shook his head, she declared she could guess, and for the next hour she and Annie and Sallie, who just then turned up, assailed him with all sorts of reasons in favour of immediate decision, and though he bantered them and laughed at them, and then most riskily tried serious argument with them, they triumphed lightly over everything he could advance, and deftly turned his own weapons against him. His mother as usual supported him, but when they ceased, she surprised them all by heaving a heavy sigh and murmuring—

" It's no bantering matter this, it's a heart breaker."

" Mother ! "

" It is ! " she cried almost fiercely, and then suddenly melting, she went on, turning appealingly to her son, " Johnny, when first I felt thy little mouth snugglin' against my breast it comforted a breaking heart ; thou's been my one comfort and hope ever sin', but oh ! I'm sore to my very soul just now."

" But, mother," he cried in keen distress, and then hesitating and looking anxiously at her, he went on, " Mother, hearken ! I'm more eager now to go than you are to send me ; I'll go just now if you'll prove to me that I am called, but I've not got the education, I've not got the gifts, and above all I've not got the call ; let God give me a call Himself, clear in my own heart, and I'll go to the end of the world."

" None are so deaf as those who won't hear."

John was cut up ; such a word from the mother he

worshipped he never expected to hear, and so oppressed by constant harassing and goaded to recklessness by this last stinging lash he jumped to his feet and cried hotly—

"Mother, you don't trust me! You think I could decide if I would. You shall decide for me! Say one word, just one word, and I'll go to the super. now."

Mrs. Ledger, pale and agitated, and full of quick remorse for her last and most unusual words, stood leaning against the mantelpiece and looking dreely into the fire.

"Thou will?" she cried, looking wonderingly and a little fearfully at him.

"I will, mother." But though his words had resolution enough in them he was bitterly repenting that he had used them.

His mother still peered broodingly into the fire, and once or twice half turned as if about to speak, but her eyes wandered back to the hot coals and she still seemed to hesitate. It was an awful moment for her; the one ambition of her life might apparently be realised by a word. She was a long time before she spoke, but at last she moved slowly to his side, put her hard hand on his head, and softly stroked it.

"John, my dear, thou'rt a better Christian than thy mother. Go thy own way; thy mother has led thee all these years, but now she'll be glad to follow. The Lord be with thee, lad; the Lord's Will be done."

It was a long speech for the silent, long-suffering woman, and John greatly marvelled at it, and from that hour not even Sallie herself was allowed to raise the question in that house.

All the same John was perfectly aware that the coming of the super.'s letter was the beginning of the great crisis; the battle had commenced, and though body and brain and heart were alike weary, he knew there could be no more rest for him until the great question was settled. Oh, what should he do? Pray? His whole life in those days was one long drawn out supplication, from the brief ejaculation of the moment, as he paced after his approaching and receding wheels at the mill, to the wearily drawn out night wrestlings that seemed to be sapping his strength. He had a feeling, too, that this incessant assailing of the Divine ear was a sort of cowardice; he was asking God to do what, in the very nature of the case, he could not do. He saw more clearly every hour that it was not merely a question as to his future, it was the supreme test of his life, and it was of the very essence of that test that, like his Divine Master, he should be left to conquer or fail alone. Again and again he faced it, and again and again he felt that the only thing he could do was to do nothing. "When you are uncertain what to do, do nothing," he remembered, had been a favourite phrase of a very judicious minister whose memory he greatly revered; but in his case such a course seemed to be only a shirking of the responsibility of his manhood. It was idle to ignore the fact that he knew quite well that if he did nothing, that, in his circumstances, would be to do everything, and his candidature would go on. Oh, if he could only have trusted himself, but the whole difficulty lay just there; he had been taught all his religious life to distrust above all things his own nature, and he wanted to be a minister. His whole being was filled with a great ambition; was not this the very best reason for not doing it? And when he had reasoned himself round to this veritable *cul-de-sac* for perhaps the fiftieth time, a feeling of utter helplessness came over him. The thing was too great for him, the fact that he was not equal to the settlement of the question was the best possible proof that he was not equal to the work involved. Was not the thing too great and grave to settle alone? Was not this

one of those rare occasions when man's unaided
reason was insufficient?   Might he not therefore
appeal to God?   Had not God in such cases
condescended to human infirmity, and when there
had been an honest purpose to do God's Will if
it could be ascertained, had not God deigned to give
some sign?

He was fighting his battle out over his work when
his thoughts first took this particular shape.   His
employment was of a monotonous and mechanical
character, and his mind, therefore, was fairly free to
think.   Dressed in the scanty clothing which the
heat necessary for the manufacture of the cotton
prescribed, and following first one wheel and then
another, piecing an " end " up here, cleaning a roller
and putting in a new roving bobbin there, he went over
and over again the same dreary mental processes.
Oh, that God would give him some indication of His
Will, His very slightest would be sufficient!   Then
he remembered having heard in class meetings and
lovefeasts the stories told by fellow members of how,
in great perplexity, God had suddenly and unmis-
takably revealed His Will to them.   They had
seemed far-fetched, credulous, and even superstitious tales to him then; but, oh, what would he
give for some such leading now!   He had always
held the doctrine of particular Providence somewhat
loosely, and with much modern reserve, but he
would have been glad to believe it now.   But his
inability to get help in this way was, of course, one
of the regular penalties of unbelief, he told himself.
Then an idea occurred to him; some of the best of
the old men he knew had a curious way of getting
rid of perplexities.   When they had come to a
standstill and knew not where to turn, he had heard
them tell how they had taken the Bible in their
hands and had prayed, and then opened the book

haphazard, and had cast their eyes on texts which had solved all their troubles at once.

It was a small thing to do, there could be no harm— No! it was for him, at any rate, a cowardly shirking of his responsibility. And yet what *was* he to do?

There was a little pile of cop skips standing against the iron pillar in the middle of the wheel-alley, and in the bottom skip he always kept a little Bible; he paused a moment, then made a dart at the skip, pulled himself up suddenly with something very like a shudder, and turned away after a broken "end." A few minutes later, however, he drew near to the skip again, and again passed it by. At last, however, with a fretful little sigh, he put his hand into the bottom skip and pulled out his Bible. His hand shook as he held the volume, and he took a nervous glance around as if afraid of being observed; then he laid the book on the cops and allowed it to fall open where it would. He dare not look, however, but followed the receding mule; but when it had finished its upward journey, and was returning, he left it and went and bent over the book once more. It lay open plainly enough, there could be no mistake; he took another frightened glance about him, and then examined the page. It was the first chapter in I. Chronicles, a mere record of names, and he turned away with a sick heart. For ten minutes more he paced about the oily floor, and at last persuading himself that this might be a trial of his faith, he closed the volume again and allowed it to fall open where it would. He did not look at it at once, but went on with his work; but presently, with a little gesture of impatience, he consulted the oracle once more. It was the fifteenth of I. Corinthians, the great chapter on the Resurrection. A bitter smile rose to his lips, there was nothing there that bore in the least upon his case, and God was showing him very clearly that he was not to be allowed to evade his own responsibility. Half an hour later, after many inward debatings, he reminded himself of the old local saying. "The third time pays for all." He had very little hope now, but a shock went through him as he noted that the page now before him had upon it a passage that was underscored. He never marked his own Bible, he rather despised the practice. Who could have done it ? He scarcely supposed it could have been done by supernatural fingers, but he was in a state now to accept anything, and so he bent shyly and fearfully over the text and read, " These shall go away into everlasting punishment," &c. ; and then he remembered that he had marked that particular text when preparing for his local preacher's examination. It was no use ; God had absolutely refused to release him ; it was not merely a decision he had to make, it was the test of his character and obedience, and he turned sadly away to his work.

A few minutes later, he noticed that it was close upon dinner time. Thursday was cleaning day, and as some of the machinery could only be cleansed standing, it was usually done in the dinner-hour, and the noon-tide meal had to be taken on the premises. John sighed again as he remembered this, for he wanted time to think and pray, but everything seemed to be against him. As the shafting overhead gave its characteristic groan and began to slacken, his mother appeared at the end of his wheel-alley ; but as he was attending at that moment to the wheel-head, and could not leave, she put down the basket against the end wall, and lifted up a letter and waved it, and placed in on the basket lid. It was some minutes before he could get to open the missive, which somehow set his heart beating. The handwriting, however, relieved him ; it was only another of Wilky's mysterious communications; so he put it down unopened and finished his cleaning. He had only ten minutes for his meal when he was able to get to it, and so the note lay neglected until work had been resumed, and the loud hum of the spindles told that all was going smoothly. Then he took out the letter and opened it with a pensive smile. There was a change in Wilky's manner; the texts were all written out this time, and there were several of them. Expressing in their mute way Wilky's anxiety, the texts touched John, and he began to read them with dimmed eyes; but when he had gone over them the second time, and the full force of their significance became clear, he gave a little gasp of surprise. It looked as though Wilky knew what he had been thinking about and doing all that morning; it was certainly a striking coincidence. Then he observed that the texts had a sort of order about them, and that one word in each selection was doubly underscored. He spread the sheet on the top of the cop skip, picked up an oil-can, and oiled a screaming spindle, and then hastening back, he read—

"They cast pur, that is, the *lot*."—Esther iii. 7.

"The *lot* is cast into the lap; but the whole disposing thereof is of the Lord."—Proverbs xvi. 33.

"The *lot* causeth contentions to cease . . . "—Proverbs xviii. 18.

"And they gave forth their *lots;* and the lot fell upon Matthias; and he was numbered with the eleven Apostles."—Acts i. 26.

All the above were written out in crabby, ill-shaped capitals, but underneath, as a sort of after-thought, there was scribbled—

> "Not mine, not mine the choice
> In things or great or small :
> Be Thou my guide, my strength,
> My wisdom and my all."

Late that night, two persons might have been seen sitting close to the table in the broker's back room, John and his former master. Wilky's bushy brows were drawn together, his bristly whiskers stood out, and his whole face betrayed keenest anxiety. John had put the fantastic idea from him in the mill, but as this was the last night before the great decision, Wilky had captured him on his way home, and had kept him there without food and with a splitting headache, trying to convince him of the wisdom of adopting the plan suggested.

For over two hours they had been arguing, and at length John, as much to get away from his tempter as with any faith in the result, had allowed himself to be persuaded into the experiment, stipulating, however, that there should be a blank slip of paper as well as the "yes" and "no." Wilky had protested that this gave an unfair proportion of chances against "yes," but after twenty minutes' wrangling he was fain to yield, and held out a stumpy fist, from the top of which three tags of tape-shaped paper projected. John put out his hand to draw, but as he touched the papers Wilky drew back his hand, and protested once more that it wasn't fair ; John, secretly hoping that his obstinancy would provoke Wilky into abandoning the experiment, stuck to his point.

At last, however, irritable through overstrained excitement, Wilky gave way, and thrust the tags of paper once more under John's nose. He sprang back as if he had been attacked by a serpent, and then turned away and stoutly declared that nothing should ever induce him to do such a thing. Wilky, nearly beside himself, stormed, and coaxed, and argued, and at length John drew near again. He held his hand behind him, fearful apparently of its betraying him ; he looked at the stumpy fist and the three ends of paper until they began to fascinate him; he sighed heavily and shrank back, and Wilky, tortured with suspense, jerked out—

"Draw, man! draw!"

John sprang away again as though he had been shot, and cried piteously—

"No, no!"

Wilky called him a coward and a shuffler, and with fierce gleaming eyes accused him of trifling.

John approached once more and put out his hand, and Wilky with drawn face and wild stare pushed the slips forward and looked at John.

"Lord forgive me," cried John, and shut his eyes tight.

"Draw!" cried Wilky, with a cry that was almost a hiss. John with a sudden deadly calmness drew one of the tags, and shutting his eyes averted his face and held out the drawn lot for Wilky to examine.

"It's a judgment," he wailed piteously, as he sank back into his chair.

John had drawn the blank.

CHAPTER XIII

THE CALL AND ITS CONSEQUENCES

THE young minder's condition as he left the furniture shop that night was one of utter wretchedness; to racking perplexities that were almost unendurable he had added a deep sense of humiliation, he had been tampering with the occult, he had been playing the game of Korah, he had reduced himself to king Saul's helpless distraction and had resorted like him to a witch-of-Endor-like means of escape. But God had been merciful, and had not answered him at all. Racked and overstrained until his brains seemed to boil, and the very roots of his hair creep, he still saw everything with almost preternatural clearness, and the various phases of the great problem were startlingly vivid as he looked at them. He had never seen so clearly or penetrated so deeply into the very heart of things as he seemed to do just then, and the inexorable conclusion had never before appeared so remorselessly irresistible. Men who were making sacrifice to enter the ministry might volunteer properly enough, but to one to whom it would be a great social lift, the only right thing was to wait until the call came. He wanted to be a minister, his whole nature seemed to rise clamorously to the chance offered, and that was the clearest possible evidence that it was only a disguised earthly ambition, and must be ruthlessly trampled down. No, in his case, nothing but the plainest and most

indubitable indication of the Divine will could justify
him in making the offer, and such an indication he
had certainly never yet had. His friends, his mother,
his sweetheart, were all so many unconscious instruments of temptation. The tempter was spreading
before *him* "the kingdoms of this world and the
glory thereof," and if he wanted to save his soul
alive, he must cry, "Get thee behind me, Satan." He
walked about for a full hour before returning home,
and the anxious looks cast upon him as he entered
the house became more serious when he declined
food and almost immediately hastened upstairs to
his own room. But nature at last began to assert
herself; the walk in the open air had brought the
blood from his brain and cooled him, and though
conscious that he was settling into dull heavy despair
he noted his condition almost gratefully. He had
intended to spend the night in prayer, but his utter
exhaustion took all desire away, nature refused to be
pushed a single point further, and with a groan of
self-abandonment he threw himself, dressed as he
was, on the bed. Half an hour later, when his
mother, distressed at the look he had worn, and the
fact that he had gone to bed without supper, stole
quietly into the room with a glass of milk, she found
him fast asleep. The signs of recent suffering on his
face wrung her heart, but she smiled with pensive
thankfulness at the soundness of his slumbers, and
setting the glass down, and drawing the bed-clothes
gently over him, she stood hovering at his side like a
wistful guardian angel. For several minutes she
brooded over him, now bending down and looking
intently into the beloved features, and now clasping
her hands and turning up her face towards the dim
ceiling, in rapt supplication. Then she moved the
candle to the little table and dropped upon her knees
at the side of the bed, and the prayer which sheer

exhaustion had intermitted was thus vicariously offered over the wearied sleeper. For one long hour the wrestling woman urged her petition, now groping in the air as if she were snatching at the garments of the Invisible, and now smiling in the passionate persuasiveness that disdained refusal. Then she stopped, and buried her bowed head in her hands, lifted a long pathetic sigh, and murmured through tear-wet fingers—

"Nevertheless not as I will—nor as he will."

The sleeper had not moved, but when she rose to her feet the anxious mother persuaded herself that there was a soft smile on the unconscious face, and so she turned away and stepped quietly out of the room and closed the door. Never a wink did this devoted woman sleep that night, and as soon as the hot coffee stall had rumbled past to its post in the market place, and the clac, clac of the clogs began to sound in the street, she was up, preparing John's morning cup of tea. Twice she went to the foot of the stairs to hear if he were stirring, but not the slightest sound could she catch.

"Well," and she drew in her lips with a painful twitch, "he shall sleep as long as he can, if he loses a quarter."

Again she listened. Oh that he would come and set her beating heart at rest! Ah, that was his door, and she, who was dying for a sight of his face, fled from the stairfoot in sudden fright. He was coming downstairs in his stocking feet as usual. He would not need to speak, one single glance at his face would tell her all. With strained intensity, she counted every step, and stared with hungry eyes at the staircase in the corner. He was coming! he was here—and in a sudden collapse of courage she turned away and ran into the pantry. Breathless and panting she stood there in the darkness, expecting, yet dreading that he would speak; but as he did not she ventured out again, but went round the tables to avoid him and kept her face carefully averted. Would he never speak! Then she took from the sideboard his breakfast-can, and began to fumble with the little screwed up parcels of tea and sugar, and as she did so, she presently ventured to raise her eyes and look at him. But John's face was averted now, and he studiously held down his head. But there was something surely gleaming from under those overshadowing brows, her heart suddenly began to melt; she dropped the can on the floor and cried in sharp distress—

"John!"

John's head dropped lower.

"John! John! Look at me!"

Yes, it was there. The face was white and solemn, and dark rings were under the brows, but the eyes! the eyes were burning with glory, glory enhanced and made infinitely solemn by a mysterious veil of self-conscious holy shame. A great awe fell upon her, she had never seen a look like that on mortal face before, and began to understand something of the feeling with which the Holy Mary must have looked on her Son, and realised dimly how the Israelites must have felt as they looked on the face of Moses.

"It's come, lad," she said at last softly, and raising his eyes more melting and yet more splendid than ever, he said in tones of almost awful solemnity—

"Yes, it's come! the burden of choice has been swallowed up in the greater burden of souls."

After an absorbed, dreamy, solemn sort of a day, John presented himself that evening at the manse, and was rather taken aback to find both the ministers awaiting him. The super. glanced a second time at him as he bade him be seated; there was a look on the visitor's face that was new. The second minister sat deep in an easy-chair on the far side of the fire, with a cigar in his mouth, and the super. took the chair in front and began to fidget, as usual, with the fire-irons.

"Well, John," he said, twirling the poker in his hands, "no use beating about the bush, you can guess why we have sent for you, eh?"

"Yes, sir."

The minister glanced again and sharply at the young minder. This was certainly a new John.

"Well, you've had twelve months to think about the matter, what do you say?"

John paused a moment and drew a long breath; both the ministers were watching him curiously—

"I'm in the hands of God and the Church, sir."

Mr. Haley turned and looked at his colleague who nodded slightly through a cloud of smoke.

"That's all right then. Well, now, my colleague and I have formed a very high opinion of your character——"

"And gifts," added number two.

"And gifts," assented the super. with a nod, "and I should like to say that we shall only be too glad to render you any assistance in our power."

"Thank you, sir," said John, fervently.

"By the way, you hav'n't had many advantages I know, you don't know anything beyond what you learnt at the Board School, I suppose?"

"I know shorthand, sir, and the rudiments of Latin and a little logic. I've made use of the evening classes at the Mechanics' Institute."

The super. raised his eyebrows in pleased surprise.

"Good! good! And what about your health? The medical examination is somewhat stiff you know."

"I never had a day's sickness in my life except when I was knocked down in Trundlegate lane."

"You've never felt anything of that since, have

you? No? Well, you factory folk look sallow enough, but you are most of you surprisingly tough."

"No harm in getting as much fresh air as you can the next few months all the same," chimed in the second minister, scrutinising a most satisfactory length of ash at the end of his cigar.

"Ah, yes, certainly! take your book into the open air whenever you can, John, but now"—and here he turned round and consulted a little book—

"There are a few questions I am required to ask you. You are not in any sort of debt, of course?"

"No sir," and John looked a little surprised at the question.

"And you don't take drams or—or tobacco"—this with a sly look at his colleague—"or snuff?"

John, getting more at ease every moment under the kindly influences of the minister's encouragement, answered in the negative.

"And you are not under any sort of matrimonial engagement, of course?"

The cleric turned to put away the book as he said this, for though he had asked the question because he was required to do so, he was already assured in his own mind of the answer.

"Well, yes, sir, I suppose I am."

Haley whisked round in astonishment; he looked significantly at his fellow-minister, whose brows were lifted, but who smoked placidly on.

"You suppose so! What do you mean by that?" and John was disturbed to detect a tone of disappointment in the minister's voice.

"I mean, sir, that there has been no formal pledge, but we are 'keeping company.'"

The super. dropped the poker with a noisy bang, rose suddenly to his feet, turned his back to the fire, pursed out his lips, and stared sternly at the bookcase against the opposite wall. The second minister's brows were raised still higher. John was astonished and a little startled; what could there be wrong in his being engaged?

" There's nothing wrong in it, is there, sir?"

" Wrong! No!" replied the minister with an embarrassed laugh, "and yet I wish it hadn't been so. You see—— But who is the young lady?"

" Miss Sarah Wood, sir."

" Who?"

" Miss Sarah Wood."

The super. threw back his head with a toss of despair; he was evidently both disappointed and alarmed, for both these good men had very definite ideas about the Woods.

John was alarmed and a little indignant; it was clear that the ministers shared the popular prejudice against the family of his sweetheart, and so in a spirit of chivalrous loyalty to his beloved he blurted out—

" She's a dear good girl, sir."

To his confusion, the simple-hearted lover's defence was greeted with a burst of laughter. When it had subsided the super. looked sideways at his colleague and the colleague looked at his superior, and off they went in another roar.

" No, no, this is too bad; you really must excuse us, John," and the super. wiped the tears of laughter out of the corners of his eyes. Then there was a pause, during which John noted that the ministers looked thoughtful, even grave, though he could see no possible reason for it. Presently the younger cleric, measuring with his eye the length of his cigar stump, said thoughtfully—

" I think you said there had been no definite engagement, Mr. John?"

" It is definite enough, so far as I am concerned, sir, but——" and John pulled up awkwardly.

M.   N

" But you are not so sure of the lady?"

John, unable as yet to see the bearings of these questions, and tortured with a fear of seeming disloyal to Sallie on the one hand, and of saying more than was strictly true on the other, hesitated, and so the super. bent over, and tapping him on the shoulder, said—

" You had better let things stand as they are, John."

" But is there some objection to a candidate being engaged, sir?"

" Well"—and the super. was evidently weighing his words—" it is not altogether a bar, you know, but the fact is the engagement, if there is one, will have to be stated on the schedule, and—and—I shall have to certify that I think the young lady suitable for a minister's wife."

" And she is, sir; she's *very* clever, and far better educated than I am; she was trained to be a schoolmistress, you know, sir."

The two ministers had another laugh. The super. held up his coat tails, and warmed his palms behind his back at the fire.

" You see, John," he explained gravely, " if you are accepted it will be seven years, possibly longer, before you can get married, and in that time many things will take place, and the Conference, from long experience, knows that these early engagements don't last. If all goes well you will go into a larger sphere of life, and your ideas and tastes will change, and if in the course of a few years you should from any cause wish to drop the engagement—well, there would be trouble, for the Conference is very strict on the point, and, I think, rightly so."

" I shall never change, sir."

" No, of course; so they all say in your position, and I've no doubt they mean it *then*, but, as a matter of fact, they do; and then comes punishment, and even in bad cases—expulsion."

The second minister looked a little embarrassed; the super. had evidently forgotten for the moment that his colleague had been "put back" two years for some such offence.

John reiterated his declaration that nothing would change his feelings, but the ministers smiled the smile of superior knowledge, and at length number two said—

"Couldn't you explain the case to the young lady and get her to suspend matters for a while? It would be much better."

"But I might lose her altogether then," cried John, in alarm, and the parsons, somewhat to his perplexity, went off into another laugh.

"Well, John," said the super. when their merriment had subsided, "I think there is nothing further to discuss to-night. We won't detain you. Of course you must push on now, and use every spare moment to the best advantage. As to this other matter, you must act uprightly, of course, but it would be better on the whole if you could go forward as unengaged," and then he kicked his colleague's foot to detain him, and as John seemed about to protest, he went on—

"Well, well, we'll think about it. Good night, John."

"She will never let him go if she knows about his prospects," mused the super., aloud, as John was being shown out.

"She'd never have looked at him but *for* his prospects," replied number two. "He's a grand lad! I should never have expected such scrupulous honour in a factory lad. He's a saint without knowing it; he'll never give her up," and the junior mused a moment on his super.'s words, and then, tossing the cigar stump into the fire, he said, slowly, " God help him if he doesn't."

Meanwhile John has started for home, eager for the joy of seeing his mother's face when he told her what had been done. But as he went along a cloud arose in his mind; it was only a little one — nothing seemed difficult now—but small though it was, he felt he would like to get it disposed of before he went home, so he turned off and made his way towards the farm. As he went along he thought rapidly. Why, this was the very thing he wanted. How wonderfully everything was working out! How good God was! He had never yet got a definite acceptance from Sallie. Lancashire people in their circumstances don't as a rule formally propose; they simply go on " keeping company" until they and everybody else accept the situation ; the decision comes when the lady is asked to " name the happy day." But this would give him the chance of getting the decisive word from his sweetheart ; she was anxious that he should go into the ministry, and if he showed her that the question had to be answered on the official schedule that would compel her to say the sweet word he longed to hear. The affair of young Flintop, which had never been fully explained, occurred to him at this moment, but it was no fault of hers if so many men were in love with her, and in his present uplifted state of mind he could not see anything bad in anybody; Sallie would be faithful enough now she was having her heart's wish.

But the young lady proved coy : she drew him on, and made him repeat all the fervent declarations of love he had whispered to her before; she found out what was at the bottom of his sudden urgency, and made him give every detail of the interview from which he had just come, and then she fell to musing, and answered his ardent questions absently. Presently she turned and seemed to measure him with her eye. It was Friday night; the kitchen was all upset with the week-end cleaning, and they were seated in the parlour where that other memorable interview had taken place. Again she looked him carefully over in a sidelong, calculating way, and then, after returning her glance to the fire and remaining silent for a moment, she put her elbow on the table, and looking steadily into his eyes, she said—

"John, you have always thought me worldly and ambitious."

There was a touch of pensive reproach in her tone, and John hastened to disavow the charge. She waited until he had done, and then went on severely—

"You thought I wanted your future position, not you."

John could not deny that such thoughts had been suggested to him, and that he had to some extent entertained them. The reproof in her voice seemed like a reproaching conscience, and he stammered out something, but instantly perceiving that he was making bad worse, he stopped confusedly. Sallie was quite aware of her advantage, and made the most of it.

"I was not vexed with you, because I—I liked you, and wished you well, but because I wanted to be a minister's wife myself."

"Oh, don't, Sallie, don't; you're cruel!"

"And if I say I love you now, I may be standing in your way——"

"You love me, Sallie! You love me!" and he made a grab at her hand, but she drew proudly back, still looking at him with calm, injured severity.

"I love you so well, John Ledger, that I will not stand in your way. You are free."

But the effort had evidently been too much for her; her face suddenly relaxed, pain and tears came into her eyes; she seemed to be dropping, but John caught her in his arms, hugged her to his breast, kissed her passionately again and again, and then began to plead his cause with her. He had been glad of the difficulty that had arisen, and had seen in it only an unexpectedly favourable opportunity of getting from her the avowal he so much longed to hear. She was an angel! she was better a thousand times than he was, and he could not, he would not give her up. She relented slowly, but at length allowed herself to be coaxed into a seat, and John talked again, and pleaded his cause most eloquently. She smiled at last, put her hand in his, gently forgave the hard thoughts of which she had convicted him, and caressed him with little lover-like touches. But she stuck to her point; knowing her power she insisted that nothing should be allowed to stand in his way, and declared that she would never be able to forgive herself if she, of all persons, should be a hindrance. John assured her over and over again that there was no danger, but she would not be moved; he should be free, absolutely free; she would tell the minister herself if he didn't, and after his examinations were over—well—well, then he would very likely think her not worthy to be a minister's wife, as indeed she wasn't, but she could bear even that if only he was doing the work of God. And John looking at her, and wondering almost to amazement at her beautiful self-sacrifice, kissed her again, and vowed that nothing should induce him to consent to her suggestion. Then she became merry again, and plucked his hair, and attempted to curl his straggling moustache, laughing all the time at what she called his preacher-like lack of business faculty.

"Let it go," she said, "get accepted, and then—

then—if you really are silly enough to want me—well, I am here."

John appeared to yield and left her, both of them happier than they had ever been during their connection with each other; but when he got away from the glamour of her influence he saw the inherent deception of the thing, and his soul revolted. He was afraid to cross the wilful little witch he had just left, but his conscience would have none of it, and he resolved quietly as he went home that, if he went forward as a candidate at all, it should be as an engaged man.

Sallie was as good as her word. The following Wednesday she went to the sewing meeting, sat near the super.'s wife, and drew her into conversation. Somebody mentioned John, and Sallie leaned over and whisperingly asked Mrs. Haley if it were true that John Ledger was to be a candidate for the ministry after all.

" You should know better than I," said the lady, and Sallie blushed a little, affected a pretty surprise, and asked why ?

" Why ? Aren't you engaged to him ? "

" I ? Oh, dear no ! " and then with another blush and a sudden drop into the confidential, she moved a little nearer, and admitted they had " walked out " a little, but were not engaged, and that, of course, this ministry question had stopped the thing, at least for a time.

Mr. Haley, when his wife detailed this conversation to him, at once saw his colleague, and then Sallie herself, and then John, and the poor man finding one lover saying one thing and the other another, concluded that there must be something between the young couple, and that the honestest thing was to listen to John's plea, and enter him on the schedule as " under matrimonial engagement." He had more scruples when it came to certifying Sallie's suitability, but even on that score, though he had an unconquerable prejudice against her, there was nothing he could put into words, and as his wife assured him that the girl was clever enough for anything, he let that go also.

The Sunday before the all-important March quarterly meeting, John took the morning service at the Chapel, in order that the super. and the officials might hear him. The elderly local preachers looked a little dubiously at each other as they consulted together on the flags of the chapel yard after the service. There was an entire absence of " style " about John's deliverances. He hadn't even divisions in his sermon.

His father, by reason of an almost phenomenal popularity in his younger days, was still the standard of comparison amongst his compeers; but John had evidently not a single one of his father's gifts, and was, in fact, a very striking contrast to him. But these good men soon found that they were in a minority, and whatever lingering doubts they may have had, they were careful not to express them either to the delighted worshippers or to the truculent and excited Wilky. The charge of plagiarism sprang up again, however, and the ministers became a little anxious as to what Flintop and his supporters might do. John was very quiet about it all. His mind was entirely at rest; he looked brighter and even younger than he had done for some time, his only misgiving now being as to how his mother and sisters would fare when his support was withdrawn. It would take all the few pound he had saved to get him any sort of outfit for college, and during his term of residence there he would be able to render them little assistance. The income from his father's business had, ever since he could remember anything, been inadequate and uncertain, and now that he recalled the fact, his father had been unusually secretive of late, which was an almost certain sign of impending trouble. Well, God had called him; that was the great thing, and He, somehow, would provide. This was the course of his thoughts on Monday, and when his day's work was done he hastened home to get to his beloved books. As he placed his hands on the "sneck" of the door he heard a sort of bellowing groan, coming evidently from his mother's bedroom. His heart stood still, and he went white to the lips. All the sweet prospects he had been dreaming of at his work were wiped out in an instant, and blank despair came down upon him as, opening the door with a trembling hand, he saw, as he now fully expected, the county-court bailiff seated by the fire.

CHAPTER XIV

AFTER ALL!

JOHN's first thought was for his mother, and, glancing round, he found her seated on a stool under the stairs, the picture of stony grief. She did not move for a moment or two, but as their eyes met the fountains of the deep within her seemed to break up, and she snatched at her apron and buried her face in it.

"That's better," said Gittins, the bailiff, a short, fat, apoplectic man, puffing away stolidly at a black pipe.

John thought it was better, too. It was a good sign when his mother could weep. He stepped forward towards the fireplace, and put down his breakfast can and basket, and as Annie, with red, swollen eyes, picked it up, he touched her with a little caressing gesture, and she burst into a fresh passion of tears.

Gittins plucked at John's sleeve and whispered sympathetically—

"Twenty-six pun five an' sevenpunce—Rose an' Crown Loan Society—Ferridge."

John's heart went cold again. He understood it all. His father had been getting out of one financial difficulty by getting into another, as usual. This time he had borrowed money from a loan society, to which Ferridge, the rent collector, had recently been appointed secretary, and the bully had evidently waited until this hour of his approaching success to deal his blow. God help them now!

At this moment another unearthly groan came from upstairs, and Sampson was heard wailing out—

"Woe is me, that I sojourn in Mesech; I dwell in the tents of Kedar."

John, forgetful of his own ruined prospects, and with an infinite sympathy for the broken-hearted woman under the stairs, felt his heart grow cold towards his father, and, as he tried to check his feelings, Gittins plucked at his sleeve again, and jerking a dirty thumb upwards and winking solemnly he cried under his breath—

"He's got 'em again!"

"A pelican in the wilderness, an owl in the desert, a sparrow upon the house-top," came downstairs, and whilst Mrs. Ledger, to whom Sampson was a man with a mind too great for the sordid details of commercial life, dried her tears and hastened upstairs to comfort her groaning spouse, Gittins leaned back in his chair and said, with another upward jerk of the thumb—

"Methodist blue devils, I calls 'em."

Annie, without a word, slipped her brother's tea upon the table, and, though his heart rose at the sight of it, John sat down to try to eat.

"Strong bulls of Bashan have beset me round!" cried the man upstairs.

John bowed his head over his cup, for the cries brought shame and resentment into his face. At that moment Wilky, looking very stern and sad, put his head in at the door. When he saw John he turned his eyes away, and was beating a retreat, though it was for his young friend that he was really looking. But just at that moment Gittins looked round, and catching the little broker's eye, he pointed upwards again with a broad grin.

"Oh that my head were waters and mine eyes a fountain of tears!" smote on the furniture dealer's ears.

The effect was magical. He thrust the door before him, waddled in fierce haste to the stair foot, gave it a savage kick to command attention from those above, and bawled out scathingly—

"Bud it isn't water—not even decent water; it's nobbut froth! Tears!" he went on, "it's other folk as has t' tears, if I know owt."

The groaning upstairs ceased suddenly, and Mrs. Ledger began to descend. But Wilky could not bear to see her just then, and John seemed an even greater embarrassment, and so he shuffled to the door and disappeared; but almost before he had gone there came another knock, and in stepped Sallie. John saw in an instant that she knew everything, but he did not observe that she was disappointed and even annoyed at finding him there. She went straight up to Mrs. Ledger and gave her an impulsive, womanly hug, that touched John deeply. Then she came to the hearthstone, turned her back upon her lover, and stood poring into the fire.

"He's got 'em; he's got 'em bad," said Gittins, flirting his thumb upwards, and nudging Sallie. She shrank away from his touch, and was leaning over to speak to her lover when "How are they increased that trouble me!" came quavering down the stairs.

"Good gracious, what's that?" and Sallie grabbed nervously at John's arm.

"It's nobbut him; he's gotten 'em again," explained the conciliatory bailiff, soothingly.

"Go out, John; go! I want to speak to—to—your mother," and John, taking a desperate swig at the almost untouched cup of tea, arose with curiosity and troubled wonder in his eyes, but he went to the door all the same, and strode with bowed head and wan face down the lane.

This was a complication indeed. He was more bewildered than anything else. What could it mean? To have all his difficulties removed and his way made clear one day, and then to be stopped by an utterly unexpected and most humiliating trouble the next, staggered him. It was a trial of his faith, doubtless, and it certainly lacked nothing in the way of effectiveness. There were no means of paying except borrowing, and if even they could do that, he certainly could not leave his mother with this additional burden upon her. He was very sure they would never be able to pay the debt, and common honesty demanded that it should be met in some other way, and met at once. He would look well pushing forward his candidature for the ministry when his beloved ones hadn't even a roof over their heads. He had saved in all about eight pounds—little enough if he persevered in his call—but where to get the rest, if he devoted what he had, as, of course, he must, to paying the debt, he did not know. It was no use going to Ferridge; he had evidently calculated the effect of his blow, and would exact his pound of flesh.

"Oh, mother; poor mother!" he moaned, and then, without exactly knowing why, he turned into Station Road and made for the furniture shop.

A strange sight presented itself as he opened the door of the back room. Wilky, in his shirt sleeves, his thick hair ruffled and standing out in tags towards every point of the compass, a pen behind his ear and another in his hand, blots of ink on his nose end, and his face working with strange emotion, was standing at a table covered with a chaotic pile of papers and accounts, whilst an old tin cash-box lay open before him, displaying a five-pound note, two pieces of gold, and a few other coins.

"Come here!" he cried fiercely, as he caught sight of John, "come here!" and dragging him unceremoniously into the middle of the room, he held him grimly by the coat collar and demanded, "Can thou swear?"

"Master!"

"Can thou swear?"

"Mr. Drax!"

"I want somebody as can swear; real, rippin' blasphemious swears! Nowt bud swearin' 'll do it! Curse God an' die! That's it! and I will! *I will!*"

"Oh, master, things are bad enough without——"

"Bad; bad! I tell thee there's things as nowt but swearin's equal to, an' this is one on 'em. Why doesn't thou swear?"

Wilky was simply beyond himself, and John, with horrified face, was trying to pacify him when a customer opened the front door. Wilky's face set into sudden sternness, and he made a dart for the shop, but John, alarmed at the thought of what might happen to the unoffending purchaser, caught him round the waist and dragged him, after a long scuffle, back into his chair, and went to deal with the person in the shop himself. When he went back he found Wilky shaking his fist at the man in the mirror.

"I will! I'll resign!" he was shouting, with red, indignant face. "Seven pound ten! What's t' good o' that! We want twenty-six! I'll send my plan in; I'll chuck up my class, I will!" and then, to John's distress, the agitated little fellow suddenly collapsed into his big chair and broke out into long, struggling sobs.

This was the very last thing John would have expected from his odd friend, well though he knew him, and his embarrassment may be easily imagined.

He waited for a moment or two wondering vaguely why this additional distress should be necessary, and then he began to talk. It would only make matters worse if he suggested the abandonment of the project so dear to them all, and yet he saw not the slightest hope. He did his best, however, and as he did not hint at dropping his candidature, Wilky gradually became quiet and at length took out his pipe.

"There isn't even time to have an auction," he cried in a deeply injured tone, and glancing round as he spoke at his very miscellaneous stock.

John understood, and shook his head. He was touched to see the interest his old friend took in his affairs, and the cheerfulness with which he would evidently have realised upon his goods for the sake of clearing the way for him; but, somehow, there lay at the bottom of all his reflection a sort of feeling that the call of which he was now so satisfied carried with it necessarily the removal of all obstacles, and so he ventured to express hopes he could not very easily justify. But Wilky was evidently thinking of something else, and puffed out great volumes of smoke, whilst his bushy eyebrows were drawn together in severe mental wrestlings. There were times when Wilky with a little effort might have raised the money required himself, but it exasperated him to think that this unexpected difficulty had come when he had even less ready cash than usual, and did not know where to raise so large a sum in the time allowed. He knew also that in a few hours all Bramwell would have learnt what had happened to the Ledgers, and the news could not fail to influence the minds of several people who would have to vote at the approaching Quarterly Meeting. If only he could think of anything he could *do*, but he could not; and inactivity just then was so irritating that he fretted and fumed and puffed away until he had infected John with much of his own restlessness. Presently Wilky began to relieve his mind by denouncing John's father, and as his judgment endorsed his friend's censures whilst his heart rebuked him for filial disloyalty, he grew more and more miserable, and finally remembering that he must take some step soon, and that his mother would be needing him, he left the furniture shop and made his way to Shed Lane. As he approached the door he heard his father's voice again, but this time the tones were short and sharp, and triumphant. "Arise, Joshuay, why liest thou thus on thy face?" was the sentence that fell on his ears as he entered, and there, standing victoriously on the hearthrug with a new, long clay pipe in his mouth and his left thumb tucked into the arm-hole of his waistcoat, was his father. "How are the mighty fallen," he went on, majestically flourishing his pipe, "and the weapons of—of—Ferridge perished!"

The look of ill-concealed disgust on John's face gave way to one of astonishment as he looked around. Gittins was nowhere to be seen. Sallie also was gone, and the tears of his mother and sisters, now more abundant than ever, were most evidently tears of joy.

"Sallie, John! Sallie!" cried the impetuous Lucy, flinging her arms round his neck with a fresh burst of relief-ful weeping.

"Sallie? What about Sallie? She hasn't——"

"She *has,* John, she has! Oh, bless her! bless her for evermore!"

"God forgive me for misjudging that dear lass!" cried Mrs. Ledger, to whom pensive self-accusation was always more easy than rejoicing, and then, whilst Sampson paced before the fire and flung off strings of Scripture that made John's flesh creep, the young minder heard what there was to tell.

Sallie had had the money with her when he went out, but she would not produce it in his presence because "he would make such a fuss," she said, with one of her most engaging little grimaces. John felt a stab of wounded pride as he realised that he was indebted for the very bed on which he would sleep that night to his sweetheart, and though he would not show it in the presence of so much glad relief, his heart was heavy within him as he reflected. It hurt his sense of delicacy to think that the girl he loved should be dragged into the sordid little troubles of their family life ; he could not allow for a moment that the debt had more than changed hands. It would have to be paid just the same, and, in fact, the kindness of Sallie laid them under the greater obligation to see that the indebtedness was discharged as soon as possible. He hated the thought that such a thing should be mixed up with the sweet experiences of love ; and he did not forget that Sallie was a Wood, and, whatever she did or said, would have very decided views indeed on the question of prompt payment. And yet his only chance of seeing the debt discharged was to stick to his present employment and abandon his candidature, but neither his own heart nor Sallie herself would consent to that. Another weary, struggling night he spent ; a little while ago he would have almost welcomed such an obstacle—it provided him with the very strongest reasons for remaining at home—but now, after the will of God had been clearly revealed to him in answer to incessant prayer, he could not, of course, hold back ; but how he was to proceed and still pay the money now owing he failed entirely to see. This was the second time Sallie had helped them in their need, and though he delighted in these acts of hers as showing the goodness of her heart, he was deeply distressed to think that she should have been put to such tests. She, when he saw her next night, was just her own gay self, and utterly refused to discuss the matter. And whilst John was pouring out his thanks and protestations of gratitude, his fate was being discussed elsewhere, for the Quarterly Meeting was in session. The weather was wild, and the super. anticipated, regretfully, that the attendance would be reduced. To his surprise and relief, however, ten minutes before the usual tea, a covered waggonette drove up to the chapel, and old Mr. Pashley got out accompanied by five others from Trundlegate, most of whom came but seldom to the gathering.

During tea, Flintop and one or two of the country local preachers seemed to have important business together, and the second minister muttered something very disrespectful as he watched their consultations. When the meeting itself opened the attendance was still somewhat below the average, but just as they were concluding the opening hymn, and the super. was counting those present, the door opened, and the stumpy form of the little broker was seen in the aperture. He wore a coat that nearly touched the ground, had the end of a lead pencil in his mouth, and there was an air of overdone unconsciousness about him as he stepped forward and led in six men who were present there for the first time. The chairman glanced with a twinkle in his eye at his colleague, but as he saw Flintop and his supporters whispering together, he began to cudgel his brains to recall the qualifications of the recruits the broker had marshalled. There was only one of whom he remained in doubt, and as his colleague assured him that the brother concerned was "all right," he proceeded briskly to business. There is much business as a rule at this assembly, but at last the question for which many of them

were waiting was reached, and the super., whose
remarks were followed by a series of confirmatory
grunts from Wilky, spoke fairly and yet confidently
of his candidate. The second minister followed and
was supported by the stewards; and the super. then
invited any others to speak who might wish.

Old Mr. Pashley broke through long years of
quarterly meeting silence to commend his young
friend. As he spoke, someone in the corner where
the Flintop contingent was seated uttered an almost
inaudible demurrer, whereupon there came a volley
of stentorian "hear, hears!" from Wilky, followed
by dropping shots from his supporters.

This put the opposition on its mettle, and Flintop
rose to his feet to ask a question.

"Could the superintendent assure them—they
made no charges—that the young brother's sermons
were his own?"

The second minister rising to his feet said that he
had heard the question raised more than once (a
trumpet-toned "Shame!" from Wilky), and so he
had taken pains to investigate the matter, and he
could assure the meeting that the young man's
sermons were absolutely his own productions.

"More nor we can say for his!" rapped out
Wilky, with a glance at Flintop.

The super. tried to catch the broker's eye, and
failing, he asked the meeting if it was prepared to
vote.

"We should like a little more——" began one of
the opposition.

"Vote! vote!" roared Wilky.

The vote was taken, the furniture dealer in his
excitement standing on a form to see how everybody
voted, and entirely forgetting to put his own hand up.

"Do you wish to remain neutral, brother Drax?"
asked the super. with a pawky smile, upon which the

little man shot up both hands, and the meeting laughed.

"Twenty-seven for, two against, and five neutral," announced the secretary, and the meeting burst into hearty applause, whilst Wilky bustled hurriedly off to communicate the result to the anxious hearts in Shed-lane.

The next three months brought many and varied excitements to our friend John. With his mother growing younger under his eyes, his sisters talking of his future with proud looks, and Sallie contriving to see him almost every day without, after all, taking up much of his precious time, he struggled away at his preparations with a light heart, and but for uneasy apprehensions about finances, and especially their debt to Sallie, he would have been lighter-hearted than he had ever been in his life; even the anxieties connected with his examinations not being sufficient to damp his pleasure. The super. arranged on the new plan that he should have plenty of practice in preaching, and the second minister undertook to act as his coach, and every spare moment he could command John spent either in his own little study-bedroom or at the house of his temporary tutor. His father, at the paint shop gatherings, hinted in terms of hazy vastness of the sacrifices he had made and the money he had spent on John's education, and whenever Wilky was not present posed as a suffering but willing martyr, who, though he loved his son to distraction and could not support the thought of parting from him, was by processes of slow but ruthless self-crucifixion compelling himself to give him up "for the good of the cause." As for Wilky, he suddenly developed an absorbing interest in theological institutions. He bought a photo of Didsbury College somewhere in Manchester and brought it home as a present to his wife, and came down with unexampled fierceness upon any of the frequenters of the paint shop who still retained and expressed any trace of the old Methodist prejudice against colleges. John passed the Synod with " flying colours," as the broker announced wherever he went for the next fortnight. The minister who heard what is called his " July " sermon spoke very encouragingly to him about it, and the super. expressed his great confidence in the written discourse which he had prepared.

When the official summons to the "July Committee" arrived by post it was handled by John's mother as if it had been a letter from the Queen, and Wilky was there a full half hour before there was any possibility of John getting from the mill in order to see and hear as soon as it was opened. Wilky showed very clearly that he would have liked to go with John to Didsbury, and as he put it " Stan' up for him wi' th' big-wigs," but Mrs. Drax put her foot upon that, and Sallie, with whom Wilky had lately become quite friendly, smilingly shook her head.

Well, John must send a "talligram" the very instant he knew the result, and Wilky would take the very first train to Manchester and bring him home in triumph. John left Bramwell on Monday afternoon, and wrote to his mother that very night to say that the candidates he had met were all so much his superiors that he begged them not to hope too much.

"That's just our John," said Mrs. Ledger with a wistful smile and a surreptitious kiss at the corner of the envelope, but Wilky was indignant with her; she was an "old maddlin" that "hadn't the pluck of a mouse, and John was a duffing noodle. The July Committee knew what it was about, and he would come out at the top of the tree. Reject him! they couldn't! they darn't! John would come back 'a full-blown minister, an' nowt else,'" and then, as a sudden brilliant idea struck him, he hurried off to Varley, the Methodist tailor, to see if he had any black cloth sufficiently good for a clerical suit.

Tuesday and Wednesday passed very slowly. Wilky could neither eat nor attend to business, and was down at the little house in Shed-lane two or three times a day rebuking the least sign of misgiving and pronouncing large and wonderful prophesies about John's future. Thursday morning brought a letter, in which John described his experiences. He said he had done better than he expected in the examinations, but enlarged again upon the immense superiority of his fellow examinees and begged them not to be too sanguine. There was no work for any of them that day. "Mother" went about with hands clasped and lips moving, and every now and then stole quietly off upstairs, they all knew for what. Sallie came once in the forenoon, and immediately after dinner arrived again, dressed and ready to wait for the expected news. Wilky fumed and fretted and put the Ledger's clock right, whilst Annie went every few minutes to the door to look for the telegraph boy. Two o'clock brought the afternoon post but no message; three came and passed, and just on the stroke of four there was a sharp knock at the door and a startled cry from all the women present. It was the telegram at last, and the boy who handed it to Annie opened his eyes with astonishment as she snatched it from him and then flung it away as if it had been some venomous thing. Wilky, with an exclamation of impatience, picked it up, but held it away from him and snarlingly cried to Sampson to open it. Old Ledger, with white face and shaking hand, received the dread missive, and then, glancing at the directions, handed it gingerly and with evident relief to his wife. She drew back with a startled little scream, and then as hastily snatched at it and hugged it to her breast. Wilky, dancing about like a cat on hot coals, shouted to her to open it, but clenched his teeth and stepped backwards as if afraid it might sting him. Then the agitated woman looked at it again, every eye in the house fixed hungrily upon her. She toyed with it fearsomely for a little while, her lips moving in prayer. With a face all awork, and shaking hands, she tore it open and looked at it, and then, with a gasp and a great cry, fell back into her husband's arms, and when Sallie a moment later stooped down and picked up the paper, she found all hope destroyed and all fears justified by one awful word, " Rejected."

CHAPTER XV

SALLIE IS STILL—SALLIE

On the afternoon of the Saturday after the events described in the last chapter, John and Sallie occupied a grass bank in the field at the end of the farm garden, with their backs to the house and the lane. Sallie's face was shadowed, her brows were slightly drawn together, her lips stood at a depressed half pout, and there was an air of weary petulance about her. John, lying on the grass by her side and watching her face anxiously, was evidently in some perplexity. Twice he had touched her arm, but she had not responded, and sat with her hat in her hand absently toying with the trimmings.

" What does the super. say, then ? " she asked, after an unpleasant pause, and glancing almost disdainfully at her lover.

" He has had a note from the chairman to say that, as far as he can make out, it is the literary paper and the medical report which have thrown me. He thinks the mission house people would have taken me for foreign work but for the doctor's schedule."

" But you wouldn't have gone abroad ? " she cried, looking down upon him with resentment, and an evident readiness to pick a quarrel.

" Yes, I would ; I would have gone anywhere, the mission field for choice ; I offered to do so, you know."

" And you would have taken me from my good

home to live amongst nasty, dirty blacks, would
you?" and she put on her hat, bridling the while
with indignation and resentment.

"Of course! Why, Sallie, I thought you understood; I thought you would have gone anywhere—
a—with me!"

"With you!" and with disdainful lip and flashing
eyes she rose to her feet. "Oh, certainly, *with you;*
any girl would go anywhere with such a grand
catch as you, wouldn't she?" and the cold sarcastic
scorn of her tone, even more than her contemptuous
manner, stung John to the quick.

"Sallie!" he cried, in amazed distress, "I thought
—I felt sure! after—after what you said that Sunday
night coming from Whittle Grove, that you would
have gone anywhere—but you are vexed. What's
the matter?"

"D-i-d y-o-u!" and she drew herself up, and
flashed anger and scorn upon him. "Then you were
very much mistaken, John Ledger. I wouldn't have
gone, and if you were accepted to-day I wouldn't go
an inch, so there!"

But John was not blind; he understood instantly
that there was something much more serious behind
all this. A great, awful dread took possession of
him; she had been faintly sympathetic when he
arrived home on Thursday night; he had seen her
twice since then, and each time she had been colder
than before towards him. He had told himself that
that was quite natural, under the circumstances, and
he must bear with her disappointment, and any little
outbreaks of fretfulness she might show. If she
loved him she would soon get over it; her love would
conquer her ambition. He had excused her thus
when her reception of him had been so much less
kindly than that of his mother and sisters. She
was different, of course; it would be a considerable

sacrifice for a proud, ambitious girl like her to marry a man who would only be a minder after all. With thoughts like these he had pacified his doubts and fears for two days, but now they did not suffice; a terrible fact was forcing itself insistently upon him.

" Sallie," he cried, with white, horrified face, " you do not love me ! "

He looked so frightful for the moment that Sallie was cowed ; she had always thought him a little limp and spiritless, but this visible agony of his was a revelation. She had not formed the deliberate purpose of quarrelling and thus breaking with him ; she knew that that was what it must come to now ; but she would have preferred to get rid of him gradually, by snubs and slights. Well, he was bringing it upon himself, and it might as well, perhaps, be done first as last. People would talk if it were done so soon, but she was smarting with self-reproach, and felt stung to recklessness.

" Love ! " she cried. " Oh, no, I don't love you ! If I'd thrown myself away as your mother did, if I'd allowed myself to be made another clog to a man struggling with poverty, if I had sunk myself to his level, and thus helped to drag us both lower, that would have been love ; but because I have some respect both for him and for myself, and want our wedding to lift us both, I don't love you. Well, I *don't* love you. I don't want to love you, so there ! that's an end ! "

John scarcely heard her ; his own thoughts and fears were so overwhelming that he could scarcely think. It seemed to him as if he had been suddenly plunged into paralysing darkness. With a great cry he flung himself at her feet, and implored her to recall her words. " She was angry ; she did not, she could not, mean what she said." For some time he pleaded thus, and Sallie, from discretion rather than relenting, gave way a little, but the interview, though John prolonged it in the desperate hope that his crushing fears were groundless, was constrained and unnatural, and he was glad at last to part in order to get time to think.

To some extent he had brought this trouble upon himself; he had allowed his own painful conscientiousness to colour his account of his experiences in the examinations, and had told his tale without one extenuating or hope-suggesting circumstance. He had enlarged upon the superiority of his fellow examinees, and the hopelessness, from the beginning, of his own chance, and had taken scrupulous care that all his friends should see the case as it actually was, and in doing so he had unconsciously done himself an injustice, and made the thing worse than it was. He had not mentioned that the decision of the July Committee was not necessarily final, neither had he said anything about the possibility of trying again another year. In truth, he was so utterly staggered by the fact that after having received what he regarded as an indubitable call, he had been refused, that he had scarcely thought of anything but the hard and faith-confounding fact itself.

For three days he had been staring with hot strained eyes into the blackness, and the first change that had come was an infinite deepening of the night. The first difficulty was confounding to him because of its mysteriousness, but the second had in it every ingredient of bitter despair. Sallie had not invited him to stay to tea, though it is not necessary to charge her with anything more serious than momentary forgetfulness, but he never thought of that, but climbed over the top of the embankment and down into the lane until he reached the old stile leading into the woods, and there he cast himself down at the foot of a mossy tree-trunk and tried to face the new situation.

And, first of all, the man in him gave trouble. He had an unconquerable suspicion of that individual, and watched all his various moods and phases with unsleeping vigilance. He was a wily, slippery, unscrupulous slave who must be kept down with unrelenting rigour, and now he saw this fearsome object springing to its feet and brandishing its chains, and utterly refusing any longer to be silenced or controlled.

He had been fooled, made a tool of, degraded. *He* was nothing; his thoughts and feelings and desires did not count. That beautiful, holy goddess, Love, which dwelt in the inner shrine of his heart, had been dragged from her throne, and harnessed like a beast of burden to the chariot of a sordid woman's ambition. But the manhood within him, outraged at the spectacle, was in open rebellion, and began to belabour him with the very chains with which it had so long been bound. It had been cast into the mire and trampled upon, but now stood up for itself and for Love. Love, real love, was so holy, so glorious a thing that neither man nor woman could despise it without covering themselves with everlasting dishonour. But this love of his had not merely been despised—it had been defiled. This angel from heaven had been dragged into the service of hell, and when she had failed in her task, had been spurned and cast aside. With his hot face in the hollow formed by the branching roots of the tree, John ground his teeth, and tore up and flung away handsful of the grass about him. His friends, even his mother, would have declared that he had no pride, but he was finding now that pride had him; it was not only there, but master, and was improving the rare opportunity by revenging itself on its stern ruler. Yes, there was no avoiding it; he, *he* was held so cheaply as to be of no account at all when he lacked certain possible prospects. The rush and tumult of his wounded pride was overpowering. He had had disappointments enough in his short life, but this was torture, this was raging madness, this was hell! For a few moments longer he lay gnashing and writhing in the intensity of his outraged resentment, and then another thought came, and he sat up suddenly. Here he was, a Christian man, torn to pieces by the raging of an unregenerate passion. The nature which he had crucified until it was surely dead had come down from its cross and mastered him. The one devil he had so painfully cast out had returned, and brought seven others with it worse than itself. A great fear rose up within him; white and stern, he braced himself for a fresh subjugation. Again and again he threw the monster, and again and again it returned to the attack. It was a long fight, and terrible, but slowly, and at great cost, he reasserted his ascendancy. He was on his feet by this time, and, with head thrown back, eyes nipped tightly together, and fingers clutching each other behind his back, he walked about, and muttered and prayed.

And just as pride and resentment got subdued, another feeling arose within him. Beaten everywhere else, the tenacious adversary came suddenly upon his rear, and struck at what was always his most vulnerable point—himself. He had brought it on himself, after all. He knew that Sallie was above him, and he ought never to have presumed. His attempt to win her and the angry pride he had just fought down were simply manifestations of selfishness. To ask her to make sacrifices for him was pride and selfishness combined. He had been doing the very thing he was so angry at in her. Then he thought of the prejudices expressed by his mother and others, and of the spirit Sallie had shown when he had refused to become a candidate the year before. They were all of a piece, and he ought to have been prepared. Sallie was not spiritual, that was all; she was moved by the ordinary prudential motives of respectable people, and if he could not offer her a position, at any rate equal to the one she was in, it was mere selfishness to be displeased with her attitude. She liked him in a way, and she had shown that if he could have offered her what she had a right to expect, she would have married him. What more could he expect from her? Ah, but she was pretty, after all, and just the bright, resourceful, prudent sort of person for a man of his rather dull spirit and unworldly ways. It would be cruel to bring her down to a position in which she would have no opportunity of using and developing her gifts; she was made to excel and lead, and what a satire on his love it would be to wish her to take the position and prospects of a working man's wife. He was quieter by this time, and the course of his thoughts seemed to soften him; the luxury of kind feelings, after all the bitterness he had felt, was sweet to him, and he grew quite tender as he reflected. If he had thought, as he ought to have done, he would have offered to release her as soon as he knew his fate, but he had held on, and had assumed that she was going to make a perfectly unnecessary sacrifice. No wonder she had been fitful and querulous; he ought to have saved her the pain of making this petty little excuse of a quarrel. And just at this point his pride came back with an utterly unexpected and confusing rush. What a muff he was! He was doing the most cowardly of all things—trying to deceive himself. He knew that, his poverty excepted, he was at least Sallie's equal; he knew that he never would have lifted his eyes to her but for her own most palpable encouragement, and he could see, if only he would, that she was a worldly, scheming little hussy, unworthy of any true man's love.

But he fought the feeling down again; it was always easy to blame himself rather than others, so he would forgive her. No! that was not the thing; he would ask her to forgive him; he would write to her and release her; that was the least atonement he could make. Yes, *he* had done the wrong, and he must undo it. And now it seemed as if the great struggle was over, but with one of those subtle doublings to which the elusive human mind is so prone, he pulled up before another difficulty. He was strangely contented with his decision; the victory had been easier than he expected. Could he have arrived at it with so little effort if he loved her as he believed he did? A change had come over him, subtle and sudden, but very real. He excused Sallie, he justified her, he pitied her worldliness. Yes, but what was this? *He did not love her!* All the rest had come with this suspicious ease, and was, therefore, now void of all virtue, because he no longer wanted her!

He had got to the edge of the wood by this time, and standing near the wicket gate, he looked hastily around him as if he had lost something. He peered wonderingly into the shadows amongst the trees, and then up at the sinking sun, and suddenly realized with amazement of heart that his own nature had outwitted him, and that whilst he had been struggling to retain Christian charity and justice towards his sweetheart, the greater thing, the deeper thing in him, the thing he had been more sure of than life itself, had somehow eluded him and slipped away— he had lost, yes, he had lost his love. A fretful vexation rose within him. He shook himself and looked appealingly at the thick trees, conjured up the image of Sallie, and dwelt upon it. He recalled her pretty ways and gay laughter, he reminded himself of her kindness in the matter of his sister, and her more recent and greater kindness when the bailiffs were in the house. He called himself an ingrate, a selfish, sulky wretch, but there he stuck. He felt grateful, forgiving, even sympathetic toward Sallie, but the old, deep love was, at any rate, stunned, and would not now move. But real love never dies; neglect, unkindness, harshness only strengthen it. Had he been deceiving himself? Had he been the ambitious one, and not Sallie? Had he been carried away by her notice of him, and had his love been after all only a subtler form of self-love?

He sighed and looked disconsolately around him, but the prostrate form of his wounded affection never stirred. Oh, this was torment, pure torment! He was sure he had loved her; he *must* love her; he *did* love her. But there was no response from within, and with a numbed, bewildered heart he strode down the footpath and back into the lane towards home. The only thing that was clear to him was that until he understood himself better he could not even write to Sallie.

A long, weary fortnight of fluctuating emotions and abortive resolutions passed over, and John remained in much the same frame of mind. He could not decide what he ought to do ; and Sallie, oddly enough, did not help him either way. There were no appointed meetings between them, but one way or another they met somewhat frequently, and it added considerably to John's perplexities that Sallie seemed as uncertain as he was himself. One day she was fairly, though pensively, kind, and the next absent, reserved, and short. As to the future, Wilky and the rest of the paint shop fraternity urged him boisterously and confidently to try again next year ; but

John could not make up his mind, because the super., who understood these things better than anybody else, never suggested such a thing, though he certainly acted as though he did not regard the case as quite settled. John had no difficulty in understanding why he was rejected, as far as the examinations were concerned, but he found it impossible to reconcile what had taken place with the direct and definite call of which he was now so confident. The only thing to do, therefore, was to wait the unfoldings of the Divine will. Meanwhile he was occupied much more constantly with his relations to Sallie. The old ardent love refused to respond to his appeals, but he sought her company because he felt that if only she would drop her wayward, undecided, and somewhat peevish manner, and be for one half-hour her own bright self, his love would awake again, and then! —Ah, then! But beyond that he could never get.

He had ceased to go regularly to the farm since their "tiff." He scarcely knew why, and Sallie did not seem to notice the change; but this sort of thing could not go on. He must get to the end of it somehow.

The super. had gone to Conference, and John had been asked to take the week-night service. He was leaving the band-room in Wilky's company, when he noticed that Sallie, who had been present, was waiting for him. As soon as they got out of the front street she took his arm with the prettiest little air of proprietorship possible, and chattered away about the sermon in a manner that reminded him of their oldest and sweetest days.

As they turned into a country lane that led by a longer way round into the road to the farm, they came suddenly upon a herd of cows, and she, with a startled little cry, clung closer to him, and he put his arm round her to reassure her. When they had got safely past, John would have withdrawn his arm, but found, with a great gush of joy, that it was held fast. Then Sallie dropped her voice and began to speak in tones only too delightful to the struggling man by her side. Halfway down the lane she stopped of herself, and sat down on the stile, and noticing that he still stood, she affected to be shocked at her own forgetfulness, and made him take the top step whilst she settled herself down on the lower one.

It was the time of the year when it is scarcely ever dark, and the air was soft and balmy, whilst a serene stillness seemed to pervade everything. Sallie looked round with a soft little sigh, leaned her shoulder against John's knee, and asked if he had ever felt such a feeling of sweet peacefulness before. John never had, but he had often been quieter within.

"One couldn't even *think* a wicked thought, a night like this, could they, John?"

John couldn't, at any rate, and he was resolving he wouldn't. She put her arm absently upon the edge of his knee, and turning her head a little backward, looked past him to the sky. John glanced at her dimpled cheek and the soft white throat beyond, and felt that life was beginning to stir at last in that leaden thing he called his heart.

"John," she said, looking up into his eyes, "when all nature seems to be breathing the name of God, as it does to-night, don't you feel as though you must go and tell everybody how good He is?"

"I do, I do," said John earnestly, and though the upturned face looked very tempting to John's unregenerate flesh, her elevated expression made the thought seem a desecration. She leaned her cheek upon the arm on his knee now, but appeared so absorbed in high thoughts as to be unconscious of the fact that John's eyes were filling with dangerous light. She dropped her eyes for a moment, and seemed to be thinking, and then, raising them suddenly, she said—

" John, are you as confident as ever that you are called to preach ? "

" Y-e-s," he replied, musingly, and then felt a stab of shame that he could even hesitate on such a point.

" So do I. If God has called you He will find you work, won't He, either in one sphere or another ? "

" Yes, in His own good time."

" Yes, God's ways are very wonderful, aren't they ? People's lives are often very different from what they expect them to be."

John agreed, and added that the chief thing was to be willing to go anywhere and do anything.

" Y-e-s."

Sallie seemed to be absorbed in some great thought outside the small affairs of ordinary life, and presently she asked, in the same musing, absent tone—

" I suppose you would go anywhere, John, and do anything, would you not ? "

" I hope so."

" Oh, I *know* so. It's noble to feel like that," and there was a mute apology and confession in the soft voice that made John vexed with himself that he was not more moved by it.

Sallie's eyes came slowly back from the horizon ; and then, as though a sudden recollection had flashed upon her, she fixed her gaze upon him and said—

" Oh, John, I'd such a funny idea come into my head to-day," and then, with a spoilt sort of gesture, which among other things brought her little hand close to his, " but I won't tell you—you'll only laugh at me."

" Yes, tell me, do ! "

But he didn't take the little hand, as he once would have done.

"Well, I was thinking"—and her hand was touching his now—"I was thinking—God moves in a mysterious way, you know—what a thing it would be if God intended you to be a minister of some other church!"

John had never thought of such a thing, and said so very decidedly.

"Well, but let me tell you"—and then putting on a very arch look—"but you wise old owls of men don't believe in signs and leadings, I know."

John, to encourage her, said that all depended, and he was getting quite vexed with the hard scepticism within him.

"Well, I never thought of such a thing in all my life before, but less than half an hour after the idea came into my head, who should come in but Miss Hessay, the Whittle Grove new vicar's sister, you know, and without me saying a word, she commenced right off and began talking about you."

"Oh, she's heard the gossip."

"Never mind that. She said her brother and she had been brought up Methodists, and that he was once a candidate for the ministry, like you, but was declined. And they thought it a very hard thing at the time, but now they see it was the hand of the Lord."

John was shaking his head quite energetically, but Sallie would not see, but went on—

"Well, she says that her brother would never have done half as much good in Methodism as he has been able to do in the Church; and she hummed and haa-ed a bit, and then she hinted that a way could be made for you, and you might get ordained, and even married, in about a couple of years."

John shook his head more decidedly than ever.

" I'm not called to the Church, Sallie."

" How do you know ?   You cannot know that ! "

" If I'm called at all, I'm called to Methodism."

" But they won't have you !   You cannot be called there.   It's stupid to talk like that."

John gave his head another weary shake ; but there had been another tone in Sallie's voice when she spoke last, and so to soothe her he felt for her hand, but she drew it away.

" I can never leave the Church of my parents ; I daren't."

Sallie drew away with a petulant little cry, and, turning her back towards him, stared with annoyance in her eyes at the opposite hedge.

" Then are you going to offer again next year ? " she demanded, half turning round and eyeing him resentfully.

John was growing a little stern, and answered gravely—

" I don't even know that—yet."

Pride, anger, and impatience struggled together in her face, whilst she tapped the cinderpath with her little foot, and presently she asked constrainedly—

" When will you know ? "

But John had begun to think of something else. He had suddenly made up his mind to speak about the thing that lay so near his heart.   His eyes glistened, and the faint lines round his mouth tightened.

" Sallie, I should like to say something to you."

A flash of curiosity came from under the long eyelashes, but the face was still sulky and averted.

" Well ? "

" Sallie, I've done you a great wrong."

" Have you only found that out to-night ? "

" I found it out some time since.   I have sought your affection when I knew that you could only respond to it at great sacrifice to yourself. I had no right—— "

But Sallie had sprung to her feet, her eyes blazing and her little hands tightly clenched. Why, this mouthing, melancholy factory lad was actually going to dismiss her—*her*!

"Stop!" she cried imperiously. "You whining old woman! I've been silly enough to think that I could put some spirit into you! Stupid that I was! You're your father's son, John Ledger, and will whine your way into a pauper's grave. Never dare speak to me again, except"—and here her native hardness and coarseness got the better of her prudence—"except to bring me the money I spent to save you from sleeping in the street! Go, sir, go!"

John went white at her words, but grew stern and strangely collected as she went on. He stood looking at her scornful, flaming face a moment until she had done, and then, with a sort of unconscious bow, he turned on his heels and left her standing there.

Half an hour later, when he reached home, he found a letter waiting for him which had come by the evening post, and as it had "Wesleyan Conference" embossed on the flap of the envelope, there were five souls consuming themselves with impatience to know the contents. Wilky was nearly beside himself, and kneeled upon a chair to look over John's shoulder as he read, and this was what he saw—

"DEAR JOHN—

"I have the happiness of informing you that you have just been accepted by Conference unanimously. You are to go to the Institution for Home work. All particulars when I return. With every good wish,

"Sincerely yours,
"WILLIAM HALEY."

PART II

THE MINISTER

———

CHAPTER I

A CASUISTICAL DEBATE AND ITS CONSEQUENCES

THREE theological students occupied one of the
studies of Didsbury Wesleyan College one miserable
day in February about eighteen months after the
events narrated in the last chapter. A steady,
depressing drizzle outside having deprived them of
the usual exercise, they are consoling themselves
with a characteristically noisy debate on a question
—always peculiarly interesting to young men in
their position—the question of the morality of
violated matrimonial engagements. The one with
his back to the door, his chair balanced on its
back legs, and his feet on the mantelpiece, is
Yewson, a third year's student, with an easy-going,
nonchalant manner, short, upstanding black hair,
and a long, impertinent nose. The one on the
opposite side of the fire, and his back to the window, is John Ledger, who is now in his second
year, and looks broader, healthier, and, at the
same time, younger, than when we last saw him.
The last of the trio is not seated at all; in fact,
nobody ever knew Max Ringley to remain long in
any one position, and during the quarter of an hour
he has been in the room he has sat at least once on
the mantelpiece itself, besides occupying in turns the
table, the top of a movable desk, and a piled-up heap

of bundles of firewood out of the coal box under the bookcase. By the time we look in upon them he has abandoned all sitting accommodation, and lies full length on his stomach with his chin propped up by long, thin hands, and his elbows resting on the hearthrug. He is evidently very tall and lank, with abundance of unmanageable yellow hair, a heavy yellow moustache, and a canary-coloured smoking cap, whilst one of his fingers is adorned with a diamond ring of some value. His expressive features change every minute, and his restless grey-blue eyes bespeak a characteristic impetuosity of temperament. He is far away the most popular preacher in the college and the worst student, in spite of the fact that he has had superior educational advantages as the son of a Midland J.P.

They were discussing the case of a former student who had been recently condemned to a longer probation for jilting a young lady.

"Conference, brethren," Yewson was saying languidly, as he tilted his chair back to a perilous angle and carefully scrutinised a slipper of tender history, "Conference is an old woman, and like other old women it sometimes loses its head and gives way to scares. Justice done in anger is usually *over*-done, and it is so in this case."

"Treason! high treason! The king can do no wrong," said John Ledger, in his invariable character of defender of recognised institutions.

"Decent fellow, Portman, too," said Ringley, staring hard at the fire on a line with his face, and wagging his head with half-regretful musings.

"Portman," resumed Yewson, "Portman was a brick, sir. But then you know, men, if the dear little things *will* hanker after the black coat and the white tie, what are we to do? You know how it is yourselves."

"No, sir!" and Ringley was on his feet and brandishing the short study poker; "we don't know what it is, and please God we never intend to know! I've heard that miserable cant until I'm tired."

"Ringley, dear boy," replied Yewson with a patronising drawl, "I love you like that! It reminds me of my own verdant youth. Bless thee, lad, we all talk like that until the evil days come when we say we have no pleasure in them."

"The fellow who gets out of a scrape by throwing the blame on a woman is a *cad!*" and Ringley brought his fist down upon the mantelpiece with a crash that made the little ornaments dance.

"Even a parson should be honest," chimed in John.

"Brethren," cried Yewson, with a bland wave of his fine white hands, "it is charming to hear you talk like that; it proves your happy innocence; to you these things are delightfully simple, the black is black and the white is white, and so you dispose of them with the most engaging emphasis. Very delightful! but very amateurish. As a matter of fact, now, the questions are usually confusing, inextricable mixtures and blendings of colours, and the black runs into the white and the white into the black until there is finally produced a shade which would defy the ingenuity of an artist to denominate. As a rule these things are delicate, subtle cases of casuistry. Moral philosophy! with all respect to our venerable, if somewhat prolix tutor—for teaching practical moral philosophy there is nothing like a bit of casuistry."

"Confound casuistry!" roared Ringley.

"Casuistry always sounds to me suspiciously like jesuitry," added John slowly.

"Beautiful!" responded Yewson.

"Brethren, your sentiments do you honour! But

come now," he went on with an air of playful argumentativeness, "let us take one or two of the simplest problems which this sort of thing presents. Referring to a remark by my excellent friend Ledger about the honesty of parsons; jilting, as it is somewhat rudely termed, takes places sometimes outside the ministerial ranks, I believe. Did you ever hear of a Church member being expelled, or even suspended, for jilting a young lady?"

"They shall be! I'll expel 'em if ever I get the chance! I'll shake the meanness out of them, the rascals!" and Ringley flourished his fists menacingly at future transgressors.

"Did you ever hear of a Church officer or a local preacher being deprived of his office for this a—a—offence?"

John was evidently beginning to be interested, but Ringley declared that he would withdraw the ticket of the President himself if he did such a thing.

"And further," continued Yewson, now quite in love with his own argument, "jilting takes place in the world every day, but it is never considered a disgrace. People don't cut a man, or even forbid him the house, for such a transgression—except of course the actual relatives of the injured party, and not always them. You hear that such and such an engagement is broken off, but it is not spoken of as a crime. You are often not even told which of the interested parties has done the deed, and nobody dreams of punishing them for it."

"Yewson," and the indignant Ringley glared at the smiling speaker with something like horror, "you're a perfect Mephistopheles. If I didn't know you, I should hate you."

"Exactly! there speaks outraged innocence. But look you! I've shown that a rule is applied to us which is applied to no other—never mind whether rightly or wrongly (for John was leaning forward to interrupt). So it is. Well now, this very delightful indignation, which warms my heart as I behold it, and which is so beautifully characteristic of my young friend (Yewson was two years the junior of the others), is all based upon the assumption, to come to our second point, that when an engagement is broken off, it is always the man's fault. As a rule it is, I grant you, but cannot your capacious minds, dearly beloved brethren, take in a case, rare I admit, yet not impossible, in which the lady has only herself to blame ? "

"No! Never!"—and Ringley, who had somehow exchanged the poker for the dust-brush, shook it fiercely at Yewson, and went on—"They're true as steel, bless 'em! too true for their comfort, poor dears ! "

"Our friend speaks out of the fulness of a large, varied, but singularly fortunate experience," Yewson went on, waving his hand at the drops of rain on the window sill, and alluding playfully to Ringley's notorious popularity with the fair sex. "Ledger, I appeal to your dispassionate wisdom. Cannot you conceive circumstances in which the gentleman, even though a cleric, has no option but to retire ? "

"No!" thundered Ringley, and John contented himself with asking—

"What, for instance ? "

"Well, suppose for instance the lady proved unfaithful ? "

"She wouldn't ! They don't, they never do ! "

Yewson waited with smiling patience, and then looking past the excited Ringley to John, he went on—

"Or suppose that, having been engaged for some

time, incompatibility of temperament should present itself ? "

" There we are ! " and Ringley threw the little brush into the coal-bin behind the green baize curtain, and began to prance about the room. " The cloven hoof at last ! The last refuge of dirty sneaks ! Lack of fortune on lady's part—incompatibility of temperament. Another girl in the way—incompatibility of disposition. Girl losing her beauty by long waiting—incompatibility of temperament. It's caddish, sir ! It's brutal ! It's damnable ! "

Yewson, as the others well knew, had commenced the discussion more from love of dialectics than from any personal sympathy with the cases he was suggesting ; but he liked talking, and as the arguments for his position accumulated before his mind he began to display more interest, and so taking his legs down from the mantelpiece and sitting up, he said—

" Without exactly imitating the youthful exuberance of language indulged in by my learned and eloquent friend on the other side, I should like to ask, through you, my lord (with a glance at Ledger), if my honourable friend takes up the romantic, shall I say quixotic, position that if a man has once given his word to a lady, nothing of any kind should ever induce him to withdraw ? "

" Yes, I do ; I say it, and I stick to it ! "

" Even if the lady should turn out a drunkard, or—or worse ? "

Ringley's jaw dropped.

" But they never do——"

" But if one did ? "

Ringley, who was quite accustomed to be vanquished in argument, looked rather staggered when the point was pressed, and turning round he glanced at John, as usual when he was in a corner.

" You are supposing an improbable and almost impossible case," said John quietly.

" But you do grant that there are exceptions to your rule ? " and Yewson seemed quite delighted with himself and his skill.

" Yes, but not many."

" But there are some; well then, each case is arguable on its own merits."

" Well ? "

" Well, suppose that some time after the engagement the fellow discovers that the girl is odd and peculiar."

"Any stick to beat a dog with," interrupted Ringley scornfully.

"And suppose that he found that there was insanity in the family, and that his girl had symptoms of it ? "

"Oh, rot ! Talk sense, Yewson ! "

" As I have known one such case, I am not only talking sense, but facts."

" Yewson, you ought to have been an Old Bailey lawyer."

Yewson bowed low in acknowledgment of the compliment, and then proceeded—

" If my honourable and learned brother will allow me, I will put an easier case still. Suppose a man gets engaged to—well, a worldly, loose sort of girl, and then gets converted and discovers gifts, and is called into the ministry: is he to continue that engagement, and inflict upon Methodism a woman who would be a perpetual disgrace to it ? "

The rapid blinking of John's eyes, and the tightening of his lips, indicated that he saw weak places in Yewson's argument; but Ringley was occupied with the general question, and was watching the third year's man with something very like horror on his face.

"Or, to take a more simple case still. Suppose a man in a lowly position; for instance, a collier—there are ex-colliers in our ministry, and fine fellows they are, too—suppose one of this class engaged to a girl of equal position. Well, he becomes a candidate, comes to college, goes out into the work. He must have a girl equal to his public position; his own tastes and ideas have also entirely changed; is he to spoil his ministry, and ruin his own and the girl's life, by carrying out an engagement made under totally different conditions?"

"An engagement's an engagement!" replied Ringley, doggedly.

"Or, to take one last case," resumed Yewson, waving his fiery opponent aside, and looking steadily at John. "A man discovers either that what he once thought was love for a girl is not love, or that the love he once had has somehow gone, he knows not how; he is not in love with any other fair maiden, he simply no longer loves the girl he proposes to marry. Which is the greater transgression, to marry a woman he can never really love, or tell her his changed feelings in time and thus spare them both, or at any rate give her the chance to set him free?"

"Out at last! the sting's in the beastly tail! a chance to set him free," and Ringley took several long strides up and down the room, gesticulating fiercely, and then coming back and shaking his fist at Yewson, he cried, "Yewson! the beast who breaks a poor girl's heart by jilting her right off is bad enough, but he's a saint by the side of the whining humbug who says he's prepared to marry her, but thinks 'she ought to know.' The cold-blooded hypocrite! I'd like to twist his measly neck for him!"

"Gentlemen of the jury, are you agreed upon your verdict?" and the advocate looked hard at John.

John seemed to have taken the argument more seriously than the others, and was evidently reluctant to answer; presently, however, he touched the end of his black moustache with the tip of his tongue, and speaking with surprising earnestness, he said shortly, almost sulkily—

"Yes, I agree with Max."

"Alas! alas! so bends my vaunting pride! I waste my fragrance on the desert air. Ah! the gong! Five o'clock, I declare. By-bye, brethren."

John watched him depart from under overhanging brows, much as though he saw the departure of an evil tempter, and then turned his head and looked gloomily into the fire.

Ringley, always most influenced by the last argument he had heard, stood looking musingly out of the window at the rain, and, after a few moments' silence, he said—

"Of course, I wasn't going to say so to him, because such arguments are, as a rule, mere sops to sore consciences, but if there was a real honest case of the kind he mentioned—I don't think there are many, of course, but if there were——"

"Max!" cried John, with an apparently unnecessary heat; "if a man has won a girl's heart and closed it to all others, and kept her waiting, he ought to marry her."

"But if he's changed——"

"Changed! he's no right to change; you might as well think of a married man changing. If he's made a mistake *he* must bear the consequences, not the poor innocent girl."

"But if he loved somebody else——"

"That would be perfidy! rank, cowardly perfidy!

No *man*, to say nothing of a minister, could ever do such a thing."

Ringley stared through the window with comic perplexity for a moment, and then breaking into one of his happy smiles, he said—

" Right you are, Johnny ! right you are, and now for the inner man."

But when his companion had banged the door after him in his usual fashion, John clasped his hands behind his head and glowered through the window, with a pained, anxious look. Then his face grew dark with inward storm, and he hid it in his hands and groaned ; for the case he had been denouncing so fiercely was, all unknown even to his inseparable friend Ringley—his own.

When he left Sallie Wood on that night of the fateful telegram, it was with the feeling that all was now at an end between them ; he could not hope, and it depressed him to feel that he did not greatly desire to do so. The hard, dead feeling he had had in his heart towards her had come back, and even the temporary desire he had had of saving her from worldliness by drawing out her better nature now seemed quixotic and almost silly. By the time he reached home he had, with many a sad sigh, resigned himself to the inevitable, and then the telegram, with its utterly unexpected message, for a time put even Sallie out of his head. But that shrewd young lady, though she had meant all she said, and probably more, on the previous evening, changed her mind with most businesslike promptitude when she heard the great news next day. She knew that John had returned himself on the official schedule as an engaged man, and would find it dangerous now to repudiate the thing. She knew, or thought she knew, his heart sufficiently well to assure herself that she could take possession of him whenever she chose, and she proceeded to play her part with characteristic smartness. She kept herself for some days carefully out of John's way, but she slipped down to the house in Shed Lane when she knew he would be at work, and delighted the hearts of his mother and sisters by enlisting their assistance in a little scheme to provide him with an outfit of underclothing; she would provide the materials, and they would all unite in the delightful labour. The thing was to be a sweet secret between them, and a wonderful surprise eventually to John. When some of the chapel people called upon her, in the absence of her father, and invited her to subscribe to a testimonial, which was to take the very sensible shape of a purse of gold, she said, with arch embarrassment and the prettiest possible little blush, that with her relationships to John she could not openly subscribe, " it would look so," but they might put down two pounds in the name of Aunt Pizer. This, as she well knew, was a tit-bit for the canvassers, who made the most of it, and before many days had passed it was known to everybody who was anybody in Bramwell Methodism that she and the young theological student, of whom they were all now so proud, were formally engaged. She appeared in public on every possible occasion by John's side, but took care never to be long alone with him, and skilfully frustrated several attempts he made to get speech with her. At the presentation meeting she wore the shy, self-conscious look of one who was personally interested in the proceedings, and accepted with pretty blushes the congratulations that were offered to her, and when, at John's home that evening, he got up to see her down the lane, she laughingly, but firmly, refused to accept his escort, but put up her red lips demurely to be kissed, and said that she had something strictly private to say to Annie and Lucy, and as the moon was about full and it was almost daylight, they must go with her to talk about—they knew what; and he (John) must go to bed and dream of being President.

The quiet assurance with which all this was done produced the distinctest possible impression on all present, and John had the feelings of a man who is being forced against his will into something very pleasant, but not quite lawful. The first thing he did with the testimonial, which the stewards had made up to £40, was to pay off the debt which they owed to Sallie. This, at any rate, he reflected, as he made the resolve, would give him an opportunity of speaking to her. The prospect of this interview led him to examine again his own heart, and the result was anything but satisfactory. His idol had been shattered; she was no longer his ideal of womanhood, but had ordinary human flaws and failings, the one he saw most clearly—worldliness—being the one for which he had least toleration. And yet she was very dear to him, and the idea which had recently come to him that he might be able to lead her out of her littleness and gradually instil larger and less selfish ideals, was strangely attractive. His heart misgave him all the same, and he felt that he was somehow weakly ignoring important and vital principles, which ought to be all-potent in his life. And when he came to think of it, it would look very awkward if he broke off with her as soon as his future had become assured; it would justify the worst things he had ever heard said about young ministers and the changes of affection which came with their changed conditions of life. He knew Sallie well enough to understand that if he took the step he contemplated she would make the very worst of it, and had the power very probably to wreck his career at its very outset. Altogether, the position was not an easy one to decide upon, and so many conflicting arguments presented themselves that he had not made up his mind when the time came to take her the money that was owing. When he arrived at the house, however, he found that Sallie had a party of young lady friends to tea, and could only give him a very few minutes. She appeared taken aback when he produced the money, and a little annoyed as well; but she took it all the same, saying, a little resignedly, that it did not really matter which of them had it; and then, as John seemed to be preparing to introduce something more serious, she slipped the money into the table drawer, and called aloud for her lady visitors to come and see the impudent man who never gave her a minute's peace, and who would not let her alone even then.

The girls came crowding into the parlour with gay, mischievous laughs, and earnestly declared that they would not give her up for a moment; and as he made for the door in mock horror, he noticed that the hand with which Sallie held open the door for him had a ring on the engaged finger. And so the days slipped rapidly by, and John could get nothing settled. Sallie left nothing to be desired in her conduct, except that she would never give him the interview he so much wanted.

But it was clear to him that she was intending him to understand that the change in his prospects had removed the only difficulty in the way, and that he might now be as happy as he wished. But, unfortunately, John was not so sure that he did wish this happiness now. Their interview on the night when he received news of his acceptance as a candidate for the ministry had made an impression upon him that seemed likely, not only never to be erased, but to grow deeper the more he thought about it. Nothing could be more charming than Sallie's manner, and he sometimes felt that he was a sulky, dissatisfied, exacting brute, and that, instead of brooding over things, he ought to accept his own happiness and be thankful, and then, when he had just concluded that it would have to be so, a feeling came to him that forbade the thought, and made him feel that to prolong the present state of things was only the conduct of a coward. Sometimes he told himself that the difficulty arose entirely from constitutional causes. Sallie was one of those natures which expanded and unfolded all their beauty in the sunshine of prosperity, but froze up and died in the cold winds of trouble. Her environment and the moral atmosphere in which she had been brought up, all tended to create in her an exaggerated horror of poverty and discomfort, and the poor girl was not to blame for these things. She would, he knew, be as bright and sweet as the most exacting lover could wish, in the life which stretched out before him, and which she evidently so much desired. Why should he not accept the situation and be happy? Sallie was light-hearted and brisk, and pushing and clever, and could rise to anything if she liked; the life he would be able to offer her would be so grateful to her that she would not only be happy herself, but would make him happy and help him on in his work, for she possessed just the qualities which he missed in himself. But whenever he got to this point, there came over him the sickening remembrance that she did not love him, or at any rate did not love him for himself, but only when he could give her the position she so much coveted. He could, of course, have had an interview with her, had he been resolute enough; but as he could never make up his mind to do what he felt would be a hard and bitter thing to her, and perhaps provoke her to reckless reprisals which might have far-reaching consequences, he rather weakly let things drift, and went away to college without any such settlement of the case as his judgment told him he ought to have had.   The day after his arrival Sallie wrote to him, ostensibly sending instructions about some stockings and other hand-knitted garments which his mother feared might be irretrievably injured in the washing.   He had, of course, replied, and so, though no word of love passed between them, a regular correspondence had been set up, and as Sallie seemed satisfied with this state of things, he had told himself that he had to be.   The poverty of his parents, and his apprehensions lest his mother should be in need, prompted him to accept offers of supply work during the vacations, and so he was not much at home ; and when he was, Sallie seemed as wary and shy of solitude as he was himself.   Of late, however, a new note had appeared in her correspondence ; her letters, which were always worth reading for their own sakes, had contained wistful little half-veiled hints of tender feelings, and latterly she had begged him to give his next holiday to his mother and her. John felt that she was missing something.   It might even be that there were at last the dawnings of real love to him in her, and so he felt he could not but meet her advances ; but when he came to write the words a sense of deception and unreality came over him, and he began to more than suspect that the love he had once felt was as surely dead as though it had never existed.

It was this letter with which he had been struggling when his friends invaded his study and commenced the discussion just reported.   That this subject of all others should have been sprung upon him struck John as somewhat singular, and the fact that his sense of right had driven him to express himself as he had done in a purely hypothetic case, strengthened his conviction as to how he ought to act in his own affair.   He was still staring at the rain-drops on the window and thinking closely. He was practically bound to Sallie, and she had many things about her that greatly charmed him. He was absolutely certain that now he could give her the position she coveted, she would prove a bright, capable, and happy little woman. Nobody would suffer by the carrying out of the engagement but himself; and it seemed more than likely that he would gain rather than otherwise, for she had just the gifts he lacked. His course, then, was clear. There were flutterings and sinkings of heart as he reached this point, but they were simply the timid caprices of his cowardly and morbid temperament, and he would tread them down.

As he reached this point, he heard the feet of his fellow-students in the corridor, as they returned from the afternoon meal. He turned round with a quick movement, then wavered a little, then turned and gazed abstractedly at a photo of his sister Lucy hanging over the mantelpiece; then, with sudden decision, he strode to a little box that propped up a half-length row of books, unlocked it, and took out a photo of Sallie, and, removing his sister's, placed the other in the frame, and then, stepping backward, looked at the picture with a smile and a sigh, and turned on his heel and hurried off to tea.

Returning a quarter of an hour later to his study, John caught the sound of Ringley's voice raised in animated speech, and pushing the door softly before him, he beheld Max standing in front of the new photo with a pen behind his ear, a Hebrew lexicon and Bible under his left arm, and a ruler in his right hand.

"Your most obedient and devoted servant, Mademoiselle," he was saying, as he genuflected obsequiously before the picture. "Your servant's most humble servant! Your gallant knight's most devoted esquire, at your service! Eyes, madam?

Yea, verily! Dainty nose and chin? of a truth! Dimples? bewitching! Your knight is a connoisseur, it would seem, madam. A sly, still-water-runs-deep sort of rogue. Look hither, my lady (placing his hand on his heart), cast your eyes over these a—a— exquisitely elongated proportions; note this enslaving hirsute adornment of the upper lip. Cast not your pearls before a—a—a—porkers; waste not thy fragrance on the desert a—a—Hebraist. Codlin's the man, not Short, my dear! Bethink thee, maiden fair! there's better fish in the sea than ever was caught! The tame, the puerile, the worthless are caught! Cast in thy dainty harpoon for the whale— the royal whale—fair fisher! Johannes! Johannes is a dreary dry-as-dust, compounded of Hebrew roots and Greek irregulars! Lift thy proud eyes to the noble Maximus! the poet! the orator! the true knight-errant, the hero of romance! the——"

"The universal lover!" broke in John, with a laugh.

"Ha! he sneers, fair damsel! Dry-as-dust is jealous! I *am* the universal lover. This poor heart embraces you all!"

"And this is he who cudgelled Yewson," laughed John again. "Oh, inconsistency! thy name is Max!"

"Consistency, sir! consistency!" cried the rhapsodical fellow, wheeling round with a sudden assumption of apparent earnestness. "Consistency is the vice of common minds! the besetment of slaves!"

CHAPTER II

THERE was most unusual animation in the dingy Bramwell station on the day John Ledger left for his first circuit. His sisters stood near him, linked arm-in-arm, alternately prompting and restraining their meek-faced mother as she gave her son final instructions as to the management of his linen and his future landlady. Sallie, dressed in quiet black, for old Zeph had recently died, stood at the other side of her lover with a pretty air of proprietorship; whilst Wilky Drax was leaning against the door-post of the booking office, and asking the new station-master whether he would ever have thought that the head of a quiet-looking fellow like John could be chock full of Greek and Hebrew; and John's father was sitting in a state of utter mental collapse, on a bench a little farther up the platform, surrounded by a bevy of elderly females, who were emulously striving to soothe the " beautiful " feelings of their friend and leader, and reconcile him to the anguish of parting with his only son.

" He shall have him," he cries one moment. " If it tears my heart-strings to flinders, I'll give him up." And then, as the females glanced at each other in unspeakable admiration of the heroic sacrifice, he suddenly collapses again, and groans out — " Me have ye bereaved of my childern. Joseph is not, an' Simeon is not, an' now—Oh, by Jings, that's the train ! "

"Ledger! L—e—d—g—e—r! Hi! Ledger! plenty of room up here!" and as John disentangled himself from the group of clinging females and rushed for the train, he beheld the yellow head and long waving arms of his college friend Ringley at the other end of the train, in the carriage closest to the engine. The race for so distant a seat disarranged all preparations and cruelly abbreviated the leave-takings, and the last thing John saw was Wilky coming waddling down the platform at the top of his speed, and shouting vociferously all the while—

"Give it 'em hot, Johnny! Plenty o' pepper! Plenty o' pep—pep—pep——"

But Max, unable to control any longer his desire to see the giver of such advice, dragged John into the carriage, and thrusting himself head and shoulders into the aperture, gazed amazedly at the rapidly receding little dwarf, and answered, with a wild wave of his long arms—

"Cayenne, sir! Best double strength Indian cayenne, sir!" and with a final war-whoop he backed into the carriage, slammed up the window, and threw himself upon his still breathless friend.

"Whatever mad freak has brought you here?" demanded John, as he wiped his hot face, for the weather was stifling.

"Only eighteen miles round, my boy! Couldn't help it! My fatherly interest, my son! My fatherly interest!"

"But"—and John eyed him over with wonder and something like alarm—"you're not going to turn up in your new circuit in that ungodly golf suit?"

"Ledger!" and Max planted himself in the seat on the opposite side of the window to John, knitted his brows, pointed his long arm, and beating time with his hand, "I'm—just—going —to—do—that—very—thing."

" But——"

" None of your billy-goat buttings at me! I'm going to do it! The ministry, sir, is making a profound mistake! It talks eloquently about seeking the masses, and coming down to the masses, and going to the masses, and all the time it wears a livery and dresses in a style that says as plain as a public-house sign-board, ' Stand thou here, whilst I go and pray yonder.' I won't have it, sir! If we are to get at the masses we must be like 'em, dress like 'em, live like 'em, eat like 'em! And, by the beard of the prophet, I mean to do it! "

" But, Max, you were always so—— "

" Never mind what I was! What I am's the question! I'm leggings and Norfolk suit and golf cap, like the man in the street! "

" Well, then, in common consistency—— "

" Hang consistency! Because I've been a fool twenty years, is that any reason why I should be a fool for twenty more? Consistency, man! consistency means stagnation, sir, and sterility! It is the pedagogue's perdition; the one little lifeless egg of the solemn old hen of respectability! "

" But a dress like that—there's moderation and decency in everything."

" Is there? I verily believe thee, my son! And that's why everything's so small and shabby and worthless! We want something drastic, something out-and-out; that's what we want! "

But at this moment the train began to slacken, and Max was soon scrambling all over the compartment for his miscellaneous luggage. They both had to change here, and as they stepped out upon the platform Max gave a shout, and then rushed headlong at the train which was just moving out from the opposite platform. Several porters gave chase, and by the time John came up he was puffing and panting, and brandishing his watch at the head porter in a vain endeavour to convince him that the train had started before the time. It would be two hours and twenty minutes before there was another train to Longhope, Ringley's destination, and so John spent the twenty minutes at his disposal in pacifying the wrath of his excited friend, and begging him to respect the usages of his class in the matter of dress. He still held out, however, but John learnt afterwards that his chum appeared on the platform at Longhope in an unimpeachable black clerical coat, light coloured knee-breeches, and a cap.

John had a compartment to himself from the junction to Partidge, his destination, and spent his time speculating on the character of the reception that awaited him. He had been what is known in Methodism as " thrust upon " the circuit to which he was going. They had invited another man, and in the earlier drafts of the stations their nominee had been " put down " for them, but in the last half-hour of " stationing " the arrangement had been interfered with, and John found himself transferred from a modest little circuit in Devonshire to the somewhat sinister reputed Partidge, in his own county. He had received no welcoming communication from the officials ; the only message, in fact, of any kind had been one on a post-card, enquiring what time he would arrive.

" Whatever you do at Partidge, Mr. John," the super. at Bramwell had said, " be sure you make friends with the Wheelers; they are the leading people ; get on with them, and you will get on with everybody."

" Beware of the Wheelers, my friend," the second minister had exhorted, " they are a stuck-up lot, I'm told, and awfully disliked. They have ruled the roost there for a generation, but things are coming to a head, I hear, so you mind your P's and Q's."

John's meditations, therefore, as the train whirled him along, were not of the pleasantest kind, and when about six o'clock he found himself pulling up opposite a great board, on which was written in letters nearly a foot long,

PARTIDGE
(Lowtown),

he looked about for a friendly face in no very confident frame of mind. When a new minister arrived at Bramwell both the stewards were there to meet him, and sometimes their wives as well, whilst quite a number of minor people found they had business at the station about that time, and the faces of Sampson Ledger and Wilky Drax could always be seen jammed against the railings of the platform on the look-out for the coming man. But John, though he lingered about the platform for two or three minutes, found no one to greet him, and was just sauntering towards the heap of luggage to select his belongings when he heard light feet come pattering behind him, a small hand was placed on his arm, and a high, clear, girlish voice cried breathlessly—

"Here we are! Hip! hip! I knew you at once. Welcome to Partidge, sir!"

Turning round, John beheld a tall, fair girl of about sixteen, with great grey eyes, long dark lashes, and piquant, expressive face, which changed every moment. She had a wealth of long, light hair down her back, and wore a walking costume of small black and white check, with a picture hat.

"Now don't look so disappointed, sir! Frown as much as you like at poor me, but don't blame anybody else. It was Hobson's choice, and even *I* am better than nobody."

John made a stiff bow to this totally novel specimen of humanity, and murmured something about being delighted to make Miss—and there he stuck.

"Betty Wheeler! But don't begin your ministerial career by telling stories. You expected the circuit steward and the super. to meet you, and you only find the steward's youngest daughter, a sort of circuit scullery-maid. Well, it is too bad, but——" and here she broke off, and stepping up to him tapped the button of his clerical coat with the handle of her sunshade, and went on, "But never mind, sir, 'the first shall be last, and the last first,' 'the bud may have a bitter taste, but sweet shall be the flower.' Everybody's gone to receive the new super., who changed his time of arrival after everything had been arranged; but cheer up, sir, you'll go with me, and if we don't have the jolliest of all jolly times—Nathan, take Mr. Ledger's umbrella and bag, and the rest can come after. This way, sir."

A moment later John found himself seated by his fair friend's side in as pretty a little pony phaeton as he had ever seen.

"You're come, Mr. Ledger, to one of the most famous towns in Lancashire," said Betty, as she snatched up the reins and screwed her little mouth into a squeaking signal for departure.

"Famous for what?" John asked, with an incredulous glance round at the long chimneys, the heavy smoke, and the dingy brick buildings.

"Famous for ugliness, sir, pure unmitigated colossal ugliness; but never mind, it's the people that make the place, and they are 'gradely folk.' We are jolly here, sir; some of us jolly bad—steady, Pindar—but all jolly. At our house we're all bricks, sir; grandmother, dad, Lady Mary, the kids, and myself. Oh, we do have larks. Mr. Ledger, can you play tennis?"

" Yes, a little."

" And golf ? "

" No."

" No! Well, I'll teach you. Can you play billiards ? "

" A very little."

" Then you'll be a match for me, but don't take on the kids; they're demons, all three of them!" and then, as another thought suddenly struck her, she turned her eyes upon him with a flash. " But we're all rippin' Methodists, out-and-outers, you know. Why, I'm a seasoned official myself."

John raised his eyebrows in polite surprise.

" Yes, I'm junior secretary of the Guild, junior leader, collector for Missions, and Sunday School organist; and the kids! why, they are up to the eyes in it—Pindar!"

The little dapple-grey, thus sternly adjured, gave a start and a hypocritical pretence of haste, but as they were approaching the second hill he soon resumed his leisurely pace.

John was looking at the busy streets through which they were passing, and the public buildings, and he was just turning to ask a question when he noticed that Miss Betty was studying him sideways, with a severely critical pucker on her brow.

" Mr. Ledger, I think I shall like you, I *do*, honest injun; but the point is, will ' her ladyship' like you ? "

" Whom do you mean by ' her ladyship ? ' "

" Who ? why Mary. She's the one, you know. Even dad's small potatoes where she comes. But you lie low a bit, Mr. Ledger; I'll find out how the land lies, and tell you how to work her."

John didn't much believe in working anybody, and couldn't for the life of him see how a female occupant of the steward's house could be of such first-rate importance, but he was too cautious and perhaps too shy to push enquiries, and merely remarked—

"She is your elder sister, I presume?"

"She is that! she's everybody's elder sister! She's the patron saint of the circuit, bless you! They called the new chapel in Brand Street 'St. Mary's' after her. She's a B.A. and a great mechanic; she invented some sort of a thing-me-gum one day, and dad says there's a fortune in it. Sing! she's the best amateur contralto in the provinces."

John felt he was conceiving a prejudice against this petticoat marvel, and, as if she read his thoughts, Betty leaned over until her light hair touched his forehead, and said impressively—

"You'll begin by hating her, Mr. Ledger, and you'll end up by adoring her; we all do. But there she is at the window! No! She's vanished, of course."

John checked, just in time, an impulse to look round, as the pony drew up before an imposing, stone-fronted, modern villa.

"Come in, Mr. Ledger! Janet, take Mr. Ledger to his room. But be sharp, sir; tea's waiting, and I'm just famished. Oh, here she is! Mary—Mr. Ledger."

"Welcome to Partidge, sir; dad's up receiving the super.; but *you're* our man, you know. We always claim the young minister."

John raised his eyes a little shyly, and looked into the frankest woman's face he had ever beheld. The brow was broad and white, and gave an intellectual cast to the whole face; the mouth was a little wide, but firm and almost masculine; the complexion creamy, with the slightest tinge of colour in the cheeks, whilst the eyes were of a deep violet, and wonderfully soft and reassuring. The little hand which he took was put out with easy frankness, and

John felt certain at once that whatever he did in the future he would never misunderstand this most uncommon specimen of womanhood.

" I scarcely understand," said John hesitatingly. " These are not my lodgings."

Betty ran off into a long rippling laugh.

" No, not your lodgings, sir," said Mary, quietly, " but your home, if you choose to make it such. Every Christian minister is welcome here, sir, but we always claim the junior preacher. Work in your lodgings, but when you want recreation and company and cheering up,well, come here,week-day or Sunday, morning, noon, or night."

The form of these words sounded, at least, a little stilted, but the frank, easy heartiness of them went to the stranger's heart, and he ascended the broad staircase with relief and even gratitude. As he came down into the hall again, Betty pounced out upon him from the smoke-room and grabbed him by the arm.

" I say, you mustn't, you know ! she won't like it. Don't you come polite piety with her. Contradict her, bully her, but for mercy's sake don't soap her ! " and she dragged him unceremoniously into the dining-room.

That night, as John rolled about in a luxurious bed at the Wheelers', he tried hard to define the impression made upon him by this singular family. They were the most unconventional people he had ever met ; there were no signs of particular politeness, but he found his needs quietly anticipated and attended to. They had very little small talk, and now that he came to notice it, no petty scandal ; but the absence of it seemed rather from taste than from either religiousness or politeness.

They were pronouncedly Lancastrian in their studious avoidance of religious talk, and yet they were keenly interested in the chapel and the circuit.

The "kids" turned out to be three great manly fellows, whose ages ranged from about thirty to eighteen, and who spoke of their Church work and official duties as if they were amusing jokes.

The father was most evidently the chosen chum of his sons, Betty was the household libertine and jester, "Lady" Mary an object of quiet but deep regard that amounted almost to reverence, and they all talked the dialect when they spoke to the cherry-cheeked old woman called grandmother.

A conscientious scruple had constrained John to mention quite early in the evening that he was an ex-factory lad, but the only change the information produced was an increase of cordiality, and they showed more inclination to talk "shop" to him.

Towards Mary Wheeler John had a curious feeling; he was conscious of a subtle, but very genuine accession of self-reliance. It was as though some long-felt deficiency had been met, and that as he approached perilous waters a pilot had come aboard his little ship.

His natural apprehensiveness warned him that this was all too good to last, and he fell asleep wondering what it could have been that made the second minister at home warn him against this most interesting and hospitable family.

In a few days he got settled down in his lodgings and was soon hard at work. And so the days ran into weeks, and the weeks into months, and he was increasing every day in his intimacy with, and respect for the Wheelers, and more perplexed than ever as to the grounds for the prejudice which he had met with amongst outsiders, and which he soon perceived was present in the minds of the people amongst whom he was now mixing. A hard student, a fastidious sermon-maker, and an almost painfully diligent pastor, he found in the house on Shuttle Hill relaxation and company, and quick but quiet sympathy, that made number seven as it was familiarly called—for the Wheelers had a sort of contempt for the modern craze for "titled" houses—a haven of comfort and rest. At the same time he was aware that he was living in an atmosphere of suspicion and petty scandal, and that the family he had grown to respect so deeply were in anything but good odour in the town.

"Yes, yes, Ledger," said the super., a little impatiently, "the Wheelers have made a pet of you and you are inexperienced and cannot see."

"I speak of them as I find them," replied John stoutly. "In the home and in the church they are always the same."

"They are so purse-proud and worldly, you know, you never hear anything spiritual in their talk."

John silently thanked God he didn't, but as he answered not, the super. went on—

"It cannot go on! It *must* not go on. I shall change the stewardship at Christmas."

"I hope not, sir."

It was almost necessary for the senior minister to carry his colleague with him in a step of this kind, and so—they were talking at the usual Monday morning preachers' meeting—he fidgeted about in his chair and cried—

"You hope not! Good heavens, Ledger, you've only to look at his face to see that he drinks."

"I don't believe it, sir!"

"But, man, it has been the talk of the circuit for years, everybody knows it; they say he never comes from the Manchester market sober."

"It's a wicked, envious falsehood, sir," and the quiet John was on his feet in indignation.

There was a momentary pause, and then the super. went on—

"I feel as if some curse were hanging over the circuit; besides he's been steward for twenty years; there ought to be a change for that reason."

"Change for that reason if you like," said John, "but for common honesty's sake let us have nothing of the other."

"Ledger, it is right to be charitable, but we've no right to be deaf and blind. We have the reputation of the circuit and the church to think of, my dear fellow, besides—and here he dropped into a portentious whisper—I'm told the firm is not solvent. I'm assured that there will be a crash before long, and I'm resolved that before that day comes I'll have him out and save the scandal, as far as we are concerned."

"And I'll prepare him for what is coming."

"What! You'll betray your super.! Good heavens, man, are you mad?"

"If you act on mere malicious rumour and get him out on a mean subterfuge, I'll tell him everything."

"You will! You'll betray me? Young man, I'll have you before the Synod!"

"I shall do it sir, Synod or no Synod."

They were standing now and glaring at each other with threatening looks.

The super. was the first to quail, however, and he dropped into a chair with a baffled, querulous snarl—

"Very well, young man, you'll do as you please, and take the consequences, but have him out I will!"

"By all means, sir, if you think it best, only go to him and tell him what you propose to do; I daresay, if you give him the slightest hint, he'll save you the trouble."

The super. answered with an angry snarl, and in

parting ostentatiously, overlooked his colleague's out-stretched hand. As for John, he went away in an anxious and indignant mood.

To think of it! He, the safest man in his college year, embroiled in a struggle with his super. before he had been three months in the work!

He had had four services on the preceding day, and was limp and washed-out, and the encounter he had just had depressed and worried him. It was madness to try a fall with his superior, and it was ungrateful and cowardly to refuse to stand up for his friends.

Oh that he were safely back in his beloved *Alma Mater*, with nothing to think of but his books! But, perhaps, he *had* been to blame; he had certainly shown a marked preference for the Wheelers. It was not right for a minister to have favourites. Perhaps if he quietly and gradually drop—No, no, it was mean, it was——

"What ho, there! Sir nose-i-th cloud! Can't you see a poor girl because she isn't a mill chimney? Take hold of this 'bike' please, don't you see I've got two!"

"Betty!"

"Yes, it's Betty, poor fetch-and-carry Betty, the circuit slave; but you cannot 'bike' in full canonicals. Oh, dear, we shall have to go back to that horrible den!"

"But, Betty, I cannot, I'm busy——"

"And *I* cannot, *I'm* busy, but we're going all the same. I promised the 'Goddess' I'd do my duty by her, and I'm doing it."

The Goddess was Betty's name for the photo of Sallie on the study mantelpiece, at which, whenever John's back was turned, she made most unladylike grimaces. She was the only "alien" who ever invaded John's sanctum, and certain cushions, rugs, flowers, and dishes of out-of-season fruit which were to be seen there had been brought by her in spite of John's polite protests. She had noticed the photo on her first invasion of the room, and thus became aware of his engagement. She pretended to be hugely disappointed, and to fiercely hate the original. She criticised the photo with reckless frankness on every possible occasion, and often roused John from pensive thoughts by chaffing him about the singularity of his taste.

" You must excuse me to-day, Betty," John said, as he took the machine from her. It was her youngest brother's, and she had brought it for her favourite minister's use.

" Excuse ? certainly! You are in for a Monday mope—I'll excuse you ! You want to write to the Goddess—I'll excuse you! You want to visit the flock—I'll excuse you ! Duty calls you and me to Bellerly, and we're going, jump up !" and without giving him time for further remonstrance she sprang upon her pretty " Swift," and darted away to John's lodgings.

John tried to get out of the trip again when they reached his own door, but his imperious little ruler waved him peremptorily indoors to change his clothes, and began industriously to oil his machine whilst she waited.

" I've a bone to pick with you, Mr. Thirdly," she cried, as they rode abreast along the highway, in the crisp December air.

" Oh, dear ! What now ?"

" What have you been doing to her ladyship ? "

" I ? Miss Wheeler ? How do you mean ? " and accustomed as he was to the reckless and startling onslaughts of his lively companion, John looked really alarmed and steered a little closer.

" You've been coming it over her some way that's certain. What do you mean, sir ? "

" I ? I've done nothing ! What does she say ? "

" Say ! That's it ! She doesn't say anything ; she talked of you often enough when first you came, but she never even alludes to you now. Now for a jolly coaster," and away she flew down the hill.

" But, Betty, you must be mistaken," cried John, when he overtook her. " I've followed your instructions most carefully."

" You've been soaping her ! "

" No ! "

" Then you've been polite, you haven't sat upon her. Have you ever made her cry ? "

" Cry ? Good gracious, Betty, I should think not."

" Tchat ! What sillies men are ! You'll never get on with her until you ' boss ' her."

The idea of " bossing " the most frank and cool-headed woman he had ever met amused John; he would like to see any one, his friend, Ringley, for instance, trying it, and he grinned as he pictured the scene. He tried again and again to get some clearer idea of the case from Betty, but failed, and just when he was giving the matter up she turned on her machine, and looking at him with the surprise of a new and rather sobering thought, she said—

" Of course you haven't been spooning on her ? "

" Betty ? "

" Of course, only men do such silly things; that would spoil everything, you know, even if there were no ' Goddess.' "

John would have liked to ask just one question more, but it seemed rather a difficult one to frame, and before he had got it ready they had arrived at his door, and Betty flew on without stopping.

After a light lunch our young preacher settled down to the preparation of a new sermon, but he found his line of thought constantly traversed by the gay Betty's mysterious conversation, and the remembrance of the altercation he had had with his super. He interpreted his own duty as a minister very literally, and so, as he brooded over the condition of the Church, and the things that were taking place about him, he found himself later in the day collecting together materials for a sermon on evil speaking. By Thursday night the discourse was finished, but almost immediately he found himself full of misgivings and wondering whether a direct attack on the popular and injurious vice was the best possible way of dealing with it; and so by noon on Friday he had put the manuscript away and was busily employed on a discourse on charity. It was late on Saturday night before he finished it, and he spent the time which ought to have been given to sleep in debating which of the two homilies he would deliver at St. Mary's the following morning. The question was undecided when he left his bedroom on Sunday, and close application for several days and the worry occasioned by his relations with his colleague had made him nervous and miserable. His style was practical and didactic; he liked to say plainly what he meant, but even the milder of the two sermons was sufficiently straight for all purposes. He had not made up his mind when the time came to adjourn to the sanctuary, but as soon as he faced the congregation his judgment seemed to clear, and he decided upon the least direct method of dealing with the evil his soul hated. He was so nervous that his first few sentences could not be heard at the other end of the chapel. Just as he began to feel at home in his work he saw Bowden, Mr. Wheeler's brother-in-law, and chief though secret enemy, lean over and whisper something to his wife. That lady referred to the Revised Version lying on her knee, lifted her eyes and looked straight at John, and then turned

and nodded with curling lip at her husband. With
a sinking heart the preacher proceeded, but a minute
later Ramsden, the poor steward, got up in his seat
with a smothered exclamation and began fumbling
for his hat ; then he looked at John, listened a little
while, and finally stepped into the aisle and made
for the door, banging it resentfully after him as he
retired.

The young preacher broke out into a cold sweat,
and before he had got another dozen sentences out,
he noticed that two or three persons had turned half-
round, and were glancing resentfully at the Wheelers'
pew. The super.'s wife and daughter had their heads
down, and were looking exceedingly embarrassed.
In the Wheelers' pew six pairs of eyes were fixed
on him with close, sympathetic attention, and this
gave him heart again. A moment later he perceived
Bowden standing up in his pew and looking round
upon his fellow- worshippers with pious protest in his
eyes. Distracted by these unwonted signs of dis-
approval John stopped, and his mind and memory
became complete blanks.

" Thar't reet, lad ! Go on wi' thee ! " shouted old
Crake from the free seats ; and as Bowden sank dis-
gustedly into his place, John resumed his discourse.
With sudden and strange confidence, he laid bare
the secret spring of uncharitableness, and, warming to
his work, with bravery now almost reckless, he sent
home-thrust after home-thrust at his startled hearers,
and then with a sudden pathetic break in his voice,
he began to plead for forbearance and consideration,
and mutual loyalty, finishing at length, in a voice
almost choked with emotion, with that exquisite
entreaty of St. Paul's—

" Let all bitterness, and wrath, and clamour, and
evil-speaking be put away from you, with all malice :
And be ye kind one to another, tender-hearted, for-

giving one another, even as God for Christ's sake hath forgiven you."

A small crowd gathered, with eyes still shining, at the foot of the pulpit stairs, and enthusiastically shook the preacher's hand and blessed him.

"Let's see, charity's another name for love, isn't it?" giggled Bradshaw, the society steward, as he bent over the vestry table counting the collection.

"Ay, but Lady Mary 'ull want summat warmer nor charity," grinned Smales, his colleague.

John glanced from one to the other of the officials with a look of mystified anxiety, and then as the meaning of their coarse jokes flashed upon him he turned and rushed, hatless as he was, out of the back entrance and home to his own study.

CHAPTER III

WHAT TOOK PLACE AT THE QUARTERLY MEETING

"SHE did! She said it! She just stood there on the rug and twisted her gloves like that (suiting the action to the word), and then she said, 'He's the manliest man I ever knew,' and then by all that's wonderful, she blushed!"

"Betty!"

"She did! My stars, Parson Ledger, but you must be a paragon! *I* never saw her blush before."

"Never?"

"Never; not even when your illustrious predecessor proposed to her. How do I know? I saw them, though they didn't see me. I couldn't help it, really—a—a—*I* didn't like your sermon."

"Why not?"

"It made me feel mean. I like sermons that make me feel teary and comfortable—but the dinner will be in, come along."

But John was in no mood for dining out that day; he resisted both the entreaties and the high-flown threats of his visitor, and fed on toast-water and biscuits the rest of the day. His poor little sermon had complicated matters indeed, as he might have known it would. It had, he felt certain, driven waverers into the camp of the enemy. They evidently regarded him as an interested partisan of the Wheelers, and his discourse as an open declaration of war. They had associated him with the peerless

Mary, and any action he might take in defence of his friends would be discounted and misunderstood. He could not think any longer of resisting the proposals of his super. under these circumstances; what a bungler he was! instead of mending matters he had made them infinitely worse. Mary Wheeler! that incomparable woman's name, linked with that of a man already engaged to be married! He writhed at the thought of it, and stamped on the floor in the bitter anguish of his spirit.

He resolved once over to go to the officials who had flung the cruel innuendo at him, and argue them out of their monstrous delusion, but the very vehemence of his effort, he reflected, would only strengthen their suspicions and justify their sneers. Presently he grew calmer; he had done his duty and would leave the rest. Nothing strengthened suspicion so much as incessant denial. He would therefore, for their own sakes, leave the Wheelers alone, and—yes—he would get some friend to invite Sallie over and make it abundantly clear, by this means, how foolish and unworthy the slander was. But when he thought of Sallie, he was conscious of a very curious feeling; a sense, somehow, that it would be unjust to her to bring her into comparison with the lovely mistress of number seven. And then his heart misgave him, the old doubts and fears he had fought down so often came to the surface again, and he tramped about the room and wrung his hands and sent up little snatches of prayer, until, before he realised it, it was time to go to Bellerly-green, where he was expected for the evening service.

Monday morning brought him a small shoal of letters—anonymous—anent the previous morning's sermon, and later on a visit and a sharp rebuke from his super.

The following Thursday morning, as he sat at his

desk, vainly trying to forget his perplexities in work, a knock came at the door, and 'Cilla, the little maid who waited upon him, came in to say that a gentleman wanted to see him, and after making her announcement she held on to the door knob, and projecting her body as far into the room as she could, she continued in an impressive, confidential whisper—

"A Catholic priest, sir."

"Show him in, 'Cilla," said John, turning his head and laying down his pen.

The "priest" seemed in a violent hurry, for he came bounding up the narrow staircase three steps at a time, and burst into the room with a noisy—

"Here we are again, Johannes! What cheer, my hearty?"

"Max!" cried John, in eager surprise, and then, as he eyed his friend over from top to toe, he cried "Max!" again.

"'Tis he; 'tis he! The same bad penny turning up again!" and rushing up to him he gave his hand a boisterous shake, and thrusting him back into his chair, looked him over with hungry affection.

"But, Max, this is never you? Where's your coming down to the masses now? Where's your doing in Rome as Rome does? Where are those worldly togs, and where, oh where, is that cherished moustache?"

Max's appearance fully justified his friend's amazement, for he had got himself up in the most extreme ritualistic attire — broad-brimmed, low-crowned, rosetted soft hat; long, black, ultra-clerical coat; cassock vest, and stock to match; a little gold cross, hanging pendant and prominent on his long-hair watch-chain; and his upper lip as bare as a table top.

"Yes, my ancient and only," he said, perching himself like a wheedling school-girl on the creaking arm of John's basket-chair. "We live and learn, my inseparable. Our beloved people are babies, and must be taught in symbols. From the Pope at one end to General Booth on the other, we are all symbolists. The great things in all great religions are the symbols. To the masses the abstract is the incomprehensible; it is the concrete, the palpable, they understand. *He* taught them in parables, and so must we."

John laughed again, and after ringing for a cup of bovril, he unearthed from behind a pile of books a little tin biscuit box, and bade his friend help himself. Whilst the appetising drink was being prepared downstairs, Max stepped from his perch and began to explore the room. He scrutinised the pictures on the walls, picked up and carefully examined every knicknack he could lay his hands upon, and finally put his long, black, gold-headed cane into a corner, hung up his hat, and throwing himself into the deep chair John had just vacated, he stretched out his long limbs until he had effectually blocked the approach to the fire.

"Yes, my only one," he resumed, puckering his brow as he usually did when about to announce his last and greatest discovery, "you rabid Protestants can see nothing in Romanism but superstition and flummery; but there's a great deal more in it than you imagine, I can tell you."

"For instance?" asked John, as he handed him the bovril.

"For instance—hand over the biscuits—we'll take that thing which most of all shocks the souls of you hide-bound respectables. Why, man, there's more wisdom in it than in the whole policy of Methodism."

"What is that?"

"The celibacy of the clergy! Wisdom, sir! Why, it's too great to be a mere human invention; it's a Divine inspiration, sir!"

"W-h-e-w!" and John laughed in amused astonishment.

"It is, I tell you! Why, since I entered the work three months and a fortnight since, I've made several marvellous discoveries, but that is the greatest of them all."

"And the newest, I suppose," laughed Ledger again.

"I mean it, Johannes; I do! If a man will do his duty to his Church and the world he must know nothing about wife or family. The Church is his wife; the people are his family. 'No man going to war entangleth himself.'"

John, who had thrown himself back upon a couch, was now shaking with laughter.

"Oh, Reuben! unstable as water!" he cried presently, "which of the six fair charmers has proved cruel now? It was six, wasn't it?"

"Six or sixty, I renounce them all! I'm a eunuch of the Kingdom of God!"

"For how long?"

"For ever and for aye. I mean it, man! Eyes, and dimples, and figures, and wonderful hair are nothing to me now. I have sterner work to do—

"'No room for mirth or trifling here.'

You primrose-on-the-river's-brim sort of fellows may go your own way, but I'm married to Mother Church. I live for my race."

"'Lord, I thank Thee that I am not as other men are,'" mocked John. "But what brought you here to-day?"

"Yammerings and yearnings, dear boy, to gaze on thy venerable visage."

"It will be venerable if I mope in this dreary den much longer. What say you to a walk?"

As they climbed the rough rain-channelled lane up
the side of Bilberry Hill, Max enlarged still further
on his last great resolve.   It was not the freak of a
moment; his striking conversions never were.   He
had seen the necessity more and more for a long
time.   A married minister was more than half a
layman.   He could never be the spiritual adviser of
the girl to whom he was a possible lover, or the man
whose rival or whose son or brother-in-law he might
become.   This generation, with its wistful private
problems and infinite questionings, its needs of and
longing for comprehension and sympathy, wanted
detachment and disinterestedness in its chosen
guides and confidants.   The man who would share
and relieve the troubles of his fellows must have none
of his own to preoccupy him.

> " A heart at leisure from itself
> To soothe and sympathise,"

was what the times called for.   He was evidently in
most serious earnest, and every objection raised by
his companion had apparently been anticipated, and
was most conclusively answered.

They found the irrepressible Betty waiting for
them on their return.   She opened her great eyes
very wide when she beheld the priestly Max, and
though she bowed with punctilious decorum when
he was introduced, she made grimaces at him behind
his back and included him in the invitation she had
brought for " high tea " with most evident reluctance.

At first Max seemed to object to this bit of dainty
earthliness, so far below the lofty moral grandeur of
the ideas he had been ventilating in the lane, but in
a few moments he was watching her every movement
and listening with more than mere polite interest
to her audacious little sallies.   He ran down the

stairs to open the door for her when she departed, and appeared not to notice the tell-tale grin on John's face when he returned. John hypocritically attempted to resume the topic they had been discussing, but the exponent of ministerial celibacy seemed to have exhausted himself, and showed faint interest. John showed him a new book, but he slipped it down under the table almost before his friend's back was turned, and did not seem at all interested in the subject of the approaching Probationers' Examinations. Presently he flung himself down on the little hard sofa, and began to kick his long legs about in most characteristic restlessness. Then in a studiously indifferent voice he inquired if there were any decent folk amongst the Partidge Methodists, and John gave a detailed and exhaustive account of the chief families in his church, mischievously omitting any reference to the Wheelers or even to Betty. 'Cilla came in to set the table for dinner, and when she had gone, Max sat up on the sofa and declared that he really wished they had not accepted the invitation out, he would very much rather have had a quiet evening to themselves. John ought, of course, to have pooh-poohed the idea, and told him all about the family they were about to visit, but with a perversity little short of maliciousness, he simply pointed out that there was no decent way out of it.

Max grumbled that he had come to see John and not to sit twiddling his thumbs in a spruced-up drawing-room with a match-making mamma and a swarm of giggling daughters.

The obtuse John rang the bell and went over to his desk.

" What's up now ? " cried Max, suddenly sitting up and watching his friend selecting notepaper.

" I'll just drop a note and ask them to excuse us ; it will be all right, I dare say."

Max stood a moment in tantalising perplexity, and then as 'Cilla came into the room he shouted: " No, no! it's all right, my girl; we don't want anything now "; and as the little domestic disappeared he sprang upon John, and seizing him by the throat he cried: " You aggravating beast! You torturer! Sit down here and tell me all about them."

John's description of the Wheelers, though it took ten minutes to give, proved painfully bald and incomplete, and for the next half-hour he was subject to a searching series of questions which came very well indeed from the lofty celibate of the morning. Max was ready to go long before the time fixed, and fumed and fidgeted until John started earlier than was necessary and took a roundabout way so as not to arrive too punctually. That night Max surpassed himself, and took the Wheelers literally by storm. He and Betty were hand and glove in half an hour. She beat him at billiards, gave him a special buttonhole of her own selection, asked him riddles until his head ached, coaxed him into singing a very innocent and ancient humorous song, and finally shocked all present by addressing him as " Father Max." The male Wheelers seemed as much taken by their vivacious visitor as was Betty, and outdid themselves in hearty Lancashire cordiality. The evening was gone all too soon, and when after a scratch supper the men folk dropped into social and political topics there was mutual delight at the discovery that on all important points they were absolutely agreed. The only thing that surprised John was that, as he watched his friend's very evident enjoyment, he noticed that he seemed almost oblivious of the chief person in the house—the queenly Mary.

Max seemed scarcely to see her, and " carried on " with Betty in a manner that would have alarmed him if he had not known him so well.

M.   S

"Come again, sir," said Mr. Wheeler heartily, as he helped Max on with his coat.

"Yes, come again, and soon," chimed in the brothers enthusiastically.

"*Don't* come again; you bore me!" screamed Betty halfway up the staircase, where she had retreated to be out of his reach.

"Wesleyan ministers never come at the wrong time here, sir. *Do* take the muffler; it is foggy outside," said the quieter elder sister; and John, who was watching the adjustment of the muffler with envious feelings, wondered to himself that Max had nothing to say to this of all women.

Ledger expected that his voluble and excited friend would plunge into extravagant praise of the Wheelers as soon as they were alone, and when they had reached the bottom of Shuttle Hill, and were turning into Broad Street without a word having been spoken, he glanced up at his companion's face and was puzzled to find it puckered into a prodigious frown of moody preoccupation. He was conscious, also, that the easy pace at which they had started had already increased into a rapid stride.

"Well, *you've* had a jolly time, at any rate," he ventured at last.

But Max was staring before him with frowning brow, in deep thought.

"They are everything they appear to be, and more, but why this break-neck pace?"

As John laid his hand upon him, Max pulled up, scowled perplexedly at him, and then, with a sudden start, strode away faster than ever.

"Max, you stupid, stop! We are not going to catch a train."

"Eh, what! Catching a train?"

Slowly he seemed to realise where he was, and dropped into an easier pace; but in a moment or two he was striding away as fast as ever, with gathered brow and dazed, far-away looks.

In despair of getting anything satisfactory out of the mad fellow, John allowed him to go his way. At the end of Broad Street, however, he saw him taking the wrong turn, and rushing after him, and seizing him by the arm and giving him a hearty shake, he brought him to a standstill.

Max looked dazedly around for a moment, laughed apologetically, took his friend's arm, and made for the road where John's lodgings were situated.

" Betty's a character, isn't she ? " said John, as they went along.

" No—yes !—that is—what did you say, old fellow ? "

" I say you're dotty, that's what I say."

" Yes, of course. Ah, ah—dotty, did you say ? "

" For goodness sake, Max, what is the matter? "

They had reached the terrace where John lived, and had unconsciously come to a standstill.

Max gazed around him with a dazed, wandering look, first on the dim street lights, and then up at the distant stars. He bent forward and surveyed the whole row of houses near them as if he were counting them, and then, scowling down at John, he asked in bewilderment—

" What were you saying ? "

" I was saying that you are demented, moonstruck, dotty. That's what I was saying."

Max appeared to realise everything all at once. He looked long and dreely at John, scrutinised the street lamps again, glanced up into the murky darkness, and then at the mud under their feet, and speaking in awed, tremulous undertones, he put his face close to John's, and said breathlessly—

" John, I've met my fate to-night ! "

John's laugh pealed down the silent street, and he

caught the mooning fellow by the arm and dragged him indoors.

John felt a little annoyed. He was quite accustomed to the wild rhapsodies of his friend, and knew and loved the heart of gold that was underneath them, but it seemed to him indecent for a young minister of six-and-twenty to be going into these wild ravings about a mere girl of sixteen. There was no knowing what the impetuous fellow might do, and it would be a sin to allow him to put notions into Betty's innocent little head. And so he determined he would speak to his mercurial friend and put a stop to matters before any mischief was done. But when he arose next morning with this intention in his mind, Max had disappeared, and though at first he was inclined to fear that he might have sallied forth to the Wheelers', on some mad errand, early as it was, he soon discovered from 'Cilla that he had taken his departure, and though a little puzzled, he was on the whole relieved and thankful. On the following Monday, however, Max turned up again and dragged John off, *nolens volens*, to number seven. John had a preaching appointment that night, and was compelled to leave his friend to enjoy himself. On his way back he called at the super.'s, and what he heard there about the growing opposition in the circuit against his friends so occupied his mind that his intended straight talk with Max was forgotten, and, in fact, as they sat over the fire at his lodgings in the small hours, John told his chum the whole story; and Max's indignation, which flamed up now, as always, against wrongdoing, excluded every other topic, and it was some consolation to him to find that his friend's judgment supported him in all he had done.

"Well," said Max, when they had talked the matter out, "you can't oppose your super., you know, and it would do no good if you did, but you must take blessed good care that you make your real feelings clear to the Wheelers."

John seemed to think that was only a poor sort of consolation after all, and when the other left him next day, he found it impossible to settle down to work. The matter seemed the worse to him because he could not help admitting that on the surface, at least, there was some justification for the super.'s attitude. Mr. Wheeler was not exactly what would be called a spiritually-minded man ; there was a hard, commercial ring about all his conversation, even on the most sacred topics. His face amply justified the suspicion that he was not sufficiently temperate, and as John was an ardent teetotaller himself, it appeared to him that the chief layman of the circuit ought to be above suspicion on that point. Of the hints about financial difficulty he could, of course, form no opinion, but rumours of that kind had, in his experience, an awkward habit of proving substantial. It appeared very mean even to think like this about people from whom he had received so many kindnesses, but he knew, on the other hand, that he was facing in this case one of the commonest tests of ministerial loyalty. The following Monday was the Quarterly meeting, and John spent the intervening time alternately resolving that he would not go near his friends until after it was over, and then rebuking himself for lack of gratitude and manliness. The result was that he found himself at number seven several times during the remaining days.

"I saw the super. this morning," said Mary Wheeler, as she handed John his tea on one of these evenings. "He looks more worried than you. We must be dreadful people to manage in Partidge.

"You are," said John playfully, "but I think the super. is troubled about his daughter."

Mr. Wheeler, who sat nearer the fire, and had not appeared to be listening, cocked an inquiring eye at his guest, and Mary said, in a sympathetic tone—

" Is she no better, then ? "

" She cannot be better without a very difficult and expensive operation."

Mary's eyes travelled towards her apparently indifferent parent, and then she asked—

" How do you mean ? "

" Miss Irene is so fragile that they fear the result of an operation unless it could be done by some specialist, and that, of course, is beyond them."

" But——" and Mary, glancing past John, looked at her father again, and stopped, and then, after watching him a moment, deftly changed the subject.

Two days later the super., looking younger than he had done for some time, came smiling into John's study and informed him that a gracious Providence had interfered to help him, and that Sir Edward Swaine, the famous Manchester surgeon, had offered through Dr. Markham, the local physician, to perform the operation on Miss Irene without charge. The conversation with the Wheelers flashed into John's mind, and he nearly blurted out his guess; but the super. seemed so certain that it was some peculiarity in the disease which had reached the great man's ears and excited his curiosity, that he had not the heart to express what were, after all, only suspicions; and when he called at number seven and " fished," they were all so very innocent that he understood that if they had anything to do with it they wished things to remain as they were. All the same, the signs made him confident he was not mistaken, and the position seemed to him to be becoming unendurable, whilst a conversation he had with Mary Wheeler that very night further increased his embarrassment.

"That is a great kindness your father is doing for the Holts," he said, when he and Mary were left alone for a few minutes.

"Oh, it is like him; he thinks of everybody but himself," she replied, as though what John had hinted at was the most everyday affair possible.

"You admire your father, Miss Wheeler," he said approvingly.

"Admire is a very poor word, Mr. Ledger. Why, sir, father is my ideal man!"

John was both puzzled and disappointed; he had given her credit for more discernment than that. He was interested, however, and so he made a perilous venture.

"He is not what you would call a great Christian. I suppose a man with his commercial experiences scarcely could be, eh?"

It was a foolish, clumsy sort of remark, but Mary had very keen religious sympathies and spoke very openly on all such matters, and yet he felt he was treading on dangerous ground.

"Father!" cried Mary, opening her large expressive eyes in most genuine astonishment. "Why, father's a saint, Mr. Ledger! a lowly saint! far away the best man I ever knew," and then she broke off with a recollecting laugh. "I see how it is; he's been opening his mind to you. Well, that *is* a compliment."

"Mr. Wheeler has never spoken to me about his own religious life."

"Hasn't he? then he *will* do; for he's taken to you wonderfully, and so you had better be prepared or he will surprise you—and deceive you."

"Deceive me!"

"Yes; don't you know? He thinks he's an awful hypocrite and a disgrace to his church. He'd give anything to be out of office; we have to frighten him into retaining it."

John really began to wonder whether he was not dreaming, but Mary, as if she were retailing the absurdest of jokes, went on—

"That's why he goes to old Crake's class; he always scolds him."

"Crake's class! Your father meets with the super."

"Yes, he subscribes and is counted in that class, but he attends Crake's, down in Bobbin Alley. Old Crake is one of father's pensioners, you know, but he talks to dad in class as though he were a hardened, worldly-minded sinner, and father likes it, and thinks old Crake and his members saints."

"But old Crake is not a fit person to lead your father!"

"Isn't he, though! You'd think he was if you saw them together. He calls father by his christian name, orders him to pray in class, and if he is absent, he comes here and scolds him for 'running with the giddy multitude to do evil' until that ridiculous man looks as thoroughly ashamed as if he had been caught in the act of theft."

John left number seven that night more perplexed than ever. Mary Wheeler was too clear-eyed to be deceived and too honest to practise deceit. If Mr. Wheeler was what she had described him to be, it was very strange that those who had known him so long should have formed such totally different opinions about him.

Early on Monday morning he hastened to the Manse to make one last appeal to the super. Before he had got many words out the senior minister interrupted him by stating that it was now too late. Mr. Wheeler's designated successor had been spoken to, and had consented to stand. And then he explained, with a little show of importance, that the specialist was expected for the operation, and somewhat brusquely dismissed his colleague. The tea before the Quarterly meeting was more largely attended than the previous one, at which John had been present for the first time, and he noted with uneasy resentment that there was an unusual number of lay preachers and extreme teetotallers present.

He had resolved, before going, to seat himself at the junior steward's table, but seeing how numerous the opposition was, he took his place defiantly at Mary Wheeler's side, sitting himself intentionally next to her father and returning the significant glances with looks of cold unconcern. When the meeting itself opened, the super. motioned to him to take his place by his side, and John followed the promptings of his own indignant heart by drawing his chair as near as possible to Mr. Wheeler's and putting his arm on that gentleman's chair back. Just as they were commencing business Mr. Wheeler got up, and in a few sympathetic words congratulated the chairman on the successful operation that had taken place that day and the encouraging reports they had of the patient, and John watched with increasing astonishment the impassive face of the senior steward as the super. explained how much he and his daughter were indebted to the generosity of the eminent scientist who had performed the operation.

Somebody was beginning to say that a resolution of thanks ought to be sent to " Sir Edward," but Mr. Wheeler somewhat unceremoniously interrupted him, and the meeting passed to the business of the day. Presently the question for which they were all waiting was reached, and a complete silence fell on the gathering as the chairman rose to introduce the election of stewards. He had a sort of pained smile about his pale lips, but his face was hard and white. A hasty glance round the room revealed to John that whilst the uninitiated were looking up with pleasant interest, the majority held their heads a little down.

"·We now come to the election of stewards," said the super., speaking with some effort. "As you are aware, gentlemen, our dear friend Mr. Wheeler has held this office for eighteen years, and you will all bear me out that he has done his work with his accustomed zeal and ability. (Hear, hear!) Mr. Wheeler does everything he undertakes well, but you will all agree with me that he has never distinguished himself in anything more than in the painstaking and, in fact, brilliant service he has rendered as the chief lay officer of this circuit. (More responses.) But our dear friend is, as you all know, an exceedingly busy man, and is occupied in all sorts of important offices and duties. It appears to me that for his sake and our own we ought not to overwork the willing horse. I propose, therefore, to release our dear friend from this particular appointment (dead silence), and give him a well-earned, though, I hope, only temporary rest."

John, whose head was on his chest, shot from under his eyebrows a quick glance at Mr. Wheeler, and noted that he seemed to be listening with a bland, ingenuous smile.

"Before we proceed any further, however," the super. went on, "I am sure it will be your wish to mark your sense of Mr. Wheeler's valuable services by a hearty vote of thanks. You would all like to speak to a resolution of this kind, I know, but perhaps I shall meet your wishes if I ask his old friend and former colleague Mr. Bullough to move a resolution."

Bullough, a short, nervous little man, who was evidently prepared for the call, rose, and in fulsome, extravagant terms moved the vote, which was seconded immediately and doubly supported, and the resolution was just being put when Collier, the junior steward, broke in with an alarmed—

"Wait a moment, Mr. Super."

At this point Wheeler leaned over, and, with a whispered exhortation, tried to induce his friend to resume his seat.

"No, no!" cried Collier excitedly; "I don't understand this, and I don't like it either. If he goes out, *I* go out, that's all."

Wheeler again tried to pacify his friend, and the chairman, whose face had become flushed, begged him to wait a moment until the resolution had been put. When that had been done, it was carried with great show of cordiality; and the super., in a long and not very coherent speech, begged the senior steward's acceptance of the vote. As John glanced at the man who stood to receive these long and strained compliments, he was amazed to find neither surprise nor resentment in his face, but only an uncomfortable and shamed impatience, as though he were anxious to get the ordeal over. A significant stillness fell all at once on the company, and men held their breath to listen.

"I thank you, Mr. Super. and brethren, for your kind words," began Mr. Wheeler. "I'm glad you have put me out, for I should never have resigned. I owe all I have and am to Methodism, and was proud to serve her. But I have always felt I was not worthy. I stayed in so long to please my dear ones, and—a—a—help a bit. May God forgive me, and make me a better man!"

The speaker paused here a moment, and John, watching the man thrust thus meanly out of office, felt a lump rise in his throat, whilst his surprise-widened eyes shone with moist light; but Wheeler was speaking again.

"Of course I cannot hand over the books with

a deficit, so I'll wipe off the little balance, and if you, Mr. Super., will just dot down the little bits o' debts on the circuit chapels, I'll—I'll see to 'em as a bit of a thank-offering."

There was a suspicious sniffing in several parts of the room as the man who appeared to John at that moment the biggest soul present sank shyly into his seat, and as the chairman, abashed and confused, rose to continue the business, a muttering broke out amongst the back seats ; two or three rose to their feet, and snatched their hats from overhanging pegs and made for the door.

"Stop! stop, brethren!" cried the super., in sudden alarm. "We have not finished."

"Yes you have!" shouted Rippon, a country official, turning round as he reached the door. "You've done now! There's nothing else you could do to hurt the circuit and shame yourselves. You've done! You've done!"

CHAPTER IV

A STAGGERING COMPLICATION

THE Quarterly meeting proved long and stormy. Collier, the junior steward, surprised and angry at the unexpected treatment of his partner in office, refused point-blank to continue his services; and the super., nonplussed and agitated, was compelled to amend his plans. Bowden, Mr. Wheeler's brother-in-law, had to be made senior steward; but nobody seemed willing to join him. Name after name was suggested, but promptly withdrawn by the person concerned, and finally John beheld the edifying spectacle of the ousted steward coming to the rescue of his enemies and appealing to the love and loyalty of his brethren not to let so important an office go a-begging. Finally, and after almost humiliating pressure, Ramsden, the St. Mary's Society steward, was pushed into the vacant position, and one of the most unpleasant meetings in the history of Partidge Methodism broke up a little before eleven. Late as it was, John felt he must see his ill-used friend home. They walked in silence until they came to the gate of number seven, and then, unable to contain himself any longer, John burst out—

" Mr. Wheeler, you're a mystery to me ! "

The manufacturer took his cigar out of his mouth, looked at his companion with mild surprise, and then said—

" How so ? "

" Well, sir, if you're not the cleverest of all clever rogues, you're the highest-minded man I ever knew."

" I'm a rogue, sure enough, but not a clever one. Come in."

Paul Wheeler, the eldest son, had been at the meeting, and so, as they entered the dining-room, they saw at once that all present knew of what had taken place. That they felt it was also clear, though all outward signs were carefully suppressed. Mary, whose eyes looked dim, gave her father a quiet lingering kiss, Paul flashed a look that told of glowing pride in his parent, whilst the others, without speaking a word, made it abundantly clear to John that they understood his awkward position in the matter, and appreciated his quiet sympathy. The conversation over the supper table was a little constrained, until the uncontrollable Betty set everybody laughing by declaring that she intended to join the Christadelphians who had lately come to town ; and then she went off into a mimic representation of " Uncle Bowden's " sanctimonious mannerisms which convulsed the whole party.

" It *is* a little unexpected," admitted Mary, as she stood holding John's overcoat in the hall ; " but I don't think it need make any difference to the cause. It isn't as if we were leaving the place, is it ? "

And John, afraid to trust himself just then, rushed into the darkness without even a formal " good-night."

And that was the last he ever heard of the nasty business from the Wheelers, though the circuit seemed as though it would never let it drop.

Ten hard, harassing weeks passed away, and the young parson found himself the prey of many anxieties. By their invitation, Sallie had visited the Wheelers during the Christmas holidays, and seemed at first highly delighted with her reception. During the second week, however, she grew petulant and sulky with John, and more than once snubbed the volatile Betty.   Of Mary Wheeler she seemed to stand in awe, but did her best to get up a little flirtation with Mark, the second son.   The day before her departure she threw decorum to the winds and invaded her lover's study.   She charged him with neglecting her, tore to pieces a little bouquet which Betty had brought the day before, and finally told him, with flaming eyes, that she did not love him and never had done, but that she would make him marry her or spoil his life.

It was never very difficult for John to hold his tongue, and he did so now, especially as this open and coarse attack had revealed to him the awful abyss on the verge of which he stood.   That he did not love Sallie as he ought to do, and once had done, he knew perfectly well; he knew just as certainly that he intended to marry her, but whether he or she was to blame for the change was not so clear, and that it was right to marry under such circumstances was less clear still.   These things made a difficulty sufficiently serious, but there was something else behind them all, deeper and darker, something so shocking, in fact, that he dared not allow it to take definite shape in his mind, but day by day he was conscious that it was growing and insisting, in spite of him, upon being recognised. Why had he changed towards Sallie? and would the change ever have been the decided thing it was if he had never met—but there he always pulled up.

And to these worries were added a number of smaller ones.   The super. was beginning to repent of having removed Mr. Wheeler from office, and John was already in fear of a rupture between his colleague and the chief layman he had been so anxious to get into office.   He was troubled also about Max's proceedings.   That volatile young man came to Partidge once a week now, or oftener, and John knew by past experiences that he could not be properly prepared for the approaching probationers' examinations. He found, also, some difficulty in retaining his respect for a man who seemed so utterly carried away by an inconsequent young creature like Betty. Not that that gay young person seemed any the worse for the experience; she seemed absolutely unspoilable, and made no secret whatever of her capricious but perfectly honest and innocent fondness for Ringley. The Wheelers, too, seemed to John culpably heedless on the point; and he could not for the life of him understand how it was that, when he had on one occasion hinted his fears to Mary, she had looked at him so scrutinisingly and then laughed with most evident amusement. In this case, however, he had got a step further than mere broodings, and had sent a long and painfully candid letter to his friend, and when he came in one morning from his before-breakfast walk, the reply was waiting for him.

He could not help smiling at the scrawly flourishes on the envelope, so characteristic as they were of the writer, but when he had slit the packet open the short note within turned his amusement into helpless perplexity.

He was addressed as "Dear, double-blinded old Dunder-head," and then there was Betty's name and a long line of increasingly elongated notes of exclamation; and then "Betty" again, and a similar rearguard of expression points. Then there was a grotesque pen-and-ink sketch of Max doubled up on a sofa, and opening a huge cavernous mouth in uncontrollable laughter. The girl's name appeared again with an hyphen between each letter, and the whole underscored half-an-inch deep, and at last a few plain words—

"Even the much-beloved examinations must stand

aside. Tell the lovely 'Cilla to lay a plate for me for dinner.

"Yours in shrieking convulsions,
"THE OLD 'UN."

John laughed; it was a characteristic epistle certainly, but what on earth did it mean? He propped it up wide open against the toast rack, and poured out the coffee. Then he glanced round for the cream, but his eyes got no farther than the hieroglyphic epistle, and he sat staring at it in bewilderment that was almost ridiculous. Then he commenced again with his food, but not a ray of illumination could he get out of the cryptic document; and he was just turning his eyes away, when he observed another letter lying where he had found the first, and which he must have overlooked. This, on opening, proved to be written in a neat but unmasculine hand, which he thought he knew, and after glancing at the flowery headline and then at the signatures, for there were two, he read—

"DEAR MR. LEDGER,

"It is our duty to inform you that, for reasons you will probably guess, we do not think it advisable that you should continue in the circuit after Conference. As Circuit Stewards we shall not, therefore, offer you the usual invitation at the approaching Quarterly Meeting. We deeply regret having to take this course, but we trust and pray that the painful discipline may bring forth its fruit in your future career.

"With earnest prayer and devout good wishes for your future usefulness,

"We are,
"Yours sincerely,
"P. J. BOWDEN, ⎱ *Circuit*
TUBAL RAMSDEN, ⎰ *Stewards.*"

There was no more breakfast for Ledger. It only needed this to fill up the cup of his bitterness, and so he pushed back his chair and laughed a hard, angry laugh. No man ever had higher ideals of ministerial life and duty than he: no man was ever more thoroughly satisfied of his call; and yet he had got entangled in difficulties which in another man he would have regarded as evidences of weakness or something worse; and his first circuit rejected him on the earliest possible opportunity. He was not merely disappointed, neither was it simply a return of his old habit of unhealthy self-suspicion. He was angry— hotly, uncontrollably angry. Fate was not simply antagonistic, she was malicious; cunning malignity could not possibly have invented any concatenation of circumstances more exasperating and shameful. He was not only released from obligation to keep terms with a fate so spiteful: he was rebellious, defiant, desperate.

He soon forgot the stewards' letter, however, and, deep in the darker perplexities that were filling his life, a sadder mood came upon him, and he began pacing the room and fighting the surly demons which had invaded his innermost life, and made his hot brain a veritable pandemonium. He had done everything, in this love affair of his, which he most condemned and hated; and was actually in the position he had always contended no straight-forward and honourable man ought or need to be in.

There was something in the situation that was almost devilish, and he bit his lips and ground his teeth in a perfect frenzy of self-torture. Time, duties, friends, were all forgotten, and he was lying face downwards on the little horse-hair sofa, when he became conscious that some one was in the room, and sitting up, he stared at the friendly face of Max

as though he were the very last person in the world
he expected to see.

Max had uttered his usual wild whoop as he
ascended the stairs, and had given the closed door a
vigorous ran-tan, but John had apparently heard
neither, and now regarded his friend as though he
were some dreadful apparition. Max's merry face
had become long with sudden alarm, a sympathy
almost womanly shone in his fine eyes, and in low
tones that betrayed the sincerity of his concern, he
cried—

"Johnny, Johnny, dear old boy! Whatever *is*
the matter?"

John looked up into the anxious face with a dazed
look; then comprehension came back to him, a sense
of sudden and sweet relief seemed to pass over him,
and lifting his eyes, full of grateful joy, he sank back
again upon the couch, and burst into grateful,
precious tears. Embarrassed and uncomfortable at
the sight of unmanly weeping, Max turned away,
took off his coat and hat, and returned to John's
side. As he did so, his eyes fell on the stewards'
letter lying on the table. There were no secrets
between these two, and in a moment more the document was flying across the room, and Max was standing on the hearthrug with a considerably relieved
face.

"Is *that* all? Come out, sir, come out!" and
seizing John, he dragged him up, and compelled him
to show his face.

"And are you ninny enough to be squelched by that
flea-bite? The skunks! The measly, little, blown-
out jacks-in-office! I'm ashamed of you, Ledger!
Why, man, it's a compliment—the greatest compliment they could pay you! Good Lord!" he went
on, more to himself than anyone else, "and Methodism is governed by fourth-rate little whipper-

snappers like these! Come here," and seizing the tongs, he pounced upon the offending letter, held it, with screwed-up nose, as far off as he could, crammed it into the fire, and pulled the burning embers over it.

Meanwhile John was recovering his self-possession. For the moment he had felt prompted to unburden himself to his friend, but his painful cautiousness checked the impulse, and though thankful and comforted by his presence, he allowed him to suppose that the letter was the immediate cause of his distress.

"Cheer up, old buckstick!" cried Max, with a resounding slap on the back. "This isn't like thee! Let the stewards go to the dogs, and the measly circuit too." And then suddenly stopping, and eyeing John over suspiciously, he went on, "There isn't anything else, is there?"

"I think I must be a bit run down," said John, apologetically.

"That's it! It's those exams., confound 'em. Well, thank goodness, I shall never have that sin laid at my door."

This was so like the man, and so ridiculously true, that John laughed, and Max, with a great leap, bawled out—

"Richard is himself again!" and then, drawing up a chair, he fell to work upon the remains of John's breakfast.

"You scapegrace! what's brought you here again so soon?" asked John, as he watched with comforting interest his friend's gastronomical performances.

"What? Ah, that's good! Ha! ha!" and the crazy fellow went off into another fit of laughter,

"Johannes," he said gaily, helping himself to butter, "do you know that you have in you the makings of a great philosopher?"

John, still sitting with his legs on the sofa, ducked his body in ironical acknowledgment.

"One of the most indubitable marks of the philosopher is wall-eyed, mole-like blindness to the most palpable, plain-as-the-nose-on-your-face facts of ordinary life."

John bowed again, but there was a glint of curiosity in his eye.

"You wrote me a solemn, philosopher-like letter about Betty"—and as he mentioned the name he rattled off into another long, noisy laugh.

"Well?" and there was the sharpness of impatience in John's tones.

"You warned me about 'Betty,' and you pleaded like a philosopher about Betty, 'B-e-t-t-y'"—and away he went again in most evident enjoyment of some hidden but delicious joke.

"Well, why not Betty?" and had Max been less entertained by his own humour, he might have noted an ominous constraint in the other's tones.

"Why not?—oh, purblind philosopher! Oh, star-gazing stumbler over mole-hills, thy name is Ledger!"

"But it is Betty you've been fooling with," and John's very lips were white, if Max had but noticed.

"Betty," cried he, still revelling in the humour of the situation, "little, innocent Betty! Why, is it possible that thy gerund-grinding brain has never seen that Betty was but a handle, a stepping-stone— the pretty gooseberry and stepping-stone to Mary?"

"Mary?"

John had sprung to his feet, and gripping hard at the back of his chair, was glaring at his friend with haggard, ashen-grey face.

"Don't, Max, don't! Not Mary!"

"Yes, Mary, of course. The peerless, the incomparable——Good heavens, Ledger! What's up?"

John stared at the now thoroughly frightened Max for a moment, and then dropping back helplessly upon the couch, he gasped in choking, terrified tones—

" Oh, Max, Max !   I love her myself ! "

Horror, shame, and intense alarm expressed themselves on the almost ghastly face at which Max now gaped dumbfounded.   A moment earlier John would have denied the fact he had just blurted out, but the utterly unexpected announcement had revealed it to him, and surprised the confession out of him.   For a long time these two stood with dropped heads, and then John, lifting shame-stricken eyes to the scared, incredulous face of his friend, burst out with reckless defiance—

" I love her !   God, honour, friends — I care not—I love her !   *I love her !* " and then, with a sudden, overwhelming recoil, and a short, stifled gasp, he fell forward in a dead swoon.

Those who had an ordinary acquaintance with Max Ringley would have been surprised to see him at this moment, but his was one of those natures which, ruffled easily on the surface, have large reserves of calm strength which astonishes onlookers in times of great and sudden pressure ; and so, with the coolness of a doctor, he laid his friend on the sofa, took off with rapid deftness the clerical collar, and opened his shirt at the neck; and then, springing downstairs, he suddenly assumed his old easy manner, and in the smoothest possible voice, asked the landlady if she had a little brandy in the house.

" Don't be alarmed, I'm not going to break the pledge, Mrs. Pride," he laughed, and then, with the little bottle in his hand, he actually stopped to admire the good woman's canary, and inquire about its breed.

The spirit was soon administered, John's clammy hands vigorously rubbed, his face fanned, and in a few moments he was opening his eyes and looking into the pitifully anxious face bending over him. His were vacant enough at first, and then comprehension came back into them. He shrank like a shamed child from his friend's eyes, and turned his head away with a low moan. Max watched him with strangest thoughts. As his passion for Mary Wheeler was his very latest affection of the kind, he regarded it as his greatest, and, in fact, his only genuine one. But the fact that his inseparable friend was now his rival, disconcerting though it was, was not the trouble that most filled his mind at this moment. Max, governed more by his intuitions than by anything else, had been strongly drawn to his constitutional opposite, as he found it in the quiet John Ledger, almost as soon as they became acquainted. John was his ideal man—quiet, sensitive, high-souled, and almost painfully conscientious, and had become his second and higher conscience, and acquired a powerful influence in his character of father confessor, not only to him, but to others of the students. He knew John's high-minded, almost overstrained scrupulosity in all matters affecting the relationship with the opposite sex, and the remorseless logic with which he applied the law of duty. And here was this immaculate, this almost revered friend of his involved in complications of the most humiliating kind. He knew but too well that John would exact the utmost penalty of the law from himself, and yet the wild, reckless, almost blasphemous language he had used revealed but too clearly the intense reality of the fatal passion that possessed him. Max was sore amazed: he stood gazing down on the passive, almost green-grey face, and pity, sympathy, and strong manly love clamoured within him to help. Just then the idea that John was his rival did not seem

to appeal to him ; he was his dear friend, in deadly
spiritual peril, and must be helped at all costs.

But how ? He pictured to himself with what
scorn John would reject such suggestions of escape
as ordinary worldly prudence would dictate ; he knew
that he would reject all help as further compromising him, and insist on fighting his battle himself ;
but as his warm heart longed to do something, he
flung himself into the low American chair, and began
to cudgel his brains for some scheme whereby he
might help his friend without consulting him. But
though, with elbow on knee and chin in hand, he
stared at the flickering coals on the fire until his
eyes felt like starting out of his head, no light came ;
the darkness grew denser and more hideous about
him, and he was in despair.

" Max ! "

The poor, abstracted fellow started as though a
bolt had struck him, and then, turning hastily, he
beheld the woe-worn eyes of his friend fixed hungrily
upon him.

" Max ! " and John turned away his head shyly,
and appealingly put out a shaking hand.

With a sudden gush of affection, Max sprang at
the pathetic palm, and gripped it with the grip of
a vice. For the space of a minute, a minute full
of emotion too deep for utterance, they remained
thus ; and then John lifted a pleading, humbled
look to his friend's face, and still holding his hand,
stammered—

" Always, Max ? "

And Max, with face awork and choking voice,
cried, " Always, dear boy ; always ! "

" Whatever comes ? "

" Whatever comes ! " and then breaking utterly
down, the agitated fellow dropped upon his knees,
and burying his face on his friend's breast, he cried,

through set teeth, " John! God do so to me, and more also, if aught but death part thee and me."

"Amen! Amen!" sobbed John in reply, and there they remained, whilst the pretty carriage clock on the mantelpiece, Max's gift to his friend, ticked eloquent endorsement of the bond just renewed.

"Sit down, old fellow, and let us think," said John at length, and the other, with red, flushed face, turned and asked solemnly—

"Hadn't we better pray?"

John blushed again with fresh shame, and then, after reflecting a moment, he pointed silently across the room towards the open door of his bedroom, and Max, with a bowed head, got up, and went and shut himself in.

An hour passed away, and 'Cilla came in to set the table for dinner. The rattle of pots brought Max from his retirement, but he shyly avoided his friend's eye, and moved nervously about from window to picture, and from picture to window again, until the meal was ready. Very little was eaten, and that reluctantly and in silence, but just as they were turning away from the table, John, who was now quite calm, raised his head and said—

"You'll help me, Max?"

"Anything on earth, dear boy. Do give me the chance!"

"Anything, Max? Think what it means."

"Anything! Anything!"

"Then if you want to help and save me, you must go and propose to Mary Wheeler to-day."

With amazement and almost resentment, Max began to protest. John waited until he had done, and then said—

"It must be done to-day, if—if you really love her."

John knew well enough how violent, and yet how

transitory his friend's fits of love had been hitherto; but it seemed to him to be the most natural of all things that this should be a serious case, considering the woman involved, and he so treated it.

Max refused, and stormed and argued; and when abuse seemed unavailing, he insisted that at least John should tell him more of his mind before he did anything.

But John was quietly obdurate, and he had so much more confidence in his quieter friend's judgment than his own, that Max presently subsided, and began to think with rueful face of the task assigned him.

It was not the first time he had proposed, and every day of the last week he had painted to himself the scene which he had begun to feel could not long be deferred; but things seemed all so different now, and he had an uneasy sense that he was about to do something the end of which he could not quite see.

And then John began to talk. Quietly and gently he extolled the fair woman now so much to them both. Then he remarked, with a sad cadence, on the equality of the match from the worldly standpoint, Max's father being a comparatively wealthy Midland squire. From that he passed on to the mutual suitability of their temperaments—Mary's queenly self-possession being the natural foil to Max's impetuosity; and he finished all by paying a glowing tribute to the character of the Wheeler family.

Several times Max interrupted with questions as to what John was going to do; but these were all quietly ignored, and at last, as his friend expected, Max's imagination caught fire, and he finally, after many protestations and frequent suspicious glances at John, consented to obey his behest, but contended for a short postponement of the actual attempt. John, however, was inexorable, and he was at last compelled to yield that point also.   It took a considerable time to get him ready.   Nearly every clean collar John had was tried and rejected ; a quarter of an hour was spent in discussing whether he ought not to pay a visit to a barber before embarking on so important an errand.   His soiled cuffs had to be judiciously turned, for John's were of altogether too shy a character to suit his taste ; and when everything else seemed in order, he suddenly remembered that he had come in worsted gloves, and as his friend's were too small, he had, cold though the weather was, to fall back on an old trick, and carry John's best kids in his hand.   He started at last, however, and John was just breathing a relieved sigh, when he came bounding back, plumped himself doggedly down on a chair, and utterly refused to go a step until John had explained himself.   And so the whole weary argument had to be gone over again, and it was perilously late in the afternoon when he got once more started.   He was back again almost instantly.

" Would it not be better, under all the circumstances, to write to her ? "

John got over this by appealing to his pride. Surely such a girl deserved something more honourable than a mere note.

Away he went once more with a sudden rush, and this time he did not return.

Left to himself, Ledger began to pace about the room in uneasy thought.   Slowly and with frequent haltings at first, then rapidly, until, all unconsciously, he was tramping about the floor in a way that greatly exercised the nerves of the landlady downstairs.   Readers of this story will think that he was well accustomed to acute mental conflict, but John felt that he had never been in real trouble before. Hitherto his difficulties had been of a religious nature mostly, but now the deep elemental passions of the natural man were awakened, and he " fought with beasts at Ephesus." Max ? They had an hour or so ago pledged themselves to eternal amity, but just now there raged within him all the fires of unregenerate jealousy, as he realised that at that moment he was perhaps in the company of the girl he now so madly loved. Mary Wheeler ? She was not something to secretly and hopelessly love ; she was something to steal, to ravish away, to fight for the possession of against all comers and at all costs. Sallie ? Right ? duty ? conscience ? These were but dry autumn leaves swept helplessly along in the mighty rush of unreasoning passion. Think ? He could not think ; he would not ! He would *have !* Mad ? Let him be mad ; he liked it, he revelled in it ! Madness and Mary were heaven. Have ? Yes, he would have, if the universe came clashing about his ears as he plucked the fatal fruit.

He did not conquer this mood ; he did not even resist it ; but it passed away of itself, and he was just beginning to shudder with horror at the awful thoughts that had passed through his mind, when there was a bang downstairs, a clatter on the staircase, and Max, with a battered hat and a bruised forehead, came staggering into the room.

" Come, John, come ! " cried the mad fellow. " There's a mob outside Wheeler's house, and they are threatening to break the windows ! "

CHAPTER V

A BANK SMASH AND A PROPOSAL

IT was not easy for John to come out of his painful abstraction all at once, and the stunning nature of the intelligence Max brought did not assist him. But Ringley was impatient and imperious.

"Look alive, man! On with those togs! It's something about a bank. 'Cilla, bring Mr. Ledger's boots. Seems to have smashed or something. Wheeler's a director—chairman in fact. Blow the bruise! Come on! Poor girls!" and dragging his companion after him down the stairs, he hurried out into the damp streets, talking excitedly as he went.

What they were going to do neither of them thought, but they were eagerly agreed that now was the time to stand by their friends.

"Some booby called Wheeler a swindler, and I went for him, and an old party interfered with an umbrella, and gave me this," explained Max carelessly, pointing to the mark on his brow. "Come on ; don't you hear them shouting ? "

Just as they turned into Nickey Lane, to avoid Broad Street, and thus get a clearer way to Shuttle Hill, John heard himself called, and pulling up, he beheld the super. making his way towards him with solemn face.

"Didn't I tell you ? Didn't I tell you ? " he gasped as he came up. "Isn't it a mercy we got him out ? "

And to the small-minded minister's astonishment,

the quiet, restrained John sprang at him like an enraged terrier.

"No, sir! *No!* It is not a mercy; it's a dishonour!—a dastardly shame! Don't you know he saved your daughter's life?"—and before the cleric could recover his amazement, Max was shaking his fist in his face.

"There's more grace in Wheeler's whiskers than there is in all the little souls in your measly, one-horse circuit!"

But just then a crashing sound was heard, and a falling of glass, and with fierce cries the two young men broke off, and dashed away in the direction of number seven. They took another bye-street, and running the length of it, turned once more, and came suddenly out opposite the house; and, as they did so, each uttered a cry, for there before them was a large upstairs window of plate glass all splintered, as by some heavy missile, and behind the window, white-faced, but calm and resolute, stood Mary Wheeler. As they rushed up, she came nearer, until her face was framed in the broken glass, and seemed to wish to speak to the crowd; but Max, dashing headlong through the throng, sprang at the gilded railings, and shouted hoarsely—

"Go back!"

Mary caught sight of them, and a soft blush mantled her cheek, but John, with a quicker intuition than his friend, had guessed what she wished to do; and springing at the railings, he had climbed lightly up the gate post before the policemen at the entrance could stop him. A moment later he was standing upright on the crown of the post, and was waving his hands and calling for silence. The crowd did not, all at once, realise the situation; but when it did, there was an outbreak of jeers and curses.

"That's him 'at's courting t' dowter," shouted some one.

"He'll give her t' sack naa (now)," jeered another.

"He'll ha' to stick his legs under somebody else's mahogany naa," cried a third, and John, heedless of everything, and only anxious for the safety of those inside the house, still waved his hands and called for attention.

Just at this moment Max uttered a sharp cry, and sprang at a man who was moving back to get swinging room for his arm, and who held half a brick in his hand. Two policemen coming up at the moment, rushed forward to stop the struggle, whilst the inspector plucked at John's coat-tail to induce him to come down.

"I'm going to speak to them and try to get them to go home."

"Then for God's sake go on, or there will be a riot."

"Friends! friends!" shouted John, as Max came back panting to the railings, and the policemen dragged the stone-thrower away to the lock-up.

"Louder! louder!" shouted the inspector in a hoarse whisper, and then, turning to the excited crowd, he cried—

"Order! Hear him! Order!"

Just at this moment a stone whizzed past John's head, and crashed into the end of the Wheeler's conservatory.

"Shame!" shouted one or two, and the policemen, glad of any help, chimed in—

"Shame!"

Comparative silence fell at last on the gathering, but dark, threatening faces were everywhere turned on to John on the gate post.

"Friends!" he resumed, "I don't know much about——"

"We want our brass," broke in two or three.

John drew himself up, fixed one or two of the more attentive with his eye, and recommenced—

" How long have you known James Wheeler ? "

" What by that ? " cried some one.

" A —— sight too long," bawled a grocer on the edge of the crowd.

" He was born in Partidge, and you have known him all your lives, haven't you ? "

No answer.

" He's lived and worked amongst you for fifty odd years, hasn't he ? "

The silence was now complete.

" Did any of you ever know him do a dirty trick ? "

Faces were clearing here and there.

" Has he ever robbed any of you of a penny ? "

There were half-reluctant nods, and somebody turned round and threatened the still muttering grocer.

" Has he done anything to shake your confidence in him ? "

" Wheer is he now, then ? " shouted a woman in dingy widow's weeds.

" Where is he !   Looking after your interests."

John knew nothing, but his confidence in his friend was complete, and he made this statement in the plenitude of a strong faith ; and as he saw doubt and fear struggling with new hope in the countenances of those before him, and realised how much this must mean to some of them, he cried, with sudden emotion—

" Oh, friends ! I'm sorry for you to-day, with all my heart."

" God bless thee ! " shouted an old man who was standing next to Max.

" But, friends," John went on, " there's one thing I'm prepared to stake my life on, and that is that James Wheeler will part with every stick he has in the world before any of you shall be injured through him—he *will !*"

" Yes, that he will, young man," cried a strange voice, and, with a sudden cry, the crowd turned round and beheld James Wheeler himself standing on the edge of the throng. He had evidently got out of a cab which had a moment before pulled up in the bye-street down which John and Max had rushed upon the scene. With easy self-possession he walked down the gap made for him by the suddenly abashed crowd, and nodding to Max, he put one foot upon the coping, and gripping the railings, raised himself above the rest and looked steadily into the faces turned up to him.

" The bank will open to-morrow morning at the usual time, and you will all receive your own," he said ; and then as though the occasion was one of no particular interest, he turned, straddled over the railings, put out his hand to John, and helped him down from his elevated position, murmuring as he did so a word in John's ear that brought the tingling blood into his pallid face.

The crowd wavered, men and women cast dazed, questioning looks at each other, and then the police becoming suddenly exceedingly valiant and energetic, they began to disperse.

Max, with shining eyes, came swarming over the railings and across the flower beds, and seizing Mr. Wheeler by the hand, began to assure him that he was a trump! a giant! a hero ! and finished by declaring—

" My old dad will give you a lift at this, sir ! He'll be proud to know such a man."

Mr. Wheeler, with a shy smile, took John by the arm, and began to move towards the house. As he opened the front door he stepped back and pushed his young friend before him, and before John could realise what was happening, he was being squeezed

M.   U

almost to choking, by a pair of long white arms; a hot, wet cheek, and a bewildering cloud of fluffy hair were being pressed against his cheek, and a shower of kisses rained upon him. Then there was a sharp cry, and John, suddenly released, beheld Mr. Wheeler enduring the same delightful sort of assault, until at length the impetuous Betty, crying and laughing together, let her father go, turned and looked at the embarrassed and evidently envious Max, and then dashed off into the house with sudden shame.

There were voices in the hall just then, and the "kids," indignant and threatening, came in to hear the details; for the mill was nearly two miles out of the town, and they had only heard the terrible news a few minutes before "stopping time."

The conversation was rapid and noisy, and of a bewildering cross-fire nature: so many things having to be told and commented upon that John was relieved when, just as Betty was opening a highly coloured description of his doings, Mary came into the room and at once attracted attention by her looks. She had been "a little frightened," she admitted, laughingly, and nobody knew then that for nearly half-an-hour she had been lying on her own bed in a dead faint. Tea was brought in presently, but nobody wanted any, and the excited young folk only drew up to the table to gratify the cherry-cheeked "grandmother."

John and Max tried to excuse themselves and get away, but nobody would hear of it.

"Friends like these must be stuck to, eh, boys?" said Mr. Wheeler, and so they were constrained to remain for a time, but later on, with many assurances of gratitude, they took their leave.

Late that same night the three young Wheelers sat pulling moodily at expired cigarettes in the smoke room, and talking in low fitful tones.　Presently the little office door that opened into the smoke room creaked on its hinges, and the elder Wheeler, without, for once, his cigar, came into the room and sat down. Complete silence ensued, but presently he turned his head and looked round as if in search of some one. Mark got up and went out, returning almost immediately with Mary, who now wore a long dressing-gown, and her wonderful hair fell in thick heavy folds down her back.　As she took her seat near her father he looked round nervously at her, and then turned his head away and began to blink his eyes rapidly.　Mary glanced at him, and then rising, stepped into the little office and returned with a cigar box which she held out to him.　He shook his head decidedly, but without daring to look at her, and so she picked two cigars from the box, laid them on his knee, and then, taking a taper, she lighted it, and still waited in silence.　With more rapid blinkings of the eyes, and a treacherous twitching about the mouth, he took the weed and taper and was soon pouring out volumes of smoke; at the same time he put out his hand and touched hers timidly, as it lay on the arm of his chair, with a touch that meant more to these deep-hearted, reticent people than a passion of emotion would have done to others.

Mr. Wheeler was clearly struggling with some well-nigh uncontrollable feeling, and the " kids " in similar plight singed their moustaches and burnt their noses' ends in vain attempts to cover their emotions behind very demonstrative lightings of cigarettes.　Silence, more painful than ever, fell on them, and then in hollow, broken tones, Mr. Wheeler faltered out—

" It's my own fault."

" Father ! "

Four suddenly stern voices rapped out this reproof,

and the father, who seemed to be sinking deeper into the chair, and looking smaller and smaller every moment, continued brokenly—

" You don't know how bad it is, children."

" No, and we don't care."

The younger men were all like their father, slow of speech, but three pairs of moist, glistening eyes were turned admiringly upon Mary, who, as usual, had found the very words they wanted.

" You lads will have to strike out for yourselves now," went on the elder man.

" We sha'n't," answered all three at once.

" But, my bairns, it's gone, it's *all* gone. We hav'n't anything left at all."

And as the big fellows looked helplessly at each other and their sister in search of a sufficient thing to say, Mary brought sudden tears into their eyes by saying, very quietly—

" Yes, we have! we've *you*."

Wheeler could not speak for several moments, and his eldest son watching him furtively, saw him driving his teeth into his cigar as though in maddening pain.

" The mill will have to go; is practically gone now," he said at last.

Shadows came upon those young faces for a moment, for that was worse than they had expected, but as they glanced suspiciously at each other, shame smote them, they called up airs of stolid indifference and almost contempt, but finally burst into nervous little laughs as their sister came once more to their rescue by answering—

" Then we'll all work together and build one twice as big."

Wheeler sprang to his feet as though he had been stung.

" We will! forgive me, children. I was a coward after all. We will! God helping us, we will!"

"Dad!" shouted Mark, as excited now as his father, "there's many a man in Partidge has begun at the bottom and won his way up *once*, but I know a jolly old fellow who is going to show 'em how to do it twice. We're on for it, daddy lad, we're all on!"

A silence fell on them for a while. Wheeler sank back into his chair and sucked eagerly at his now unlighted cigar.

"I don't quite see what we shall do—yet," he said, in slow musing tones, "but God——"

And before he could get the dilatory words out, Mary said, shyly—

"There's my little patent."

"M-a-r-y!" and Wheeler's suddenly excited shout seemed to ring through the quiet house as he leaped to his feet and stood gazing at her. Then he turned away, and looking with wet-eyed appeal from one of his stalwart sons to the other, he said: "Didn't I say she was God's angel in the house, and the best member of the firm to boot!" and then, before she could prevent him, he had picked her up in his long arms and was hugging her to his heart and showering hot joyful kisses on her face. When he at length released her, as her brothers all looked very like making similar attacks, she retreated towards the door.

"An unprotected female must protect herself," she said, with something of Betty in her momentary manner, and with a long sweeping curtsey she vanished.

Something very like cheerfulness seemed to have entered the hearts of those she left behind her, and very soon they were deep in conversation on the details of the bank crisis and the arrangements and sacrifices necessary to clear the good name of Wheeler.

"We shall do it, lads," cried the older man, as

they rose to separate; "they can rob us and impoverish us, but they never shall disgrace us." And as the sons uttered each a fervent "Never," he led the way upstairs, crying heartily: "And now for Mary's patent. Bless her!"

Next morning, Mr. Wheeler was early at the bank. It was an old black and white structure which had originally been in the centre of the town, but which with the growth of the neighbourhood had been left very much to itself, and now stood back behind high railings in the narrow old Market Street. The institution itself was a very old-fashioned one, doing a slow, safe business amongst the aborigines of the district. It had been held in the greatest regard, and was always considered particularly safe. A new manager, however, who had been appointed some three years before the crisis, early announced his intention of clearing out the cobwebs and rousing the concern out of its musty ways, and he had carried out his threat only too well, and the unexpected collapse of a firm very deep in its books had brought about the immediate difficulty. Mr. Wheeler, as an old townsman, had always had a quiet ambition to hold shares in the bank, and having unexpectedly come into possession of a parcel of scrip some months before the new management took hold, he was soon put upon the directorate, because of his position and influence more than for the value of his holding. He had, however, caused a flutter in the dovecote by tartly critising the "new ways." And suddenly the crash came, and he discovered that his fellow-directors were either men of straw, or had ingeniously covered themselves by overdrafts, and he had, perhaps, unwisely expressed himself about the matter at the first sign of danger; thus producing uneasiness and a nasty "run," with such consequences as we have already seen. Practically he was left either to shuffle and edge as he might have done and thus save his possessions, or face the matter out, which, as he well knew, meant the loss of all he had.

He was greeted with mingled groans and cheers as he approached the excited crowd of depositors, but he only winced when somebody flung the word " Methody " at him. Punctually at ten o'clock the doors were opened, and payments made. At first there was a violent scramble and much cursing, but as depositor after depositor came away satisfied, the stream slackened, and in a hour had become quite manageable; and by the time the dinner-hour was reached the demand had almost ceased, and a few customers had even brought their money back. Meanwhile, Mr. Wheeler was busy enough in the back office receiving visits from friends, and reports from the chief constable about the search for the manager, who had disappeared the day before. Fellow-shareholders also visited him and abused him for having brought the thing upon himself and them, and for his quixotic conduct now that the worst had come. Old friends, business men from other towns, wired offering assistance, or called upon him and suggested "perfectly safe" and "honourable methods" whereby he might save himself and evade, or at least postpone, his liability. Having failed in this argument, some of them began to abuse him as the enemy of his family, the robber of his children, and the spoiler of his sons' prospects. To each and all he replied with the same smiling firmness, and went on paying out through the clerks the demands made. Then it was reported to him that the run had stopped, and going into the counting-house to peep at the crowd still standing about, he was accosted by a rough-looking old fellow, in shabby fustian and a greasy silk hat of antique fashion.

"I've towd thee monny a time as thou were a foo'," he cried, glaring savagely at the temporary banker, "but now thou knows it, I reacon," and then with a curious spasmodic movement on his face, he drew out a parcel of notes amounting to about £40, and pitching them on the high counter, said, snappishly, "Here, tak' care o' them."

It was old Crake the leader, and Mr. Wheeler's eyes glistened as he handed back the money, and begged the old man to go home.

"Oh! it's sperritual pride now, is it! The lunger I live the more I sees that needle's eye as t' Master talks about. Here, lad! thee tak' it," and with a sternly indignant glance at Wheeler, he stepped up to a grinning clerk and handed him the notes. The only responsible director then shrugged his shoulders and retreated into the inner office, and the old fellow flung after him the most applicable Scripture text he could think of—"Pride goeth before a fall, and a haughty spirit before destruction."

Wherever James Wheeler appeared during the next few days he was greeted with something like an ovation, and even on the busy Manchester Exchange men stood by as he passed, took off their hats, and made attempts at cheering. Many condemned the action as unjust to himself and his family, for his responsibility was after all a joint one. More than one little committee was formed to try to compel him to stay his hand, but they produced no effect. The mill, a fine modern concern, the envy of many, was held over for a little time, to see if anything could be done to save it to the family, but Wheeler proved so fastidiously scrupulous, and his sons so stubbornly infatuated about their father, that nothing was accomplished, and when in growing admiration his fellow shareholders in the bank insisted upon purchasing and presenting him with the house in

which he lived, he peremptorily stopped the movement, and insisted that it would require all they
could find in the way of cash to help the bank upon
its feet again.

The super., as the result of John's hasty words,
had an affecting interview with his ex-steward, the
details of which have never leaked out, but from that
day the minister went about declaring that " he was
not fit to black Mr. Wheeler's boots."

When the Quarterly meeting came, there was a
special vote of congratulation sent to the ex-steward,
and an invitation to the now all-popular second
minister to remain in the circuit. The stewards,
the authors of that stinging letter to John, were
most fulsome, and when John quietly but firmly
declined, a large party headed by old Crake
absolutely refused to accept the refusal, and insisted
that he must be made to stop, even if Conference
had to be invoked. During these exciting times, and
in spite of imminent examinations, Max came to
Partidge every third or fourth day, though his own
circuit was forty miles away. But though John and
he talked much and often about the Wheelers, each
noted it as an odd thing that the other never alluded
to the dread subject that was so constantly in their
thoughts. Max, glowing with intense admiration of
the conduct of his friends, was now absolutely certain
there was only one woman in the world for him, and
he revelled in the delicious thought that in their
misfortune his projected proposal would be a delicate
compliment, and show the family that he had a soul
above mere worldly considerations.

Every time he came to Partidge he had within
him the fixed purpose of proposing to Mary before
he returned, but on each occasion John's strange and
significant silence, and the increasing pallor and
pensiveness of his face, touched the impressionable

fellow's heart, and he decided to wait until his friend should speak. Then came the examinations; times of torturing humiliation to Max, but when they were over, and he had thrown the last erratic sheet of Hebrew aside, he startled John and the examining minister, by shouting—

"And now for Rose Cottage and Paradise!—Paradise lost to Paradise regained."

It was known to both of them that the Wheelers were removing to their new home that very week, and Max waited impatiently until the more painstaking John had finished in order that he might, as he expected, be asked to call at Partidge *en route*, spend the night, and, of course, see the Wheelers.

Rose Cottage was a little old-fashioned house on the other side of the railway, and was the place to which James Wheeler had taken his bride when he was only a cashier. They found their arrival anticipated, and Betty met them with a long bamboo curtain rod as a sort of wand of office and showed them over the new residence. Everything looked very cramped and small after the beautiful home they had so often visited, and there was a smell of paint and whitewash, but Betty was in high spirits, and did the honours with lavish descriptive embellishments and serio-comic gravity.

"Step forward, gentlemen, mind that two-and-eleven-penny umbrella stand! Walk this way—the reception room; don't knock the gaseliers with your head, Mr. Ringley!"—and she showed them a small front room which was to be used for state occasions, and thus went from room to room. "This, dearly beloved brethering," she cried, standing before a closed door, "is the refectory, or, as the Revised Version has it—the kitchen! Our *chef* is at this moment preparing dyspeptic instruments of torture, and is not on view, so we will ascend." On the

second storey she vaguely indicated with a majestic
sweep of the hand the various rooms, and uttered
the single word "dormitories," and then pointed
to the door of a room over the drawing-room on
which was a sheet of paper covered with letters in
different stages of intoxication, and which made up
the significant announcement: "THE PROPHET'S
CHAMBER!"

Thus introduced, they spent a delightful evening,
and Max kept the thoroughly weary and pensive
John up into the small hours as he enlarged on
the "splendid humility" of the Wheelers and the
incomparable charms of Mary.

Next morning, he was strangely restless and absent-
minded. Several times John caught him studying
him with scowling brow, as if he longed to introduce
the fateful topic, but was uncertain as to its reception.
They both knew that he ought to be back in his
circuit, for to-morrow was Sunday; but he fidgeted
about, looked up the time-table, started several
conversations which he somehow could not maintain,
and at last turning shyly to his companion, he asked,
bluntly—

"What about this girl?"

John paled a little, drew himself together, went
over and dropped some old post-cards and used
envelopes into the fire, and then said—

"Go and ask her to-day."

Max started, and looked a little taken aback, John
was always so downright and blunt; then a smile
came into the corners of his mouth, and it was clear
that the suggestion was very much to his mind.
But his face shadowed suddenly, he looked hard out
of the window a little while, and then stepped up to
John, and taking him by the shoulder and looking
with earnest, scrutinising gaze into his eyes, he asked,
softly—

"And what about you, old man?"

There was a pause, he could feel John's frame shaking under his hands, and at last the answer came—

"Max, dear old fellow, it's of God's mercy that you are the man. My guilty love is so strong that my religion even is too weak for it sometimes, but I am helped and hope to be saved by—by—b—y—by my love to thee. Go, ask her, and the Lord help and prosper thee!"

Max's head had dropped upon his breast, his face went pale and red and pale and red again, his eyes were shining with a strange, struggling light, and at last he set his teeth together, clenched his fist, and shouted, with drawn, agonised face—

"I will never see her again!"

But John knew him better than he knew himself, and so, after waiting for the height of his passion to subside, he began to talk as of old. Max held out most obstinately, and repeated his last declaration half-a-dozen times, but at length, and as usual, he yielded to his friend's greater firmness, and about eleven o'clock, morning though it was, he sallied forth on his mission.

Two hours passed; long, terrible hours for John Ledger, and at last, on the stroke of one, he heard the steps of his chum on the stairs and began to shake like a leaf.

"Well?" he cried with painful eagerness, almost before Max had got into the room. But the Romeo, with sphinx-like face, began to put away his hat and overcoat with most painful deliberateness.

"Well?" cried John again, with emotion that made his voice shake. But Max walked coolly to the window, thrust his hands deep into his pockets, and stood gazing moodily out of the window, and actually humming a medley of fag-ends of tunes.

"Speak! Speak, man! You are killing me!"

And then Max turned round, surveyed John critically from head to foot, and then going close up to him and seizing him by the button of his coat, he said, in tones of unalterable conviction—

"Ledger! the woman that will ever get a proposal from me again isn't made."

"She refused you?" cried John, with a sudden swelling of the heart that frightened him.

"Refused me! Why, man, she laughed at me!"

"Never!"

"She laughed at me, and looked like a seraph all the time. She licked me all over with sweet words like a mother tabby with an obstreperous kitten. Sweet! she was sugar itself; she was butter and honey! Why, man alive, I thought once she was going to kiss me!"

"But she didn't refuse——"

"Didn't she? Not in so many words, she's too confoundedly clever for that. She didn't even offer to be a sister. She stroked me down and smiled and smothered me in compliments, and smiled and said: 'How kind of me!' and smiled; and then, when I was feeling like a silly fool, if she didn't raise her big eyes and cock her dimpled chin, and ask as demurely as an old maid, if I didn't think there was something the matter with the health of Mr. Ledger. No, no, *Mister* Ledger, once bitten twice shy! No more proposing for yours truly."

CHAPTER VI

MAX RINGLEY HAS AN IDEA

IT was clear to John Ledger, when, on Max's departure to a too long neglected work, he had leisure to think, that after all his friend's affections had not been very deeply engaged, and he thought with glowing admiration of the delicate kindness of Mary, who had evidently contrived to satisfy or at least to silence Max without too seriously hurting his self-love. How she had done it was by no means clear from Max's hyperbolical and disjointed descriptions, but that it had been done effectually and with the least possible pain was very manifest. John was glad—selfishly, wickedly glad. The few words his friend had slipped out about Mary's concern for him meant nothing, of course, but they seemed unutterably sweet, and he would believe they meant something in spite of reason and right and everything else. That his passion was hopeless, and mad and guilty as well, he knew; but that it was *his* passion, the one great overmastering passion of his life, he knew also, and did not at that moment wish it otherwise. To love was enough, and every other consideration was relentlessly shut out. And just when the guilty dream, as he regarded it, was most intoxicating it began to slip away. He tried to fix it, strained his soul's eyes after it, clutched at it with mad desperation, but it faded before him like a dissolving view, and he was left alone in the outer darkness. The severe strain of self-repression during the last few weeks had drained his strength, and that, with the exhaustion of his examinations, had reduced his vitality, and he was in that limp physical condition in which all mental ideas, especially those of a pensive nature, become vivid even to exaggeration; and every feature of the dreadful *impasse* in which he found himself stood out with startling distinctness. The worst fear of his life was more than realised, and he, the fastidiously conscientious, was steeped in basest guilt. He had not even been equal to the demands of elementary morality, and proposed to himself to stand at God's altar and vow to love a woman he knew he never could love; whilst solemnly pledged and spiritually married to one woman, he had allowed himself to love another. To one of them it was robbery, and to the other, grossest insult.

The position was bad enough when considered thus, but when he thought of it as it was related to God, and then remembered that he was not a mere man but a teacher of Christian morality, the blackness of darkness came upon him, and he would gladly have died at that moment to escape the torture. But there was no escape; there was even no relief. He was lying on the little horse-hair sofa, his eyes nipped tightly together in acute anguish. Self-pity came more than once to his aid, but seeing in it only another and a deadlier foe he resisted, and hardened his heart against himself.

In life's great extremes he had been taught to seek God, but now he felt that as the difficulty was of his own making, it could only be dealt with by himself, and that to ask God to help him out of a trouble from which there was a clear, if almost impossibly hard path of duty, was to further insult an already outraged Deity.

He rolled about on the couch and groaned; and then a little patch of grey appeared; it could scarcely be called light, but it was some little change from the dense darkness that enveloped his soul. He grew quiet, removed his hands from his face, and lay staring at the white ceiling. Then he rose, went to his desk, and took out a bundle of letters and glanced them over. Yes, there was something there; there was quite sufficient in those letters to at least palliate his offence, for Sallie had written very harshly and recklessly sometimes; he could give her up definitely and then make some atonement to God and his conscience by resolving he would never marry at all. Then he woke from his reverie with a start, flung the letters from him as though they had bitten his fingers, and stood looking down upon them on the floor as one who watched a hissing, mesmerising snake. There was anger, horror, disgust on his face now, and presently with a cry he made a plunge at the letters, and, lest they should tempt him again, gathered them in his hands, threw them with a little gasp into the fire, and stood watching their destruction with painful interest. The little clock struck six, and remembering that to-morrow was Sunday he smiled bitterly, and flung himself once more on his couch.

"No, there was no way out"; even the desperate course he had pacified his conscience with so long now seemed not only wicked but impossible. There was one thing to do, and one only; he shrank from it, resisted it, spurned it, but there it was, certain, clear, irresistible: *he ought to resign the ministry for which he was no longer fit.*

And then he thought of his mother and Wilky Drax, and all the other kind friends who were so proud of him and interested in his welfare, and as this touched a tender chord his hot eyes grew moist for a moment; but the thought was soon lost in the reflection that when connexional discipline had been satisfied, the intrinsic sinfulness of what he had done would still be there, and as his mind reeled under the ever growing burden, he longed in that excruciating moment that he might die.

There was a local preacher in the pulpit at St. Mary's next morning, for the now popular second minister was reported ill—the examinations, it was said—and Betty Wheeler and her brother Paul were absent from the chapel, presumably looking after the sick man; and late on Sunday evening a pale, still woman bordering on sixty got off the train at Partidge and was piloted to John's lodgings, whilst a marble-faced girl, with restless manner and wistful eyes, moved absently about at Rose Cottage, guessing, perhaps, some little of the truth, but painfully perplexed all the same.

Meanwhile Max had reached his own circuit. So absorbed was he in his rejection by Mary that he had allowed himself to be taken past the junction, and had to journey some twelve miles further on, and get round to Longhope as best he could. His lodgings were almost palatial as compared with his friend's, and he looked round with a little sigh of thankfulness upon the orderliness to which his landlady had reduced things during his absence, and he was just ordering his tea when the good woman came in with a message that one of his parishioners was ill, and had sent for him. Conscience-smitten and anxious, the impulsive fellow forgot about his hunger, and a few minutes later his coat tails were seen flying round sundry street corners, and his supporters, glancing after his retreating form, turned to each other to remark upon the wonderful devotion of their young pastor; for Max, being exceedingly popular as a preacher, could do no wrong, and his many admirers saw devotion and self-sacrifice where, in an ordinary man, they would have observed nothing but the bare performance of duty.

An hour later he sat at his table absently consuming his chop and musing on the many incidents of his recent life. He sighed and wagged his head, and with clenched fists vowed perpetual celibacy as he thought of Mary, but grew still and sad as he reflected on the condition and difficulties of his comrade. The absent-minded emptying of the cold dregs of his teacup into the sugar basin instead of the slop bowl, however, brought him back; but in a very brief space he was once more asking himself what John ought to do. It was not long, however, before he got a step further, and began to wonder what he could do himself to assist in the disentanglement. A hare-brained idea of suggesting to John that they should both volunteer for work in some remote corner of the mission field, and thus leave all their perplexities behind them, flitted for a moment before his mind, only to be dismissed by the remembrance that John would never be a party to any such scheme. Then the novelty of the situation brought a smile to his lips. Hitherto he had been the one to get into scrapes, and John had had to devise the means of deliverance; but now the positions were reversed, and the unwontedness of the situation tickled him exceedingly, and he spun a piece of dry toast round on the tip of his finger and chuckled. Then he wondered if there was any discreet, elderly minister to whom he could go for counsel; but not being able to recall any, his mind flitted to Mary Wheeler. She was so clever, so clear-headed, so high-minded, that he was sure, if she cared, she could suggest a way out; but remembering all at once that he suspected Mary of secret fondness for John, he saw that she would certainly refuse to have anything to do with

the matter.   From Mary his mind travelled easily to
Sallie Wood.   Following, as he generally did, his
instinct rather than his reason, he had decided long
ago that the union between John and Sallie ought
never to be consummated, and he was not quite aware
that in his heart of hearts he had designed his friend
for his own sister.   He had never seen Sallie, but
he had an immovable conviction, he knew not why,
that she was not good enough for John, and it would
be an infinite pity if the poor fellow sacrificed himself, as he felt certain he would do if left to his own
devices.   He wondered musingly what sort of a girl
Sallie was: whatever her disposition she would be
madly in love with John—any girl would be.   But
perhaps she was not; women are a queer quantity—
Max was getting the cynicism of experience all at
once—perhaps she had never learnt to value him as
he and the rest of his college friends, tutors included,
had done; and then a wild, ridiculous, but most
alluringly daring idea flashed into his mind, and he
threw back his head and grinned as he thought of it.
How would it be to go to Sallie unknown to
John, and——

"Telegram, sir; boy waitin' for hanswer."

Max started as he heard the announcement, and
then thought, with a queer little pang—

"What if John has——"

But he tore the salmon-coloured envelope open,
and read with puzzled face—

"Waiting answer to letter.   Wire reply.
                                    "CLOUGHTON, Bramwell."

With puckered, scowling brow he stared at the
telegram, rubbed his left ear violently, and frowned
again at the incomprehensible message.   Then suddenly remembering, he plunged at the mantelpiece,
and grabbed at a small heap of unopened and hitherto

forgotten letters. He ran his eye hastily over the postmarks, picked out a note with the Bramwell stamp on it, tore it open and glanced rapidly over the communication. As he read he raised his brows and cried "Ah!" now and then in complete surprise; then he knitted his forehead, threw the note down absently on the table, and turned and glared at Mrs. Spudder in intense thought. The landlady understood her man by this time, and stood quite unconcerned, knowing well enough that he did not see her. After thinking thus for a short time Max turned to look for a reply form, and Mrs. Spudder had, of course, to find it for him. Then he scribbled a few words, added a tip for the messenger, scrambled into his coat and hat, and dashed off to see his super.

The letter informed him that the Connexional Evangelist had suddenly failed them at Bramwell through illness, and that as the arrangements had all been made, and the season was late, they could not now postpone the fixture. They had heard of him through Mr. John Ledger and others; would he take the vacant place? The writer was a friend of his super.'s, and was writing him by that post to ask that Mr. Ringley might be released from his ordinary work for ten days. The missive concluded with an earnest and flattering appeal to Max to come and help them. An hour later a telegram accepting the invitation had been sent, and Max was back in his study trying to realise the new situation. He was so excited he could not sit still; pacing up and down his large, long room, stumbling over kicked-up edges of carpet, running against inconveniently placed chairs, he scowled and tittered, scowled and "Pshaw-ed" again, uttering between whiles all sorts of odd ejaculations.

Coincidence! It was no mere coincidence; it was a direct and most palpable Providential leading. He would see Sallie, get to know her, and in ten days, perhaps a fortnight, what might not be done!

The opening was so startlingly opportune that there must be something in it, and his sanguine temperament led him to feel that his friend's difficulties were already disposed of.

He would be very diplomatic, trust him for that; no rushing headlong at it, and spoiling the whole game; he would study her carefully, make sure of his ground step by step, and then——

And the light-hearted fellow hugged himself in rosy anticipations of brilliant strategic success. His heart grew soft again as he pictured to himself the relief and comfort it would be to the too scrupulous John.

"Dear old boy! why, there was not anything on earth he would not do for John."

All at once he pulled up abruptly, the tender look vanished from his face, and a blank expression took its place, accompanied by an almost frightened gasp, and then the comic side of his last great idea came upon him, and he threw himself into his elaborate mechanical reading chair, and rolled about and held his sides in uncontrollable laughter.

"Ye gods! Ye gods! it will kill me! Lark! There never was such a lark!" and then, springing out of his chair, he cried, "Max! Max! she might *transfer* her affections, she *might*!" and away he went with another roar.

"Imagine, sir! the lady suggests a simple swop! She reads poetry and suggests Miles Standish to thee, Max! Oh, scrumptious! Oh, glorious!" and dropping helplessly into his chair again he drew up his legs and crowed and laughed, and crowed and laughed again.

When at last his hilarity had exhausted itself, he began to really look at the idea. He saw, of course, how wildly outrageous and hare-brained it was, but that only made it appeal the more attractively to his romantic, topsy-turvy nature. How it would startle the respectables! How the " saints "—Max had a prejudice against " saints "—would lift up holy hands in horror, and turn up the whites of their eyes! How their college chums would grin and the old Governor look grave, with a glint in the tail of his eye! Yes, it was a magnificently audacious idea, and intensely fascinating on that account. It would beat a novel, he told himself, and carry confusion into the ranks of the " uncu guid." It did not occur to him that he would be simply transferring John's difficulty to himself; he only saw the fun of the thing and the happy escape that would thus be provided for his friend.

Gradually he grew quieter, a gentle light stole back into his eyes, and the corners of his mouth tightened a little. A photo of his friend stood on the mantlepiece, and he presently got up and began to look steadily at it. A long sigh escaped him as he gazed, and then he cried, nodding at the picture, " It's mad, my boy, of course! It will never come off, as you say! but Johnny! dear, good old Johnny! if there *is* a chance of it, and if she *is* passable, and if there really is no other way out, mad and crazy though it is, here's the chap that will do it! " and then gazing wistfully at the face in the photo until his eyes grew wet, he said slowly and almost solemnly, " Yes, dear boy! here's the chap that will do it."

He had appointments at country places on the following day, and as he walked from village to village he repeated to himself his vow that nothing should induce him to go to Partidge again, and on his return journey he made the resolution four or five times over with ever-increasing intensity; but on Monday morning he was the first person to alight

from the 9.57 train at Partidge station.   Circumstances alter cases, of course, and the fact that in a
few days he was due at John's circuit town of Bramwell made it absolutely necessary that he should
interview his friend and get all the information
possible as to the character and condition of those
he was about to preach to ; and this was surely a
sufficient reason for waiving otherwise adamantine
resolutions.   He knew nothing of what had taken
place since he left John, and so was astonished to
find his chum in bed with his mother attending him.
John was propped up in bed with a writing-board on
his knees, evidently composing a letter, but his
appearance had changed so shockingly during the
thirty odd hours since they parted, that for the
moment Max was too alarmed to notice John's
manner or occupation, until a furtive attempt on the
sick man's part to hide his correspondence attracted
his attention and excited his suspicion.   And just
then the doctor was announced, and to Max's
increasing alarm he was accompanied by a physician
from Bellerby, a retired man who had great local
fame.   He withdrew and wandered about restlessly
in the study until the consultation was over.   They
were not very long he noted, with relief, but as they
were leaving the local medico came over to him and
said in subdued tones—

   " You are Mr. Ledger's friend, I understand ? "

   Max bowed and turned a suddenly whitened face
to his interrogator.

   " Ah—ah—would you mind slipping down to my
surgery in about ten minutes? We should like to see
you."

   Max felt his heart beating, but as the doctor
departed, Mrs. Ledger came out of the bedroom and
with anxious face asked what they had said. Max
told her, and then as he watched the face grow pale

and the lips quiver, he felt his own eyes were getting dim, and with a sudden pathetic impulse he bent over and reverently kissed the drawn face of the mother of his friend.

"Mr. Ledger seems a reserved sort of man, Mr. —a—a—Ringley," said the doctor, when Max, still anxious and nervous, sat down in the consulting room.

Max nodded his head and looked at the physicians inquiringly.

"Well now, you are his friend, his closest friend, I understand. Is he fairly open with you—a—a— about his private affairs, you know?"

"I know all there is to know," and Max licked his parched lips.

"Has he had any great shock lately that you know of? I don't want to know what it is, you know."

"No," said Max rather bluntly, and then he almost regretted having spoken so hastily.

"He has no financial troubles, or—— "

"Of course not! he's my friend!" and he seemed to think that answer more than sufficient, but the doctor was not quite so clear about it.

"Have you noticed that he is troubled about any theological matters?"

"If he were I should have known it. Of course he's just passed a very stiff examination."

"Yes! yes! That is something, no doubt, but you see, this is more than overstrain— " and then he turned to his colleague and they conversed in an undertone for a moment; presently he turned and looked calculatingly at Max, and then resumed slowly—"You have never heard that there is insanity in his family?"

Max was getting angry; a hot reply rose to his lips, but curbing himself he said gruffly—

"I've never heard of any such thing."

There was another and longer consultation, and then the specialist turned and began to move about the room restlessly, with his hands in his pockets.

" Your friend, Mr. Ringley, has no disease upon him whatever, but he's frightfully run down, his vitality is very low, and the fact is the trouble is mental. He is the victim of some fixed idea, probably a hallucination; the index finger of his brain, so to speak, does not move, and that, as I need not say, is most dangerous. He needs no physic; he must be kept active; change of scene and occupation are imperative, and if you know anything that is likely to be troubling him you must get it out of him or get him to forget it."

Max asked several questions and was courteously answered, but he got very little more light; nothing, in fact, but the oft-repeated injunction to get at the bottom of his friend's troubles and take him away somewhere. Max returned in a perplexed and anxious state of mind; some of the things he had heard relieved him immensely, but the others so exactly indicated the danger he was so well aware of that he was almost frightened. Some of the duties enjoined upon him, he knew he could discharge better than anybody else, but in the graver and more delicate things he was profoundly mistrustful. Constitutionally he needed some one to lean upon, and had had that privilege during the last three years with John, but in this case he must act alone, and the prospect made him very uneasy. One moment, on the return journey, he started off with a plunge to carry out his instructions, and the next he found himself standing staring at the pavement and wondering how he must act. He ran over in his mind a list of college friends who might possibly assist him, but found no one in whom he could confide so delicate a business. Then he had a notion of going right away to Sallie and telling her the whole truth, and appealing to her goodness of heart to release John of her own free will, but as he could not be certain that John would accept of any such solution, he was compelled to abandon that also. A great longing came over him to throw resolution to the winds and go and consult the Wheelers—Mr. Wheeler particularly—but as he could not decide that it would be quite fair to his friend to do this without his consent, that hope had to be relinquished like the rest. He had arrived at John's lodgings by this time, and as the period of action was now come, he darted upstairs and bounced into the bedroom with much of his usual boisterousness. Mrs. Ledger met him at the top of the stairs, and checking a mad impulse to hug her, he whispered a few words that brought the light back into her eyes, and then dashing past he bounded into the room, crying, " Come out o' this! Arise and shine! No more malingering nonsense here! Get up, sir! Get up, I say—where's that water jug?" and he made a snatch at the quilt and gave a jerk to it, when he suddenly caught sight of the letter John had previously concealed. It fluttered out with the corner of the bedcover, and John, who was beginning to smile in a wan sort of way, uttered a cry of alarm and put out his hand for the epistle. Max, hurriedly justifying himself by the instructions he had received, took a glance at it as he picked it up, and noticed that it commenced " Dear Mr. President." He could scarcely suppress the exclamation that rushed to his lips, but with a hasty covering joke about love letters he flung it back to the sick man, and then resumed his clamour for John to get up. " He says you're foxing, man! You're coming the old soldier! Get up, I say! Where *is* that water jug?"

John, however, was engaged in concealing his

unfinished letter, and so, to flatter the idea that he
had noticed nothing, Max resumed his blustering
demands.

"Up, sir! I'm in command now! Valet, sir?
certainly—at your service! Twenty pounds a year
and parquisites! Stockings, sir? here you are!
Shaving water, sir? hot, sir? why, of course!"

Laughing in spite of himself as the mad fellow
rattled on, John was soon up and dressed, and as
the fire had now been lighted in his own room, he
joined his nurses and listened listlessly whilst Max,
with his ridiculous comic embellishments and his
own reservations, detailed the instructions he had
received. Then he evoked the ready sympathy of
Mrs. Ledger by describing himself as suffering
acutely from brain-fag in consequence of the strenuous
efforts he had made at the recent examinations, and
when this, as he hoped, produced another faint smile
from John, he plunged into an account of the invitation he had received for the mission at Bramwell,
and as that brought fresh inspiration he announced
that he should stay with them all the week, and then
they would all adjourn together to John's old home;
his instructions were imperative, and he was going
to carry them out; John was to do no work for a
month at least. This last statement was, of course,
purely apocryphal, but he leaned back as he made it,
and avoiding John's eye, bestowed a complicated
wink on the anxious mother. Taking her cue from
him, the old lady fell in with the suggestion eagerly,
and when John attempted to demur he was met by a
stentorian schoolmaster-like "Silence!" and sternly
informed that he was under authority. After a
light repast Max sent for a conveyance, and mounting
the box took them out for a long drive, keeping
John close to his side and chattering away with
riotous banter that opened Mrs. Ledger's eyes again

and again and made her wonder whether this could really be a minister of religion and her son's chosen companion. But he soon found that he had undertaken no easy task ; his mirth, being forced, tired him strangely, and Monday was one of the longest days he had ever spent. Whenever, during the drive, he glanced at John, he found him abstracted and painfully depressed, and as he only replied in monosyllables, it became increasingly difficult to maintain a conversation. As Mrs. Ledger occupied the only spare bed in the house, and he did not intend to let John out of his sight, he contrived that it should be agreed for them to sleep together at least for a night or two. All the evening he tried to interest John in books, and found that the only subject he cared in the least for was next year's examinations, themes Max's soul hated. But he conquered his repugnance and commenced reading aloud, only to discover that the other was not following him, but was evidently absorbed in his own gloomy reflections. In bed that night he got the first opportunity for quiet thought. How ever was he to get through a week like this ? and what would be the end of all these cruel entanglements ? To whom could he go for counsel and support ? Why ? oh why had God allowed so extremely conscientious a man to wander into this hopeless *cul-de-sac* ? Over and over again he turned his harassing dubitations, and then he heard the clock strike twelve, and turned over with a fierce resolve to go to sleep. All at once he remembered about John's unfinished letter. He knew instinctively that it was his formal resignation as a minister—the headline made suspicion all but certainty—what else could he have to write to so high an authority about ? But what had become of it ? It had not yet been sent, he was sure, and he must take care that it never was. John had certainly not

posted it yet, and he must see that he got no opportunity of doing so.   What was there in the letter?
John had never alluded to it—a most suspicious
circumstance.   They understood each other entirely;
if he could get hold of the letter and destroy it,
John would understand that no such thing could be
done with his consent and whilst he was there.
Should he get softly out of bed and try to find it?
He had no scruple either in reading or burning it;
he was only carrying out his instructions.   John had
been very quiet now for nearly an hour.   Was he
asleep? He raised himself upon his elbow and
looked over, and then sank back with a smothered
cry, for the patient lay on his back with his eyes
wide open, and evidently unconscious where he was.
Max's head dropped on the pillow with a groan.
How much longer was this miserable torture
going on?

On Tuesday Sallie came, accompanied by the Bramwell super.'s daughter, and Max, whilst welcoming
the interesting diversion, soon found fresh cause for
worry in the confirmation of his previous suspicions.
She was fussy enough about John for a few moments,
but soon showed to his friend's jealous eye that her
concern was not very deep.   He had arranged for
another drive, and was surprised and a little excited
when Sallie proposed to sit by his side on the box.
He could not deny that she was pretty, and certainly
exerted herself to be entertaining, and by the time
John and he went to see them off at the station, he
and Sallie were on the best possible terms.   It was
always easy for the impulsive fellow to imagine
himself in love with the last fair woman he had met,
and he began to think that really his ridiculous and
outrageous idea of solving all difficulties by stealing
his friend's sweetheart was not so altogether wild and
mad as he had thought.   Sallie did not attempt to

conceal her delight at the prospect of his coming visit to Bramwell; though Max would have liked her better if she had been more interested in the fact that John was going too. He slept soundly that night, and it was as well he did, for next day was wild and wet, and they were condemned to a long endurance indoors. John seemed uneasier than ever, and more than once announced his intention of going out, rain or no rain; but on Max making it clear that he would go with him, he seemed to grow more resigned, and abandoned the project. "That letter," said Max to himself. It proved a draggy, depressing, never-ending sort of a day, and as Max saw his friend sinking and growing more haggard every hour, he grew desperate and resolved to thresh the matter out again, even if it were only a fruitless repetition of old arguments. When they had retired for the night, therefore, he closed and locked the bedroom door, and startled John by challenging him about the letter. To his surprise the dejected fellow seemed glad to talk, and so they began, and step by step and point by point went over the whole ground.

"It only wants strength," cried John, at the end of an hour's hard contention; "it only wants manliness and a little common honesty to put the whole thing right."

"How?" and Max stared at his companion, half anticipating the answer.

"How! I must do the plain right. I must set Sallie free, I must resign the ministry I am no longer fit for, and I must stamp the image of Mary Wheeler out of my heart."

"Never! you shall not! God is not a monster! Some way will open if you will only wait, man!"

"God!" shouted John, and his whole frame shook with emotion. "Is God the condoner of sin? Are we to use Him to save us from the consequences of our own folly? Are we to expect Him to do for us what we can do for ourselves, and what for the sake of our own spiritual discipline and development we ought to do for ourselves? God is mercy, God is love, but God is not *soft*."

It was no use: Max the healthy-minded, the nimble-witted, the incurably-sanguine, had hoped to carry his point over John's feebleness by clamourous and impetuous rush of argument, but he soon realised that whatever might be the matter with his friend's body, his mind was clear enough, and saw everything with vivid, inexorable, even exaggerated distinctness; and so, after another long hour of haggling, which became more than once quite peevish, they ended where they had begun, and neither of them slept a wink that night.

Returning from a drive, abbreviated by the weather, next day, they found a note waiting them containing an invitation from Rose Cottage to spend the evening; and Max, weary and disheartened, allowed himself to be comforted by the thought that some help would surely come to him out of this visit. At the last moment John turned stubborn, and it was only when Max refused point blank to go without him that he yielded. The afternoon passed rather drearily, and it was a relief to more than one there when the male Wheelers came home. John even seemed to rouse up a little, for Mr. Wheeler made so much of his mother that he was touched by it, and exerted himself to be agreeable. All the same, every time he was left to himself he was found with bent head absorbed in painfully sad reflections. Mark Wheeler had rigged up a little lathe in an upstairs back room, and made some pretty articles of furniture, and as Mrs. Ledger expressed interest in his work, and there was also a

model of Mary's patent to be seen there, the whole
of those who were talking with the young mechanic
adjourned upstairs, and Max, gnawing his thumbs
and fighting with his perplexities, suddenly found
himself left alone with Miss Wheeler. She had been
playing for them, and still sat on the stool toying
absently with the piano keys. He watched her
furtively for a few minutes, but presently raising his
eyes he caught her looking at him. She neither
blushed nor smiled, but got quietly up, slipped
between him and the sofa arm, sat down close to
him, and then said gently—

"Mr. Ledger doesn't seem much better, Mr.
Ringley."

Max, nearly at his wits'-end with preplexity, felt
that those soft tones were sending the cup of his
troubles brimming over, and so he raised his head
and answered chokily—

"No."

Mary sat looking at him sideways, and then with a
sudden impulse she leaned forward, and placing her
hand shyly on his with a momentary touch she
said—

"God bless you! Mr. Ringley, you're a true friend
to him."

Max's head dropped suddenly on his breast; he
turned away his eyes, and then, with a swift change,
he looked up into her face, and in a voice trembling
with feeling he stammered—

"It's nothing to what he's been to me. Oh, Miss
Wheeler, there'll never be another John Ledger!"

It was the Wheelers who had arranged for the
specialist, and so, using the little information she had,
Mary, after another long pause, said—

"It is some mental or spiritual trouble, I
understand."

Max did not answer all at once; slowly, however,

he raised his head again and looked at her until the colour began to rise. Ah! this was a girl indeed! Here was a heart that could feel with him if only he dared tell her. His was not the sort of temperament to have to bear lonely burdens. Oh, that he could talk to somebody—her, for instance! He would tell her a little—nothing compromising, nothing that he ought not, but just enough to let her see where he was, and evoke her precious sympathy. No!—Yes! Well, he would be very discreet, and so as he talked, and the wonderful face he was watching grew soft with tender interest, his sore heart opened more and more, and he was soon pouring out the whole story. But he was not going to break his trust even under these gracious circumstances, and so he only mentioned that there was *a* second lady, of whom he was careful to speak in the third person. Mary was utterly unconscious, or seemed so to him. With parted lips and moist eyes she hung upon his words, until, gazing at her and absorbed in the witching glamour of her flattering and tender sympathy, he suddenly slipped out the wrong pronoun, and she was on her feet, the blood surging up through neck and cheek, and her whole face dyed in crimson. For a moment she stood in speechless embarrassment, and then, as footsteps were heard coming downstairs, she turned and rushed away, leaving him covered with confusion and shame, and more miserable than he had ever been.

How he got through the rest of that evening Max could never tell, and though Betty surpassed herself in audacious banter, he never rallied, and was heartily glad when the time came to depart. The only thing that interested him was the reappearance of Mary, but when at last she rejoined the company, except that she was a little paler, he could detect nothing that gave him any clue to her mind. When they were departing, however, as the little lobby did not give room enough for them all at once, Mary brought his coat into the little dining-room, and as she helped him on, she whispered—

"Mr. Ledger's troubles are very great, Mr. Ringley," and as he turned to look at her, wondering why she should make so very common-place a remark, she went on, "but none but a good and true man would ever have them; have faith in God, dear friend!"

CHAPTER VII

HOW SALLIE FOUND HER HEART

To the surprise of everybody at Rose Cottage, the reserved and almost stately Mary seemed almost gay in her high spirits when the visitors had left them. She hummed a tune, and smiled as she removed her father's shoes and playfully put on his slippers; she pulled Betty's long hair, and then kissed her for apology; she slipped into the little drawing-room, and strummed a few bars almost wildly on the piano, and then broke off abruptly to speak to their solitary domestic, whom she greatly astonished by addressing as "dear." Presently she broke out in earnest praise of Max for his devotion to his friend, but turned her head away in secret tears as her father expressed concern about John; in fact her whole conduct was so unlike her ordinary demeanour, that the men-folk went to bed mildly wondering what had come over her. The house was so small that she and Betty had to occupy the same room, but to-night she bustled her sister off before her, and having also got rid of the servant, she extinguished all the lights in the kitchen and lobby, and then, retreating to the warm dining-room, turned up the gas, and throwing herself into a big easy-chair, abandoned herself to thought. She was evidently profoundly affected; her eyes swam with soft warm light, her perfectly white skin seemed to gleam as from some deep, powerful, inward pleasure, and she sighed once and again with infinite contentment—

"He will not!" she murmured, with proud, confident joy, "he will not even for me"—and then, clasping her hands together, she cried, "Let him be true, O God! Let him conquer! Let him stand the test, and be a man, and do what Thou wilt with me!"

She sat musing in silence, and then, gazing absently at the jets in the little gas fire, she went on—

"Love him! Yea! If he fails I'll love him for the grand struggle he is making; but if he conquers, if he conquers, I'll be proud to kiss his feet!"

The glow of excitement faded slowly out of her face, and a long fit of pensive musing followed. All at once she started to her feet, crying—

"But it is wrong to love him! I'm committing the very sin I want to see him conquer!"

She turned half round with a repudiating gesture, and drew herself in as though shrinking from some suddenly discovered reptile; her breath came in short, quick gasps, and she cried out in a sort of holy horror—

"I'm expecting him to do what I cannot do myself."

Slowly, and as if all her strength had suddenly failed her, she sank down upon her knees, and bowing her head over the table and covering her face with her hands, she moaned—

"*Now* I know! *Now* I understand what he suffers! Poor, poor Mr. Ledger!"

For fully five minutes she remained motionless where she was, and finally, throwing back her head and revealing a drawn, vehement face, she cried—

"I cannot! I cannot! I do not ask to have him. Let him win his battle, Lord! Let me love him in secret and in silence for ever! O God! Great, good God! I am only a woman!"

   *   *   *   *   *

Max returned to John's lodgings that night in a very uneasy, fluctuating condition of mind. He saw now why Mary Wheeler could not care for him, but he saw also what serious complications might arise from his foolish confidences. But, after all, Mary knew the exact position of things now, and he could not entirely condemn himself. She was a wonderful girl, and he felt towards her all that quiet trustfulness which she contrived to inspire in the minds of all who came to know her. On the whole, therefore, he would like to have encouraged himself, and perhaps would have done so but for two puzzling facts. One was that he could no longer disguise from himself that some change was coming over John which he did not know how to interpret, and the other that Mrs. Ledger gave ominous indications that she had got to the end of her patience, and would not much longer be kept without a fuller explanation as to the condition of her son. He knew that examinations and over-work and recent friction in the circuit would not serve any longer as explanations, and he would either have to invent something else or tell her the truth. He had carried out the doctor's directions with painful exactitude, and had never left John for a moment night or day, except when absolutely compelled, and then for the fewest possible minutes. But all that Thursday Mrs. Ledger had given signs of wanting to speak to him alone, and he began to feel that if he did not heed her there would be fresh complications.

As they were retiring, therefore, he made a little signal to " mother " as, to her great delight, he had taken to calling her, and when John had dropped upon his knees by the bedside, he threw a dressing gown over his shoulders and joined the waiting mother in the other room.

With the simple directness which reminded him of John, she went straight to the point. There was not only something wrong with her son, but that something was of the most serious character, and they were keeping it from her. Did Max know what it was? He had grown confident, almost conceited, about his diplomacy during this very trying week, and so he gave her an evasive reply, which was the amplest confirmation he could have furnished of her fears; and the next moment she had put her finger on the very spot.

When she mentioned Sallie, he was startled, but when, in the very next sentence, she plumped out the name of Mary Wheeler, Max began to look at her as though she were something uncanny. There was a strained silence between them after he had made his half-unconscious nod of admission, and then, with a long, soft sigh, she said—

"Sallie's been very good to us all—but she's shallow! You know she never cared for him, for himself——"

"I think Miss Wheeler's more like the sort of girl for——"

"Her!" interrupted the anxious mother, "H-a-y. Ay, she's solid gold that creature is; she's good enough even for him."

There was a movement in the adjoining bedroom, and they both glanced nervously towards the door.

"It's hard! It's terrible hard!" moaned the poor mother.

"We must help him, mother! We must do something! What are we good for if we cannot help him now?"

Mrs. Ledger looked up in a little alarm, and seemed about to object, but then another thought came, and she dropped her eyes, and looked wistfully into the dying fire. "We munnat meddle! It's between him and his Maker, you know"—and then, lifting her head, with rapt face and glistening eyes she added, "We must help him as Moses helped Joshua. He's fightin' t' Malekites in t' valley, and we mun pray in t' mountain. We shall be in good company, you know."

"Good company, mother?"

"Ay, Miss Wheeler's prayin' for him this very minute, and we mun help her.—Good night, my lad," and making a shy, hasty snatch at his hand, she hurriedly kissed it, and moved off to her own bedroom.

Max heaved a sigh of relief; somehow his burden seemed lighter, and he almost burst into a cry of thankfulness when, on re-entering his bedroom and leaning over, he found John, for the first time, to his knowledge, that week, fast asleep.

The patient was distinctly better next morning; he talked a little after breakfast, and conducted their family devotions himself. His face was pinched enough, and his eyes looked sadly hollow; but self-possession and interest in life were evidently coming back to him, and Max struggled between hope and misgiving. It looked as though John had won his battle and made up his mind, but how? What had he concluded to do? and Max would have given much to have had the answer to these questions. They were to leave in the forenoon, John and his mother going straight home, and Max returning to his circuit until next day, when he would join them at Bramwell. He had so many things to think of that he only returned to the pressing anxieties connected with John now and again. Many a time during the Friday evening he laughed at himself and his fantastic plan for delivering his friend, and though at bottom he saw its quixotic and absurd character, there was something about it that fascinated him, and he found himself saying that if the worst came to the worst and Sallie improved as much on acquaintance as he felt she very easily might, all women being wonderfully delightful and trustworthy to him, he would make a plunge of it, and astonish John by taking the "stumbling-block" out of the way. Once the question insinuated itself into his pleasantly dreamy meditations, "How would John take such a manœuvre?" but he shut it out again. The wild, romantic absurdity of the idea vastly entertained him, and he did not know that the fact that it would, in all probability, never be tried made it the more delightful to speculate upon.

"Ye gods!" he chuckled as he sat over his Quaker oats that night, "ye Gods! what a cackle there would be! Stealing the sweetheart of his greatest friend! Ha, ha! Max, my boy, you'd be the talk of the Connexion for once! Abominable treachery by a probationer! The Conference paralysed with indignation! It's spicy! It's nuts!"

Then he flung his spoon into the large teacup that had held his food, and as the occasion seemed to justify any recklessness, he groped in a box at the side of his bookcase, and pulled out a faded and precarious cigarette, and in brazen defiance of Connexional regulations, lighted it and flung himself back into his reading-chair, stretched out his long legs, and chuckled again. "The Bramwellians will mob me," he grinned; "the diminutive broker will call me 'Judas,' and threaten my life; the 'saints' will be horrified; the Chairman will insist on a minor Synod; brother Ringley will be hauled up before his betters, and then—then—Mysterious collapse of the prosecution! Pathetic plea for the prisoner by the prosecutor, and—and—and—Tableau!"

At her father's death Sallie had improved her worldly appearance, and had gone to live, with Aunt Pizer as a housekeeper, in a pretty little villa next door but one to the super. She was left better off than was expected, and had set up a little governess car, which the super. occasionally had the loan of, and so Max, notwitstanding the great crazy plan he had in his head, was rather taken aback when the minister, after a hearty greeting, led the way to the station gate and introduced him to Sallie herself, seated with the reins in her hand, evidently waiting for him. She received him effusively, made him sit next to her, complimented him on his healthy appearance, and then rattled off into an animated and most flattering description of the grand doings they were expecting during the mission. This was playing into his hands with a vengeance; but, to his own surprise, it rather ruffled him, and he asked somewhat gruffly—

" How's John ? "

Sallie left the super. to answer, and before they were out of the station yard she was leaning over towards him, to the peril of the driving, and telling him that they were all very glad indeed that the Connexional evangelist could not come. He was to be entertained at the Manse, and Sallie, who was evidently on the best of terms with the occupants, came in to tea, and kept him in conversation and pressed dainties upon him until the poor fellow was out of countenance, and wished her far enough. What disgusted him most was that John was not there, and that Sallie never alluded to him, and, in fact, showed no concern for his welfare, but even kept Max half an hour in the drawing-room consulting him about the hymns to be used at the services, even after he had announced his desire to go and see his chum. And next day it was worse. She sent him some flowers to adorn the breakfast table, insisted on driving him and the rest of the occupants of the house to chapel, though the distance was short, and Max had scruples about unnecessary Sunday labour. At any other time he would have been pleased with the excellent taste she had displayed in her dress, but now he felt irritated as he glanced at her, and listened to her chatter with an inward resentment he had difficulty in keeping out of his face. She was delighted with his sermon, and with affected shyness declined the invitation to dine, insisting that he would want a " nap "—a thing which Max detested on a Sunday. She came in, however, to tea, and spent the rest of the day with them.

" Where's John ? " he demanded abruptly, as they were walking home after the evening service. " And why is he not dressed in clericals ? "

" Isn't he ? I never noticed ! You see, we know him so well, we don't observe."

" It would be better for you if you did know him," Max thought, but what he said was simply a muffled grunt.

The services, in spite of the lateness of the season, were a great success. Max had the golden mouth ; in the pulpit he was irresistible, and very delightful results began to manifest themselves, and the little town simmered with excitement. On Monday Sallie came with John in the governess car, and insisted on taking them both out for a long drive ; and on Tuesday the experiment was repeated, but by this time Max had conceived a feeling towards Sallie which made him barely civil to her. The services seemed to be doing John good ; he entered heartily into them, and Max was delighted that anything could appeal to him and bring him out of his hopeless lassitude. It was decided to continue the gatherings to the end of the second week, and Max's chief anxiety was how to deal with the almost indecently prominent attentions of Sallie. But on the Thursday he never saw her all day ; she was absent from the

Bible reading service in the afternoon, where she had hitherto generally sung a solo, and did not turn up at night; and he discovered by a cautious question that she had not been, as he hoped, with John. On Friday, inquiry by the Manse people elicited the information that Miss Wood was unwell, and Max had so strong a prejudice against her, that he had not the charity to believe in her excuse, but suspected her crafty angling for sympathy.

Max was in trouble with himself. He had always had such faith in all women, and this girl was actually making him feel mean and suspicious towards them. He would see her at Jericho before he would ask after her again. The idea of delivering his friend by running away with Sallie still seemed to him a triumph of brilliant strategy, but he also realised that it was impossible as far as he was concerned. He *could not*, even to save John Ledger.

The second Sunday, a day long to be remembered in Bramwell Methodism, passed away. Such congregations, such "unction," and such delightful results as the oldest Methodist had never seen before. Wilky Drax, with whom Max had struck up a violent friendship, refused to open his shop at all on the Monday, but spent his time standing at the paint shop door bareheaded, and tackling any unregenerates who gave him the opportunity about their "souls."

On Monday morning, however, Max declined an invitation for a drive with the super., and went and hunted John up, with the intention of having things out with him. John responded promptly enough, and they strolled out and down the old lane beyond Ledger's house.

"That is where Sallie was born," said John languidly, as they passed the farm.

" And the place where you went courting, eh?

Now, old fellow, where are we? I'm getting out of my depth."

"Just where we were," and the old haggard look came back into his face.

"Ah!" and Max pulled up and looked searchingly at his friend. "Johnny, old chap, I was beginning to hope; you have seemed so much better this last few days."

"Yes, one cause of anxiety has been removed."

"What's that?"

"I can see clearly enough that—well, that it will not break her heart."

"Ah! Good! Then if *she* doesn't make a fuss——"

"Ah, that's another thing! That is just what she would do, unless she had another string to her bow, of which I see no sign. I was afraid that I was slighting a true woman's love, but I don't think now she ever really cared for me."

"More fool she, then. But 'all's well that ends well.' We shall worry through now."

"How?"

"How? Well, if she never really cared for you, you've done her no great harm. Throw her over, and serve her right. If the worst comes to the worst, you'll only get put back a year or two, and Mary will wait."

"Oh, Max, will you never see?"

"See what? It's all right, isn't it?"

John wearily shook his head.

"Well, of all the—— But what's the hitch now?"

"God!"

"God? Ledger, I could shake you! You're morbid, man; you're dotty!"

"Max," and John spoke in that deliberate, quietly-decided tone at once so inexorable and yet so irritating to his friend, "God took me, a poor factory lad, and lifted me into this holy ministry, and I have dishonoured myself and brought pain and shame upon others by ceasing to love the woman I was pledged to, and—oh, bitterness of hell—loving another woman."

"But hang it, man!" cried Max, at this dogged repetition of a statement he was utterly weary of hearing; and then he broke off and demanded sullenly, "Well, what's your gnat-straining prudery going to do next?"

John blinked his eyes and winced, and then, drawing himself together, he said slowly—

"The least I can do in gratitude for the fact that Sallie is not injured is to prevent Methodism having the pain of expelling me. The money Methodism has spent upon me shall not be lost. I'll earn my own living, and preach every Sunday as a layman—if they'll let me."

And that was only the commencement of the argument. For over an hour they went at it, ding, dong! Max shouted and gesticulated, dropped his voice, and nearly cried in tender expostulation; bullied, almost threatened, until at last, nervous and excitable with the results upon himself of his preaching efforts, and utterly exasperated at John's relentless interpretation of the situation, he turned and snapped out a sentence he would have given worlds to recall the very next moment—

"Confound it, man, don't be such a Pharisee! She *is* injured after all—— Oh, Johnny, don't! Dear old Johnny, don't! I didn't mean it! Forgive me!"

But the mischief was done. In the state of mind into which John had brought himself, he saw at once that, though Sallie might still be heart-whole, yet in the judgment even of his friend he had done her a great injury, and at least had interfered with her chances of becoming suitably and happily married.

This appeared to Max a ridiculous refinement of the facts, but to John it was terribly real, and though he still clung to his one little crumb of comfort, the iron had been forced into his soul once more, and he gave himself up to fresh self-reproach.

"Then you've made up your mind?" said Max fiercely, after another half-hour's struggle.

John sighed, looked at his friend with eyes that wrung Max's soul, and then said quietly—

"I shall write to the President to-day."

Max had to struggle with his emotions for some time, and at last, putting his hand on John's shoulder with a half-caressing touch, so natural and yet so irresistible in him, he asked, with the suspicion of tears in his eyes, and voice that was almost choked—

"Dear old fellow, grant me one last request."

"What is it?"

"Wait one week; just one little week. I feel sure something will be done before then. If *you* ought to leave the ministry, where am I and lots of others of us? Wait a week; just one week."

"It would have been all over a fortnight ago but for you; will you promise me not to ask me again?"

"I promise."

"Then I will wait one week, but nothing will come of it; nothing *can* come of it."

They parted presently, and Max, perturbed and infinitely saddened, left his friend at the door of his mother's cottage, and was plunging along the street, when, glancing aside, he caught sight of Sallie Wood, and she was actually trying to pass him unobserved! Yes, and it was not prudery. She was confused and shy, but entirely without affectation. As their eyes met, it came into Max's mind to appeal to her to release John. He would tell her the whole truth, and surely she would have some sense and some mercy. But the sight of her face touched him; her evident but inexplicable embarrassment puzzled him; and he began to wonder whether she was in some spiritual trouble. Common politeness prompted him to ask after her health, and to enquire where she had been the last few days. She seemed to be angry at her own confusion, and recovering with a great effort, explained that she was not very well, and then put out her hand to part. In sheer astonishment he let her go, and walked back to the Manse more perplexed and distraught than ever. He soon found himself pitying the girl. She was fond of John after all, and had found out something which was giving her great distress. When she came once more to the afternoon meeting and took the solo, she looked so tenderly and wistfully sorrowful that he called himself a brute for his hard thoughts, and began to fear that he had been doing her a wrong in urging John to break with her. And so the time slipped by. The mission closed on the Friday night, but there was to be a grand tea meeting on the Saturday for the reception of the hundred and sixty odd new converts, and Max had been prevailed upon to stay for the gathering, although it would mean reaching his own home about midnight. During the time he had been in Bramwell the fantastic idea of proposing to Sallie as a means of relieving his friend had been driven from his mind by his unconquerable dislike of her, and now the soft-hearted fellow was beginning to turn to it again out of sheer pity for her. Successful always with women, save for one memorable instance, and sustained by that harmless sort of vanity so characteristic of such natures, he did not greatly doubt that he could comfort her, and really it was a hard case to be robbed of a husband, and especially such a husband as he felt certain John would make. " Poor girl! poor little thing!" he said to himself again and again. "She has a heart after all, and she's pretty. She's prettier than ever now she's in trouble and ill."

All this affected his nerves, already unstrung by the excitements of the mission, and on Saturday morning he was so restless he could neither read nor think. He would require a sermon for his own pulpit at Longhope on the following morning, but, though he shut himself up in the super.'s study, he only seemed thereby to be giving a better opportunity to the worrying enemy to harass him. Nothing could he think of but Sallie and John, and John and Sallie, and then Sallie and himself. More than once the impulse came upon him to rush out and tell her how John felt, and then if she *did* seem cut up about it, why he must comfort her—he must, even if she were very disconsolate;—but he never got further than that.

Then he wondered whether it would do any good to unbosom himself to that motherly soul, Mrs. Cloughton, his hostess. Yes,—but no; the remembrance that the things that burdened his heart were others' secrets as well as his checked him, and he got no further. At dinner he ate so little that his hostess insisted on dosing him with *nux vomica*, and he was too weary and sick at heart to resist.

"It is May day, Mr. Ringley; go out into the garden a while, it will do you good," said the motherly soul, and Max, indifferent what he did, sauntered forth presently into the sunshine. There was a large kitchen garden behind the Manse into which Max had never been, but after wandering aimlessly about in the front for a few moments, he raised the catch of the trellis gate and entered. The super. joined him for some time, and then was called away to attend to a caller. Max was glad to be alone again, and wandered up and down the neatly trimmed paths, pondering the difficulty which had taken such hold upon him. Scarcely knowing what he did, he strayed toward the bottom of the garden, and spying a seat,

flung himself down upon it and was soon absorbed
in fretful musings. Presently he heard footsteps
approaching, and expecting to see the super. returning
to him he raised his head, but there was no one
in sight. The footsteps came nearer; they were
evidently behind him, close to him in fact, and just as
he was looking round they stopped. Where was he?
and who was the new-comer? As softly as possible
he took a survey of his position, and discovered that
the seat on which he sat leaned against a summer-
house in the next garden. The building was old and
covered with climbing plants, and as he gazed stupidly
at it he caught a glint of colour amongst the twisted
stems. Half unconsciously he leaned forward and
noticed a long crack half hidden with the foliage,
and through the crack, of all persons in the world,
Sallie Wood! He drew a long breath; it seemed as
if Providence were throwing him in this girl's way,
unless indeed she had seen him come out and was—
but he dismissed the unworthy thought. Then he
recollected that as Sallie's house was round the
corner from the Manse she must have a garden
behind that touched the one he was in, and that she
was therefore in her own grounds. Had she seen
him? Should he speak to her? Could he keep sufficient restraint upon himself if she turned pathetic—
but before he could settle these points he heard a
sound like a sob, and was compelled to have a second
peep. Yes, it was she. She wore a dainty dress of
some light material that suited her admirably, and he
felt a thrill of admiration as he glanced her over from
head to foot. But what was this? She was crying,
and crying with her face uncovered, in evident
unconsciousness of any other presence. The sight
of her made his heart melt. He would speak to her at
any cost and get to the bottom of these things. But
at that moment there were other footsteps, and as he

peeped again through the handy crack, lo! John Ledger came round the curve of the box-edged path and approached the rickety summer-house. Max could not have moved at that moment if his life had depended upon it. Sallie did not rise, did not even raise her head as her lover came up, and when he seated himself on the edge of the seat opposite to her she still continued to look ruefully at her pretty shoe. With a strange, fascinating feeling, as though conscious that this was no chance meeting, Max watched the couple from his questionable vantage point.

"John"—and Sallie, whose voice sounded inexpressibly tender to the susceptible watcher, raised her eyes with an expression in them that was new to Max—"John, will you be absolutely frank with me if I am with you? I never have been, alas! but I will be now."

John raised his eyes in weary surprise and simply nodded.

"John, do you really love Mary Wheeler?"

Max in his concealment gasped, and John sprang as if stung to his feet.

"Don't think I'm going to scold you, John dear, or reproach you—I've lost a love I never knew how to value—but I do want to know. Do you, John?"

And her tone was so humble and pleading that Max felt he could have hugged her.

"Yes, Sallie!—God forgive me!"

There was another pause; some deep, strong emotion was shaking Sallie's very soul. At last, however, she raised her tear-dimmed eyes and asked—

"With all your heart and mind and soul and strength, John?"

John, staring as if he saw an apparition, mechanically nodded.

"And do you feel that—that the world would be a blank and a wilderness if she were not in it?"

" Yes, but——"

Sallie had risen and gone close to her lover; she now raised her hand and checked his words.

"And do you feel mean and cheap in her presence, and common, as though she belonged to some superior kind of beings and you were unworthy to speak to her?"

John had evidently no more amazement left in him, and simply nodded stupidly again.

"And do you feel that if you could serve her, be her slave, do anything that would give her pleasure, that *that* would be the greatest joy on earth, even though she never looked at you?"

Once more, dazed and almost breathlessly, John said "Yes."

She paused a long time now, with her head down; when she raised it, her face was flushed and red and her eyes gleamed with tears.

"Then go to her, John dear, and be happy! and may the good Lord bless you both."

Max, with dimmed eyes, stared at the crack, and felt he wanted to jump over the wall and kiss her, and John, overwhelmed by this most amazing and unexpected denouement, simply fell back in his seat and sobbed.

Max could not, of course, attempt to leave at this point lest the others should find they had been overheard, but as he was struggling with a conscience that was calling him hard names for eavesdropping he heard a soft sound, and looking through his spy-hole he saw Sallie on her knees and her arms round her lover.

"I didn't know, John! I didn't!" she cried piteously. "I cannot bear it, when I think how deceitful and mean and cruel I have been, but I didn't know!"

"Didn't know what?" asked John, almost as much moved as she was.

" I didn't know what it meant to be—to be—to be in love."

" In love ? "

" Yes, in love ! Oh, John, I'm in love ! and if you have suffered one thousandth part what I suffer now I'm sorry, oh, so sorry ! "

" It cannot be, Sallie ; it must not——"

" It can ! It must ! I'll go to her myself. I'll beg her on my knees to love you. You are worthy of her, and I'm a poor, wicked, selfish girl."

But for the boards between them Max would have been picking her up and kissing her, and as it was he made sounds which if the others had been less absorbed they must have heard. He felt also a strong anger arising within him against the cold-hearted John.

" I tried to be true, Sallie," began John again, but she interrupted him.

" True ! you were true ! Why, John, you loved me once—really *loved* me ! But, oh, I never loved you ! and now I am justly punished."

And Max began to think that John had some bowels after all as he answered—

" You shall not be punished, dear. I'll conquer my wicked passion. I'll love you, Sallie. I always should have loved you if you had been like this ; but now we'll be married, dear. I'll conquer it and you will help me ! "

" Conquer it ! " and she was on her feet in indignation. " You cannot conquer it if it is real ! You must not ! It is a holy thing ! It is irresistible ! Oh, John, how *can* you ? "

" How have you found all this out ? " asked John suddenly, after a long silence, and he was in his heart secretly suspecting that even this might only be one of her wiles.

" Found it out ? Love ! Love has taught me ! I love, myself, at last, and now I know. Oh ! how could

I have been so cruel to you, John? for you really loved me once; now didn't you?"

"Yes, Sallie, I did, and——"

"No! No! I love another! He will never look at me! He is high above me, and I am but dirt under his feet. I shall never be with him, never be his, but oh! to love is enough; it is bliss! it is heaven itself, only—only it is so painful," and with this inconsistent little confession she hid her face in her hands and the tears dropped through her fingers to the ground. "I cannot tell you who it is, John. I will never—never—Oh yes, I will. I *must* tell just one person in the world! It is—it is your—Oh no! what am I saying? I dare not! I dare not!"

But John saw it, and Max, sinking through the floor with fright and wonder and pity, and he knew not what besides, gave a sudden gasp and then sprang back and was discovered. He wanted to flee, but his feet refused to do their office, and he could not have moved whatever had depended upon it. John came hastily to the other side of the boards and gasped "Max!" and Sallie, with a frightened, woeful little scream, that remained with Max for many a day, fled, and when at last he started after her, shouting apologies and explanations, she rushed indoors and fled to her room. Max was so consumed with shame and distress and pity for the poor girl that he could not be pacified, but John held him back and quieted him and made him sit down and talk.

The two friends parted presently, John in a state of mind he would have found it impossible to describe, and Max consumed with one great resolve to see Sallie and apologise and propose to her. On that point he was immovable; he called twice at her house and pressed to be allowed to speak to Sallie, but was refused. He came back to Bramwell

on Monday by an early train, more intent on his
purpose than ever, only to discover that Sallie had
gone to London and would not be back for an
indefinite period. Then he would go to London
after her! Poor dear girl, she must be sick with
shame! Was there ever so cowardly a thing done
to a woman since the world began? Why, if it were
only as an atonement or reparation for the wrong he
must win her, but besides, she was pretty and sweet—
and John! why John hadn't loved her was at that
moment incomprehensible to him. But neither Aunt
Pizer nor anybody else could give him any address
where he would be likely to find the girl he thought
he was now in love with. He stayed all night arguing
with John, who was even now almost as severe upon
himself as he had ever been, and on Tuesday morning
there came a tender, plaintive letter from Sallie to
her old lover, urging him to go to Mary Wheeler
and be happy, and threatening that if he hesitated or
tortured himself any more she would write to Rose
Cottage herself. By the afternoon post of the same
day came a letter to Max from the same source. A
shy, timid, touchingly humble message it was,
appealing piteously to him to keep her secret and
never attempt to get speech with her. Max cried
like a great girl as he read it, and vowed that if he
had to wait until he was fifty he would have her, and
her only. It took some time to get John entirely
convinced that his course was now clear, but when
Sallie wrote a second time to say that she was so
grieved at the trouble she had wilfully given him and
all the deceptions she had practised upon him that
she had written to Mary Wheeler asking her forgive-
ness, John felt that something must be done now,
and so he returned to Mary and his work. Work,
the great healer, soon brought back the natural
buoyancy of his mind, and although Mary held back

for a time, she let him see how proud she was of the struggle he had made with his conscience, and soon made him a happy man. Wilky Drax got himself into hot water by waiting upon Max when he was one day in Bramwell and offering him sage and characteristic advice to be aware of Sallie Wood, and the friendship between the two was only preserved by Mrs. Drax's gentle intercession. Mary's patent proved a little gold mine to the firm; they were soon back in the old house; the old bank became also a paying thing once more. When John and Mary were married, Max, who had almost forgotten his passion for Sallie in his devotion to his last hobby, photography, "took" the bridal party, and had a characteristic quarrel with the bridesmaid, but notwithstanding these things the Bramwell people stick to it that Mr. Ringley will marry Sallie Wood, and the Partidge folk are just as certain he will marry Betty.

Latest reports concerning him, however, state that he has been announcing some very original views on the celibacy of the clergy.

Sallie has become a sister of the people.

THE END.

BRADBURY, AGNEW, & CO. LD., PRINTERS, LONDON AND TONBRIDGE.

THE COMING
OF THE
PREACHERS

Bibliographical note:

this facsimile has been made from a copy in the
British Museum
(04410.f.29)

THE COMING OF
THE PREACHERS

The Coming of the Preachers

A TALE OF THE RISE OF METHODISM

By
JOHN ACKWORTH

LONDON: HODDER AND
STOUGHTON   27
PATERNOSTER ROW 1901

Printed by Hazell, Watson, & Viney, Ld., London and Aylesbury.

PREFATORY NOTE

ENGLAND in the time of John Wesley was a country of small towns and villages. Roads were few and bad, and means of intercommunication primitive and mostly expensive. There was, therefore, an isolation and remoteness about provincial life which we in these times find it difficult to realise. But the majority of the inhabitants of Great Britain lived in these same self-contained and unchanging townlets; and this story is written to illustrate the rise of Methodism, by showing how that great movement came to a representative small borough, and how it affected the lives, characters, and interests of the inhabitants.

PATRICROFT, 1901.

v

CONTENTS

CHAPTER I

A DANGEROUS FLIRTATION

"OH, plague on't! I never shall o'er-master it—never!" And the fiddle slipped from under her dimpled chin and dropped to her side, whilst she sank into an elbow-chair, raised her black brows, and puckered her forehead, a picture of pretty, half-earnest despair.

And her teacher, standing at her side with a piece of resin between his fingers, looked down upon her with hungry eyes. Alas! that was all he could ever do when, as now, he was able to watch her unnoticed; for though he was a very wise and sober young man, who prided himself much upon his self-control, he lost nerve and sense and everything else in the presence of this tantalising young beauty.

And she knew it, and played upon it, and did as she liked with him, and then sent him from her presence to grind his teeth and teach himself to hate her; for though he was only her uncles' apprentice, just out of his time, and she was an heiress in her own right and the next owner of the business, and had been to London and even to the Bath Wells, he felt

himself as good as she was and far cleverer;
but at the same time he knew only too well
that she would scorn a mere journeyman, and
was as ambitious in her way as he was in his.
Oh for a peep into that incomprehensible little
heart!

They had grown up together. From the first
week of his apprenticeship he had been her slave;
he had made and repaired her "babies" (dolls),
and smuggled gingerbread animals for her from
the, to her, forbidden fair. When she was quite big
he had carried her home from local routs, lest she
should wet her dainty slippers in the rutty, muddy
lanes, and had compromised his own conscience
by surreptitiously purchasing for her contraband
literature from the travelling chapmen. Later
still he had bought, out of his scanty earnings,
that wonderful new story book about a certain Mr.
Robinson Crusoe, and in the long winter evenings,
when her uncles were at the Hanover Arms, he
had sat in the tall-backed chair in the parlour
and read to her.

Even after that ever-memorable visit to the
capital she had, after a while, returned to
the old intimacy, though now, alas! it was
often interrupted by temporary, though very
irritating, assumptions of superiority, with quite
as sudden and embarrassing lapses into the old
affectionateness. But for the last two years they
had been drifting further and further apart, for
she was more frequently "my lady," and he,
warned by repeated snubs, was learning to know
his place.

Recently, however, after an unusually lengthy fit of loftiness, occasioned, he suspected, by the attentions of a certain young lieutenant home for a visit, she had become suddenly very complacent, and had finally cajoled him into teaching her to play on the fiddle, and this was her fourth lesson.

Hitherto the practices had been to Mark Rawson periods of delicious misery, for, for the first time in his life, he had found "young mistress" a dull scholar. She was clever, that he knew, and could learn anything she gave her mind to, having acquired quite a local reputation for her skill upon the harpsichord. But upon his beloved violin she either could not or would not make any progress, and so he was tortured with the suspicion that she was only using the instrument as a means of bringing them together. But if so, why?

Was she changing her mind about him now that he was free of his apprenticeship and a full journeyman? or was she only consoling herself with him because of the defection of the officer? He would be no man's stopgap! Even this bewitching creature should not make him forget what was due to himself. He was not her equal quite, but he was a man, and free and ambitious, and she should not play with him though she were ten times as enslaving as she was.

These and many like thoughts were racing through his brain as he stood looking down upon his fair pupil.

"Nay, mistress, try again.   'Twas but that
the fingering was wrong," he said at length,
keeping the utmost restraint upon himself as he
spoke.

"Fingers!   My fingers are cobbler's thumbs,
methinks"; and, passing her fiddle-bow into the
left hand, she held out the other with a gesture of
mock disgust, and displayed a dainty little thumb
and four pink fingers, a little too short for correct
shape, but soft and tender as a babe's.

Mark gazed at the gleaming digits and the
slim wrist and round little arm, bare to the elbows,
and felt the teacher in him giving way to the
man.

"Naught's amiss wi' the fingers," he said a little
constrainedly.   "Look at mine," and he stretched
out a strong, sinewy palm and held it within a
few inches of hers.

"Oh, la! what a monster!" and with a gay
little laugh she rose to her feet and put her hand
close to his to compare them; in the comparison
she touched his thumb with hers, and it thrilled
him to the toes.   Then she dropped her fiddle-bow
and held up her other hand, to show that it would
take both hers to equal his, and as she touched
him again Mark had to fight with a mighty
impulse to take the two pink-and-white morsels
in his grasp.   In his struggle the tortured teacher
sighed, which brought a quick glance from the
fair tormentor, and, letting her hands fall to
her side, she said in meek, almost apologetic
tones:

"Let me try but once again," and turned

and picked up her instrument. For several
bars he heard the lesson faithfully reproduced,
and then, just as he was glancing round the
room, still intent upon the music, there came a
rasping discord and a petulant cry of despair from
the pupil.

"The wrong finger again! the wrong finger,
mistress!" he cried, raising his hands in deprecation.

"Well, well, I did as I was told. Look there!"
and she came close to him and showed him her
finger still pressed on the string.

"Ah, but t'other finger, mistress."

"How? That?"

"Nay, nay! the other, the third. Ah! but not
there!"

Two or three times she changed her fingers, but
still they were not satisfactory.

"Why, do it thyself; put the fingers on the
place thyself—put them on. Thou art not afeared
to touch them!"

And Mark bent over and took the fingers in
his and adjusted them to their places, whilst his
own tingled, and he felt he was blushing like
a girl. It took a long time to arrange so small a
matter, for the lady either could not or would not
understand, and at length he put his hand under
hers, as it clasped the neck of the instrument,
and, bending his finger over the strings, showed
her exactly how each finger was to be placed.
The instruction was carefully given, and the
fair pupil showed such innocent intelligence and
apparent desire to learn that all Mark's doubts
of her melted away, and as she began gently to

draw her hands from under his, prudence and pride, and all things else, vanished; and, grasping the little fingers in his, he raised them hastily to his lips and kissed them passionately.

The fiddle slipped down upon a lambskin rug at her feet, and Mark, glad to hide for a moment his burning face, stooped down and picked it up. He dare not look in his mistress's face, and if he had done he would have been no wiser, for her own feelings were so divided at the moment that her only safety lay in keeping expression out of it. But now he was raising his eyes to hers, and so, to cover her thoughts, she burst out mockingly:

"So, so! our new journeyman is amorous! But I had forgot, he is *free* now."

Mark winced at the cutting double meaning she put into her "free," and, with dropped head and sullen Dutch courage, he muttered:

"I am not free, mistress."

"Not? How? Why this finger bussing, then? Am I a cook-maid or a sewing-woman?"

Under this cruel cut Mark's great frame quivered in every limb, but the long-pent-up feelings of his heart were now too near his lips to be checked even by this, and so, with a painful effort at self-control, he clenched his hands together, and said:

"Mistress, for my great liberty I humbly crave your pardon. I could have worshipped you and loved you, and held my peace, but you have not let me! You have encouraged me, and then flouted me. You have been betimes kindly cruel and cruelly kind. You have deceived me, you have tempted me ; but now, by the great God, you shall hear me ! I love you, and I hate myself for loving you. You have unmanned me ; you have humbled and enslaved me ; you have bewitched me ; but were I to become your equal to-day, were you the only woman left in Britain, I would never, never ask you to wed me !"

She was below the medium height, but as she drew herself up and lifted her great brown eyes to his she looked a very empress. She brushed back an unruly lock of hair with imperious gesture, her lip curled haughtily, her bosom heaved under her lace tucker, and she was just about to fling at him an annihilating retort, when a sudden change swept over her, tears rushed into her eyes, her whole body collapsed, and she would have sunk helplessly to the floor if he had not caught her in his arms.

"Oh, what have I done? what have I done?" he cried distractedly. But the limp little figure on his left arm sobbed on. "Forgive me, dear mistress ! oh, forgive me, I—I—— Oh, heavens! the master!"

In the side of the room there was a door leading into the shop, in the upper panel of this door was a small window, and as Mark lifted his head he caught sight of a round snub nose and two chubby cheeks, surmounted by a pair of rolling grey eyes, flattened against the glass.

The hitherto limp and sobbing maiden recovered herself with startling suddenness, and with a sharp, scared cry rushed into the extreme corner of the room, and darted off upstairs. Mark drew himself together and turned toward the door. The jolly face had disappeared from the window and the latch of the door rattled a little significantly. Then there came a series of hardly forced little coughs, followed by another movement of the " sneck," the door opened slowly, and in came the junior member of the firm with whom Mark had just finished his apprenticeship.

He was a broad-set, middle-sized, comfortable-looking sort of man, who only wanted a little more colour to suggest the old English country squire. His brown wig was rather carelessly put on, and showed some tags of red hair under its edges. He wore a long-waisted, ample-skirted blue coat without the heavy collar that was then " the mode," an equally large waistcoat plentifully sprinkled with snuff, blue breeches and stockings, and buckled shoes. He sauntered with slow, shy, apologetic manner into the parlour, blowing the air of an old roundel through his still well-preserved teeth, and ostentatiously ignoring the prostrate violin and the disarranged furniture. Once or twice he pursed out his lips and gazed up at the dark oak joists above his head, and finally pulled out an enormous brass box of snuff, and helped himself.

Mark, meanwhile, was trying to recover himself. He had picked up the fiddle and hung it upon a nail between the window and the cupboard, pushed away the elbow-chair so recently occupied by his mistress, and was stooping down to poke the wood and turf fire when Mr. Ebenezer turned to him, and, with an air of sudden confidence, put his hand on his shoulder ; and whilst Mark was wincing in anticipation of some mild request for an explanation of the recent scene, he said in low, serious tones :

" Mark boy, I've bottomed the Muggletonians."

Mark, on whose face relief and amusement were struggling together, replied with an overdone simulation of interest :

" Ah ! truly ! that is good hearing, sir."

Mr. Ebenezer took another pinch of snuff, stared hard and musingly at his employee, and then, as the puckers of a stern conviction gathered on his brow, he said :

" Mark, Muggletonianism is balderdash ! "

" Worse than the Aminadabs, sir ? "

" Aminadabs ! "   And here Mr. Ebenezer's thoughts seemed suddenly to take a wider range. " Mark boy, the Aminadabs are sly and slow, but, rabbit them ! they are mighty sure.   Brag is a good dog, but Holdfast is better.   ' Fast bind, fast find,' that's the Dabs, boy !—that's the Dabs ! "

" 'Tis you for nosing out heresy, sir," murmured Mark admiringly.

" Heresy !   Ah, that minds me," and putting down his snuff-box on the table near him, he dived into the capacious left-hand pocket of his coat, and produced two or three tracts evidently fresh from the printer's, and in a few moments he and Mark were deeply engrossed in discussing the titles ; for in 1744 theological pamphlet literature was very abundant, and, of course, very popular.

The tracts, with their long, involved, and bellicose titles, proved very interesting to one, at least, of the men who were examining them ; but just as Mr. Ebenezer had got engrossed in a description of the bearings of a very fierce controversy with which one of them was connected, the door leading from the shop opened again, and in stepped Mr. Josephus, the senior partner of the firm, and Mark was glad of an excuse to retire.

With a respectful salutation to the newcomer, he slipped away, and was soon standing in the little back office with an account-book opened before him. Once and again he dipped his quill into the ink-pot, but on each occasion he paused, pen in air, and stood staring hard and absently over the screen into the shop.

He was not exactly handsome, though his face was square and clean-cut, and had an air of strength about it, but there was a restlessness in his eyes and a tightness about the lips that suggested constant internal conflict, and made those who watched him uncomfortable. His masters were hatters, and had a slow, old-fashioned business in the equally slow and steady-going market town of Helsham, in the north Midlands. They were comfortably off and lived simply, and had both reached that period of life when men want to carry things easily.

Consequently, when, about two years before the time of which we now speak, they had ascertained by actual testing that their apprentice was a smart, trustworthy lad, they had brought him out of the cellar workshop, and had placed him in the office, and, in course of time, he had come to have the whole of the business of the firm in his hands, and had, with the assistance of a salesman, set his masters at liberty to pursue their own hobbies. For these two old gentlemen were both faddists in their way. Ebenezer, as we have seen, was a theologian, though of a somewhat eccentric order, and Josephus was a politician and a town councillor.

Their niece was also their ward, and though she had been an alarming addition to the bachelor family when first she arrived, she not only easily established herself, but very soon became a wilful tyrant, whose whims they would never cross themselves nor allow any one else to cross if they could prevent them. She was, in a small way, an heiress, and as she grew to womanhood had developed a somewhat striking beauty.

That she must marry well the two old fogies had long since settled, though they lived in painful uneasiness under the consciousness that when it came to matrimony she would not be likely to consult their wishes, except they should happen to coincide with her own. But they had a duty to perform to their brother's child, and in a dull sort of way they intended to do it.

And all this was known full well by their recently enfranchised apprentice, and provided matter for meditation to him as he stood reflecting in the little back office. He was not likely to forget that he had become indispensable to his masters, and that they could not carry on without him, neither did he overlook the fact that tradesmen's daughters had sometimes been known to marry their father's apprentices.

Overlook it? That was one of the things that complicated the situation. It was one of the stalest of stale jokes amongst apprentices and young journeymen, and the subject of chaff in every pothouse frequented by their class in the country. Hadn't he himself been teased about it times without count? Was it not the most popular theme of the chapbooks and ballads hawked and sung at country fairs? The thing had become a sort of scandal, and a very sore point with all self-respecting tradesmen; so much so that he knew it would make one of his greatest difficulties, and he smiled bitterly as he imagined the scorn with which the proud young beauty, before whom he had just bemeaned himself, would receive any such idea.

In any case he would have had a difficult task, requiring infinite care and long patience, and now, behold! he had spoilt his chance for ever by losing control of himself and estranging his mistress, perhaps permanently. But the bitterest thought of all to this proud, sensitive fellow was that he had abased himself in his own eyes. He had allowed passion and pride to carry him away, and stood condemned at the bar of his own conscience.

Why was it that she had such power to unman

him and make him do what both self-interest and
self-respect forbade? He had acted like a baby,
like an undisciplined cur ; and as he thought of
it he jammed the feather end of his quill into
his mouth, and gnawed at it in bitterest self-
reproach.

CHAPTER II

FEMININE DIPLOMACY

WHILST young Mark was grinding his teeth and inwardly cursing his own impetuous folly and pride in the shop-office, his two masters were fidgeting about in the parlour, looking for signs of the evening meal. Mr. Josephus, who was tall and thin, was dressed like his brother, except that he wore a somewhat imposing bag-wig, and the three-cornered hat he took off as he entered was more severely cocked, as became a man of his public pretensions. The room they occupied was a long, narrow apartment with a mullioned window of exceptional width opposite the shop door. It was wainscoted all round, and at one end was a wide fireplace with a florid Queen Anne grate, whilst at the opposite one was a shelf-rack containing pots of delph-ware and a few articles in china, and on the lowest shelf a row of pewter plates.

Besides the door into the shop there was one near the window that led down into the cellar kitchen, and another at the end of the pot-rack that led to the upstairs rooms. The furniture was for the most part heavy and ugly, and included several stiff, high-backed chairs and an uninviting settee.

Mr. Josephus grew impatient, and stamped on the oak floor under his feet as a signal to the maid to bring up the food. Mr. Ebenezer was evidently uneasy also, but for a different reason. He lifted his wig and scratched underneath it, took out his snuff-box, and commenced to polish it on the knee of his breeches, and glanced restlessly every moment or two in the direction of the door through which his niece had so recently disappeared.

Presently Kerry, the maid, a stout, middle-aged woman, deeply pock-marked and covered with perspiration, came in with an aggrieved air and began to place the pewter plates on the table, and at the same instant a step was heard overhead, and a moment later the young mistress appeared. She looked none the worse for her fit of crying, and though she shot a quick, inquiring glance at Uncle Ebenezer, she put on a bright look and an easy manner, and drew up to the table.

"Kerry, you draggletail! your hair's all a tousle. How oft shall I tell you not to come before your masters i' that way? Will you never be aught but a slut?"

"Slut I—fatkins!" and poor Kerry was almost crying in her indignation. "Is't not the brew-day an' the fair-week? and hesn't the racketing Peter been wi' the small coal, an' me wi' me pore head lifting and lurchin' wi' the megrims?"

Mr. Ebenezer lifted his head with sudden interest.

"What, woman! again? Hast lost the humlock out of thy shoe? Plague take thee! I'll ha' thee blistered! But here, wench, here, I've a new remedy." And, fumbling in his capacious waist-coat pocket, he pulled out a bit of dried horse-radish, carefully screwed up in the page of an old tract. "Go, powder that, woman! Powder it fine, mark thee; and then snuff it up thy nose, and—here, here,"—for the overpowered domestic had eagerly accepted the strange prescription, and was making off to try it at once,—"when the pain passes, come and tell me. Dost hear me?"

Kerry, mollified by her master's sympathy, and eager to commence experiments, vanished down the stairs; and Uncle Ebenezer drew up to the table and took a long pull from his pewter pot of home-brewed ale.

The food, which consisted of wholemeal bread, barley cake, and salt pork, was consumed for some moments in silence; and then the young mistress, who had evidently been preparing the question she now asked, raised her eyes, and, glancing at her portly uncle, inquired:

"Well, uncle, has Peggy Dimmock's dream come true?"

"True! Ay, has it? She was brought to bed this very morning at six o' the clock, an' it's twins; that's what the double primrose meant!"

"Bless us!" And then, after momentary hesitation: "But the parson says dreams are all rubbish, Uncle Tebby."

"Parson!" and the old man's face expressed the

loftiest possible contempt. "What do parsons know about such great matters?—dreams! What was't Mayor Astbury dreamed the night Queen Anne died? What was the signification of Holam, beholding lambs in harvest, when he slept in the stage waggon? Didn't the Jacobites come forthwith? Not give heed to dreams! Why, girl, what does Providence send 'em for?"

Young mistress appeared to be only half convinced, and, after another moment or two of musing, she asked:

"What does it signify to dream of a funeral?"

And here for the first time Mr. Josephus joined in the conversation, and both brothers answered promptly:

"A wedding."

The elders were now watching her with quickened interest, and waiting for the information they feared might be given.

"*I* dreamed of a funeral last night."

Uncle Ebenezer darted a quick glance at his brother, and that worthy seemed to find difficulty in swallowing the food he had in his mouth. But Mr. Josephus was not to be easily frightened, and so, with a look that belied his light words, he said:

"Tut, tut! 'tis but a fond girl's whimsies."

Mr. Ebenezer put his hand up hastily, as if to check him. "Was it a mean funeral or a fine 'un?" he demanded seriously.

"A fine one, an' there was a white pall on the coffin."

"It *is* a wedding," and Mr. Ebenezer looked

2

at his brother with graphic significance. "Was there aught on the pall, flowers or the like?"

"There were nests, uncle."

Ebenezer's jaw dropped, a long soft sigh escaped him, and after looking solemnly at his niece a moment or two he shook his head, and said sadly:

"Thou'll be married, girl," but he did not add, as the omen might have justified him in doing, "unfortunately" married.

Christiana, as she was called in honour of Bunyan's heroine, laughed at her uncle's lugubrious tones, and then, lifting her hands, cried in mock indignation:

"La! Uncle Tebby, you wouldn't have me an old maid, would you?"

Ebenezer felt in his heart of hearts that was just what he would have liked, and then, realising all at once what a selfish old curmudgeon he was to desire such a thing, he blinked his eyes very rapidly, nipped them tightly together, rubbed the end of his snub nose, and stammered huskily whilst he gazed hard at his niece:

"Kinty love, thou must never leave thy poor old uncles"; and then, with a sudden flash of illumination, he opened his eyes as wide as he could, and, looking significantly into the laughing brown orbs opposite to him, he added: "The young spark that wins thee must take us too; he must live here, Kinty— here!"

The real inwardness of this communication was

of course lost upon the silent Josephus; but Kinty understood that it was her uncle's way of signifying to her that if the scene of which he had been the unintentional witness a little while before meant anything, he for one would not oppose. And so, with a light blush and a covering little laugh, she rose from the table and made for the kitchen; whilst Uncle Ebenezer turned round and drew the three-cornered elbow-chair up to the fire.

Mr. Josephus was already smoking, with his back to the shop door, and as Ebenezer settled in the opposite corner and prepared to follow his brother's example, he shot stealthy glances now and again towards the senior member of the firm. Having lighted his pipe, he took off his wig, and put it in the little recess where he usually kept his tobacco and snuff; and then, settling down in his chair, he sat watching his brother, and following out his own confused reflections. What was the meaning of the scene he had witnessed? It did not in the least surprise him that Mark Rawson should aspire to the hand of his mistress, for though he knew him to be perfectly trustworthy, he knew also that he was bold and terribly ambitious.

It would solve many awkward questions if Mark could succeed to the business, but what a come-down it would be for their little queen, and how all their friends would jeer about it! And what about his niece? If she was going to tamely give herself away to a penniless apprentice, why then he was, and always had been, entirely at sea in his estimate of her character? And her act would be in absolute contradiction to the whole spirit of her life and aspirations hitherto. In the many playful little banterings he and she had had together on this always interesting subject, it had been taken for granted that she would marry somebody distinguished and be a great lady. And certainly it would be a huge mistake if she did not, for she was in every way fitted, in his poor judgment, for any position in life, however exalted, and would, if he understood her, make herself and everybody about her miserable if she had to be bound down for ever to the drudgery of a common tradesman's wife.

He felt his head beginning to ache ; the working out of problems was not at all in his way. Oh that he could tell Josephus about it ! And that brought up a further complication. Would it be right to betray his niece and tell his brother? On the other hand, would it be right to conceal so very important a matter from him? If ever the matter was properly adjusted he knew full well that his strong, silent brother would have to do it, and, on the other hand, he knew that Josephus had very definite ideas as to Kinty's future, and very ambitious ones too. He was not accustomed to abstract reflection, his brother generally did it for both of them ; he feared to open his mouth lest he should make matters worse, and yet he was too uneasy to be silent, and so he finally took the weak man's policy and began to drift and talk.

"Bad dream, bad dream!" he muttered, looking hard into the fire and solemnly shaking his head

But Mr. Josephus did not take the bait; he simply looked lazily at his brother through the tobacco smoke and puffed on.

Ebenezer glowered for a moment at the andirons on the grate, then scowled, and looked round at his wig, brought his eyes back uneasily to his brother, and then ventured:

"After sweet meat comes sour sauce, brother."

Josephus seemed to be still immovable, but after a moment's pause he leaned as far back as the very straight back of his chair would allow, and replied:

"As to common dreams, brother, pish! but this one is fair and true; she has been bidded for this very day, no other."

"A-h!" and the clouds began to lift from Ebenezer's mind; Mark had been speaking to Josephus earlier in the day, and the scene of which he had been the accidental witness was the natural sequence. Very right and proper. And he blew a long wreath of smoke from his pipe, and sat meditating complacently. "Well, brother," he said at last, with a sort of half-reluctant contentment, "'a bird in the hand is worth two in the bush,' after all; but I reckon 'every man thinks his own geese swans.'"

Josephus scowled, and turned to his brother a look of perplexed inquiry. But Ebenezer had already returned to his favourite topic, and presently drawled out musingly:

"A Friday's dream on Saturday told
  Will sure to come true e'er the day be old."

Josephus's curiosity was allayed, and the two sat in silence for some time. At last Ebenezer, with another small sigh of resignation, remarked:

"Well, he hath served us punctually and truly, and hath earned the reward. Faith, 'tis like to Jacob and Rachel," and then as his memory made a sudden effort he laughed, and added: "Gad, but I nearly spoilt their bussing and clipping though, hang me!"

But Josephus had risen to his feet, wonder, perplexity, and indignation expressed on his countenance. "Service? reward? What has thy addle pate got in it now? Who was bussing and clipping?"

Ebenezer began to fear he had made a terrible mistake, but was now too curious to try to recover himself, and so he blurted out:

"Who? who but our man, Mark."

Josephus's face was past all describing; he opened his tight little mouth and gasped.

"Mark!" he shouted at length, "the beggarly apprentice! Teb, thou art crazed, man. Mark!" and he looked round the room in utter amazement and disgust.

And just at this point the door from the kitchen opened, and in stepped one of the subjects of this tangled discussion.

"Niece, Niece Christiana, what's this billing and clipping with a beggarly apprentice? Hast forgotten thyself, woman?"

Now Kinty made it a point always to stand up to Uncle Josephus when he "hectored" her, and guessing at once that Ebenezer had betrayed her, but done it unwittingly, she set herself at once to defend him and herself as well.

"Why shout that fashion, uncle? I am not deaf, and I am not a child."

"'Shout!' it would make the dumb shout. Hast no pride, wench—no self-regard? Marry a dirty apprentice out of Tan-pit Lane! Why, woman, I've been solicited for thee to-day by the Mayor for his son."

The piece of information contained in the last outburst had its effect at once on Kinty. It touched her vanity, though it embarrassed her decision; and so to gain time and conciliate her uncle, at any rate for the moment, she said:

"Uncle Josy, whether maltster, or hatter, or pedlar, the precise choice rests with the woman, does not it?"

This clever reminder that the grand suitor he had got for her was after all only a tradesman, like Mark, was the nearest to a retort she dare venture upon just then; but it angered her uncle as she, in the thirteen years she had lived with him, had never seen him angered. He drew himself up, clenched his fists as if he had difficulty in preventing himself laying hands upon her, called her a baggage, an impertinent hussy, an ungrateful madam, and then, with a sudden flash of resolution, darted forward toward the door with the evident intention of bringing the offending apprentice to book.

"Uncle, let alone!" and stepping between him and the door, she drew up herself to her utmost height, and flashing upon him a look of proud defiance, she cried: "I can take care of myself, I hope; but if you interfere, by Heaven, I *will* marry him!"

"Kinty woman, Kinty!" cried Uncle Ebenezer, with coaxing expostulation.

"Well, uncle," and there slipped into her voice a little tremor she knew but too well how to use, "I would not disoblige my dear foster-fathers, but I am not a baby or a goose of a kitchen wench."

Josephus, beginning to feel rather ridiculous, muttered several vague threats of which his niece diplomatically took no notice, but allowed him to slink back into his chair. Then she drew nearer to him, and with a soft word or two tried to mollify his wrath, and spoke in such a light, patronising way of Mark that he was effectually hoodwinked. Presently she put her hand on the arm of his chair, and after indirectly providing an opening for him to speak of the offer he had had for her hand, she began to adjust the bow of his wig with her fingers, dropping every now and again some little word which encouraged him to discover all there was to tell. And when he had given her all particulars, Josephus began to inquire what she thought about the matter; but that did not suit her cue at all just then, for she wanted time to think, and so she fell to accusing them of wanting to get rid of her, made them laugh by hinting that Uncle Ebenezer must be wanting to get married himself, and then, having brought them into the most pliable humour possible, she suddenly became pensive, was sure she was a great trouble to them, vowed they were the dearest of dear uncles, and that she loved them so much that he would have to be an " exquisite pretty fellow " who would tempt her to leave them.

By this time Mr. Ebenezer's eyes were swimming, and his chubby cheeks quivering with emotion, and even Josephus, who was more vulnerable on the point of affection for his niece than any other, began to clear his throat and rub his bare chin in a most uneasy manner.

Whilst she had been talking Kinty had also been listening for certain well-known sounds in the shop, and as she heard the shutters put up one by one, and the great heavy bar placed across them, and a few minutes later the front door banged, she knew that Mark had gone home for the night, and was therefore out of her uncles' reach. That point secured, she began to hum a little tune, and drew a low stool near the fire and commenced work upon a sampler-frame, at which sign her uncles rose and made off for the tavern, and she was left alone.

The premises stood some few steps above the street, and there was a side entrance in a passage. As soon as she heard the footsteps of her uncles die away down the entry, she paused ; the sampler gradually slipped from her knee to the floor, and she sat musing over the events of the day.

Presently she rose from her seat and put the sampler away, peered through the leaded window for a moment, drew the curtain, stood wavering near the staircase leading down into the cellar kitchen, and then, with sudden decision, turned and ran upstairs, and in a few minutes reappeared with a large horn lantern in her hand and covered from head to foot with a long, dark cloak.

CHAPTER III

THE WISE-WOMAN

IT was quite dark when Kinty stepped gingerly out of the passage and down the steps into the street, and she paused for a moment to get accustomed to the change. Then it came over her that she was exposing herself to serious risk, for though the night was young, and her uncles' shop stood in the main street of the town, it was none too safe for a young female to be out. She glanced back hesitatingly at the outer or street door she had just closed, and then turned to gaze through the darkness at the few dim sputtering oil lamps that lighted that part of the town. Then she looked musingly at her own lantern, and at last, with an impatient shrug of her shoulders, she set off down the badly paved street.

Before she had gone many steps she uttered a startled little cry as the lamplighter, darting from an entry down which he had evidently come for a short cut, nearly ran against her. A little farther on she had to pass the noisy Hanover Arms, in the big back-parlour of which her uncles usually spent their evenings; and there was a big round lantern stuck on a post standing before the hostelry, and she had to cross to the other side of the road to avoid being seen by any one who might inform her relatives. Safely past this danger, she began to grow more nervous, for the lights in the street grew fewer, and, except for an occasional gleam from the lantern of some wanderer like herself, she seemed to be going towards total darkness.

At the bottom of the street she took a quick turn to the left, and entered a lane that seemed to lead out into the country. There were still houses on each side of the road, and a feeble light came from some of the windows; but the sounds of life that had assured her in the High Street now grew fainter and fewer, and except for the dull whirr of some spinning-wheel, or the click of the shuttle of some belated weaver, she could hear nothing.

Still hastening on, she presently came to a number of low-lying gardens, and here her heart began to beat more quickly, and, holding up her lantern until it was nearly level with her eyes, she broke into a run. A hundred yards or so farther on she came to a cottage, a low, thatched building, standing some few yards back from the road. She knew there was a puddle somewhere in front of the cottage that sometimes assumed the proportions of a pond, and so, lowering her lantern, she carefully picked her way to the door.

There was no latch visible, but Kinty slipped

her hand up the inner edge of the jamb and took hold of a knotted string, which she pulled, gently pressing forward with her elbow at the same time. But the door did not open, and after giving the string another tug, she rapped smartly, and held her breath to listen. She could hear, away in the distance, the creaking and groaning of the heavy baggage waggon due in the town that night, and which was now evidently struggling down the steep hill into Helsham, but not a sound of any kind came from the cottage within.

"Goody! Goody Wagstaffe, open! 'Tis a friend. Open quickly!"

At first there was no response, but just when Kinty was getting out of all patience—for she knew that the occupant of the cottage must be at home—there was a slow shuffling tread on the inside of the house, a very deliberate sliding back of heavy wooden bars, and then the door opened a little, and the visitor was bidden to enter.

"Bless me, Goody, how cautious you are! The footpads would never trouble *you*."

"Five times, young mistress—five times in eighteen years have they visited this little cot. But step in—step in and sit." So saying, Goody Wagstaffe led the way into the cottage.

She was a very tall woman, with large, sharp features, a long, skinny neck, greenish eyes, and a sullen expression. She wore a coarse linsey-woolsey dress, with faded damask bodice which evidently had not been made for her, and her abundant grey hair was almost hidden under a

large white cap adorned by a rusty black ribbon.
Save that her attire looked threadbare she had an
air of gentility about her, and her person and her
house were scrupulously clean.   The room into
which Kinty was now ushered was small and
low; the walls, where they could be seen, were
whitewashed, but they were covered for the most
part with oddly arranged shelves, or hidden behind
pieces of furniture which looked—like their owner
—somewhat out of their element.   Over the open
fireplace were shelves containing dried herbs, some
in paper and some without.   There were similar
packages on shelves nearly all round the room,
for Goody Wagstaffe was a somewhat noted
herbalist.

At the side of the disproportionately large fireplace stood a spinning-wheel with hanks of wool
and empty bobbins, and against the wall behind
them hung a large woman's hat, such as is now
called " Welsh," but which was a not uncommon
head-covering amongst women of the lower classes
at the time of which I write.

There was no light in the room save what came
from the fire, but even that made Kinty's eyes
blink as she accepted the dame's invitation and
came towards the centre of the room.   The chair
that was brought out for her was evidently kept
for such purposes, for it was a specimen of the
stiffest high-backed chairs of the period, and was
altogether out of keeping with the rest of the
furniture.   As Kinty settled herself in this seat,
her hostess turned her back to her and became
absorbed in the contents of a large iron pot on

the fire, from which were escaping a mixture of strange odours, none of which could be said to be inviting.

" 'Twas mighty dark as I came hither, Goody," began Kinty, putting back her velvet hood.

"Too dark for a maid to be abroad," replied Goody gruffly, and still keeping her back to her visitor, whilst she glowered dreely into the pot on the fire.

Kinty's face fell ; this was not at all the reception she had expected.

"Why, good dame," she cried, "what ails ye? I could but come ; I have something to ask thee, something great."

The dame gave another surly grunt, but did not turn round. There was an awkward pause, during which Kinty's buckled shoe was tapping uneasily upon the sanded flags. In a moment, however, the dame turned half round, and, glancing suspiciously at her visitor, she said :

"Ye never come in the daylight, mistress."

"The day ! I cannot ; I dare not !"

The dame looked Kinty over as she made this last assertion, and then, suddenly turning to her bubbling pot once more, she muttered up the chimney :

"What cannot be asked in the daylight sha' na be answered i' th' dark."

Kinty was amazed ; she had never found her friend in this mood before. What did it all mean ?

"Goody," she cried, "what's amiss? There's naught to be frightened at—nothing."

"Nothing!" and here the wise-woman turned round upon her visitor. "Nothing! Is the ducking-stool nothing? and the stocks, and the town's lock-up, nothing? is the name of evil-eye and witch nothing?"

"Tut, tut!" began Kinty, thinking to relieve the dame's mind by making light of her apprehensions. But the old woman was evidently in great distress.

"Tut!" she cried indignantly; "but when ye've been twice in the goose-green pond, ye'll not say 'Tut!' When ye've been thrice afore the bench for casting the evil-eye, ye'll not say 'Tut.' When the constable watches your door like a cat at a mouse hole, ye'll not say 'Tut.' Ah, no, pretty mistress, what's play to you may be death to me."

Kinty was aghast at this totally unlooked-for outburst from one who had always been so tractable, and raised her brows at the aspect of the case thus forcibly presented to her. She could not question the fact that the wise-woman's reputation had of late made her an object of suspicion, and, to do her justice, she was shocked to think that any action of hers should bring her friend into trouble.

But she was a very resolute little woman, and had no idea of giving up the object of her visit; and so she dropped into a sympathetic, soothing tone, listened attentively to the long and tedious details the old woman entered into, and, when she judged that the proper moment had arrived, she raised the skirt of her dress, revealing a yellow quilted, silk petticoat, and from a hanging-pocket attached thereto she pulled out a small parcel of real Bohea tea, and a little snuff-box well filled with the then all-popular dust, and pressed them upon the dame.

Then she asked a number of politic questions about Mother Wagstaffe's medicines, and at last came round to the real object of her visit, and declared, with apparently adamantine resolution, that, after what the dame had told her, she would never think of pressing her or troubling her in any way. At this, as the clever little schemer anticipated, the dame relented, and offered to gratify her curiosity for this one last occasion. But no, Kinty would not hear of it, and rose to go, and of course her hostess could not reconcile herself to sending so generous a friend away unsatisfied, and so made her sit down and say what she had come to say. And so, though with a very pretty pretence of reluctance, she told her dream, and affected the utmost astonishment when the dame interpreted it much in the same way as her uncles had done.

Having now got the dame interested, she ventured to ask her if there was any means of ascertaining whom she was to marry, and when the wise-woman hesitated, she appeared not to care to have the question answered. Next her hand was examined, and her eyes, and a certain little mole on the lobe of her left ear, and then she was told that she had two lovers, both of whom were devoted to her, and both of them exceedingly jealous in disposition, but that

3

she could not make up her mind which of them to take.

"But, Goody, I know all that; I want to know which of them I *shall* take," she said, when the dame stopped.

"One is tall and strong and proud and—and poor, and the other is short and slow and rich."

"Yes, yes," cried Kinty, following the old woman's description with hasty nods of the head; "but which of them shall I take?"

The wise-woman took her visitor's hand again and examined it carefully; then, still bending over it, she crooned out in tones that made her visitor thrill:

> "What you would, that you will not;
> What you would not, that you will."

The enigmatical nature of this preposterous and evasive prediction was exactly to the mind of the maiden who received it. It was paradoxical and mysterious, and would provide much food for speculation; and so, after repeating it over two or three times to make sure she had got it correctly, she turned to go.

"'Tis lonely for you living thus, Goody," she said sympathetically, as she picked up her lantern.

"Ah, mistress, mistress, I'm the most solitary woman alive, and what have I done—what have I done to merit it?"

The poor old Goody seemed strangely moved

by the light words of her friend, and her tones
were so pathetic that Kinty turned to look at
her, and then, with an impulsive little movement,
suddenly put her arm round the lonely woman's
neck and kissed her.

"Bless thee, pretty mistress! Heaven bless
thee for that," cried Goody, the tears suddenly
springing into her eyes ; and, with a quick change
of manner, she drew her visitor back into the
little cot, and, taking her two hands in hers, she
said solemnly : "Pretty maid, the heart that spoke
in that kiss is a sure heart ; in the storm that is
coming follow that ; with lovers and friends and
enemies alike, follow that ; thy heart is thy fortune,
thy heart is thy safety. Oh, pretty maid, follow
that, follow that !"

And still murmuring "Follow that, follow that,"
she gently pushed her visitor to the door, and then,
slipping back, snatched her tall hat from its peg,
and, catching up Kinty at the edge of the pond, she
drew her down a back lane, and conducted her by
a shorter cut home.

Meanwhile Mark Rawson had gone home with
a sore heart and an aching brain. The events
of the day had tried even his strong nerves, and
he felt dejected and irritable. Nothing would
have relieved him so much just then as a hearty,
satisfying quarrel with some one. But it was an
additional grievance to him that there was no
chance for that in the home to which he was
hastening.

His sister, though as spirited and proud as
himself to all the world, was sweetness and

docility to him. She worshipped him, in fact, and though young enough to have ambitions of her own, forgot everything personal in her intense devotion to the interests of her only brother; and it was the ideas instilled and sedulously nurtured by herself which had begotten the ambitions that now so powerfully influenced his life and thoughts.

But of late she had become afraid of her own success. Mark was too proud to be very communicative, but she had not studied his every whim and change of mind all these years for nothing, and what she saw of her brother gave her very serious misgivings lest he should be led to overreach himself.

She was a sewing-woman, and during Mark's apprenticeship had acquired a fairly good connection amongst the tradesfolk of the town. Since he had become " free," however, she had somewhat curtailed her labours, and as her brother now came home every day, instead of as beforetime on Sunday afternoons only, she devoted all her spare time to his comfort. For some days now she had been very uneasy about him; she had divined his affection for Mistress Kinty, and, whilst she had no selfish wish to keep him to herself, she was frightened at the idea of his casting his eyes so much above himself. She had told him, when he was but very young the wonderful story of Dick Whittington, the London apprentice, who became Lord Mayor, and since then she had purchased every chapbook offered to her which told a similar tale. Her efforts had been only too successful, and she began to tremble for the results.

As Mark entered the cottage and took off his small, three-cornered hat, she saw at once that he was unusually depressed, and forgetting everything else set to work to comfort him. She was "turning" a bright-coloured waistcoat for him, and as he strode past her and threw himself disconsolately upon the settle in the open fireplace, she lifted her head from her work, and smiled.

"Tired, laddie?" she asked with gentle sympathy. And when he did not respond she went on: "Take heart; there's heavier troubles than tired bones."

Mark gave an impatient twist; even sympathy was irritating just then.

"Boneache is easier than heartache, an' sooner cured also."

Mark sighed heavily, and wondered to himself what she would say about those who were afflicted with both these calamities.

"'Tis not poor workers only who suffer; their masters smart sometimes. There are heavy hearts under silk garments in this very town to-night."

A gleam of interest shot into the listener's eyes, and he raised his head from his breast and looked inquiringly at his sister.

"I've been to a great house to-day, an' talked to a proud woman, an' I came away thanking God I wasna her."

Mark seemed determined not to be interested,

but common decency seemed to demand that
he should say something, and so he asked curtly:

" Where hast been ? "

" To Widow Gatts, the currier's, an' both the
young masters were drunk in the house, and that
before noon.   She was that distraught she couldna
direct me, and when she spoke of ' the young
masters,' an' ' the young masters,' with a tear in
her voice, I thanked God for a good brother,
though only a journeyman as yet."

There, the little compliment she had worked
up to was out at last, and though she blushed
as she uttered it she glanced up wistfully into
Mark's face, and was disappointed to note how
little effect it had upon him.   He caught, however,
at her last word.

" Yet," he cried, " yet !   Oh, Nance, drop
that !   'Tis a dream, woman, a will-o'-the-wisp.
What I am that I shall be—a journeyman !"
And then, turning his head away with something very like a sob, he groaned : " A common
journeyman."

Nancy was now seriously alarmed ; there was
evidently something more than common the matter
with her brother.

" Nay, nay," she cried.   " Take hope, laddie.
Rome was not built in a day."   And she stepped
up to the side of the settle and put her hand
on his forehead.   But her touch seemed like a
sting to the tortured lad.   He flung away her
hand and jumped to his feet with something very
like a curse, and then, as he looked at his sister's
pained and flushing face, a gush of tender penitence

came into his heart. He dropped down on
the bench again, and, burying his head in his
hands, groaned out a sob that shook his whole
frame.

Relieved by the outburst, and keenly ashamed
of his manner towards the sister who doted upon
him he felt constrained to explain himself.
Vaguely and hesitantly at first, but presently
little by little the whole of his recent experiences
were told, and in a few moments Nancy knew
all there was to know. And the telling relieved
them both. Henceforth there would be no need
of concealments and evasions, and each could
speak openly to the other upon any aspect of
their struggle that might present itself. Nancy
was not only comforted, but encouraged; she had
feared something worse, and there were incidents
in the story just narrated which to her were of
the most promising character. At any rate, there
was no reason to give up the project so dear to
them both. Mark must rise; and though the
way they had chosen was beset with difficulties,
they were young and accustomed to sacrifices,
and she saw no reason why they should not
succeed.

"Young mistress is thy quarry, lad; to it with
her, and let naught stop thee," she said, as a
sort of summing up of the whole case.

Mark sat for a moment musing, whilst the light
of the little candle shone dimly upon his face.
Presently he replied with a regretful shake of
the head:

"'Twas my runagate tongue that did my

business. She'll hate me for't—she can but hate me."

"Tut, man! care not for that; women love a masterly man. To her, and good luck to thee."

Mark sighed again, and stooped down to unfasten his shoes, and Nancy turned away to prepare the supper.

CHAPTER IV

A METHODIST

WHILST Mistress Kinty was paying her clandestine visit to the wise-woman, and Mark was discussing his difficulties with his sister, Mr. Ebenezer was enjoying his invariable pipe and glass at the Hanover Arms. This ancient hostel, which stood about a hundred yards lower down the High Street than the hatter's shop, was a sort of local posting-house which had fallen on evil times. The stage-coaches to and from the north used to pass through Helsham; but some few years before the time of which I write the route had been changed, to avoid the great hill on the side of which the town stood, and so the tavern had lost much of its importance.

In those good old times, also, it had been known as the Bull's Head; but though there still remained some dim outline of a fabulous bovine monster on the creaking signboard that swung on a bracket over the door, the title had been changed in honour of the reigning house. The front of the inn was paved with cobble stones, and the tavern itself stood one step below the level of the road.

The first room to your right as you entered was called the parlour ; and it was here that Mr. Ebenezer and his cronies, and, in fact, many of the notables of the town, usually foregathered. It was a dark and low apartment, the walls of which were plentifully adorned with out-of-date notices of "cockings," stage-coach bills, lotteries, and the like, relieved here and there by badly drawn and clumsily framed pictures of famous long-distance coaches.

As it was still winter, the latter end of February, in fact, there was a bright log fire burning at the far end of the room, and at the side nearest the window a long table occupied nearly the whole length of the apartment. Mr. Ebenezer, being a leisurely sort of person, was generally one of the first to arrive ; and when he entered on the night in question the only persons present were the vicar of the parish, who occupied the three-cornered chair at the end of the table, and a stranger, who sat meditatively consuming a meal of havercake, cheese, and small ale.

"Ha, parson, you've beat me again," cried Ebenezer cheerily, and, dropping into a seat near the fire, he took a long, careful scrutiny of the stranger. The parson at the other side of the fire deigned no answer ; his head was thrown back and his chin projected, and he was evidently lost in thought. Three others entered now, one of whom was Mr. Josephus. Each man, as he looked round for a seat, saluted the minister ; but that individual might have been a statue for any apparent impression the greetings made upon him ; and Mr. Ebenezer, as he made room for his brother at the fire, leaned forward, and, jerking his fat thumb parsonwards, solemnly winked.

Mr. Josephus raised his brow at this signal, and a quiet smile played round his mouth, for there was sure to be entertainment when the parson was in this mood. The other newcomers glanced at the cleric and then at each other, took huge pinches of snuff to conceal their grins, and then began to call loudly for the drawer (potboy).

Large quart tankards of ale having been served, Mr. Ebenezer, without speaking, pushed his towards the minister ; but that official did not condescend to notice the friendly offer, and still kept his head in the air. He was a short, spare man, with red, bibulous face and twinkling grey eyes. He wore a grey wig, slightly powdered, neat bands, and neat, but somewhat threadbare, clothes.

" All Papists ordered to leave London, gentlemen ; traveller upstairs just brought the tidings ! " cried the landlord, opening the door and closing it again after he had delivered his announcement.

For the next ten minutes this choice and exciting piece of intelligence was discussed in all its bearings, and more than one present cast a suspicious glance at the stranger still quietly consuming his supper.

" Did not I tell you that would come next ? " demanded the black-wigged haberdasher, who sat with his back to the stranger. "I could see what was coming by that last packet of tracts my merchant sent me."

"T-r-a-c-t-s!" sneered a rusty voice on the other side, and as the company turned round the parson was seen with his nose buried in Mr. Ebenezer's pewter.

They waited for the minister to continue, but he only wiped his lips with the back of his hand, and throwing back his head laughed sarcastically:

"Tracts!"

"Those printers print nothing but tracts these times," said Mr. Josephus; and his stout brother, seeing an opportunity for a quotation, chimed in:

"'Of making of books there is no end.'"

The tankard, which was again being raised to the minister's lips, stopped on its way, a wrathful frown appeared on the parson's face, and, rising to his feet pot in hand, he stepped into the middle of the room, crying indignantly:

"Books, Mr. Tebby! You don't call tracts books, surely? Tracts are to books what black dogs [false coin] are to honest shillings. Tracts sir! tracts are the scum of literature. Fiery darts of the wicked! Grub Street fleas come out into the country to take the air."

Here the irate parson strode the length of the room, shaking his wig in righteous indignation and still holding the pot in his hand.

"They hit the Church cruel hard sometimes, truly, sir," observed Swigge, a mild little tailor, with a melancholy eye and a drooping, pensive nose.

This remark was intended to be sympathetic and to have a mollifying effect; unfortunately, it had the very opposite, for the clergyman, who had just reached the door in one of his perambulations, suddenly whisked round, and, glaring fiercely at the tailor, cried:

"Church, sir! hit the Church, sir! And why not? they are only following the country. Any stick is good enough to beat a dog with. They are in the mode, sir, in the very pink o' the fashion. Hit her, sir! The Government hits her, and the nobility hit her, and the common people hit her, and why shouldn't the lousy Grub Street ink-flingers hit her, too? She's down, sir, and every dirty scullion may give her a kick."

The little tailor looked as though he were about to demur to this very violent condemnation, but thinking better of it he simply helped himself to a pinch of snuff and solemnly shook his head; in which non-committal sort of response he was joined by Mr. Ebenezer.

By this time the vicar, for such he was, had finished his ale, and holding up the pewter to the candle, he carefully scrutinised the empty vessel, and then put it down on the table with a significant bang. Accepting the hint, two or three of his companions called for the "drawer" and had the pot refilled, upon which the minister, with a grunt of acknowledgment, took the vessel in his hand, and, pulling out a chair that stood against the table, he turned it round and drew up to the fire between Mr. Josephus and the haberdasher. Then he pulled out a little black pipe, upon which he was offered tobacco by both the haberdasher and Mr. Ebenezer, and, having carefully charged and lighted, he stretched out his black-stockinged legs to the fire, and fixed an injured, protesting gaze upon the picture of a main of fighting cocks over the mantelpiece.

"Gentlemen," he said, puffing out great clouds of smoke and wagging his head with half-drunken solemnity, "the country's doomed, the Church is doomed, and we shall all go to the Pope and the devil."

"Nay, master vicar," remonstrated the tailor diffidently, "not so bad as that ; there are some true Christians left yet." And then, glancing round the company to invite corroboration, he continued : "We are all good churchmen here."

The vicar burst into a scornful, sardonic laugh. "Churchmen, ha ! ha ! yea, verily" ; and then, bending forward, with a fierce scowl, he demanded : "Friend Swigge, when was you last at church ?"

The little tailor's face suddenly fell, and he glanced somewhat uneasily at his friends ; but they, being in no better case than himself with respect to their parson's accusation, turned their eyes away and smoked on in stubborn silence.

"Churchmen !" laughed the vicar again. "Ha, yes ; we are all churchmen, true loyal churchmen, but we never go to church ! The country is full of Protestants, loyal Protestants ; but the tithes are not paid, and the churches are empty, and the people are become jackasses and—and pagans !"

" There's the meeting-houses, sir——"

But the tailor was not allowed to proceed. The vicar jumped to his feet, and his red face became almost purple.

"What!" he shouted, "flout you me with meeting-houses! Pest-houses, sir! puritanical sink-pots, sir! papistical Guy Fawkes conspiracy-holes, sir! Meeting-houses!" he went on with growing indignation. "The country's got a plague of 'em, sir; they are blotches on the face of the country, they are pock-marks on the social body. Pock-marks," he continued, as the full fitness of his simile opened out to his excited mind, "that's what it is to a nicety; the country's got the meeting-house pox, i' Gad, an' by the Lord it's got it bad."

As the parson finished this tirade, which was furious even for him, Mr. Ebenezer shook his head at the tailor to warn him not to pursue the dangerous topic, and the rest, taking the hint, held their peace, whilst the cleric settled himself in his chair and continued his complaint in somewhat milder tones. The subject of meeting-houses was evidently a sore one with him, and in a moment or two he was denouncing the two " conventicles" existing in the town in his sternest tones. The buildings themselves were anathematised as "rat holes," "heresy shops," "soul traps," and the people who frequented them dubbed "Schismatics," Windbags, Fanatical Enthusiasts, and Creeping Jesuses.

Mr. Ebenezer, who was a sort of religious connoisseur, and amused himself by patronising every new belief that came under his notice, seemed a little uneasy under the parson's sweeping abuse; but presently the angry man passed on to other grievances, and became more serious and depressed as he proceeded. At this point, however, the landlord sauntered into the room; but, perceiving that his spiritual adviser was on his high horse, he quietly slipped into a seat by his side and commenced to twiddle his thumbs, every now and again turning over a huge quid of tobacco in his mouth, as the minister's words stimulated his thoughts.

The vicar scarcely deigned to notice the new-comer, but went on to enlarge upon his own hardships and the awful degeneracy of the times. People couldn't come to church, and when they did come they fell asleep and snored like grampuses, or got up and went out when the sermon was reached. As for Holy Communion, it was a dead letter.

"Cockings, sir!" he cried, turning hastily upon the landlord, who had been whispering something to Mr. Josephus—"Cockings, sir! Oh, yes, we can go to cockings any hour of any day, or bull-baits either, or spring fairs; and as to hearing, we can stand by the hour to listen to some pickle-herring of a quack in the market-place; but when it cometh to worshipping, we are employed—we are detained. Ah, yes; surely, surely."

Then it came out that all this moralising had originated in a discovery the good man had made that very day, which was that at Nat Bagshaw's, the Blue Lion in Rosemary Lane, they had on the preceding Sabbath held a cock-fight.

"What are we coming to, neighbours?" he demanded. "A Sunday cocking! A gathering of dirty, swearing tinkers and gamblers and pimps and blacklegs in Helsham on the Sabbath day! Why not hold the fair on Sabbath, an' be done?"

But again the vicar caught some of the landlord's whispered words to Mr. Josephus, and, leaning sideways over the arm of his chair, seemed anxious to hear more ; and, in fact, he was so intent upon listening that he forgot the subject upon which he was holding forth, until a sudden hiatus in his language, and glances of surprise from his hearers, brought him back to himself, and he plunged off once more, though not now with the same vigour as previously. As he mourned over the gambling, the immorality, the drunkenness of the times, the poaching and smuggling and illicit dealings in spirits so prevalent just then in the country, his voice grew solemn and then pathetic, and the company began to watch him in the expectation that this sermon would end as others delivered under similar circumstances had ended, in a maudlin burst of tears. But as they watched him they observed that he was once more listening eagerly to the conversation going on in an undertone between Mr. Josephus and the landlord, and as he listened and leaned further and further over his chair-arm his words grew more and more disjointed, and all at once he jumped to his feet.

"What, man!" he shouted, glaring at the

4

landlord; "the scurvy, bandy-legged cocks of Harewood beat ours! Let them come on! Bring them up, I say; we'll show them what the genuine old Helsham Shakebag can go! Two guineas on the old shakebag! and no villainous foreign spurs, neither."

With an indulgent smile at the suddenness with which the sportsman had overcome the divine in their vicar, the rest of the company, rather thankful for the diversion, turned their attention to the business in hand, and were soon engaged in a discussion about a challenge which had been sent to the landlord to fight a main of cocks with the men of Harewood. For the Hanover Arms possessed the largest cock-pit in the town, and the gentlemen present, the parson included, were chief patrons thereof.

In the midst of a discussion which soon became very animated, the stranger, who all this time had been sitting unnoticed in the far corner, rose to his feet, and after looking for a moment at the scene before him, and then ostentatiously clearing his throat, he stepped up to the fire-place, put his hand on the vicar's arm, and asked seriously:

"Sir, are not you the vicar of this parish?"

The clergyman, who was deeply interested in the sporting question under discussion, turned round somewhat impatiently, and when he saw that his questioner was a stranger he made a low bow, and answered:

"The same, sir, and at your commands."

"You have been speaking, sir, of the prevailing

sin and wickedness of the nation and of this parish."

The vicar paled a little; he did not at all relish the stranger's manner.

"Well, sir, and what of it?" and he put on a defiant air.

The stranger paused a moment, looked the cleric up and down deliberately, and then, fixing him with his eyes, he said in slow, weighty tones:

"Well, sir, if God *is* the Heavenly Father of all this nation and all the people in this parish, and if Jesus Christ *did* wrestle and agonise and die for us all, and if He be our daysman and advocate, then, sir, He must at this moment be raging against you like a lioness robbed of her cubs."

Every eye in the room was now fixed upon the speaker. He was a tallish man, with a long, large-featured face and soft, pleading eyes. He was dressed in a respectable dark-brown suit in the fashion of the period, with grey stockings, plain shoes, and a bob-wig; and as he stood, still looking at the parson, that worthy went red in the face, and began to bridle with indignation.

"And who might *you* be, sir, that speaks thus to your betters?" he demanded angrily. "Some babbling conventicler just out o' Bedlam, I'll warrant me."

"Sir, I am a poor sinner, a brand plucked from the burning. I have no learning, sir, and no gifts; but if I had your position, sir, and your talents and your influence, it should go hard with me but I would stop some poor sinner going down to the pit, and win some little trophy or other for my great Redeemer's crown."

Mr. Josephus had drawn himself up, and with his back to the fire was looking at the speaker with veiled contempt, whilst his brother had pushed his way to the front of the little group, and was gazing at the stranger with wondering, even admiring, eyes. The rest of the company were looking at the vicar as if they were sorry for him ; and as if he understood their feeling and resented it, the parson threw up his sharp chin, and, surveying his questioner loftily, replied :

"I am an English clergyman and an honest man, sir, and when I want instruction or assistance from such as thee I'll ask for it, and until I do stick thou to thy conventicle and thy whining."

The stranger seemed to have difficulty in finding his voice ; he never took his eyes off the vicar, however, and at length, speaking in low, restrained tones, he said :

"Good sir, if I have spoke unadvisedly with my lips, I pray your pardon ; but you have spoke of the sin that abounds in your town, of the Sabbath-breaking, and the gambling, and the godlessness. For two days now I have walked about here myself, and have seen the ignorance and deadness and sin and misery, and my heart hath burned within me. I have yearned over these lost souls with the spirit of the travailing Redeemer, and as I hearkened to your words just now I thought I saw the Saviour of the world stretching out His hands over this good town and crying, 'Woe is Me for My hurt! My wound is grievous. My tabernacle is spoiled, and all My cords are broken : My children are gone forth of Me, and they are not. For the pastors are become brutish, and have not sought the Lord,'" and taking off a low-crowned, broad-brimmed hat, he made a stiff bow and left the room.

The vicar stood staring at the closed door for some time after the departure of the stranger, and presently, with an awkward laugh but a much soberer expression of countenance, he turned to the landlord and demanded to know what the "impertinent Jack-pudding" meant. The host could only state that he had stayed in the house since the day before, and declared himself as much perplexed as his reverence as to what was the man's business in Helsham. Mr. Ebenezer was confident that the fellow was a Muggletonian, and the little tailor was sure that he belonged to some of the schismatical sects. The landlord thought that he was more probably an Anabaptist, but as the company were familiar with people of that creed the suggestion was not very helpful and lacked the element of novelty, and just when speculation was getting exhausted the vicar sprang to his feet, and cried :

"What a muddlehead am I! Why, certainly, certainly!"

As this exclamation was not particularly informing the company waited until the parson should become more explicit, and so, after looking from one to the other of them, as though inviting confirmation for a statement he had not yet made, but was sure they would endorse, he finally stepped over to Mr. Ebenezer as the one most likely to be interested in the announcement, and said :

" Why, Mr. Tebby, he is a *Methodist !* " And before any one could ask who and what a Methodist was, they heard a ringing voice crying in the street outside :

"God willing, John Snaith will preach the Gospel in the market-place to-morrow morn at eight of the clock."

CHAPTER V

AN OLD-TIME FAIR

" P-A-R-S-T nine and a clear night," broke on Mistress Kinty's ears as she hurried down the backyard towards the kitchen door. A soft little cry of alarm escaped her, for she realised that her uncles might just be returning home, and would be scandalised to discover that a young female had been abroad alone at that late hour, and so she hastened indoors, and ran upstairs into the parlour, and thence to her own bedroom.

But even then she must have been caught but for the fact that the watch had detained her uncles at the end of the side-passage, and was giving them the details of a recent capture of a footpad, who was now in safe custody at the watch-house. The candle she had left lighted when she went out had burnt itself away, and was now filling the room with its characteristically evil odours as she entered, and she had to make haste and light a second one, which she had provided, lest the maid, who would follow her, she knew, in a moment, should discover that she had been guilty of the wastefulness of leaving a burning candle for two hours.

She had got all this put right, however, and was just settling down into a chair when Kerry came up with the warming-pan, which she industriously rubbed between the sheets of the great bed to the accompaniment of a tune which she hissed, ostler-like, through her teeth. Kinty grew impatient, for she wanted to be alone; but it was only after the third bidding that the servant took herself and her sulphur-flavoured pan away.

But even then Kinty found it very difficult to collect her thoughts. This had been a very eventful day, far away the most momentous in her life hitherto, and now that she came to the end of it, she was perplexed to know what was likely to be the outcome of it all. She knew the mayor's son well enough, and liked him, and was not greatly surprised at the offer which had been made, for he had shown her very particular attention at occasional routs at which they had met during the winter.

He was rather above her in station, and very well-to-do, and it would be a match such as she might be proud of. And she *was* proud of it; and her eyes sparkled again as she thought of the envy of certain young lady friends of hers when her engagement became known. She would of course have a grand wedding, and that pleased her too, and in a few minutes she was absorbed in a vision of a pretty house on the outskirts of the town, with at least two domestics, and perhaps even a page-boy. Yes, it was in every way a most desirable match, and she could see no reason whatever why she should not be very happy.

"Thy heart is thy fortune; follow that, follow that."

"Oh, gracious! what was that?"

Kinty was no more superstitious than any other girl of her age and class at that time, but she started, shrank back into the low chair she was occupying, glanced nervously around the room, and then smiled as she remembered those were the words the wise-woman had spoken with such strange earnestness a little while before, and that it was but an odd trick of her memory that brought them back so strikingly at that moment. But why had they come back just then, and with such alarming distinctness? And she drew her elbows closer to her side and checked a tendency to shiver.

In a few moments her thoughts had carried her away again, but this time she was thinking about her visit to Goody Wagstaffe. Why, if her acceptance of the mayor's son was so easy and satisfactory a thing, had she ever gone to see Goody at all? And then she thought of Mark, and a smile played about her little mouth.

He was really a "very pretty fellow," only so terribly real and earnest about everything. She greatly enjoyed their dallyings and little flirtations together, and she had no greater pleasure in life than to work Mark up to making one of those rash and terribly vain speeches of his, and then bring him to her feet in abject repentance again.

But the smile died away as she realised all at once that these delightful little entertainments would now have to cease if she accepted the young maltster. She could see Mark's face, with his stern brow and flashing eyes, when he learnt that she was engaged, and there crept into her heart something as near to fear as she had ever felt in her life. And the more she thought of this aspect of the case the less she liked it, and at this moment the wise-woman's words came back to her with most troublesome persistence:

"Follow thy heart, pretty maid; follow that, follow that."

Kinty twisted impatiently in her chair and petulantly shrugged her shoulders. It really was very disturbing, and, after all, she could not, no, she could not give up her intercourse with her journeyman lover. Questions of right and wrong began to arise very awkwardly in her mind, but she put them back and returned to what had hitherto been the chief rule of her life, her likes and dislikes.

Of course she could not think seriously of marrying Mark; but she liked him, or, at any rate, she liked his attentions, and it was a real hardship to have even to think of giving them up. She *wouldn't* give them up, and she rose with a pettish jerk and began to undress. It was a real hardship to be interfered with in this manner. Why hadn't the young maltster waited a little ? Why was her Uncle Josephus so very anxious to get her married ? Of course, she would not do anything really bad or foolish, but it would be much better to let her go her own way ; and with that she slipped into bed and buried her head in the big feather pillows, still protesting against her unpleasant situation.

Well, neither her uncle nor the young maltster should have it all their own way ; she would lead them a dance yet, though of course she would have to yield eventually, but for the present she would enjoy herself—but then she heard once more with a distinctness that made her start up and draw the bed-hangings :

" Follow thy heart, pretty maid ; follow that, follow that."

As she was dosing off to sleep, Kinty remembered that next day was the fair, and that suggested to her an idea for another delightfully risky after-dark excursion, which, whilst it would gratify her own dear whim, would also provide her an opportunity of pleasing Mark, and with these comforting reflections she fell asleep.

In the morning she was awakened by the sounds of voices engaged in angry altercation. Listening a moment, she became aware that Uncle Josephus was scolding Mark in the shop, and so, with all possible haste, she dressed quickly and made her way down into the parlour.

She arrived on the scene just as her uncle was coming into the room, with his small, thin face still red with anger and the lips of his little mouth pursed out indignantly. His countenance changed as he saw his niece, and as it was not his cue just then to quarrel with her he gave her a pleasant greeting and drew up to the table. And just then Mr. Ebenezer entered, full of the preaching which he had just attended, and of the wonderful sermon he had heard from the mysterious stranger of the night before.

His mind was greatly exercised also, because the preacher had shown signs of hoarseness, and he commenced an animated discussion with Kinty as to whether rubbing the soles of the feet before the fire with garlic and lard, or the taking of powdered nettle-roots, was the best specific for this particular disorder.

As the fair day meant a busy time in the shop, the two brothers knew that their services were required at home, at least for a time; and so, though Mr. Josephus mentioned twice over that the "cocking" between their town and Harewood would commence at eleven, Mr. Ebenezer did not take the hint, but gave every indication of his intention of attending to business. Mr. Josephus wanted him out of the way, the farther the better, that he might have his niece to himself whilst they discussed the important subject of the offer for her hand; but Ebenezer either could not or would not take the hint, and though he went into the shop again and again, he returned in a moment or two, so that his brother could not get his business opened.

Kinty, however, understood it all, and knew that Uncle Ebenezer was lingering about of set purpose to protect her, and felt grateful to him.

A few minutes later Mark came into the parlour to call first one and then the other of his masters to the shop to assist in serving an unusual rush of customers, but they were soon back again, and Mr. Josephus, as the hour stole round towards eleven, went again and again to the far end of the room and scrutinised the hanging clock. Both brothers were as fidgety as they could well be, and at last, with a grunt and an impatient gesture, the elder one snatched his cocked hat from the peg near the shop door, and darted off to the popular sport.

Mr. Ebenezer, who was in the shop as his brother passed through, returned to the parlour almost immediately, and after pacing about the floor and chuckling to himself as if he had accomplished something, he nodded his head significantly at Kinty and made off to the cock-pit.

When Mark came in about noon to snatch a hasty meal, Kinty found him exceedingly sulky and taciturn. She plied him with all the special dainties which Kerry had provided for the fair— raised pork-pie, salt beef, white bread, and preserved gooseberry tart, with watered sack to wash them down. But he ate on in surly silence and answered her questions in laconic monosyllables. One thing, however, she discovered, that the scolding she had heard him receiving from his master had no reference to herself, and that Mark knew nothing of what was impending.

Later in the day, as the business slackened, the young hatter came into the parlour with excuses for so doing that were not too serious, and so Kinty ventured to open her attack upon him. She inquired into the causes of his morning's disgrace, and expressed, both in word and manner, a quite unusual resentment towards her uncle for his unfairness. And this opened the way for a few delicately hinted, but very effective compliments upon Mark's business abilities.

Then, as she watched him thawing under the process, she put her elbows upon the table and, propping her chin with her hands, she hinted to him that she would very much like to see the fair, but that she was like nobody else, she had no one to take her about, and her uncles would, as she well knew, not return home till late.

When he comprehended what she really meant, Mark's brows went up and he shook his head very seriously. Then he shot at her a glance of wondering surprise, and though she felt the implied reproach, she was only the more determined on that account to carry her point, and so she talked steadily on. Her voice grew softer and lower as she spoke, and there presently crept into it a coaxing cadence which Mark found it very difficult to resist.

A helpless sense of drifting came over him; he was under a spell and could not help himself. One or two stock objections about her uncles and their anger if they ever found her out, as they easily might, and about the questionableness of her presence in such a scene as they both knew they would witness, were advanced by him; but the irresistible force of her almost humble pleadings and her bewitching personality bore down all before them, and when he returned to the shop he had consented to be her escort on this risky and compromising excursion.

It was none too safe to have the windows exposed after dark on the fair night, and so Mark had to put the shutters up an hour earlier than usual, and by the time it was quite dusk he was waiting in the passage next to the shop for his fair companion, who, however, exercised the privilege of her sex and kept him there for some time. Presently she appeared, covered from head to foot, as on the previous night, with a dark cloak and hood, so that Mark breathed a little sigh of relief as he saw that she would not be easily recognised.

It was a strange scene into which the two now plunged. The narrow main street of the town was ablaze with light from a long row of gay stalls which stood along one side, and the upstairs rooms of the business houses were also illuminated, so that it was fairly easy to see one's way. But even then Kinty stumbled into a great hole in the cobble-stone pavement, and before she had recovered from the shock a country clown, with a drunken female on his arm, came staggering out of a byway and sent her reeling into the arms of her companion.

Uttering a little cry of dismay, Kinty paused, and then, with a coquettish little gesture, put her arm into Mark's, and he, with his blood all at once coursing madly through his veins at her confiding little action, hugged the trembling limb close to his side and moved briskly and boldly along.

The street seemed full of drunken people, and the taverns as they passed them sent forth streams of blasphemy which made Mark shudder, pagan though he was, and he glanced apprehensively down at the little hooded figure at his side.

The street opened out below the Hanover Arms and formed an irregular square. On one side of the square was the court-house and market-hall, now in darkness, and on the other was the fair-ground, crowded by a struggling, screaming, swearing mass of humanity. And here Mark pulled up, hoping that the whimsical little beauty at his side would be intimidated by the spectacle and wish to return. But, with an imperious " Go on ! art frightened ? " she pushed him forward, and the next instant they were in a ring of evil-smelling country joskins, who were listening to, and evidently hugely enjoying, the singing of some ballads. The few words Mark caught were so obscene and filthy that he jerked his companion away, whether she would or no ; and she, in resentment, stopped before a man who in raucous tones was trying to sell chapbooks whose very titles were sufficient to make Mark blush.

In trying to escape from this scene they found themselves blocked by a couple of men who were pushing their way recklessly through the crowd with raree-shows slung round their necks, and a moment later they arrived, breathless and sore, before a booth, on the outside stage of which a man, holding a lighted link in his hand, was inviting the public to see a real " Blackamoor " walk the tight-rope.

Thinking this was as innocent an entertainment as they were likely to find, and anxious to get his companion into a quieter place, Mark suggested that they should go and see the rope-walker; but Kinty curled her lip and glanced across to where some performers in tawdry finery were announcing that the most diverting play at the fair was to be performed.

On their way thither, however, they found their path blocked by a couple of quacks who were evidently in fierce competition, each worthy being assisted by a bawling "pickle-herring" (clown) who was out-shouting his master. One was extolling the virtues of a wonderful cure brought from the West Indies by an old mariner, and the other was offering a magic face-wash that was warranted to remove every trace of pock-mark; and before they could get through the crowd of half-drunken rustics who were listening open-mouthed to these men, there was a bustle behind them, and they were thrust back, as the constable came along, assisted by two or three men carrying long halberts, and who were dragging a woman to the watch-house who had been discovered surreptitiously selling short scraps of lace and remnants of velvet upon which no duty had been paid.

This episode, however, drove them into a corner, where the tide of struggling, reckless life rolled past them, and they could stand and look on.

Mark would probably have spent his evening amongst this roistering crowd if he had not been attending upon his mistress, and would have thought nothing of it; but somehow her presence gave him a new delicacy, and he glanced down upon her in the hope of finding some sign in her face which would have encouraged him to propose a return.

But though the woman in Kinty was asserting itself very vigorously just then, she turned away her face, and he saw nothing but the overhanging flap of her hood.

And so the two stood there and looked round on it all.

The noise was deafening, drums beating, fiddles and Lancashire bagpipes screaming, and voices of every tone and character blending with the other sounds, making a perfect Bedlam.

"Let us go," said Mark, at last; and as his companion made no reply, he began to force his way through the crowd. Before they had gone many steps, however, Kinty stopped again before a puppet-show, on the outside stage of which a fantastically dressed posture-master was going through some startling acrobatic feats. Kinty was evidently interested; but a querulous little cry escaped her, as two great rough country-men in smock-frocks came along and blocked her view, and Mark felt a strange impulse to snatch her up in his arms, and lift her high enough to see. But at that moment the acrobat stopped his antics, and turned a scared face up towards the sky. The eyes of the company around followed him, the music at some of the other booths ceased, a great, awful hush fell on that cursing crowd, and all eyes were turned upwards.

For a moment Mark could not make out what it all meant; but just as a series of shrieks burst from the rough women near him, he caught sight of a light in the heavens, and there, careering majestically across the darkened sky, was a great blazing four-tailed comet.

For a moment or two Mark scarcely realised what was taking place; but as the silence spread over all that multitude, and he glanced round at the sea of white, upturned faces, an icy chill crept down his spine, and his heart rose into his throat as if it would choke him. The fiery messenger in the heavens seemed to be casting on him a fearful spell, and he stood riveted to the spot.

The crowd about him was affected even more than he was; the only sounds that could be heard were low, smothered moans; and, just when the tension of horror was highest, a man pushed hastily past him, and a moment later the awful silence was broken by a deep, ringing voice crying in tones that seemed to pierce every heart:

"Behold! the Bridegroom cometh.   Behold! the Bridegroom cometh."

CHAPTER VI

THE FIRST OF THE PREACHERS

THE shock that passed through Mark's strong frame as the piercing words just quoted rang in his ears seemed to shake the very foundations of his being; he felt as if the hour of doom had come, and they were all about to be dragged to judgment. The fact that he could not see the speaker seemed to heighten the weird effect of his words, and as text thundered after text he felt that his heart was becoming water within him.

And those about him seemed to be, if anything, more affected than himself; the majority were still watching the course of the fiery monster above their heads, and gasps and smothered wails escaped them as the comet changed its appearance, the four tails being reduced to two, and then suddenly increased to six. Here and there a terrified female was shrieking out for mercy, whilst "Prepare to meet thy God," and "Behold, He cometh with clouds," and other such texts went ringing over their heads.

Then by a sudden, simultaneous impulse the crowd began to scatter and run, some in one direction and some in another; and in the vacant places thus left Mark could see the forms of solitary persons kneeling on the ground, with hands held up to heaven in agonising prayer. And at this moment he had another shock. So intense was his preoccupation in the phenomenon and its effects that he had forgotten his companion; but all at once the light touch on his arm became a dead weight, there was a long, low moan, and he just put out his arm in time to prevent Kinty falling to the ground in a dead faint.

Something very like a sob escaped the distressed youth. What was he to do now? He had no knowledge of how to restore fainting females, and he dare not ask assistance for fear of discovery. He paused a moment, looked hard across the fair-ground, as if calculating the distance he would have to travel, and then, snatching up his burden and clasping her to his breast, he pushed boldly forward towards his mistress's home.

He was a strong, young fellow, and Kinty was small and light, but she began to feel very heavy as he staggered along; and just as he was approaching the edge of the ground and was about to enter the street, he discovered that it was blocked on all sides by crowds of staring, terrified people, who had swarmed out of shops, houses, taverns, and alleys to gaze on the terrible portent above them.

A cry of disappointment and fear escaped the struggling youth, for the only other way to the shop was much farther round and very dark;

but without a moment's hesitation he turned and staggered along the edge of the fair-ground towards the back street. Just as he was entering it he heard a long, quivering sigh close to his ear, and became conscious that his precious burden was recovering. But the moment Kinty opened her eyes she caught sight again of the flaming messenger, and with another wail and a shudder she flung her arm round Mark's neck, and cried in terror:

"Oh, save me, Mark! save me! I'm thine, Mark! thine only! save me!"

Mark, with his heart leaping in his breast, and his ears tingling with tumultuous joy, hugged the frightened form closer to him, and staggered pantingly on, avoiding a fleeing woman here and a sprawling drunkard there, and at last reached the back door by which Kinty had entered the night before. And here Kinty begged to be set down; but when he had released her he found that the cautious Kerry had bolted the yard-door, as it was fair night, and, however inconvenient, they would have to go round into the High Street and enter by the front.

Carefully retracing their steps down the muddy, uneven lane, they had just reached the corner, where a little covered passage led into the street, when a low, deep roar quite close at hand startled them both, and Kinty, uttering a frightened cry, once more snatched at Mark's arm, and was barely pacified when he assured her that it was only the bull that had been brought to the Hanover Arms for to-morrow's baiting; and, before they could recover their composure, they had collided against a watchman, who, with his cocked hat far back on his head and his lantern in his left hand, was trying to cover his eyes with the cape of his great-coat to keep out the sight of the terror in the heavens.

When they reached the open street again, they found that it was impossible to steal along under the shadow of the buildings, for the sides of the street were lined with gaping, muttering men and women, who were speaking together under their breath, and wonderingly speculating what this great sign might mean. There was nothing for it therefore but to make a dash up the middle of the road; and even this was not very easy, for once they had to skirt round a sedan-chair, the bearers of which had set it down when they first saw the comet, and could not be induced either by the threats or entreaties of the terrified occupant to resume their labours. And their troubles were not over even when they reached the passage to the hat-shop side-door.

As she put her foot upon the step Kinty gave Mark's arm a nervous, confiding tug, and begged him to stay there until she saw how things were indoors, for if her uncles had not returned she felt she dare not stay in the house alone. She rapped hurriedly on the door, but there was no answer. She tried again, with no better result.

Then Mark, who was standing in the entrance of the passage, came to her assistance, and when after two rattling ran-tans they received no response, he suddenly remembered that there was just a chance of being able to enter by the workshop. He stepped outside and went down the stairs under the shop window, and to his surprise found the door a little ajar—evidently somebody had entered quite recently. He beckoned Kinty to follow him, and they threaded their way down through the workshop towards the door that led into Kerry's domicile. There was a light there and the sound of voices, and at that moment their tense nerves received another shock as they caught a long, plaintive wail.

The door from the workshop opened into a narrow passage, at the right-hand side of which was another door, and as Mark glanced across he observed that this second door was partly open, and there in the kitchen, reclining on a short bench, was Kerry, evidently in a state of collapse, and standing over her, coaxing and comforting, was Jerry Duccles, one of their workmen.

"Kerry, woman! Lawks a massy, Kerry!" groaned Duccles, evidently not much less alarmed than the domestic, and standing over her with a helpless look of distress on his face. But Kerry only threw up her arms and tossed back her head, and wailed again.

"'Tis the Lord, Kerry; 'tis the Lord wi' ten thousand of His——"

"'Tis the devil! 'tis the devil!" wailed Kerry, shaking her tousled head and hugging her fat hands together; "'tis the devil wi' his brimstone tail! Oh, Lordy, Lordy!" and she immediately ran off a long screaming rigmarole of quotations from the Prayer Book and the Burial Service.

Duccles was clearly at his wits' end ; he had recently been dabbling in millenarian doctrines amongst some new religionists who had come into the town, and he was not quite sure whether the event that was terrifying them all was a fulfilment of the prophecies he had listened to, or a judgment on him for deserting the dissenting meeting-house in Cobble Alley.

"Kerry !" cried Kinty sharply, for she was too frightened herself to see the ridiculousness of the situation. But as she brushed past Mark and suddenly appeared out of the darkness of the workshop, covered as she was in dark hood and cloak, Duccles gave a yell and made a plunge at the scullery, whilst Kerry threw up her arms once more and with a piercing shriek rolled off the bench to the floor.

Mark rushed forward to pick her up, crying as he did so to Duccles not to be a "jackass." He found the task he had undertaken altogether beyond him, but when Duccles at last ventured to come forth from his hiding-place and assist, they managed to get the still inanimate domestic into a chair, and after treating her to burnt feathers, asafœtida drops, and some of Mistress Kinty's Hungary water she was pleased to "come to," and at once began to protest that she wasn't one of the elect, and didn't want to be taken up with the "forty hundred and four thousand."

It took some time to pacify the poor soul, and when that was accomplished, and Mark had led the way upstairs with a candle in his hand, the Hungary water was required for Kinty herself, and Mark was only too glad to stay with her and try to relieve her fears. But he was no more free from the superstitions of his time than she was, and paid his attentions with a nervous and absent air. Many a time during the last hour or so he had thought of his sister, alone in their little cottage; but even now he dared not suggest departure, lest he should offend the wilful little woman to whom he was devoted.

Presently, however, Kinty heard footsteps in the passage, and ran to unfasten the door, whilst Mark skipped down the stairs into the kitchen, and thence through the cellar workshop into the street. The crowds had thinned somewhat, but, in spite of the nipping air, little knots of men and women, most of them with bare heads, were still standing in the doorways discussing the phenomenon.

Here was the parish beadle, who, with his hands in the pockets of his great-coat and his staff most unbecomingly tucked under his arm, was explaining to a company of scared-looking women and youths that the sign in the heavens was connected with another rising of the Jacobites. Outside the Hanover Arms the parson was entertaining a mixed company, who listened, as they had never listened to his sermons, whilst he tried to make them understand some of the principles of astronomy;

but his explanations about nebulæ and excentric orbits, rudimentary and even self-contradictory as they were, were received by the majority of his hearers with all the apprehensive unbelief of fear.

As Mark turned out of the High Street towards his home he had to cross the north corner of the town-hall square, where he came upon two men in the stocks, who had evidently been forgotten in the general scare, and who were giving vent to all kinds of unearthly groanings ; but whether it was because they had been left alone after their sentences had expired, or because they shared the general terror about the comet, Mark was not able to decide.

At the bottom of the next short street he came upon a company who were standing in a windless corner and listening to a tall, sour-faced man, who, by the aid of a lantern lent by the watch, who himself held it aloft on his staff, was reading to the company lurid descriptions of the horrors which were to overtake the ungodly when the saints were caught up into the air ; and just as he approached his own little dwelling, Mark found a Quaker, who was trying to allay the fears of some of his neighbours by explaining that the fiery portent meant an invasion from France, the return of the Jesuits, and subjugation to Rome, because of national oppression towards Dissenters.

By this time the young hatter was feeling confused ; the whole thing was terribly real to him, and he had no doubt whatever that something strange and wonderful was impending, but the explanations he heard were all so mutually contradictory that he was bewildered. In this frame of mind he pushed once more for home, and was surprised, and a little disappointed, to discover that his sister was absent. Somehow he felt he could not sit down; he looked at the little fire, and was disappointed to find that it did not require stirring; he walked two or three times across the sanded floor, went to the door and looked out, came back again and stood wavering before the fire, and then, with an impatient little gesture, threw off his cocked hat, put on a hosen cap, and stepped out once more into the lane.

Instinctively he looked up at the shaft of fire in the heavens, glanced absently up the lane and then down again, and the next moment he was lounging aimlessly along towards the country. The pleading, impulsive little sentence his mistress had used as he carried her out of the fair came back to him like sweet music, and was instantly banished by superstitious apprehensions of danger.

As he strolled on the unwonted stillness of the town on such a night impressed him, and he listened once and again for the sound of the strange preacher's voice. Then he remembered that the sermon must be over long ago, and once more his thoughts came back to his mistress and the sweet words she had used. " I am thine, Mark ; only thine," she had said, and as he turned the words over again and again they sounded sweeter at each repetition.

He was still moving slowly along, he cared not where; the town was behind him; he had passed the last straggling row of cottages some minutes ago; the air felt fresher, the stars shone out with a frosty clearness, and but for the presence of the flaming monster above him he could have enjoyed the solitude.

"Ha! what was that?"

He pulled up in the middle of the lane, and his heart gave a jump, and then began to beat rapidly as he became conscious of the near presence of some human being. It sounded like a moan; no, like the murmur of a stream, for it was continuous. It was on his right hand, and certainly close to him.

In the nervous condition in which recent experiences had left him, he began to feel strangely afraid. And now the sound had ceased. No, there it was again! What could it be? or, rather, *who* could it be? for it was certainly something human.

Then he grew ashamed of his own fear, and with an effort stepped to the side of the lane. An old wall separated the road from the pasture beyond, and the ground fell away from the wall inwards. He stopped, cautiously peeped over, and almost instantly ducked again, for there in a little hollow in the field, and quite near to him, was a kneeling figure, and a man with white, anguished face turned up towards the blazing comet was evidently praying. It was only another poor wretch scared like the rest of them by the fiery messenger. Was it anybody he knew ? Ha ! and raising his head once more to the edge of the wall he was just about to peep when he heard the voice again.

" Oh, spare ! good Lord, spare the people ! Is Thy mercy clean gone for ever ? doth Thy promise fail for evermore ? Hath God forgotten to be gracious? hath He in anger shut His tender mercies? O Lord, merciful and gracious, slow to anger and of great mercy, spare us but a little while ! Let it alone this year also ! Truly our cup is full, truly we are a seed of evildoers, children that are corrupters ; we have forsaken the Lord, and have provoked the Holy One of Israel to anger ! But spare us, Lord, most holy ! Oh, hold Thy hand ! hold Thy hand !

> Oh, take away Thy rod,
> Oh, take away Thy wrath ;
> My gracious Saviour and my God,
> Oh, take a gentler path."

The vehement earnestness with which this prayer was uttered was a revelation to Mark ; it was something he had never seen the like of before and did not at all understand. Whoever the suppliant was it was not fear that was moving him. There was such a confidence, such a conscious-ness of power with Omnipotence, such reverent familiarity, and withal such intense sympathy with others in the prayer, that Mark felt he had never before understood what supplication was, and he was just raising his head over the edge of the wall for a last look at the wrestler when the man he was watching rose suddenly to his feet, and Mark's amazement was complete when he discovered that the suppliant was the very respectably dressed stranger whom Mr. Ebenezer had pointed out to him that very day as the Methodist preacher.

CHAPTER VII

OPPOSITION

MARK did not sleep well that night; the experiences of the day had been too exciting to allow of that; and when he started from home for the shop next morning even the remembrance of his mistress's impulsive words seemed to afford him little satisfaction, and he found it easy to remember the natural captiousness and whimsical uncertainty of Kinty's disposition. As he held her in his arms and struggled through the crowd with her the night before she seemed to be already his, but this morning he could think of nothing but the difficulties in the way, and prepared himself to find his lady-love in her most distant and standoffish mood.

So engrossed was he in these uncomfortable thoughts that the morning greetings of a string of countrymen who were driving ponies into town laden with homespun cloth passed unheeded by him; and he was just turning down out of Wet-salter's Yard into the market-place when, hearing a voice, he raised his head, and discovered that the square contained some hundreds of people, who were standing round the market-cross listening to the man he had seen at prayer the night before.

Mark hesitated a moment; the crowd seemed to consist chiefly of draggle-tailed women, loose, dirty-looking men connected with the fair booths, and little knots of wool-workers in their leather breeches, striped linsey-woolsey aprons, and gay neckerchiefs.

Mark had no stomach for such company just then, and was turning away to avoid the gathering by taking the causeway, when he caught sight of the Dissenting minister, whose broad, Quaker-like hat was visible against the pillar on which the town-hall stood. A second glance revealed several respectable tradesmen standing at non-committal distance, but earnestly listening to the preacher; and on the outside of the crowd he observed a pudgy form, which he at once recognised as that of Mr. Ebenezer.

Mark strode across the worn cobble-stones, and, taking his place by his master's side, respectfully gave him the morning's greetings. Mr. Ebenezer rolled his eyes round to see who was speaking to him, but without even turning his head, and then raising his hand, he impatiently motioned to Mark to be silent and to listen, and immediately became absorbed once more in the preacher's utterances.

Thus admonished, Mark made an attempt to attend, but as he could never remember to have been interested in a sermon in his life, he had no expectation of succeeding. To his surprise, however, he found the discourse attractive;

though, even to his uncultured ear, the English of the speaker was somewhat homely, and occasionally even uncouth.

But Mark soon lost sight of all this in his growing surprise. Why, this man actually believed what he was saying! He was using terms with which Mark had been more or less familiar all his life; but he used them as though they represented facts, realities, and tremendous personal interests. He seemed to assume that religion was a practical, every-day concern for common people, and that the Bible and Prayer Book were to be taken literally.

And then the scene in the field the night before came back to him; and his surprise was increased as he all at once noticed that the one was the natural complement of the other. If the familiar words the preacher was now using represented actual facts instead of hazy, poetical abstractions, then his agony in prayer the night before was quite natural; but that they *did* represent facts was a thought so utterly novel to Mark that he revelled for the moment in the pure luxury of a new sensation, and with raised brows and wondering half-smile turned to speak to his master. But at this moment a horn was blown, summoning the wool-workers to their employment; and the assembly began to break up, though the preacher still continued his discourse. Uncle Ebenezer turned to go with the rest, and Mark immediately joined him.

As they went along, Mr. Ebenezer seemed

to be in a brown study; but just as they entered the High Street he pulled up, and as though Mark had been advancing some argument he could not accept, he cried in protesting tones :

"But there's naught of Fifth Monarchy doctrine in that, nor millenarianism neither!"

Mark, who knew the old man's peculiarities, smiled a little, and answered :

"Why, no, sir ; I trow not."

"Then is't papistry? is't solifidi-ism? is't wet-quakerism?" and Mr. Ebenezer's tone and look indicated that he was prepared to deny that the doctrine they had just listened to represented any of the above-named religious cults.

Now Mark had never heard of some of the beliefs named by his master, but knowing what he was expected to say, he simply shook his head, and answered :

"Nay, nay, sir! You'd have nosed it out if't had been."

They went up the steepish street until they approached the hat-shop. And just as Mark was turning into the door the old man pulled up once more ; and seizing him by the arm, and puckering up his face until it became one vast wrinkle of conviction, he said :

"Mark, Methodism is balderdash!"

"I believe you, sir! truly," replied the journeyman, stepping forward to assist the shopman, who was taking off the great bar from the shutters. But as he went towards the passage with one of the implements, Mr. Ebenezer took hold of his coat lapel and went on with, if possible, deeper conviction :

"But take me, boy, if yonder bawling ranti-pole 'bides long i' old Helsham, ther'll be mischief —mischief, boy!" And with that the old fellow waddled off up the passage to breakfast.

Before Mark had been on the premises many minutes he was made aware of two facts: first, that Mistress Kinty was in her frostiest and most distant mood; and, secondly, that as both his masters had been brought home drunk the night before, he must expect an unusually hard time of it with Mr. Josephus. The first discovery, though it did not surprise him very much, increased the depression with which he had been struggling ever since he awoke; and the second, though quite a usual thing amongst men of his masters' class, rather surprised him. But the fact was that they, like many others of their associates, had done their utmost to allay the fears created by the appearance of the comet in excessive libations. It was therefore a relief to him when the senior partner of the firm remained in the parlour; but had he known what was taking place there he would probably have preferred to have endured any number of snubs in the shop.

The fact was Mr. Josephus was having an unexpectedly good time with Kinty. She had slept less even than her lover, and got out of bed in the worst possible humour with herself. She was overwrought and nervous with the exciting experiences of the previous night, she was angry with herself for having made that impulsive and very awkward confession to Mark, and was of course inclined to visit the consequences upon his head. She felt resentful and sore, and it was most provoking to recollect that he would be entertaining quite ridiculous hopes, and would probably take the earliest opportunity of still further pressing his suit.

And then there was her uncle; she could not much longer put him off, and as Mark's attentions now seemed only irritations to her, she finally determined that she would save herself trouble and get out of her little perplexities by consenting to the young maltster's proposals, as far, at any rate, as yielding to her uncle's wishes was concerned.

Over the breakfast-table, therefore, she managed to maintain some sort of conversation about the awful occurrence of the night before, and was relieved to find that her guardians knew nothing about her expedition with Mark. As it happened, too, the shopman, knowing how welcome such exciting news would be, had brought word that one of the quack doctors at the fair had been caught stealing some of the showmen's goods and had been arrested, whereupon it had transpired that he was a notorious escaped horse-thief, who was suspected also of highwayman proclivities; and Mr. Ebenezer hastened away to be present when so interesting a character should appear before the magistrates.

Everything favoured Mr. Josephus, and to his surprise and delight Kinty did not try to avoid him, but sat still, and allowed him to introduce the pregnant topic. She did not surrender all at once, by any means, and at best her consent was tentative and strictly conditional; but that was much more than he had expected to get, at least without resorting to threats, and so presently he sauntered off to his usual rendezvous at the Hanover Arms in a highly satisfied frame of mind, going so far even as to stop in the shop as he went off and inform Mark that he might close at midday and take a holiday.

On his way down, however, he met Mr. Ebenezer, who was returning with a disappointed and rather disgusted look on his face, for the romantic story told by the shopman turned out to be nothing more than a squabble between two rival quacks, one of whom was said to be "straight like" a certain notorious horse-thief who had been executed some time before, and whose bones still hung in the gibbet on Hango Hill at the town end.

Josephus was in such great good-humour that he condescended to sympathise with his brother in his disappointment, and they adjourned together to the tavern. Arrived there, they found the parlour nearly full of men of their own class, whose conversation was divided between the fiery visitant of the previous night and the doings of the Methodist. The morning was cold, and the theological group held the fireplace; the two brothers, therefore, made their way to the end of the room, and soon were ensconced in chairs.

"Sit, sit," cried the little tailor impatiently, and then, turning to the chandler who sat next to him, he proceeded: "Sink me, goodman, but 'tis true! They are an off-cast of a dirty Rooshian sect called the Moravians, who forbid to marry, and have all things common, including wives."

"I tell ye, neighbour," and the chandler, who was large and fat, helped himself to a huge pinch of snuff, "that Westley has sold himself to the evil one, like to that Mephibosheth as was wrote about in a book long sin' by one Marlowe. Sir, if he do but come into a room like this, honest men begin to bark like hounds and foam at mouth, and simple women go possessed."

"They tell," and Mr. Ebenezer, who was the speaker, dropped his voice into a tragic whisper— "they tell that he toucheth for the evil. Is't not high treason?"

"Treason belike!" cried the little tailor. "Ay, an' he bringeth out of trance, an' casteth out spirits."

"Treason!" echoed the landlord, who had just joined the company. "A traveller by the coach told me no longer gone than yesterday that 'tis ascertained for certain in the city that he is chief of the Jesuits and is the head agent of the Papists to bring back the Pope an' the Pretender."

"Gentlemen, be done!" cried the vicar, who so far had been strangely silent, but who now raised his voice to command attention. "Let me tell you the pure truth. This Wesley is a simple adventurer; he was sent about his business from Oxford University for scurvy doctrines and cullionly tricks. He had to abscond from our American colonies for treasonable practices and meddling with women. The Church has done his business by closing her doors against him, and so he goeth about preaching to, and living upon, greasy rake-hells and trollopy kitchen wenches," and with an all-sufficient look of conclusiveness the reverend gentleman leaned back against the fireplace and surveyed the company.

At this moment there strode into the parlour a tall, well-built man, who wore his own hair, a broad-brimmed hat a little too high for a tradesman's, a long, dark, closely buttoned cloak, black stockings, and plain leather shoes that were fastened with laces. He did not seem very much at home, and his presence seemed to impose a restraint upon the company, whilst the vicar drew back a little and looked anywhere save at the newcomer.

The conversation seemed likely to get stranded, but Mr. Ebenezer, who apparently was the only person present who was not afraid of the latest arrival, set the ball rolling once more by turning round, and asking:

"Well, sir, what think you o' this new doctrine? I saw you was present this morning."

"Doctrines, goodman! call you those Bedlamite ravings doctrines?" And then glancing solemnly round the company, but avoiding the parson's eye, he went on, in deep, serious tones: "Ah, neighbours,

I was not astonished upon the awful appearance last night—I expected it."

" Expected it ? " cried several voices at once.

"No other!" and the big man, who was the leading Dissenting minister of the town, and was feared rather than respected for the austerity of his opinions, drew himself up, and, waving his left hand as if preaching, went on : " Look on the condition of the nation ! the ice-cold deadness, worldliness, and wholesale simony of the Church ; the debauchery, the gambling, the unclean living and wickedness in high places amongst the quality ; the sordid grovelling, beastliness, and drunkenness amongst common people ; the gaming, the smuggling, the dealing in uncustomed goods amongst all classes. Why, sirs, this, this merry-andrew, hedge-and-ditch spouting is of consequence ! 'Tis a sign of the times, and followeth in order. The last outflow of national iniquity and the first sign of coming doom hath ever been the upspringing of false prophets. And are they not now here at our very doors and upon our very streets ? "

An uncomfortable silence followed this outburst, for even those who were discussing incidental astronomy in the background had been arrested by it, and Mr. Ebenezer and his associates slowly shook their heads, whilst the parson buried a rather scornful face in an ale-can.

As nobody replied to the minister, and as his presence did not seem very acceptable, he presently moved towards the door, but almost before he had disappeared the parson was on his feet, and shaking his fist towards the entrance, he cried :

" The Pharisee ! the whining Roundhead ! Would he have the world turned into a puritanical vinegar barrel ? "

And then the irate vicar plunged off into a long tirade against sour-faced religion, and from that he passed to a defence of the town in which they all lived, and in utter obliviousness of his own lugubrious lamentation of the previous evening, he commended the peaceableness, good neighbourliness, and respectability of the old borough.

A word from the little tailor suddenly switched him off on another tack, and he enumerated all the religious institutions in the locality : his own parish church, with its venerable associations and its accommodation for nearly a thousand worshippers ; St. Barnaby's, on the opposite side of the town—and here the audience were surprised, as much as they could be by anything their vicar might say, to hear him pronounce a modified eulogy upon a brother clergyman of the rival parish—the Dissenters' meeting-house, represented by the gloomy minister who had just left them ; the Anabaptist conventicle, which was known locally as Scapegoat Chapel, though for what reason does not appear ; there was also the little Quaker meeting-house in Tan-pit Lane, and a nondescript denomination whose habitat was continually changing ; and if all these were not sufficient to provide for the religious needs of the population, he demanded to know what was.

"As regards these preaching Methodists," he went on, "'tis my place to put down all heresy and schism and fanatical enthusiasm, and, by the great Lord, I will!"

"Sir, sir, do you intend that?" and, to the astonishment of everybody present, the Dissenting minister, who had stopped in the passage on hearing the vicar's voice, and had, therefore, listened to the whole of his furious harangue, came back into the parlour and strode up to the parson in an attitude that was almost menacing.

The parson looked dashed, but, stepping back a little, and surveying the Dissenter from head to foot with deliberate astonishment, he demanded:

"Sir, am not I a man of my word?"

"If you are a man of your word," replied the Dissenter, concealing his irony and contempt with difficulty, "and if you have authority to put down schism and fanatical buffoonery, you will exercise your office and purge this good town of these Methodistical abominations."

"Ah, that will I," responded the vicar, politically ignoring the sarcastic tone of his brother minister, "and request your good offices to assist me, worthy sir."

At which conciliatory offer the company murmured its pleasure, and, a moment or two later, the minister had reluctantly consented to take a seat, and the old Hanover tavern saw the surprising spectacle of these ancient adversaries conspiring with the rest of the company to rid the town of the offending evangelists, the vicar securing the more cordial support of his rival by stipulating

that, in the interests of the Churches they represented, he and the Dissenter must of course be
kept out of the business.

Half an hour later Mark was astonished to
see his masters and the vicar pass through the
shop into the parlour, and his surprise was
increased when Kinty summoned him into their
presence.

"Ah, the very fellow!" cried the vicar eagerly
as Mark entered, and then he glanced curiously
at the table, and from that to the sideboard, as
if in search of something.

"Kinty woman, bring his reverence a tankard,"
cried Mr. Ebenezer; and as the young mistress
hastened away, the cleric surveyed Mark's stalwart
proportions with increased satisfaction, and again
murmured:

"The very man."

Kinty, returning almost immediately, set the
home-brewed before their visitor, and sitting down
at the edge of the table, looked inquiringly
from her uncles to Mark, and then back again
to the vicar.

"Journeyman," said Mr. Josephus, clearing his
throat and nipping his lips together, "hast seen
these rattle-headed preachers that are come to
town?"

"Yea, master," answered Mark, glancing inquiringly from one to the other of the company.

"Well, they are corrupting the town and
frighting good people out of their wits."

Mark nodded, and once more glanced round
the company.

"Well, thou art a stout, limbersome fellow, and hast great say, I'll warrant, wi' the apprentices, and art ready to addle an odd guinea or so an' please thy masters ?"

And again Mark nodded, but with much more deliberation.

"Well, man," and Mr. Josephus seemed almost angry that his serving-man did not respond more eagerly, "there's horseponds in the town and claypits, and a chance for a mighty fine marlock ; what says ta ?"

Mark hesitated ; he was about as innocent of religiousness as the gayest youth in the place, and was too intent upon his own ambitions to have much interest in anything else ; but what he had seen of the preacher had certainly not prepared him to take the lead in persecution, for that was evidently what his master hinted at.

"We'll take account of the watch an' the constables," said Mr. Ebenezer encouragingly.

"Tut, tut ! the chicken-heart is afeared," sneered Mr. Josephus.

It was perplexity rather than fear that was restraining Mark, but the thought behind Mr. Ebenezer's well-meant encouragement and Mr. Josephus's jibe touched his tenderest point, and as at that moment he caught Kinty's eyes eagerly fixed upon him, whilst her lip was already beginning to curl in contempt of his cowardice, he realised that this refusal just here might seriously affect his cherished projects, and so with a plunge and a stammering disavowal of hesitation he consented to carry out his masters' wishes.

CHAPTER VIII

A MISS-HIT

AFTER his interview with his masters and the vicar, Mark returned to the shop in a somewhat uneasy state of mind. He knew little about these Methodist preachers, and really cared less, but he had no more objection to a rough-and-tumble frolic, with them as the victims, than any other lusty and godless young fellow in the town. But he had developed the habit of late of regarding himself as something more than an ordinary apprentice, and it appeared to him that if his masters had shared that idea, and had any serious thoughts of encouraging the great dream of his life, they would not have selected him for this particular task.

Moreover, they had associated "Big Barny" with him in the arrangements, and he was one of the most disreputable roughs in the town, which made it all the clearer that his employers regarded the business as suitable for persons with no scruples of respectability, and classed him amongst the common ruck of men-servants. This was gall and bitterness to him, and he had a momentary feeling of anger against the evangelist.

Thinking of him, however, brought up before his mind the scene he had witnessed in the Tan-pit Lane meadows the night before, and as that haggard face rose once more before him, his resentment gave way to something not unlike sympathy. He could not forget, either, the sermon he had heard in the market-place, and putting these two things together he began to realise that, to say the least of it, the enterprise he had undertaken would be carried out, as far as he was concerned, in a reluctant and half-hearted fashion.

Then he thought of Mistress Kinty ; half-measures would certainly not satisfy her, and he knew perfectly well that though she might care very little about a thing herself, when she had once taken it up she would resent any laggardliness on the part of those who served her, and would in fact make the thing a personal one.

And after all, he could not stand on trifles as he was situated ; the great thing was to gratify his mistress, and any "fan-dangling" scruples of his own must be relentlessly crushed. He could drown every preaching pilgrim in the kingdom, he felt, if it would help him to attain the great object upon which he had set his heart. It would strengthen and stimulate him if he could have an interview with Kinty before he went off to his task ; and his masters would be certain to go to the bull-baiting, which always took place on the second day of the fair.

It commenced usually at two o'clock, and, if he could find means to occupy his time so as to be left in the shop when it was closed for the half-holiday, he would get his wish, and know better what to do.

Just then he discovered from Kerry that the vicar was staying to dinner, and, as this would mean that he could not dine in the parlour, he felt that he must stay behind after the workmen had gone to be sure how he stood with his tantalising and captious mistress. He assisted the shopman to close at the appointed time, sent the workmen off for their holiday, and then stole down to the cellar kitchen to beg a little dinner from Kerry. He had scarcely commenced his meal when he heard light footsteps upon the staircase, and a moment later the young mistress came into the room.

To his great gratification she was in her most gay and genial mood, and rallied him upon his new distinction as captain of the heresy-hunters; and had he not suspected that her tone was that of the gratified mistress, rather than the interested sweetheart, he would have been, at any rate as long as she stayed, completely happy. She left them all too soon, however, and Mark hastened back to his books in the shop. It was necessary he should find something very important in these to provide a sufficient excuse for working on a holiday, and so he tried to interest himself as much as possible in the accounts.

Once he made a little excuse to go into the

parlour, only to discover that Mr. Ebenezer had fallen asleep in his elbow-chair, and gave no signs of awaking.   There was a mischievous smile on Kinty's face as Mark forgot what he was supposed to have come about, and beat a hasty retreat ; but whilst he was brooding at the desk, over what that particular flicker of amusement might mean, he heard a low tap on the little glass pane in the door, and, turning round, beheld the laughing face of his mistress peeping gaily and encouragingly down upon him.

It was getting time for him to be off and make his preparations for the baiting of the preacher, which, it had been suggested, should take place that very night, if the good man ventured to resume his unpopular ministrations.

But Uncle Ebenezer still slumbered placidly on, and Kinty either would not or could not wake him.   Mark began to fume, for his nerves had been tried somewhat by recent events, and he was becoming very anxious.   Would Mr. Ebenezer never wake up ?   Might he not make the great bull-baiting an excuse for arousing him ?   Mistress Kinty came twice to the slight "quarrel" of glass, but her signal was always one of caution.   Presently, however, there was a slight stir in the parlour, Mark heard voices in conversation, and a moment later Mr. Ebenezer opened the little door and stepped down into the shop, which was, of course, now almost dark, as the shutters had been put up.   Mark had lighted a candle, and stood leaning against the desk in the little screened office.   Mr. Ebenezer waddled yawning to the office with his wig all awry, as usual.

"Ho, ho, Master Mark!" he chuckled, "we are great; we are a very pretty fellow now! Champion of the Church, i' gad! A proper George o' the Dragon! Defender o' the Faith, no less. Ho, ho, ho!"

Mark turned half round towards his master with a protesting smile, but Mr. Ebenezer only chuckled the more, and went on:

"Down with 'em, boy! Down wi' the sects an' the schisms. Down wi' the 'hisms' an' the 'ations'! Down wi' the balderdashers!"

"But what harm o' the Methodists, sir?" asked Mark, with a pucker of perplexity on his brow, but a smile about his lips.

"Harm, boy, harm!" and, pursing out his lips and pulling down his brows in sudden appearance of sternness, he went on: "What a plague, man! They are the pests o' the nation; honest folk are madded with them. They'll bring a Bedlam on us!" And then, stepping back and shaking his fat fist, he went on: "But I've judged 'em, trust me. I smell 'em all out. I snuff, an' I sniff, an' I nose 'em out. Boy, 'many talk o' Robin Hood that never shot wi' his bow'; but 'ye cannot catch old birds wi' chaff.' I've sounded 'em, sir, sounded 'em all—Anabaps, an' Presbies, an' Blue Lights, an' old Muggletonians, an' all—an' I tell thee they be fanaticals, ale-froth, balderdash!"

Mark felt a sudden prompting to tell his master about the preacher he had seen at prayer, but a most unusual feeling of reverence seemed to restrain him, and he turned to the desk again with an odd little sigh.

Mr. Ebenezer caught the sigh, and opened his round eyes wonderingly. For a moment he stood contemplating the young journeyman with meditative eye, helping himself the while to huge pinches of snuff. Then he began to blink rapidly to assist thought, shut up the snuff-box with a loud snap, and stepping up to Mark, smote him heavily on the back, and cried in a thick whisper:

"Take heart, boy, thou'rt i' luck. 'Give a man luck an' throw him into sea,' 'Faint heart never won fair lady.' This will do thy business. ''Tis an ill wind that blows nobody good.' Take heart, boy, take heart!"

"Ah, sir!" sighed Mark, affecting a deeper dejection than he would have admitted, in order to draw the old man out, "have not I heard you oft say, 'Look not too high, lest a chip fall in your eye?'"

"Tut, tut, man! 'kissing goes by favour.' Am not I for thee? Is not the little baggage indoors for thee? Is not the parson?—the parson! Why, man, he had a thought to buy thee a great book— Mister,"—and here he scratched his wig vigorously to stimulate his memory,—"Mister Foe's great book for 'prentices, no other. What is't? what is't? Plague o' my addled head! *The Compleat Trades- man*. Busk out the Methodists, an' thou win'st the rubber."

Now all this was milk and honey to Mark. The old man had never spoken with such unequivocal plainness before, and so to lead him on still further he shook his head, and sighed :

" Ah, sir ! but 'one man had better steal a horse than another look over the hedge.'"

" C-h-u-t ! What's downed thee so ? Take heart, man ; 'a man's a man if he have but a hose on his head.' To her man, to—— Great God, what's that ? "

This abrupt outburst was caused by some commotion in the street. There was a long, bellowing roar, followed by a series of terrified shrieks and the trampling of many feet. Without pausing to listen, Mr. Ebenezer rushed to the shop door and flung it open. Quick as lightning, however, he sprang back with a cry and a curse, and banging the door to, flung his broad back against it, and set his heels to the floor, evidently resolved to hold the fort against all comers.

" 'Tis the bull, boy ; the bull's loose, and he's after the Methodist."

Puffing and panting with his unusual exertions, his mouth all a-work, and his round eyes almost starting out of his head, the old fellow looked so comical, that when he mentioned that the bull was after the Methodist, the situation struck Mark as exceedingly comical, and he had difficulty in restraining his laughter.

Stepping to the door, however, he induced Mr. Ebenezer to release his hold, and gently opened it. He could see nothing but a stream of scared and shouting men and women going past, and so, venturing a little farther, he presently got upon the shop step, and glancing down the street, he saw the Hanover Arms' bull, all covered with gaudy ribbons, tearing away up the hill, and bellowing and foaming at the mouth, whilst a few yards behind it was the Methodist preacher with his coat torn from his back, and a great wound in his temple, from which the blood was flowing and covering his face.

Mark felt his heart go suddenly sick; he was not squeamish, he felt no more the brutality of the rough horse-play so common in his day than did any other young fellow of the times; but at this sight he felt his whole nature stirred, and hot indignation began to surge up within him. He drew a laboured breath, and was just making way for Kinty upon the doorstep when he heard another shout, and turning round saw Big Barny run up behind the preacher, lift a flail into the air, and bring the swinging end of it down on the poor fugitive's head, felling him to the ground.

With a fierce curse and a howl of outraged indignation, Mark sprang into the street, rushed through the crowd, and with a well-planted blow behind the ear, sent Barny staggering to the earth, and then stooped down and, putting his arm under the fallen preacher, raised his head, and facing angrily round used language we cannot print, and defied the howling mob to come a step nearer. For a full minute he faced the angry multitude, and then a groan and a movement from the man upon his arm drew his attention once more in that direction. He found that the preacher was not quite unconscious and wanted to get up. Gently raising him, and glancing round for a resting-place, he led the sufferer to a little side street, at the end of which was a low grassy hillock.

Slowly, and with much pain, the stricken man, leaning heavily on his conductor's arm, was conducted to the selected spot, and Mark, having laid him down and bidden a small boy fetch a pot of water, took off his own neck-cloth, and began to stanch the wound in the man's temple. The crowd, abashed and somewhat intimidated, stole slowly up towards the two; but Mark's manner was so threatening that they were fain to keep their distance.

"Bless the Lord, bless the Lord," murmured the sufferer as Mark gently examined his wound.

"Yea, 'tis lucky you are alive, good man," said Mark soothingly.

The preacher opened his eyes, looked hard at Mark, and gently shook his head; then, as Mark saw that he wanted to say more, he paused, and watched a tear as it escaped from the preacher's eye.

Suddenly a smile of touching gratitude suffused the stained face, and in low, thankful tones he murmured:

"Counted worthy—counted worthy."

"Nay, nay," cried Mark, with a lump in his throat; "thou hast done naught worthy o' this, good man."

The sufferer groaned and shook his head; and

then, lifting his eyes up to Mark's, with a look that brought back to him the scene in the meadow, he sobbed:

"Worthy to suffer shame for His name."

Mark's emotion, when he understood the reference, was strange and deep, and brushing away a tear, he bound up the preacher's head; and then raising him gently to his feet, handed him over to a tinker of the town, who now came forward and announced himself as one of the sufferer's friends. Mark was surprised to hear the man's claim, for he had been known in the town, as long as he could remember, as a violent and worthless character. But as he was now beginning to recollect himself, and realise what this strange act of his involved, he was glad to be thus released, and presently strode through the shrinking crowd back to the shop.

Mr. Ebenezer had disappeared, and Mistress Kinty was standing against the railings leading down from the street into the workshop, and he was free therefore to pass through. His mind was in a perfect whirl. He saw at once that what he had done would seriously affect his cherished plans; he could not face Kinty until he had recovered command of himself, and so, after a moment's thought, he slipped down the back stairs into the workshop below, that he might be alone.

Sitting down with his back against the dye-vat, and flinging his feet upon a heap of hat-blocks, he gave himself up to very harassing cogitations. His soul melted again as he thought of the cruelty

to which the preacher had been subjected, and
in his heart of hearts he could not blame himself
for what he had done. And yet it had been an
expensive and foolish effort. He could not,
in common consistency, any longer pretend to
lead the attack upon this preaching; and if he
did not, he realised that his refusal would appear
worse in the eyes of his friends than if he had
never undertaken the task.

The one way that seemed to have presented
itself of ingratiating himself with Mr. Josephus
was now closed, and he felt perfectly certain that
Kinty would despise him, and haughtily pit her
own claims upon him against any considerations
either of humanity or anything else.

Once more, therefore, he bitterly blamed himself for hot-headed impulsiveness, and almost
wished that he had never interfered in the
matter. What was the preacher or his peculiar
doctrines to him? But it always had been so;
again and again he had spoilt his chances by
his impetuousness and lack of self-control, and
it seemed that the older he got, and the more
need there was for restraining himself, the less
he was able to do so. Why had he interfered
in what was, after all, a mere——

" Marky, come hither."

It was the voice of his mistress calling from the
head of the stairs, and in a mood of surly self-
disgust he obeyed the summons, and stepped up
into the parlour.

There was anger and scorn in Kinty's pretty
face as, with hang-dog look, he appeared before

her; but had he been able to lift his head, he might have observed that her expression changed as she watched him, and a gravity that was almost anxiety began to manifest itself.

"What is this, thou'st done?" she asked presently in cold, restrained tones. There was no encouragement in that voice, and Mark, with dull desperation, lifted his head, and commenced his story. But as he talked, his own interest in the scene of which he had been so prominent an actor returned, and in spite of himself he grew animated, and could not help thinking that Kinty was affected too.

She shuddered once or twice at the most harrowing details, and covered her face with her hands; but, dropping them again as he told of the preacher's martyr-like joy, he perceived that her eyes glistened, and there was something very like a tear in them. He talked, therefore, longer than he needed; but when he had finished she froze him again by the chilling question:

"And what will Uncle Josephus think upon this?"

Mark had nothing to reply; that aspect of the case maddened him, and he shook his head, and set his fine teeth together grimly. And then this perplexing and utterly unfathomable little beauty began to speak.

She had a difficult part to play, but she performed it with the consummate tact of which she was mistress. She ignored altogether the scene with the preacher, and confined herself to admonitions on self-control. Her object evidently was to encourage him, but to encourage him without in any way committing herself. And she succeeded to perfection.

He saw, as he had never been allowed to see before, that she cared for him, at least, in some way. He perceived, also, that she was very anxious that he should conciliate by every means in his power her Uncle Josephus; and why that, if she did not wish him to realise his great dream? It was not often that she was serious like this, and though she committed herself to nothing, she managed to infuse fresh hope into her lover, and finally send him away more in love with her than ever, and more determined than ever to move heaven and earth to obtain her.

Before he left the premises, however, Mark ascertained from Kerry, the maid, the reason for the appearance of the bull in the street. It appeared that, just about the time for the baiting to commence, the preacher had begun a service in the market-place, and many of the people on their way to the sport, still impressed by the recent terrifying appearance of the comet, had stopped to listen.

The popular entertainment was for once, therefore, neglected, and the landlord in his chagrin had bidden his men take the bull out and let it go at the preacher. The infuriated animal rushed eagerly enough out of the ring and the yard, and nearly dragged the ostler who held the rope off his feet; but when it was suddenly called to face the crowd in the market-place, neither yellings nor beatings could induce it to charge them, until, goaded by an unusually savage assault upon its flanks, it had dashed into the crowd and upset the speaker, scattering the people in all directions. Then it had broken loose from the conductors, and, turning again upon the poor evangelist, had chased him up the High Street, and it was just at this point that Mark had appeared on the scene.

CHAPTER IX

DISGRACE

IT was past five o'clock, and the sun was setting, when Mark left the hat-shop, and he had scarcely got into the street when he was made aware that his recent defence of the preacher had been keenly resented by his fellow townsmen, or, at least, by the lower class of them. As he passed along, jibes and threats were flung at him by half-drunken men in holiday attire, and when he got opposite the Hanover Arms, which he would have been willing to pass unobserved, he was challenged by a big hairy man who held two bull-dogs in leash, animals which had been cheated of their rights by the disappearance of the bull. Before Mark could reply they were joined by the landlord, and the young hatter was treated to abuse too coarse to be set down here. Mark, who was in mortal fear lest his masters, who were in the parlour, should come out, had to swallow his pride, let the men abuse him, and get away as quickly as he could.

The fair was in full swing when he reached the market-place, and so he dodged to one side, strode hastily along under the shadow of the buildings, and was just emerging into the by-lane, when, as he was passing the entrance of a square of miserable cottages called Weaver's Croft, he heard his name called, and before he could look round found himself confronted by the bulky form of Big Barny, who was evidently three-parts drunk.

"Ho, ho, Master Knob-knuckles!" cried the brawny giant fiercely, as he spread out his legs and set his arms akimbo, so that Mark could not possibly pass; "thou com'st precisely. Knuckles, is't? So, then, knuckles be't," and then, waving one arm towards the entry of the croft, he raised his voice and shouted: "The game, lads, the game! High! Tester, high! Smaw-toes, hither, hither!"

A moment later Mark found himself surrounded with a scowling, cursing ring of loafers, in tight-fitting hosen nightcaps, greasy leather breeches, and heavy clogs, who laughed and gloated over their victim with unholy delight.

"Souse 'un! Duck 'un!" shouted one or two.

"Nay, nay, good fellows," cried Barny, "'tis knuckles he liketh, an' knuckles he shall have!" and then, turning jeeringly to Mark, he went on: "To it, 'prentice, to it then!" and began to square up to his opponent.

Now Mark was in a quandary; he knew that he had but to give the proper signal, and a score of sturdy lads of his own class would have been at his side in a few moments. But he was only too well aware that to embroil himself in a disreputable street-fight was the surest way he could possibly

take to forfeit what little claim to respectability
he possessed, whereas he needed every bit he
could command if he was to accomplish his end.
It was fair-time too, and a small affair on these
occasions, as he knew, often developed into a
serious riot. He hated the thought of it, but he
must get away from this at whatever sacrifice of
present dignity, and so he cried:

"A barley, a barley!"

Before the words were out of his mouth, however,
he received a swinging blow on the forehead,
which made him see stars, and sent him staggering against the side wall. With a gasp and a
yell he set his back to the wall, put his fingers
to his lips, sent forth a shrill double whistle,
and then, springing forward, charged his cursing
enemy.

"'Prentices, a rescue, a rescue!" shouted voices
here and there, and whilst Mark was struggling
with his enemy, some half-score of sturdy youths
had flung themselves upon the loafers, and with
fists and cudgels and plentiful execrations were
dealing vengeance to all and sundry. The loafers
backed down the passage towards their own
dominions, and the eager assailants followed them,
whilst women began to shriek, children fled in
terror indoors, and windows and heads were being
indifferently broken.

Then there was a cry of "Constable." The
Crofters as quickly as they were able vanished
indoors, having more to fear from the representative of the law than their opponents, whilst
Mark, struggling and rolling over with his enemy

on the ground, was taken possession of by the legal officer, and a few moments later found himself, still panting and breathless, in the town lock-up.

The room into which he was thrust was a filthy hole, three or four steps below the level of the road. Sewage from the shambles had recently percolated through the wall and stained it half-way from the floor with great slimy patches, whilst pools of loathsome matter lay along the wallside, and the whole apartment was filled with a sicken-ing stench. But had it been more abominable than it was it is doubtful whether the young hatter would have felt it, for he was undergoing almost indescribable sufferings in his mind. At any time a squabble with such characters as those with whom he had just been in conflict would have been nauseous to him, but just now it was the refinement of torture, and marked the very nadir of all his ambitions.

Each aspect of the case as he turned to it seemed more tormenting than the others, and there appeared to be no spark of hope anywhere. The long, sleepless night he passed in that sink-hole of a place seemed almost short to him, so utterly absorbed was he in his own painful reflections ; and when, without even having been asked to wash or eat, he was ordered to appear before the mayor, he shuddered at the contem-plation of an ignominy he had scarcely as yet thought of.

Now the day after the fair was usually a very busy one for the magistrates, but the comet had appeared again the night before, and though it did not produce such terrors as upon its first advent, it so effectually intimidated the people that there was very little employment for their worships. Twenty minutes, therefore, after the court opened, Mark and his burly companion were ushered into the justices' room, which was often used for such purposes on unimportant occasions. Mark's heart went sick with shame as he followed Barny, and he flushed and bit his lip as he perceived that Mr. Josephus sat by his worship's side.

"What! cullion! thou here again?" shouted the mayor, assuming angry indignation he did not quite feel, as he caught sight of Barny. "What did I tell thee when thou wert here Wednesday se'nnight? 'Tis the gallows thou art after, no less. What's the charge, constable?"

"'Sult an' buttery, y'ur wash'p, an' breaking King's peace. Be done, thou Jack-pudding" (this to Barny, who was muttering).

Barny was a sort of privileged rough. To begin with, he was a native of the town, and a good-tempered, jolly, somewhat convenient sort of ruffian. He was also an occasional and unofficial constable's henchman, having a very neat and expeditious way of dealing with obstreperous offenders. He was, moreover, a most reliable authority on game, and tasty dishes could be procured by his assistance when otherwise they were unobtainable. He was a constant visitor at the back doors of the local magnates, and spirits of undeniable quality, tobacco, and

8

even lace for the ladies, passed from his possession to theirs at ridiculous and highly suspicious prices.

The excise officer had made him a special study, but without any satisfactory result, and he was known to have privately expressed the opinion that the "beaks" of Helsham were all swindling smugglers, and this though Helsham was at least sixty miles from the sea. Appearances, however, must be kept up; and so his worship put on his very sternest look, glared fiercely at the bigger of the prisoners, and demanded what he had to say for himself. Barny had nothing to say, but rubbed his face with a great dirty hand, and looked sheepishly at his worship.

The mayor continued to glare at him sternly, and at last he said:

"Thou great hulking vagabond, I'll send thee to Bridewell!"

Then he leaned over the table in front of him, and held a whispered but not very serious consultation with the clerk, shaking his wig, and appearing as resolute and inflexible as though he were dealing with a notorious highwayman. Then he turned round, and pretended to consult Mr. Josephus—who was not a magistrate—and, finally, leaning back in his high-backed chair, he once more resumed his withering stare at the prisoner; and presently, shouting it out as if he had been condemning the whole town to summary execution, he cried:

"Take him away to the stocks."

Barny bobbed a clumsy bow, and made haste to depart with the constable's assistant; but

Mark went white with horror. The stocks! was he going to have the last ignominy of worthlessness placed upon him? He would die for very shame!

There was silence in the court for some time after Barny's departure, broken only by the scratching of official quills; and then the mayor, lifting his head and putting down his pen, demanded, as savagely as before:

"So, then, young hot-blood! what cock-an'-bull tale hast thou fetched wi' thee?"

Mark, with parched throat and cracking lips, stammered out an apologetic explanation; but the magistrate broke ruthlessly in upon him:

"Sink me, rapscallion! dost think to come the London Mohocks here? I'll ha' the peace kept, I assure thee, or I'll have every scurvy 'prentice o' ye pressed!"

Mark ventured to continue his plea, and this time the mayor listened, taking prodigious pinches of snuff, and muttering and shaking his wig as he did so.

There was a long silence when Mark concluded his defence; the mayor was still watching him, and evidently meditating. Presently, speaking with chilling deliberation, he said:

"I've a thought, young rantipole, I've a thought to send thee to the post" [whipping-post].

Mark was about to say something to mitigate the severity of the sentence, but the man in authority stopped him with a wave of the hand and the constable pulled him by the sleeve and cried:

" Silence ! "

And then his worship took up his quill and proceeded to read Mark a characteristic lecture, made up partly of extravagant threats and partly of well-meant, if somewhat coarsely expressed, counsels ; finishing his deliverance with the information that because of the respect he bore Mark's " worthy master," and the good character that townsman had given him, he would be set at liberty. But he must be very careful not to come there again.

But this unexpectedly merciful treatment had a totally different effect on Mark to the one produced upon the more experienced Barny. Every overwrought nerve in his body suddenly seemed to collapse, he had to struggle with an hysterical desire to shriek, and finally his pent-up and struggling emotions found vent in a loud sob. Before he could speak his thanks, however, the mayor had risen, and Mark was hustled downstairs, and a few moments later found himself in the arms of his sister, who had been waiting for him outside.

There was nothing very unusual in a " pretty fellow " of an apprentice embroiling himself in a street row, for such things were of almost daily occurrence, and, under ordinary circumstances, Mark would have made the best of matters. But he was wounded—self-wounded—in a very tender point. It was not merely that his pride had received a stab, though that was bad enough to bear ; he had brought down his grand castle of hope with his own hand, and by reducing himself to the level of an ordinary, roistering apprentice had effectually frustrated his most darling ambition.

His sister understood the true inwardness of all this, and whilst by every little affectionate attention she could think of she tried to soothe him, she kept silence on the main subject until such times as she could speak with effect. Hungry and dirty, nauseated with the vile stink of the jail, that seemed somehow still to cling to him, and sick at heart with his own humiliating reflections, he flung himself down on the settle near the fire and gave himself up to his own bitter thoughts. Like a wise woman his sister fed him, and induced him to change his clothes, and then she conveyed to him the most comforting and interesting bit of information she could think of; namely, that the Methodist preacher had left the town; adding in her anxiety to comfort him an apocryphal little embellishment to the effect that the departure was "for good and all."

These things revived him a little as he sat up to review his situation in the light of the fact just stated. But he was not in a condition to be encouraged; the disappearance of the preacher, which the day before would have been welcomed by him, now appeared as a fresh misfortune, as it robbed him of a chance of rehabilitating himself in the eyes of his masters and their niece. At this moment his sister reminded him that he would be missed at the shop; but the thought of how he would be received there made his heart sink again, and he was just about to make a peevish reply, when a broad shadow fell across the window, the door opened, and in stepped Uncle Ebenezer.

The old fellow entered the house with every appearance of hurry upon him, but, catching sight of Mark's woebegone face, he suddenly burst into a great laugh, affected to treat the affair as an excellent joke, quoted some remarks of his brother's intended to convey the idea that he looked at the matter in an even less serious light, and then, assuming a sudden look of earnestness and haste, he explained that the agent from Bewdley had arrived with some wonderful samples of caps, and that nothing could be done in the absence of the indispensable Mark.

Mark was touched by the old man's clever contrivance to get him back to business, and started off with him in better spirits than he had had for some time. But, on the way to the shop, he discovered that the Methodists were not quite done with, for though the preacher had indeed departed, he had made some eight or nine converts, and they had taken a disused loft belonging to a carpenter in Pie Lane, and were intending to hold meetings there; so that, hinted Mr. Ebenezer, as he panted after the now eager journeyman, there would be plenty of fun yet, and plenty of scope for the resources of Mark in his character of champion.

Mark's reception at the shop was as cordial as it could well be; in fact, when, an hour afterwards, he had got back to his old place behind the screen he soon convinced himself that it was far too cordial. It was just the kind of treatment they might be expected to extend to a roistering but indispensable assistant, but not at all the sort of thing they would offer to one whom they regarded as a probable future member of the family.

However, the position was, after all, somewhat relieved. His feelings towards the new sect were those of keen resentment, as the cause of all the trouble through which he had recently passed, and though he still retained some sympathy for the man he had defended, he had none for the people he had left behind, and would feel no scruple in disturbing their devotions.

Pie Lane was situated in the low-lying part of the town to the left of the market-place, and not far from Goody Wagstaffe's cottage. When, therefore, the business of the day was over, Mark made his way in that direction with the idea of reconnoitring the position with a view to future operations; for the more he thought of it, the more clearly he saw that it might provide him with the means of restoring himself to favour and assisting his great project.

The loft proved somewhat difficult to find; but presently he noticed a woman with a lantern going down a passage into what seemed to be a stable-yard. Keeping carefully out of sight, he followed her, and presently came to a two-storeyed building, in the upper room of which there were lights. The woman climbed the wooden outside stairs; and 'as she opened the door Mark caught the sound of a voice, raised as if in supplication, which assured him that he was on the right track at last. He paused a moment to decide what was best to do. Then he determined to have a look at the gathering if possible, and was just gliding round to the side in search of some means of getting a peep through the window, when a hand was suddenly laid upon his shoulder, and, turning round with a start, he found himself face to face with Goody Wagstaffe.

"Zounds, woman! but you frighted me!" he cried, and was superstitious enough to step back to avoid the wise-woman's eye.

Goody never moved; she stood there in the darkness, and Mark could see and almost feel the flash of her piercing eyes.

"Boy," she said sternly, "what is't thou art upon? Playing the fox?"

"Ay, Goody! Foxing the Methodist geese," laughed Mark a little nervously.

Goody stood for a moment irresolute. Then, taking a step towards him as he shrank into the shadow of the loft, she said in low, solemn tones:

"Then let the fox beware o' the farmer. ''Tis a fearful thing, laddie, to fall into the hands of the living God.'"

Mark shuddered involuntarily, and then his gorge began to rise. He was not to be intimidated by witch-like ways and terrifying quotations of Scripture, and he was just about to make a sneering reply, when the old woman turned suddenly from him, saying as she did so:

"Come away, come away. I have a thought to tell thee something." And she started down the yard.

The people in the loft overhead had just commenced to sing, and Mark suspected that the old woman was simply trying to draw him from the spot, and so he hesitated; but Goody, knowing human nature better than he did, stalked on towards the passage, and Mark, wondering why he did so, followed her.

When they reached the lane he hesitated, and if only the strange woman had turned round to speak to him he could have left her there, but as he peered through the gloom he saw her crossing the marshy ground towards her cottage, and in a dazed, aimless sort of way he plodded after her. She did not turn round even when she reached the door, but raising the latch strode inside and silently pointed to a seat. But Mark resented this assumption of control, and remained standing, as a protest and an assertion of his independence. Goody stirred up the smouldering fire until the room was filled with its light. Then she took off her long cloak and Welsh hat, moved her spinning-wheel farther away from the hearthstone, and, facing abruptly round upon Mark, said:

"Thou art to captain the persecutors, 'tis said."

"And what of it?" demanded Mark sullenly.

The wise-woman's manner suddenly changed. She came close up to her unwilling visitor, looked steadily into his face for a moment, and then, in a voice so tender and pleading that he found it difficult to believe it was hers, she said :

" Boy Rawson, if poor lone old Goody were lost in the black darkness upon Mowley Moor, wi' the storms beating round her, an' she found a little lantern to help her, wouldst dash the light from her hands ? "

" Goody ! " began Mark in indignant repudiation ; but the wise-woman stopped him by a touch on the arm, and went on in even softer tones :

" An' if a poor lost soul in the bottomless pit had crawled to the mouth, and was just climbing out, wouldst pick her back into the flames and the torments again ? "

" Goody ! " exclaimed Mark again ; but she checked him once more, and coming close up to him, put her hand gently on his breast, and asked :

" Hast got a heart, Rawson ? A true human heart, that feels and lives and hopes ? "

" Ay, mistress," replied he, in tones that were husky.

" An' hast got friends that love thee and help thee and speak sweetly to thee ? "

" Ay, Goody, ay ; but why all this ? "

The wise-woman looked steadily at him without speaking for quite an embarrassing space of time ; and then, dropping her head, she faltered sadly :

" Poor Goody has had nor heart, nor hope, nor friend for sixty weary years."

Mark felt a lump in his throat and dimness in

his eyes, and was just about to offer a sympathetic word when the old creature lifted her head again, and, with eyes that shone with a strange light and gleamed with soft, beautiful tears, she went on:

"But, Rawson, the heartless woman has found a heart, and the friendless one has found a Friend, and the hopeless woman has got a sweet hope. An' she got all these wi' the Methodists. Oh, let 'em a-be, Rawson; for poor Goody's sake, let 'em a-be!"

Mark made no attempt to conceal his emotion at this touching appeal; he dropped into a seat, hastily brushing away a tear, and presently commenced to argue the question with her. But Goody's heart was in her argument, and he soon found he was overmatched. She told him stories of the doings of the Methodists that made the tears come again, she posted him thoroughly in all the details of Mr. Wesley's history and work, and then had sense enough not to press him for a promise.

It was late when he left the cottage, but his mind was in such a state that, instead of striking for home, he returned to the lane and followed it across the moor until it brought him out at the top of the High Street. He turned down the street to get home through the town, and presently found himself passing the hat-shop. For a moment he paused to look at it and remind himself of all the proud hopes it contained for him, and as he stood gazing up at the dim shadow of the swinging sign-board, the house door opened,

Mistress Kinty's silvery voice reached him, and there, in the lighted doorway, stood the maltster's son in elaborate tie-wig, bright blue coat, and laced hat, and it was evident he had been spending the evening with the Kirkes.

CHAPTER X

WOMEN'S WILES

NOW it must be remembered that Mark knew
nothing of the proposal for Kinty's hand which
had been made by the maltster mayor on behalf
of his son. But he was perfectly well aware that
she might have any one of a score of the "sparks"
of the town, and it had been one of the tantalising
uncertainties of his position that, though she
mixed with them freely enough upon occasion,
he could not discover that she had shown
particular favour to any. The scene he had
just witnessed came upon him, therefore, with all
the stunning effect of a great and unwelcome
discovery.

The young maltster was about the most
dangerous competitor he could possibly have had.
In the fine-drawn social classifications which
obtain nowhere so completely as in an old-
fashioned country town like Helsham, this young
man was just sufficiently above Kinty and her
uncles in position to make the match a most
desirable one in their eyes, and the young fellow
himself was so sober and steady-going as to

preclude any hope that he was merely carrying on a flirtation.

Neither was it possible to regard this as an ordinary social call, for the elaborate way in which the visitor was got up and Kinty's own appearance precluded any such supposition. She was dressed in her very best—a low-cut, full-hooped damask gown, with short sleeves and bodice laced down the front, whilst her head was adorned with a cap which was turned up over the forehead, giving something of the same effect as the all-fashionable " commode " ; and Mark, standing in the darkness, whilst she was surrounded with light, could not be sure that her face had not upon it several of those eccentric patches which ladies of any pretence to fashion so much affected at that period. Evidently, therefore, this was a visit of ceremony, and about the most complicating circumstance which could have presented itself at this juncture of Mark's affairs.

As a linkman, who had been standing in a passage near Mark, now appeared to conduct the visitor home, the young hatter beheld an amount of bowing and curtseying which roused the devil of jealousy in him, and he backed into the entry out of which the man with the torch had come, and, setting his back against the wall, poured out a stream of hearty execrations upon the ways and wiles of women.

Then he fell to pitying himself and cursing the fate that had caused him to be born poor, but breaking off suddenly from this fruitless exercise, he rushed into the street again, shook his fist fiercely first at the closed shop and then up at Kinty's lighted bedroom window, and wildly vowed that in spite of pride and prejudice, and scurvy money-loving, and the deceitfulness of women, he would have his way, or know the reason why. But his fierce resolution passed away in its own expression; and breaking down in a bitter, despairing sob, he turned and stalked savagely off home.

Nancy, his sister, received him with all the old affectionateness; but when she saw his face and heard his story of the day's experiences she looked disappointed and even impatient; and when at last he had finished, she turned her head away, and, stooping down, lifted her spinning-wheel away from the fire.

"Ah! 'tis a bitter business," sighed Mark, more to invite her sympathy, which he felt he needed, than with any thought that she could help him. But to his surprise she did not reply.

"'Tis naught but ill-luck, an' scurvy fortune, an' ill-natured enemies for poor bodies like ourselves, to be sure," he complained querulously.

"Ay, truly thou hast a great enemy," she sighed, absently unroving the weft from her bobbin.

Mark looked up with curiosity; but she had apparently nothing more to say. After a moment's pause, however, she went on:

"One that would undo thee, though the fairies themselves wrought for thee."

Mark, who had dropped upon the settle, now

raised himself on his elbow, and looked keenly at her, evidently expecting her to proceed; and she, wetting her fingers upon her lips, and applying them again to her yarn, slowly proceeded:

"Naught can be done till *he* is overed with."

"He? Who? Get on, wench! Who?"

"Thyself."

"Self! S-e-l-f! As how?" and Mark sprang to his feet, and glared at her in indignant amazement.

"Thy own silly baby's heart, an' what thou fondly [foolishly] calls thy 'feelings.'"

"Oh, Nance! thou art madding me! Speak out, wench!"

And Nancy flung her bobbin from her, and, turning to him, cried indignantly:

"What hast thou to do wi' pale-faced preachers and their whinings? What hast thou to do wi' witch-wives, whimsy-whamsies, an' crocodile's tears? Thou hast to climb, man; thou hast to rise! Get thy mastership an' thy well-to-do wife, and then have thy fill of feelings, an' it content thee."

Through all that was left of that night Nancy urged upon her brother these considerations of worldly prudence, and though she was not herself satisfied with the result of her effort, Mark went to bed trying to convince himself that she was right, and that the only thing for him to do was to smother down his own susceptibilities, at any rate, until such times as he could indulge them without damage to his worldly interests.

In his own little chamber under the thatched roof, another idea took shape in his mind. Whilst he was under these feelings, and before anything could occur to change them again, he would take the final plunge, as far as Kinty was concerned. The suspense in which he had lived of late, aggravated as it was by the incidents that had recently transpired, had become unbearable, and therefore, for better or worse, he must know his fate.

He scarcely slept that night, and when he arose next morning he found himself in a fretful and nervous state of mind, and the task he had set himself seemed much more difficult than it had appeared the previous evening, whilst his better nature began to assert itself most embarrassingly and to plead for the wise-woman and her Methodists.

And on this part of the question he found great comfort in the reflection that the preacher had gone, and would, he hoped, never appear in Helsham again; so that his "feelings," as his sister had sneeringly called them, would not be appealed to again, and thus one source of danger was removed.

Realising this, he began to wonder whether it was necessary to carry out the other resolution he had formed, that, namely, which bound him to come to an issue with his lady-love, and though he came to no definite decision on that point, he felt that at any rate the demand for instant action was not so pressing.

Before he had been long at the shop, however,

he forgot all about his troubles, for his masters took one of their periodical fits of interest in business, and had the account books brought into the parlour, where, arrayed in long night-dresses (dressing-gowns), with hosen caps on their heads, and an open snuff-box before them, they endeavoured to get some idea of the state of their affairs.

Mr. Ebenezer soon tired, and in the middle of the forenoon toddled off to the tavern, but Mr. Josephus stuck to the business until he had ascertained how things stood. Just as they were concluding and Mark was receiving some final instructions about future stocks, Mr. Ebenezer came back with the thrilling intelligence that the French were preparing to invade the country in the interests of the Pretender. This very effectually extinguished all Mr. Josephus's interest in business, and he and his brother made off to the tavern to discuss the news.

So far, Mark had seen very little of Kinty; she seemed, in fact, to be as busy in her way as her uncles had been in theirs, and the balancing of the books had had to be done to the accompaniment of the buzz of the spinning-wheel.

Some time, however, before the departure of the brothers she had laid aside her work and served them with a little " nooning " repast, and poor Mark felt himself ridiculously uplifted when she gave him a portion out of the same jug as his masters, which was a quite unusual favour.

When they were left alone he felt himself
strangely embarrassed, and did his very utmost
to try to finish the work that was left him
to do upon the accounts.   But the more he
tried to concentrate his mind the less successful
he was, for Kinty somehow hovered most tantalisingly about him, and seemed to be in an
unusually gracious mood.   Then he took to
watching her furtively, and dropped his eyes
hastily upon his books when they met hers.

His work was about finished, but he dallied
with it and lingered on, hoping he knew not
what.   He was engaged in a most careful and
quite unnecessary repair of his quill when,
without the least warning, Kinty, who was at
that moment somewhere behind him, put her
small hand on one of his shoulders, and leaning
over until her hair brushed his cheek, covered
the open page before him with her other hand,
and said with playful impatience :

" Plague upon your silly writings !   Shut up,
and talk with me " ; and suiting the action to the
word, she leaned over still farther and closed the
ledger.

With a nervous laugh he pushed back his chair
and turned to look at her, and she, retreating
until she stood with her back to the fire, put
her hands behind her, and looking curiously
down upon him, said:

" Marky, what wouldst give for a mighty
great secret ? "

Mark felt his heart stop, and then set off again
at a great rate.   Had she never thought more

seriously of him than to be willing to tell him
about her grand sweetheart, as though he had
no concern in the matter at all?

" Nay, mistress, I am no guesser," he stammered
confusedly.

" Toots! but thou *shalt* guess, Master Sober-
sides."

The reproof conveyed in the name she gave
him admonished Mark that she was more in
earnest than he thought and than her manner
seemed to indicate, and so he made shift to do
her bidding ; but just as he was about to speak
a sudden impulse came into his mind, and without
waiting he blurted out:

" 'Tis that you have got an admirer."

The answer was entirely unexpected, he could
see, and it was by no means clear that it was
welcome ; but he was committed now, and must
brave it through ; and so he fixed his eyes upon
her steadily, and she, wincing somewhat under
his gaze, drew a long breath, and, more soberly
than she had hitherto spoken, demanded :

" And have I but *one* admirer, Mr. Journeyman?"

Mark's heart was getting hot within him.
What right had she thus recklessly to drag him
against his will into this most dangerous of all
topics? She knew she was torturing him, and
seemed to enjoy it ; and so, unable to keep the
words back, he said bitterly :

" Ah, but the rest are toys to be sported
with and cast away."

When he had spoken he would have given

worlds to have the words back. Kinty flushed, drew herself up, looked him deliberately over, and then answered :

"Shifty shy-cocks and pluckless would-if-I-dares deserve no other."

Lashed by her cutting taunt, and maddened by the tantalising uncertainty in his own mind, he sprang to his feet and, snatching at her hand, cried :

"Dare, mistress, dare! I will dare all hell at a word from you! A word! ay, a nod, a look! I will dare aught to reach you!"

Kinty drew her hand away, stepped back from him, and then, raising a face in which the colour was coming and going in a manner Mark had never seen the like of, she looked him full in the eyes and said quietly, repeating his last words :

"Anything on earth—but the Methodists."

"Methodists!" shouted he in amazed indignation. "Curse the Methodists! I'm bewitched of the Methodists! Oh, mistress, speak the word, give me but one little hope, and I'll sweep every Methodist in the kingdom away."

As he uttered this reckless speech he was conscious that Kinty was studying him in a curious, searching sort of way. He thought she seemed pleased for a moment; then he was as sure she was disappointed, and in the end she laughed at his extravagant wholesale offer to exterminate a whole sect, and availed herself of the opportunity it seemed to present of returning to safer subjects.

" Bless me, man, thou art a fire-eater ! " she cried ; and then, dropping into one of the stiff-backed chairs, she said lightly, " But this lover o' mine is a mighty pretty fellow, I will assure thee."

And do what he might, he could not bring her back to the all-important topic. She began to tell him who this lover of hers was, and went on to repeat all the good things she had ever heard of him. She enlarged on his position and probable income, and indulged in very free comments on his appearance. Then she gave him particulars of two or three previous " affairs " her suitor had had, and concluded by hoping that he would not be a ravaging Methodist-baiter.

Mark listened to her with listless self-disgust. Once more she had baffled him and beaten him. Him ? Why, she could twist him round her finger, the bewitching, maddening little baggage ! He had made his grand effort and was no nearer, and as he listened with decent politeness to her rambling, irresponsible talk, he wondered whether he ever would get anything out of her.

But just then the shopman, with a red face, came in to ask his help with a customer who wanted unduly to " cheapen " a hat, and he rose to attend to business. As he left his chair, however, Kinty rose from hers, and as he was opening the little door into the shop, she put her hand on his arm, and with a curious little movement which was more nearly like a caress than he had ever received from her, she said seriously :

"Is thy heart upon' this Methodist-hunting, Mark? thy own heart?"

And Mark, surprised and perplexed, turned round and caught in her eyes the same studious, inquiring look that had puzzled him before. But the question suggested such a sweet thought to him that he answered eagerly:

"Ay, mistress, ay; my heart's to pleasure you."

And to his dismay she turned quickly away and hid her face, and he went into the shop wondering in what new way he had managed to offend her.

When he had disposed of the grasping customer he returned to the parlour, but Kinty was gone, and he was compelled to give himself to his work in the office once more. But it was only a pretence; he was too excited by what had taken place to be able calmly to resume his occupation, and there were so many new questions to be discussed that his quill got dry again and again without ever having been put to paper.

Somehow he felt relieved in spite of himself, but when he asked himself why, he could give no satisfactory answer. It was evident that she was not greatly smitten with her lover of the night before, or she would not have discussed him so freely.

And why was she so concerned about his attitude towards the Methodists, if she had made up her mind to accept the other man? And then he recalled her curious look at the crucial moment when she was making him vow to persecute the despised sect. She could not be supposed to be anything but anxious that he should try to please her and her uncles; but if she were pleased, she showed it in a way that was most unusual to her.

But there! What *was* unusual to her? The only thing that was certain about her was that you never could be certain of her; at least, that had been his unhappy experience. And yet that look exercised his mind a great deal; it might mean nothing, but at any rate it made him uneasy, though in a strangely hopeful sort of way.

Well, he could but wait and hope, and if he had been in the habit of praying at all, he would perhaps have concluded that at this juncture of his experiences the first thing to make supplication for was that the Methodist preachers might never come to Helsham again. Just when he had reached this point, and was still musingly toying with his quill, he heard a man crying something in the street, and strolling leisurely to the door he opened it, and heard:

"Mr. Charles Wesley will, God willing, preach the Gospel at the market-cross to-morrow morning at eleven o' the clock."

CHAPTER XI

THE COMING OF WESLEY

HELSHAM, usually the dullest of places, was lively enough now. Rumours of the wildest and most exciting character arrived from one source or other almost every hour anent the political situation, and the honest tradesmen, roused to patriotic ardour one hour, and plunged into mournful forebodings the next, found it impossible to stick steadily to business, but leaving their affairs to their wives or assistants, gathered in little knots in the streets, receiving and assisting each other to digest the highly spiced stories which seemed to spring no one knew whence or how.

The taverns of course drove a flourishing trade, for the regular frequenters of each hostel foregathered at their own particular house of entertainment and turned it into a sort of committee room of political exigencies. Then the sound of the drum began to be heard in the streets, and the gay ribbons of the recruiting-sergeant were seen at many an ale-house door.

Press-gang rumours also made their appearance, and there was lamentation in more than one lowly home over a sturdy bread-winner carried off to serve his country in the approaching wars. And, as if these were not enough, about the middle of the afternoon of the day when Mark tried to come to an understanding with his mistress, the grave and reverend seigniors, who were discussing Jacobitism in the Hanover Arms' parlour, were startled to hear the news concerning the intended visit of Mr. Charles Wesley.

The vicar, who as usual was leading the conversation, received the information with a string of objurgations too violent to print, and members of the select circle near him turned and looked at each other as if to ask if so very provoking an announcement could by any possibility have truth in it.

"Methodism!" shouted the little tailor. "I tell ye, neighbours, 'tis jesuitical devilry! 'tis the popish wolf i' sheep's clothing."

"This very morn, no other," said the courier, who still wore riding-clothes and spoke in slow, weighty tones, "'twas told me in Purstock town that this same Charles Wesley had prayed for the Pretender in the open street."

"An excellent fine Government have we in these times, of a truth," sneered the tailor indignantly; but as this was getting perilously near to treasonable language, the landlord interposed and asked them to have regard for the reputation of the "house."

Then Mr. Josephus broke in and demanded why this rascally preaching was not put down by the proper authorities; and, acting on this suggestion, it was decided to send for the mayor, and if necessary press upon him the urgent importance of taking the matter into his own hands and forbidding the preachers the town. But the messenger returned with the information that his worship had that morning been called away to the county capital on business connected with the threatened invasion, and so it was decided to interview the town clerk.

That worthy, who was a seedy little fellow in an enormous wig that nearly hid his thin, bilious face, joined with his friends in denouncing the preachers, but explained, with many parenthetic regrets, that there was no law to punish the offenders *now*, but that he believed if a score or two honest lads could be got together who would take the law into their own hands, why, then the authorities were really so very much occupied with important matters of State that they might do what they listed without any excessive danger of being brought to account for it.

And then Mr. Josephus spoke up ; he was really intensely indignant. It had been bad enough when an unknown representative of this " fanatical " new religion had invaded the town and made such a disturbance, but when they had got over that, and were just settling down to their ordinary, easy-going life, to be threatened with a visit from one of the " heads " of this new craze was simply intolerable, and he, for his part, would find money, or anything else that was needed, to put a stop to such intrusions.

Having thus gradually worked themselves into

a sort of informal committee of ways and means, the company proceeded to make arrangements for the reception of the obnoxious preacher. The recruiting-sergeant was to be interviewed and plied with drink until he should promise to lend his drums for the occasion, and these, with similar instruments already belonging to towns-people, could be trusted to make noise enough to drown the voice of the most stentorian preacher.

The town clerk, having explained that, much as he should enjoy the fun, his office forbade him taking any open part in it, and the vicar, with much more sincerity, having bemoaned the fact that he must keep in the background for similar reasons, the little tailor was told off to secure the assistance of Big Barny, and Mr. Josephus undertook to repeat his former arrangement with the apprentices.

Some objection was raised to the matter being committed to Mark again, but Mr. Josephus felt that the former failure somehow reflected upon him, and he therefore insisted on the matter being left in his hands, in order that he might redeem his character by the thoroughness with which he should wipe out his former disgrace.

By this time it was quite dark, and when Mr. Josephus, with his brother and the vicar, arrived at the hat-shop the lamp had been lighted, and Mark was at his place behind the screen, struggling with the emotions which had been awakened by the announcement with which we closed the last chapter. Mr. Josephus bade him follow them into the parlour, and Mr. Ebenezer, dropping behind his companions, bestowed on the young journeyman a significant and complicated wink.

As soon as they were seated, and the vicar had paid his compliments to Kinty by means of a can of sack, Mr. Josephus opened the business by informing Mark of the coming of Mr. Wesley. Mark nodded, and, without exactly knowing why, stole a glance at his young mistress, who, however, seemed so occupied in making Mr. Ebenezer put his wig straight that she did not observe him.

He was now informed that there could be no more " shilly-shally " about dealing with the Methodists.   Mr. Josephus denounced them in terms of severest scorn, and demanded that Mark should prove that he was worthy of being regarded as a loyal townsman by at once making arrangements for a rigorous treatment of the religious invaders.   Mark attempted to raise an objection, but his master, who seemed to be in one of his rare talking moods, waved his hand and stopped him, and the journeyman had to listen to all the suggested plans, together with a long lecture on his duty to his masters and his country, rounded off with a number of vague hints of reward.

Again Mark would have interrupted, but Mr. Josephus, having got well a-going, found it difficult to stop, and, as he had partaken more freely than usual of intoxicants, he was in a most voluble mood, and once more launched out into a denunciation of the Wesleys and their followers, retailing a number of more or less embellished

stories of the reported doings of these " disgrace-
ful and criminal" religionists. Mark, though he
attempted to speak as already indicated, was only
too glad for his master to go on, for he was never
in a less fit condition to answer, and found it
impossible to make up his mind.

At length, however, his master's harangue came
to an end, and every eye in the company was
turned to him. He drew a long breath, hesitated
a little, rubbed the oak floor with one foot, and
then, raising his glance to his master's face, he
was just about to make an evasive reply when
Kinty, who was watching him closely, broke in:

"La! uncle, but I should like to see this
horrid preaching-monster—an' hearken him."

And whilst Mr. Josephus turned to her with
a snap, and the vicar lifted his hands in pious
horror, Mr. Ebenezer gave a chuckling sort of
laugh, rubbed his wig with the hand that held
his snuff-box, and, totally oblivious of the fact that
he was sprinkling his clothes with the pungent
dust, cried out:

"I—fatkins, an' so would I !"

And before any one could stop her, Kinty
had added:

"'Twould be vastly entertaining—better than
a gibbeting."

Josephus was dumbfounded. What would this
highly licensed madcap of a girl suggest next?
He looked from her to her equally frivolous uncle,
and then at Mark and the vicar, as if appealing
to them to know whether they had ever heard
of so outrageous a suggestion, and was just

opening his mouth to rebuke her as she deserved when Ebenezer broke in :

"No harm, brother ; he won't swallow us. 'Cursed cows have short horns.'"

And then Kinty took up the tale again. Very cleverly and cautiously she talked, appealing most deftly to that strong curiosity so deep in rustic natures, laughing gaily at all her uncle's fears of her getting corrupted by the preacher, and assuming always that, after they had gratified her whim, the design in hand could be carried out according to arrangement.

And her chief point made an impression. Neither her uncle nor the vicar was proof against the wish to see and hear, for once at any rate, a character that had become nationally notorious, and so, though Mr. Josephus held out for some time longer, when the vicar, under the spell of Kinty's bright eyes, went over to the enemy, he was compelled to surrender, though he did it with the worst possible grace, and with the strict stipulation that when they had once gratified a curiosity for which he pretended great contempt, but which he was conscious of not being entirely proof against himself, he should be no longer balked of his purpose.

Mark, to his immense relief and equally great astonishment, was therefore dismissed for the present, but with strict injunctions to hold himself in readiness to carry out his master's wishes at any moment of the coming day.

Next morning Mr. Josephus discovered that the feeling Kinty had expressed was by no means an uncommon one, a good many people in the town, who expressed the utmost horror of the new doctrines, confessing to a strong desire "for once only" to see and hear one of the chief exponents of them; and it became clear to him that, whatever the final issue, Mr. Charles Wesley might be sure of a great congregation when he appeared.

By ten o'clock little knots of people were already beginning to assemble at the cross,—smock-frocked labourers from the country, with here and there a "renter," as the tenant farmers were called; workmen of all sorts, idle apprentices, a chapman or two plying their wares, small tradesmen and their assistants, tavern-loungers, wool-croppers with their striped aprons and hosen caps, and women with white head-coverings and gaudy print dresses.

All these, and many more, gradually came to make up a crowd, which, as the appointed time drew near, must have numbered nearly a thousand persons. Except on fair-days, such a crowd had not assembled in Helsham market-place for many a long day.

Kinty, in a flat straw hat that drooped a little over the ears and gave her a coquettish look, came to the preaching in the company of Mr. Josephus; for her favourite uncle had grown impatient, and started off some twenty minutes before them. A little cry of disappointment escaped her as she came up and discovered that with her stature it would now be almost impossible to see, and she was looking round for some vantage-ground, when the currier, whose shop stood at the corner of the street, end on to the market-place, came forward and invited them upstairs into his storeroom, the flap door of which, when opened, commanded an excellent view of the whole square.

Here they could both see and hear; and Kinty, glancing over the crowd, perceived Uncle Ebenezer standing close up to the little knot of Methodists who were evidently waiting for the preacher. His wig was down into the back of his neck, and the cocked hat that held it in its place showed serious signs of falling behind him. It was evident that he, at any rate, was entirely engrossed.

A little farther from them stood the vicar, with the corners of his mouth drawn peevishly down, and his eyes constantly wandering towards Big Barny and a gang of roughs who occupied the middle of the road, and who were armed with cudgels and small bags of dust and stones. Close against the wall, under their feet, the occupants of the store next observed a band of men with drums, old cans, and superannuated musical instruments, upon which they were evidently growing impatient to perform, while the constable and two stout assistants formed a little party to themselves, and studied with dubious eyes the preparations of Barny and his colleagues.

Kinty was looking for Mark, and at last she spied him standing alongside Goody Wagstaffe, and listening with evident embarrassment to something the old dame was saying. At this moment her attention was attracted to a rough-looking fellow, evidently a small-coal man, who, mounted upon a donkey which he was trying to drive into the crowd, was flourishing over his shoulders a long flail-like thing, the lash of which had bladders strung upon it, with which he was belabouring all who came within his reach.

This was too good fun for a man of Big Barny's tastes to resist, and so he darted forward, and was just grabbing at the bladder-whip when some one touched him from behind, and springing round with a foul curse upon his lips, he found himself face to face with a carefully dressed and evidently very gentlemanly clergyman, who politely asked to be allowed to pass. Barny's long arms fell to his side, his jaw dropped confusedly, and, with a blundering apology, he stepped back ; and then turned and stared with amazement at his comrades, for the person who had spoken to him was Charles Wesley. With a clumsy respectfulness, amounting almost to awe, the crowd fell back on each side, and the preacher strode to the cross.

Taking his stand upon the worn steps, and facing the crowd with respectful confidence, he gave out a hymn, and almost immediately commenced to sing. The inhabitants of Helsham had very little knowledge of hymnology, and so with the exception of two or three who stood nearest to the preacher nobody joined in at first. But the tune was taking, though somewhat plaintive, and first one and then another took up the unwonted exercise.

The preacher read out the verses one by one ;

the words were bright and warm, and the chorus was irresistible. Soon the greater part of that immense company were singing, and that with heart and relish, and when at last the hymn ended there could be no doubt in any person's mind present that Mr. Wesley would get a hearing for once.

The prayer, which was long and impassioned, was followed with keenest attention by the now numerous occupants of the currier's store doorway, but whilst they were not able to catch in any single sentence the slightest phrase which could be applied to Jacobitism, there was that in the supplication which rebuked them, and made them feel something akin to shame.

After a portion of Scripture had been read and another hymn sung to an old psalm-tune well known to all, the clergyman began to preach. Some one tapped a drum as the text was announced, but so many angry heads were turned round sharply, and so many people cried "Hush!" that the venture was not persevered with. In two or three moments after he commenced, the preacher had such attention as the vicar had never been able to boast of during his whole ministry, and necks were craned forward and hands were placed behind ears in order that not a syllable might be lost.

The effect seemed to Kinty to be something uncanny, and whilst her own heart fluttered as some of the burning words forced their way down to her conscience, she became aware of a strange, subtle, sympathetic influence that was moving

the crowd at her feet. A moment or two later
the sensation became audible ; a soft, low, moaning
hum rose to her ears, and the crowd seemed to
be under some wondrous spell.

The man with the donkey had got down from
his seat, and was standing gazing at the preacher
spellbound ; Big Barny, with dropped jaw and
raised eyebrows, was leaning heavily over the
shoulders of a little man before him, and Kinty
caught the gleam of tears in his eyes ; whilst
Goody Wagstaffe, a few feet from the preacher,
was turning up to heaven a face that shone with
a wonderful light.

Kinty heaved a great sigh and looked again
for Mark, but as she scanned the heads of the
crowd she saw a couple of thin arms suddenly
thrown up, and there broke upon her ear the
most awful shriek she had ever heard.

Before she could draw her breath a man's
voice came from the outer edge of the crowd
in a cry that was despair itself, and as she
stepped back into the store in terror, a woman,
standing just under the doorway, threw herself
headlong upon the crowd, and began to pour
out the most repulsive and horrible blasphemies.

The scene that followed haunted Kinty's
imagination for many a day. The preacher's
voice was drowned in the wails of frantic men
and women ; respectable townsmen, heads of
families, stood there and sobbed like children ;
others fell on their knees and began to cry for
the Divine mercy ; women suddenly burst forth
into weird hysterical laughter, and passionately

hugged each other ; and, to complete the picture, the roughs in the background began to beat a wild ran-tan on their drums.

The preacher stopped now, and sprang fearlessly into the midst of the crowd, vainly striving to subdue the emotions his words had aroused, and administer comfort to those in genuine spiritual distress.   And at this moment Uncle Josephus took the terrified and almost helpless Kinty and led her away from the door.

CHAPTER XII

AN ATTACK

AND whilst Kinty and her uncle were making their way home, Mark Rawson still stood watching the scene we have just described. He was about as innocent of religion as any other healthy young pagan of his time, and whatever tendency there might have been in him in that direction was checked and almost smothered under the strong ambition which had recently taken possession of him.

He had, however, quite his share of that native reverence for sacred things which lies deep in the breast of every human being, and is the surest thing to which the advocates of religion can appeal. In his conception of things, whatever religion was or was not, it represented the decencies and respectabilities of life, and the scene upon which he was gazing produced in him a strong but very complete revulsion of feeling.

Religion! To connect these outrageous scenes with holy things was nothing short of blasphemy. It was more like Pandemonium, and about the likeliest thing he could think of for bringing

Christianity into disrepute with all well-disposed persons.

There, a few yards from him, was Big Barny grovelling on the cobble-stones and smearing his dirty face with tear-stains, whilst he bellowed and slobbered like a whipped schoolboy, and just behind him stood his draggle-tailed paramour, " Yorkshire Peggy," who was tearing her matted red hair with one hand, and clinging with childish terror to the cloak of Goody Wagstaffe with the other.

Groans and sobs and occasional bursts of hysterical laughter filled the air, and even decent tradesfolk and respectable women were wringing their hands and making strenuous efforts to get at Mr. Wesley to speak to him. Mark was outraged ; scorn and indignation burned within him ; and when the carpenter in whose loft the Methodists held their private meetings rose from his knees, where he had been speaking to a sobbing girl, and touched Mark on the elbow, saying as he did so, in what to the young hatter seemed tones of whining sanctimoniousness, " Will you also be His disciple ? " Mark felt strongly impelled to knock him down, and turning away, with eyes that flashed with scorn, and a lip that was curled in intense contempt, he hissed out :

" Thou scabby shoulder-clapper ! " and strode angrily back to his work.

" That thee, Mark ? " called out Mr. Josephus as he entered the shop, and proceeded to hang up his cap in the little office.

" Ay, ay, sir," answered Mark, hesitating, as he turned to his books.

"Then come hither, man—come hither!"

Promptly obeying the summons, the marks of his recent disgust still traceable on his face deepened as he discovered Kinty, sitting limp and wan in the elbow-chair, whilst Mr. Josephus, agitated and angry, was pacing before the fire, impatiently waiting his subordinate's appearance; and the vicar, with the inevitable can of liquor at his elbow, sat drumming his fingers on the table.

"Well, what think's ta o' matters now?" demanded Josephus, glaring fiercely at the young journeyman.

"Think, sir?" cried Mark, impatient to disburden himself; "what can I think? 'Tis witchery!—witchery, no less."

"Witchery?" shouted the parson in husky tones. "'Tis devilry!—hellish devilry! Conversion, sir?—i' gad, but they've converted me to-day! Devils, say you?—yea, truly; I believe i' devils *now*, legions o' devils, an' possession o' devils. Sink me, but I believe it all now!"

"What is the Government about?" began Mr. Josephus. But, jumping to his feet as if he had been struck, the vicar burst out again in wrathful scorn:

"Government, sir? Government is passing Toleration Acts an' Conventicle Acts, an' manufacturing Jacobites by wholesale! Gad! we shall all be Jacobites soon out o' pure compulsion!" and then, scared lest any one should have heard his rash and treasonable words, he glanced quickly round and sank back somewhat abashed into his chair.

But nobody there objected to his violent language, Mark least of all. He was studying Kinty, and instead of finding her as he expected, scornful and mocking, he observed that she was silent, timid, and woebegone. He was indignant.

It took no little to intimidate that bright and plucky little woman, and the fact that she had been so affected was the strongest possible evidence of the outrageous nature of the incidents they had just witnessed. There must be no further dallying with an evil of this sort. His mind was entirely made up. Pity and toleration were worse than wasted on wretches who brought terror and madness amongst their fellow-men.

He was ready for anything, as eager now to commence as he had before been reluctant, and ere they had talked many minutes a scheme had been sketched by which all future public preaching should be stopped, and even the meetings at the "loft" brought to an end, even if they had to resort to the extreme course of burning the building over the heads of the Methodists.

But at this moment Mr. Ebenezer came waddling into the parlour, and everybody turned to look at him, and then at each other, for the old fellow's appearance was such as to excite the utmost concern.

He seemed suddenly to have become a smaller man ; his garments hung loosely upon him, and what of his face could be seen from under his forward-tilted hat was ashen grey in colour,

His hands hung heavily upon the sides of his great-coat pockets, and he brought a flavour into the room which told that he had been drinking.

He did not speak as he entered, he did not even raise his head, but shuffled to his seat in the chimney-corner, and dropped into his place like an overwearied traveller.

Mark watched his old master with concern, and with an inward curse laid the change he saw at the door of the objectionable new religionists, against whom he vowed summary and terrible vengeance. Kinty also seemed distressed, and went quietly over to her uncle ; and, slipping her tiny hand into his, sat on the arm of his chair, mutely assuring him of her sympathy.

Then the vicar started the conversation again ; but Mr. Ebenezer seemed to be quite uninterested, and was soon, in the excitement of the discussion, forgotten.

All through that day and the next, whilst Mark was maturing his plans for attacking the Methodists, Kinty was engaged in nursing her uncle ; and whenever Mark went into the parlour, he was dismissed in the fewest possible words, and could get no opportunity of speaking to his mistress alone.

Mr. Ebenezer developed gout, and sat in the corner with his right foot enswathed in cloths, and engaged in a series of exceedingly interesting experiments with various famous local cures for his disorder. This doctoring seemed to divert the old fellow's mind, and he was somewhat more cheerful, the concern of his friends being chiefly shown in their curiosity to ascertain exactly how he had been affected by Mr. Wesley's preaching.

That this was the original cause was very clear, and that he had been strongly moved by it was also apparent; for the appearance of gout in his great toe was the almost certain consequence of any extraordinary mental excitement. But how precisely the affair had affected him, and what his present opinion might be, they had no means of finding out, for he was most unusually taciturn.

The only thing that really interested him was some new remedy for his old enemy, and in the course of some forty-eight hours he had tried treacle poultices, in which both he and Kerry the maid had much faith, elixir of vitriol, raw beefsteak plaster, a decoction of tansy, and was just arranging for a sort of primitive vapour bath, when the vicar called on the Methodist business, and immediately prescribed a preparation of elder buds.

On the third morning, therefore, after the now notorious sermon, when Mark stepped into the parlour on some matter of trade, he found his old master sitting with his bad leg upon a chair, slowly sipping elder tea, whilst a pile of pamphlets, all of which were in some way connected with Methodism, lay on the table before him.

To Mark's surprise, the patient scarcely noticed his presence, but kept on reading the pamphlet he happened to have in his hand, every now and again taking off his great horn glasses and polishing them on the corner of the tablecloth, sighing heavily as he did so. At this point, however, Kinty came in, accompanied by Kerry, who carried a large bowl of some herbal decoction for the purpose of fomenting the invalid's foot, and Mr. Ebenezer rather astonished Mark by asking the domestic what was the latest news about the Methodists.

He grew more surprised, and a little suspicious also, when Kerry, as if expecting the question, began a long story of the changes which had been produced in the town by Charles Wesley's sermon.

Big Barny and Yorkshire Peggy had made arrangements to be legally married, as a condition of membership amongst the new sect; Tommy Rolls, the man who had carried the bladder-whip on the day of Mr. Wesley's visit, had sold his dogs and rabbit-snares, and declared his intention of abandoning poaching for ever; whilst Eli Glass, the keeper of the Fox and Grapes, a disreputable ale-house in the lowest part of Tan-pit Lane, had handed over to the custom-house authorities certain spirits which he had been in the habit of retailing, but which he was not certain had ever had duty paid upon them, and had poured out his stock of small-ale into the "goyt," with the avowed intention of never selling intoxicants again.

Mr. Ebenezer seemed very strangely interested in these details, and so far forgot himself as to set his foot into the nearly boiling herbs; but though he drew it back again with a yell, and

repeated it when Kerry, on her knees, accidentally
touched the inflamed toe, he was most un-
accountably indifferent, and soon had the serving-
woman running over a list of persons in the town
who had shown leanings towards the obnoxious
sect. When she finished her tale with the im-
formation that so many people now attended
the Methodists' services that the loft was too
small, and they were on the look-out for a larger
building, he lapsed into a brown study, out of
which even his interest in his own disordered
member was not sufficient to recall him.

Mark did not like these symptoms at all.
Surely the old man was not coming what the
sectaries would call "under conviction"! Now
that he was in a fair way for ingratiating himself
in the good graces of Mr. Josephus, it would be
a pretty complication if he found Mr. Ebenezer,
whom he so greatly respected, against him.

And then there was young mistress. Why
was she so very silent and shy these days?
Why was it that she had never given him the
chance of exchanging words with her since the
day of the now famous sermon?

But, after all, these were minor matters;
the Methodists themselves had helped him out
of a great difficulty, and had put it into his
power to get on terms again with the all-important person upon whom the fulfilment of his
ambitions depended, and he would make the
most of his opportunity, and strike whilst the
iron was hot.

Mr. Josephus had been most unusually amiable

these last few days, and had told him not to spare money, time, or pains to accomplish the task he had now formally undertaken, and he had had so much encouragement to proceed from both the vicar and the landlord of the Hanover Arms that there was no longer any room for hesitation.

Besides, every day that passed over was giving a chance to his rival. He had discovered, by diligently plying Kerry as he sat over his meals in the kitchen, that there was something in the visit of the young maltster which he had so accidentally been witness to, and he could not help wondering how it was that that young man remained quiet so long. For, as far as he could ascertain, he had never been to the house since. At any rate, every day the formal proposal which he dreaded so much was delayed was a day gained for him, and he was determined to make the most of his opportunities.

On the fifth morning after the scene in the market-place, as Mark was engaged in a prolonged and irritating struggle with an old farmer who was " cheapening " a beaver hat, who should walk into the shop but his worship the mayor, who inquired in a very surly voice for Mr. Josephus. He was evidently suffering under great, though suppressed, excitement, and gnawed chafingly at his under lip as he waited for Mark's answer to his question.

The young hatter went suddenly cold, and with clumsy embarrassment ushered the magistrate into the parlour, whence, as he absently struggled with the haggling customer, he caught sounds of loud-voiced and apparently angry discussion. Then Mr. Josephus came to the parlour door and beckoned him to join them, and he was compelled to leave the old farmer to the shopman, whilst he went with beating heart to do his master's bidding.

The mayor, who had all along been regarded as shamefully indifferent to the disturbances caused by the Methodists, now seemed to have found some cause for great resentment ; he was white to the lips, and his utterance, which was never very clear, had now become confused and sputtering in the excess of his anger.

" 'Tis preposterous ! 'tis an af-af-af-affront to the majesty o' the law ! 'tis rebellion ! rank, staring rebellion, no less ! " he roared, smiting the table with his fist, and glaring round the room as though appealing against any gainsayer.

" Why doesn't your worship bring the law on 'em ? " asked Mr. Josephus in respectful perplexity.

" Law ! Law, says you ? That's where it b-b-b-ites, man ! 'Tis the law that has done it ! 'Tis your new Riot Acts an' your Toleration Laws that stop us ! Putting down disturbers ! Why, man, 'tis the very thing that causes 'em all ! " And then, breaking suddenly off and making a grab at Mark, he seized him by the lapel of his coat and went on excitedly : " Sithi, youngster ! go to it ! to it, man ! Purge 'em out ! burn 'em out ! drown 'em out ! and, by the great Harry, I'll give thee five gowden guineas ! "

A deep groan came at this moment from somewhere behind the magistrate, and whipping petulantly round he discovered Mr. Ebenezer sitting in his accustomed corner, and apparently entirely engrossed in the condition of his toe.

The diversion, however, caused Mark to look round, and the pride he was beginning to feel at being regarded as of so much importance by the chief men of the town suffered a sudden shadowing as he perceived Kinty looking at him with sad and somewhat anxious eyes. But the mayor had resumed the discussion upon the Methodists, and Mark soon forgot everything else in the flattering sense of his own importance and the gain he was expecting to make out of his undertaking to lead the persecutions.

They talked a long time, and it soon became clear to him that he must act at once if he desired to retain either the favour of the maltster or the good opinion of his master; and so, after a long discussion of ways and means, Mark was released for the day from his service in the shop, and so set at liberty to carry out his arrangements for uprooting the intrusive sectaries.

He started on his errand in the highest possible spirits, though he could not help reflecting with regret how much easier his task would have been if he had gone forward with it before Mr. Wesley's visit, for then Big Barny, the small-coal man, and several others could have been got together at a moment's notice. But they had now gone over to the enemy, and he had to

refuse to allow himself to think how awkward
these men might make it if they were inclined
to show fight.

As he proceeded with his task, however, his
difficulties seemed to increase. Slinger, a roistering apprentice whitesmith, replied to his invitation
by looking him solemnly in the face, and quoting,
"Touch not Mine anointed, and do My prophets
no harm"; and two roughs, who were brickmakers,
offered to pray with him, whilst Corny Steep, the
maltster's waggoner, handed him a tract, and
exhorted him to make his "calling and election
sure," and he soon discovered that he was not
only making no progress with his scheme, but
was forewarning the Methodists themselves of
the danger that threatened them.

Eventually, however, he had to swallow his
pride, and apply to the ostlers and stablemen at
the Hanover Arms, and the other old posting-
houses of the town, and these, with the assistance
of a band of young quarrymen, formed a company
which in numbers at any rate was more than
satisfactory; and having fixed the corner of the
lane leading down to the carpenter's shop as
the rendezvous for the evening, Mark hastened
back to the shop to inform Mr. Josephus of his
success.

Punctually at eight o'clock he made for the
place appointed, and found his band already
assembled. At his bidding, they lighted their
lanterns and then darkened them, and followed
him down the entry, only to discover that the
place was in total darkness. Staples, a red-haired,

out-of-work "drawer" (potboy), suggested that they should break into the workshop underneath the loft, and with the shavings set fire to the building; but as the mayor had warned him against such an extreme course, Mark withheld them, and dismissed them for the night, after arranging for a similar meeting the following evening.

Later on the same night he discovered that, as he feared, the Methodists had got wind of their intention, and had taken refuge in a dwelling house at the other end of the town.

Next evening they met with a similar experience, and though to satisfy some of the more impetuous spirits Mark attempted to find out where the "fanatics" were met, he was not successful, and he had some difficulty in persuading his assistants to re-assemble yet once again on the following night. Mark's forces were somewhat depleted when they came together, but he learnt as soon as he arrived that the Methodists were already in the room, two or three indeed having passed to the gathering whilst his comrades had stood waiting.

With the same arrangements as before they stole quietly up the entry and into the yard, and to their delight found that the Methodists had commenced to sing. At a word from their leader the gang divided and surrounded the building, standing sufficiently far back to be able to see the dim light through the windows. The tune was soft and plaintive, and the singers were evidently few in number.

"Hold, boys! tarry till I whistle and then fling all together. Take me?"

Various husky grunts came in response, there was a moment or two of silence, broken only by the droning of the tune within the building, then a shrill whistle, followed by a shout and a whiz of stones and the crashing and shivering of glass.

"To it! another!" shouted Mark, and as cries and groans came from inside crash, crash, came the stones once more.

Howls and shrieks, the scuffling of feet and the overturning of seats could now be heard, and a moment later the door of the loft was flung open, and the tall form of Goody Wagstaffe appeared at the top of the stairs.

"Mercy, neighbours, mercy!" she cried, lifting her long thin arms in supplication.

"The witchwoman! Duck her! To th' pond wi' her!" shouted some one; and in less time than it takes to describe the poor old soul was dragged from her place, hoisted upon the shoulders of four strong young fellows, and a moment later a piercing shriek and a loud, heavy splash announced that the barbarous wretches had fulfilled their threat.

Meanwhile Mark and the others had forced their way into the room, where a scene met them which at any other time would have made the young hatter sick with shame and resentment In the middle of the room knelt two women, with blood trickling down their faces and arms lifted up to their Maker in prayer for deliverance.

Into the dim corners wives had been thrust by their husbands, who stood before them with white, set faces, evidently resolved to defend their beloved ones at any cost, and here and there men and women were struggling over benches and the prostrate forms of their fellow-worshippers towards the door.

"Out o' this! Out o' this, you snivellers!" shouted Mark; but his own sick heart took all the menace out of his words, and he was just leaning forward to see more distinctly in the dimness, when he caught sight of a little white face, which, with closed eyes, was turned up to the roof, and in the midst of the uproar he heard a song, the words and tune of which were both strange to him, come forth from the bruised and bleeding mouth of a maiden of about fourteen summers.

> " Other refuge have I none,
>   Hangs my helpless soul on Thee
> Leave, ah, leave me not alone,
>   Still support and comfort me.
> All my trust on Thee is stayed,
>   All my help from Thee I——

but here, perhaps fortunately for Mark's feelings, a great, hulking fellow seized a bench and was lifting it through the window, but one end of it caught the rude, wooden, six-branched candlestick which hung in the centre of the room, and brought it down with a tremendous crash upon the little singer's head.

In spite of himself, Mark uttered a fierce shriek;

but as the room was now in total darkness, all
he could do was to grope forward towards the
now prostrate singer. Before he could reach her,
however, there was a loud shout outside, the
youths behind Mark were pushed violently forward, and the deep voice of Big Barny was
heard calling on the rioters to desist.

Mark struggled hard to reach the singer, but
the more he pushed one way the more he was
pressed the other. All at once he felt the cool
night air on his cheek, he was lifted from his feet
and carried in the press for three or four yards,
then a wild blow struck him somewhere on the
side of his head, he felt himself suddenly whizzing
through the air, and when he came to himself
he was lying on the ground underneath the steps
leading up to the loft, with a head that felt as if
it did not belong to him, and a leg that was
twisted under him and broken.

CHAPTER XIII

THE FLAX MILL GOSPEL

BEFORE he could quite realise all that had
happened to him Mark had swooned again, and
when he next recovered consciousness he was
lying on his sister's truckle bed by the fire at
home, and the irascible local apothecary was
busy setting his limb. The pain in that member,
however, was as nothing to what he felt in other
parts of his body; he was sore all over, and
his head sung and swam again if he moved it
ever so little. He had fallen or been pushed
from the top of the unrailed staircase of the
loft, and his sister and the other volunteer
nurses in the room were giving thanks in incoherent terms to Providence that he had not
been killed outright.

The apothecary snapped and swore at him
as if it were a crime to have broken a limb;
and Mark was heartily glad when the operation
was finished and he was bidden go to sleep.
But that soon proved to be impossible, and he
spent a weary night struggling with pain that
every hour seemed to grow worse.

Immediately after breakfast next morning

Mr. Ebenezer, still lame, and limping on a stick, arrived, bringing with him a local bone-setter of great repute, and in spite of Mark's feeble protests, his suffering member was subjected to a long and not too gentle examination, the bone-setter pishing and pshawing and shaking his head, and finally announcing that the leg was not set at all, and that the patient must during the night, have suffered agonies.

Mark, though scared at the prospect of a second operation, was compelled to confirm this latter statement ; and so the limb was once more subjected to professional treatment, and the poor sufferer groaned and almost screamed under the hands of his tormentor. He was soon, however, aware of a change in his own feelings ; and when his visitors had left him it was not long before he had dropped into a nice refreshing sleep, from which he awoke later in the afternoon to find Mistress Kinty bending anxiously over him.

During the next few days he began to realise that this accident of his seemed likely to turn out very much to his advantage. The young mistress was most anxious and assiduous in her attentions, and showed a concern which was far in excess of anything that could be expected from her merely as the niece of his employers ; the only drawback being that, although his sister very considerately gave them many opportunities, Kinty never would remain alone with him, and so he could not, contrive as he would, get a chance of speaking to her about the matter that was always uppermost in his thoughts. Moreover, there was a gravity and soberness in her manner which was to him most perplexing, and which he could not any longer put down to mere concern for his recovery.

The mayor also sent little delicacies from his kitchen nearly every day, and twice during the first fortnight of his confinement came to see him. Mr. Ebenezer's attentions, though somewhat embarrassing, were only what he might expect from the kindly heart of the old man, and but for the fact that he produced almost every time he came some new salve or lotion, and insisted on its being used, Mark would have been glad enough to see him.

The most encouraging circumstance, however, was the conduct of Mr. Josephus. That worthy came every day, and often in a roundabout way dropped remarks which showed Mark that he felt that the accident had been brought about in an endeavour to oblige him, which of course was the sweetest possible medicine to the sufferer. In addition to these things, Mark rejoiced to discover that he was being sorely missed in the business. Mr. Ebenezer made no bones about it, but as he saw it gratified the patient, he enlarged to the point of romance upon the inconveniences they were suffering, and the impatience they all felt for his recovery.

But Mr. Ebenezer, as Mark well knew, took little interest in the business, and it was to his brother that he looked for signs of his own importance. And certainly these were not want.

ing, for almost every day the senior partner of the firm would come in, ostensibly to inquire how he was progressing, and then in an off-handed, clumsily disguised manner make a business remark, which would lead Mark to reply as he knew he was expected to do, and supply the information that was required ; whilst once, and sometimes oftener, each day the shop-man would come down post haste with some question which required an immediate answer, and which showed the young hatter how very important he was to the well-being of the business.

One thing, however, greatly troubled him ; whilst he was thus laid aside, the way was entirely open to his rival, and he made no doubt that that young gentleman was making the most of his opportunities. This was a matter upon which he could not ask questions except very cautiously, and all he could ascertain was the information which Kerry, who came down every day with some dainty from the young mistress, imparted, that, as far as she could observe, there was no change in the situation.

Judge, therefore, of his surprise and delight when his sister came hurrying into the room one afternoon about a fortnight after the accident, with the amazing but delightful information that the young maltster had turned Methodist, and had been driven from home by his indignant father and disinherited. The more he reflected on this intelligence the better he liked it.

The way was now fairly open to him. That Mr. Josephus would follow the mayor's example and repudiate with scorn the pretensions of a man who belonged to the hated sectaries he was absolutely certain, and the inconveniences to which they were being put by his absence from the shop were working for him as no amount of pleading on his part could have done.

Mr. Josephus had already hinted that they would have to remove him to the shop as soon as it was safe to do so, in order to have him at hand for consultation; and when that came about, and he was left, as he knew he would be, many hours of the day in the parlour with the young mistress, he was confident that with the feelings she had already betrayed towards him, he would not be long before he accomplished his heart's desire.

As to the Methodists, he felt a little weary of them ; and as this accident of his had served his purpose with his master more effectually than any amount of heretic-baiting could have done, he would be glad enough to wash his hands of them altogether. He had heard without much interest that they were supposed to be entirely disheartened by their persecutions ; the loft had been left in such a state on the night of the attack that it was not possible to use it again, if even it had been safe to do so ; and nobody else would lend them any sort of building in which to assemble, and so Mark's sister who was his chief informant, supposed they had heard the last of them,

Mark was not so sure ; but he was glad enough to know that he would not be troubled any further about them, and almost grateful to them for having captured his rival, and thus removed one of the most serious dangers to his prospects.

Meanwhile his injured limb progressed somewhat slowly, and this exposed him to the torture of having to take a succession of infallible remedies prescribed by Uncle Ebenezer for the purpose of "bringing him on," a compensating consideration being that his master had conceived a violent prejudice against the then all-popular bleeding, and he was therefore delivered from that infliction.

Five or six weeks thus passed away and the spring was creeping upon them, the days grew longer and the air softer, and Mark was getting out of all patience to be about again. The bone-setter, however, was inexorable, and he was not even permitted to be removed, as he so much wished, to the shop. Lack of active occupation robbed the patient somewhat of his natural rest, and he found it impossible to sleep long after dawn.

On a certain Sabbath morning, about the end of March, he lay wakeful and reflective in his little bed by the fireside, feeling somewhat oppressed by the unusual warmth of the air and the closeness of the room. By the aid of his long walking-stick he had succeeded, after several attempts, in unloosing the fastening of the little window just behind him and opening the aperture, when his ears were delighted with a stream of delightful bird melody that came pouring into the room, heightened as it was to him by the balmy sweetness of the fresh morning air. No other sounds could be heard, except the distant lowing of cattle and an occasional footstep in the lane, and he surrendered himself to the influences of the occasion and felt his soul bathed in soothing, yet healing and purifying peace.

For an hour or more he lay steeping himself in the quiet influences about him, and was just beginning to think it was time to wake his sister, who, since his accident, had occupied his own little bedroom under the thatch, when suddenly the stillness was broken by a man's deep voice apparently close to him. It sounded like some one reading aloud, and before he had time to think whence it came, there rose in the air the solemn strains of the Old Hundredth, sung, evidently, by a goodly number of mixed voices.

"Good Lord!" cried Mark, "'tis the Methodists!" and, with a protesting frown and a gesture of petulant disgust, he flung himself back upon his couch. But the music clung to him, seemed, in fact, to wrap him round, and before the hymn was finished he found himself listening to it attentively, and finding in it something that harmonised somehow with the sweet stillness which at first it seemed so rudely to have disturbed.

Then the singing stopped, and Mark began to wonder where the sounds came from. At first he had concluded they were holding an open-air service in the lane, but the solitary man's voice he could now hear, evidently raised in prayer, seemed to come in through the little window, and so, dragging himself to his feet, and groping for his crutch, he moved cautiously to the open casement and looked out.

Yes, there it was. Standing end on to the back of the cottage, so close that the near corner obstructed the light of the little window, was a comparatively large building which, as long as Mark could remember, had been used as a flax mill. He recollected now that during his illness he had heard that it had been given up, and he understood at once that the Methodists must have got hold of it by some means and turned it into a meeting-house. The nearest window had a swinging flap for its upper half, and that was open, and this was the reason he had heard so distinctly.

For the moment a curious, almost superstitious, feeling took possession of him ; it appeared as if some mysterious powers were at work on behalf of these hated religionists, and he might, after all, have to attribute his late accident to occult agencies, he did not care further to define.

But the leader of the service was raising his voice, and Mark soon perceived that he was praying. He could now hear every word distinctly, and what a prayer it was ! Instead of the droning, sing-song, lifeless sentences to which he had been accustomed at church, this petition glowed with intense reality. It seemed to Mark as if the suppliant were in the very presence of some one from whom he was desperately yet confidently intent upon wringing some immediate concession. He pleaded boldly, almost passionately, and yet with a reverence that seemed all the truer because it was not expressed in words.

It was a long, roundabout supplication, but Mark felt as if he could see some great shining personality with whom the suppliant was pleading, and when at last the petition came to a close, he heaved a great sigh and fell against the cottage wall profoundly impressed.

Just then he heard an exclamation behind him, and, glancing round, discovered his sister making her way to his window. With an impatient but decisive gesture he waved her back, and when she persisted in speaking he almost hissed out, "Hush!" Unconsciously he had thrust his head farther into the casement, but all the sounds he could catch were voices speaking in conversational tones together with the very puzzling clinking of pots, for the fact was the worshippers were holding a love-feast, only Mark had never heard of such an institution.

Presently they began to sing again, this time a lively, swinging tune which, before Mark could fairly catch, changed into a sort of duet, shrill voices of women being followed by the deep bass tones of the men, and then the women again, and so on for some little time, until, but for the catching nature of the music, Mark could have smiled at the, to him, ludicrous performance. After another short pause he heard a strange voice speaking—a woman's—but he could not catch the low tones, and when she raised her voice, she became at his distance incoherent.

Suddenly the deep tones of a voice he knew reached him, and Big Barny began to tell the story of his long life of wickedness and his subsequent conversion, with all the blessed consequences both for him and the woman who was now his wife. Then there was another sing, two or three more speakers followed, and Mark listened spellbound to a tale that moved his very soul, coming from the evidently excited Goody Wagstaffe.

By this time he had got his head halfway through the window, and his sister again remonstrated with him, only to be rebuked with even a sterner impatience than before. The love-feast had for the time, at any rate, entirely captured him, and as he strained his whole attention to hear, he now caught, soft and low, the hymn which the little maiden had sung in the loft on the day of the attack.

It seemed to vibrate through Mark's whole nature; but whilst he listened it stopped, and some one—evidently the little girl before named —was speaking. But he could not hear, only, after he had listened for some time, he just caught in tones of growing excitement : "God bless our enemies ! Jesus died for our enemies ! 'Twas only one little wound on my head, but He was wounded all over for me—and for them."

Mark felt he was choking, and drew back,

catching as he did so the chorus of Amens! with which the finish of the child's "testimony" was received. A moment more, and he heard the leader praying again, and as he placed his hand on his thumping heart that he might hear what was being asked for, there was a shuffling of feet in the flax mill, and realising that the meeting was over, he sank back and fell upon the little bed overcome.

And now it seemed as though a long lazy, and conveniently docile conscience had suddenly awakened, and was taking vengeance for its past ill-treatment. Every scene in which he had taken part against the Methodists came back to him with startling vividness, and drove deeper the iron into his soul.

For some moments he lay in agonised thought, and would have relieved himself with groans, or even tears, but for the presence of his sister. Twice she summoned him to breakfast, but he took no heed; and it was only when she came and pulled his hands away from over his eyes, and sneeringly asked him if the Methodists had "madded" him, too, that he roused himself and drew up to the table. It was little that he ate that morning, and his sister grew angrier and more scornful as she vainly pressed first one little dainty upon him and then another. He felt more like himself, however, after the meal, and suggested to Nancy that his accident must have made him weak and nervous; and she, not to let him off too easily, retorted that he always had been weak where he ought to be strongest.

He was content, however, to escape thus easily, and spent the whole morning trying to get rid of the impression made upon him by the love-feast, and convince himself that his conduct towards the new sect was quite justifiable. Somehow, his reasoning, however conclusive, brought him little relief, and he found himself growing strangely pensive and irritable.

In the afternoon, however, when church was over, Mistress Kinty called to see him, and she looked so bonny in her Sunday clothes, and was so very bright and cheerful, with something of her old gaiety of manner, that he forgot everything else whilst she was present. Then Mr. Josephus looked in, and before he was well seated commenced to tell his young friend that the vicar had just turned away half a score Methodists who had the "owdaciousness" to come to the sacrament. The old master, Mark thought, seemed unusually bitter, even for him, against the hated religionists, and he soon discovered the reason.

"Why, sir," he said, "the Methodists have got the flax mill."

It would appear that Mark had unconsciously touched an angry wound somewhere upon his master, for the old man jumped excitedly to his feet.

"Flax mill, i' Gad! flax mill! Ay, ay, they've got the flax mill, sure enough," and he laughed bitterly, as though there were some unknown hatefulness in the circumstance.

Mark scarce knew how to reply to so mysterious

a remark, but he was saved the trouble, for Mr. Josephus suddenly rose from his seat, and stepping across the sanded floor bent over Mark and demanded fiercely :

" Where got the Methodists three hundred pounds? the scurvy scratchbacks haven't a guinea among them."

" Nay, nay, sir. Where ? " asked Mark, looking up into his employer's face inquiringly, and waiting for further light.

" Where ? What drivelling old doze-pot 'ud do the like, save one. 'Tis *him*, man, him, I'm telling thee ! "

Now " him," however devoid of grammar, was usually the term with which Mr. Josephus indicated his brother, and Mark's eyes opened wide, and he gave vent to a prolonged " W-he-w ! " That was a complication indeed, and he sat back in his chair and looked at his employer with a long, wondering stare, as if to assist his amazed reflections. It was evidently only a shrewd guess at present, but for the next few minutes Mr. Josephus poured out upon his absent and eccentric brother all the maledictions he could command, his wrath being intensified by the fact well enough understood by Mark that easygoing and placable as Mr. Ebenezer was, he was not easy to manage on the side of his cranks.

This then explained much in his junior master's conduct which had been perplexing, and he realised that in trying to oblige one employer he had inadvertently estranged the other. And he did not forget either that where Mistress

Kinty was concerned, Mr. Ebenezer might easily
prove a more dangerous opponent than even
his narrow-minded brother.

For some time, therefore, after Mr. Josephus's
departure, Mark remained in anxious thought
over this new complication, and the experiences
of the morning were crowded out of his thoughts.
A little later, however, Mr. Ebenezer called at
the cottage, and was just the same jovial kindly
soul as ever, and Mark felt considerably relieved
when he made no allusion to the new sect.

There was no service at the church in the
evenings, but Mark's sister, as the night was
fine, went out for a much-needed walk in the
fresh air, and he was left—not altogether un-
willingly—by himself. He was tired by this
time, and lay down on the little bed to rest ;
but whilst his body reposed, his busy brain
was as active as ever, and he was just going
over again the events of the day when he
heard singing once more, and realised that the
Methodists were holding another meeting.

Somehow, the thing disturbed him strangely.
He got up, banged the open window, and
began to pace the floor. Then he laughed at
his own weakness, and told himself that he would
go through with the scheme on which he had
set his heart, " Methodists or no Methodists."
The music seemed to irritate him, and he limped
to the door and stood in the opening to be away
from the sound.

But the more he tried to escape, the closer
the thing seemed to cling to him. He muttered

something very like a curse, and looked up and down the narrow lane in vain search for something or somebody to distract his attention. Then he sneered at himself for his cowardice, came into the house again and resumed his pacing of the floor.

Presently he made a sudden dart at the back window, but pulled himself up, called himself a fool, and stood waveringly in the middle of the room. Gradually, however, he edged towards the casement, told himself he would just ascertain what sort of meeting was being held, toyed hesitantly for a minute or two with the fastening, and then flung back the window and listened. The meeting had now been in progress for some time, and the worshippers were singing again. He had heard them use the tune before, and thought he would amuse himself by learning it from them.

The music came to an end presently, but he still lingered at the window. Then he heard the preacher—if such he was—read a portion of Scripture, to which, however, he paid small attention, and he was just debating with himself whether he would not retire from his place, when the speaker raised his voice, and Mark distinctly heard, "How shall we escape if we neglect so great salvation?" read out as a kind of text.

The reader, who now began to preach, had a coarse voice and was evidently uneducated, but before he had uttered half a dozen sentences Mark was listening with all his powers. His leg, his former resolutions, were now all forgotten, and with craned neck and bated breath he drank in every word. The voice of the preacher got higher and higher, then dropped for a moment, but soon rang out until it was almost a shout. Mark was gripping the window frame as though his life depended upon it.

On and on went the sermon, and deeper and deeper drove the iron into Mark's soul. He was white to the lips, his breath came short and fast, a sense of utter and awful lostness took possession of him, and when at length the preacher, with a jerky peroration, rang out once more the "How? how shall we escape?" Mark burst into a great broken-hearted sob, and fell back on the bed, crying in a pitiless, hopeless wail:

"God ha' mercy! God ha' mercy on me a sinner!"

CHAPTER XIV

CROSSING THE RUBICON

AND whilst Mark lay thus on his little bed struggling with feelings which were all the more distressing because they were so new and strange, his sister was " taking the air " and entertaining herself with thoughts of the pleasantest possible character. At last they were in sight of the goal, and the weary hopes of many days were about to be realised.

They had been singularly fortunate, of late especially, and things which at one time were difficulties, had turned out to their advantage and the furtherance of their cherished plans. She had turned away from the town, and was making for the country; her step quickened under the stimulating nature of her thoughts, and she threw up her head and smiled to herself.

For years now she had cherished this great ambition for her brother, and it was from her that he had first received the suggestion upon which they were still working. The position to which they aspired, though difficult, was not impossible, and of late everything had favoured them. The accident that might have been so serious, seemed to have been sent by some good fairy to help them, for certainly it had produced an effect upon Mr. Josephus such as no mere Methodist-baiting could have done; and though she still anticipated that he would demur to Mark's proposal, and even be nasty for a little time, she made no doubt in her own mind but that they would eventually succeed.

As for Mistress Kinty, she had had, by means of this same accident, quite wonderful opportunities of studying that impetuous young lady, and had not neglected the occasion. The little impulsive, but highly characteristic self-revelations which she had given, were, equally with her succeeding lapses into self-conscious reserve, instructive to the all-observant Nancy; and she felt no manner of doubt in her mind that, however wayward and captious that young lady had been in the past, now Mark had only to ask and have. And ask he should; and that before he was many days older.

The impatience of the brothers to get him once more upon the premises boded nothing but good, and she expected that before next Sunday, at latest, Mark would be once more in his place; though, of course, able to do nothing except superintend. But that also, when she thought of it, was the best thing that could be for them. In his lame condition he would receive much consideration, and almost certainly spend most of his time in the parlour.

Altogether it seemed to the delighted girl that they were on the eve of the realisation of their ambitious hopes, and she turned round and stepped back to the little cottage humming, though it was Sunday, a merry little country catch.

"Fegs! 'tis a man's trick precise!" she cried light-heartedly, as she opened the door some twenty minutes later and found the room in darkness. "Mark, what art thou about i' th' dark, man?"

And as the fire was almost out, she groped in a little cupboard on the door-side of the mantel-piece for the flint and tinder-box, by which means she speedily procured a light, railing gaily the while at her brother for his man-like negligence.

"Where is a, where is a? Dreaming o' love an' fortune belike," she laughed, struggling with the obstinate candle, and then, as she discovered her brother lying full length on the bed with his face buried in his pillow, she broke off, and cried: "Good God! what's this? Mark, Mark! what's amiss?"

Mark hugged the end of the pillow to the side of his face and groaned.

With a cry, half-alarm and half-impatience, she jerked the pillow away from him, and, setting the candle upon the table, gripped him by the shoulders and turned him over until she could see his face; and then, as she caught sight of his drawn, agonised expression, she fell down on her knees by his side, and, pressing her face against his, began to beseech him to tell her what had happened.

Three times, with increasing earnestness, she

repeated the question, and at last, with another groan, he turned his head away and muttered something about the Methodists, and, at the same moment, she caught the cold spring air that came in through the still open window, and comprehended something of what had taken place. At that moment she felt she hated the new sect as she could hate nothing else under the sun ; but, warned by what had happened on a previous occasion, she checked herself and remained with her face against his, struggling to obtain the mastery of her feelings.

For some moments they continued in this position, and Nancy was just about to make a coaxing request for explanations, when Mark lifted his pale, suffering face to hers, and said with an earnestness that left no doubt as to the seriousness of the case :

" Nance, I'm accursed ! 'tis the finger o' God on my leg, like the Bible man wi' the shrunk sinew. Nance, oh, Nance ! I'd gi' my life an' every hope that's in it if I'd ne'er put finger on those people. Nance, dear Nance, I'm accursed ! "

She could not help it : rage, scorn, and maddening fear carried her away, and disregarding all prudence, she for the next ten minutes poured out upon the obnoxious sect every epithet of contempt and bitter hatred she could command. Twice, at least, Mark tried to stop her, but her anger was in full flood and swept his remonstrances before it.

Then she turned upon him, and in bitter, biting phrase mocked at his cowardice and spiritlessness.

To this he listened with limp, exasperating
indifference, and brought back all her alarm and
anger by finally turning away once more, and
groaning as he had done fifty times that night,
" God ha' massy upo' me, a sinner."

This sort of thing was utterly beyond Nancy.
Spiritual sorrow was not only something unknown
to her, it was incomprehensible ; she felt baffled
and entirely nonplussed, she had no one to help
her, no friend to whom she could turn in this
great perplexity, and as a sense of all that was
involved as far as she understood it, came upon
her, followed by a realisation of perfect helplessness before trials and difficulties of such a peculiar
character, her strong, tenacious courage broke
utterly down, and she burst into a passion of
weeping.

This appealed to the man in Mark ; he got
up and tried to soothe her, and the more she
pushed him away and upbraided him the more
persistent he became in his consolations. He
put his arm around her—a thing he had never
done since they were children. Then he tried
to kiss away her tears and pacify her agitation ;
but it was long before he made any impression ;
and the mean little candle burned down into
the socket, and finally went out in a smoky
sputter.

Still they sat on in the darkness, and presently
Nancy found her tongue again and began to
reason with him. Then he told her just where
he was, and though she could not understand
his feeling, she comprehended that he was

chiefly troubled lest he should have brought some curse upon himself by his conduct towards the Methodists. She strove hard to reassure him, and belied her own feelings by mocking at his apprehensions, but in a gentle, coaxing sort of way.

Then she took up the talking herself, and deftly appealed to his great pride by showing him what a triumph the Methodists would make of his change of front, even though he never joined their society. Proceeding, she pretended to break confidences, excusing herself by the special pressure of their position, and gave him details of what Kinty had said and done, using her own vivid imagination for the purpose with growing effect. From these things she passed to a survey of their position, and appealed to him not to spoil the great dream of their lives just when it was about to be realised.

Her confidence visibly affected her brother. He shook his head at her most hopeful statements, but she was quick enough to know that it was only the unbelief that loves to have more proof offered to it; and so she talked on. Then she pointed out that all that was necessary was that he should brighten up, and keep his own counsel until he had got Kinty; after that, if his conscience was not at rest, he could do whatever he liked, and nobody would stop him.

Everything that a busy brain and a keen sense of the desperateness of the situation could suggest, she urged upon him, and, as she presently discovered that he was being influenced, she talked

on, going over and over again the same arguments ; and at last, long after midnight, she
allowed him to go supperless to bed with the
confidence that she had not laboured in vain.

It scarcely needs to be stated that Mark did
not sleep that night. As soon as his sister had
left him, the whole of his old feelings came back
upon him with redoubled force. As he tried
to analyse them, he found, as his sister had
asserted, that they were largely superstitious, or
at least he tried to persuade himself so ; only
he was conscious of something behind his fears,
dark and awful, which he had not yet had
courage to face, but which he felt certain
would not long be kept back.

The position was exceedingly tantalising, and
he felt more than a little of his sister's resentment as he realised how completely indulgence
in these apprehensions would forfeit all that he
had lived and worked for. Mr. Josephus was,
he knew, as fierce as ever in his opposition to
the new sect, and was only waiting his recovery
to resume operations. And what if he refused
his master ? He shuddered as he pictured the
scene. Mr. Josephus's blazing wrath, and the
even more terrible scorn in Mistress Kinty's
pretty eyes. Was ever a poor wretch in so
torturing a position ?

But morning brought Kinty in her very gayest
mood, and Mark felt both fears and scruples
melting away in her seductive presence. She
brought a message that he could be done without no longer, and that Uncle Josephus was

coming down with a sedan-chair some time in the forenoon to fetch him to the shop ; and she arched her brows and looked with bewitching mock-seriousness at Nancy, as she explained that she did not think it at all impossible that Mark might be kept at the shop altogether, at least for some time, and until he could walk freely and safely to and fro.

And the welcome he received at the shop went further to undo the work of the day before. Mr. Ebenezer was uproarious, and insisted upon celebrating the occasion by opening a bottle of wine and treating the shopman and the men in the work-cellar to sack. Mr. Josephus showed quite as much pleasure, only in a more dignified way ; whilst Kerry, bringing in the wine, gave him a boisterous hug, which set Kinty off chattering about " privileged persons " in a most delightful and tempting way.

Mr. Josephus was anxious to get at the books, but his brother would hear none of it, and it was late in the afternoon before anything of a business nature was attempted. Mark soon found plenty to occupy his thoughts, and so his relations to the Methodists were thrust relentlessly into the background.

Thus the time slipped away, the days passed into weeks, Mark's leg was getting rapidly better, and he was able to go about on it, though not for any length of time. His days during this period were times of delight, for everybody made so much of him and Mr. Josephus was so frank in acknowledging his indispensability that much of his old pride came back, and he already saw himself in possession of the establishment and the dainty little woman who adorned it.

As for Kinty herself, she was most delightfully, and yet tantalisingly changeable, as was natural to her. Sometimes she became almost bold in her advances, going so far indeed as to suggest that the dangerous music lessons might be resumed, and then she would have most perplexing and tormenting fits of shy reticence, during which he scarcely saw her.

The gossip, too, of both shop and parlour disturbed him, for in sleepy old Helsham during these times the people found little to talk about but the Methodists. Every day Mr. Ebenezer brought some interesting detail about the doings of the sect, and Mr. Josephus and the shopman waxed eloquent together about the way in which they were spoiling the sport of the town by drawing into their circle first one and then another of the townsmen, until it was scarcely possible to get up a decent cock-fight at all.

Then the vicar would call, pouring out wrath and indignation, and complaining about the impertinence of the Methodists, who insisted upon coming to church, causing that venerable building, which, in recent times, was almost empty, to be nearly filled with worshippers. It was easy to hear and forget these things in the day-time, but when night came and the young hatter was alone, he had to fight the battle over again, with the uneasy conviction that he was not overcoming his misgivings, but that, in fact, they were slowly gaining the ascendency.

Night after night he struggled with his restless, unsleeping conscience, and the small hours of the mornings usually found him making some temporary truce in order to get sleep. But next night he had to face one more broken vow added to all the rest, and he soon realised that he was in the grip of some power that was steadily acquiring a stronger hold upon him.

By this time he had gone back to live at home, and he had to put on the best appearance he could, in order to lull the watchful and jealous vigilance of his sister. She was constantly urging him to make the great plunge, and propose formally to Uncle Josephus for Kinty's hand, and it was an added difficulty with him that he had to be constantly inventing excuses for delay.

Meanwhile, his feelings were undergoing a subtle, but profound and significant change. A chilling sense of loneliness came upon him ; it appeared to him that he had gone before his Maker, supported by the company and cheers of his neighbours, and that all at once he had awakened to the discovery that he was deserted, and stood alone in the dread Presence. Slowly he became conscious that mere superstitious fear and apprehension of punishment as a persecutor was receding in his mind before another and a stronger feeling. The Methodists, and everything connected with them, seemed to fade into the background, obscured by a much more important question.

Then he awoke to the fact that he no longer cared as he used to do about his position at the shop and the furtherance of his great scheme, and Kinty and all the proud and tender thoughts which her name suggested seemed to be parts of a long bygone dream. Steadily but relentlessly it was forced in upon him, that he had a personal relationship with the Deity, and that religion was not merely a national or social affair, not such in any true sense, in fact, at all; but a personal one, and that the one question for him, greater than all other and before all other, was his own position as an individual in the sight of his God. The world and its affairs were mere shadows about him; this was *the* question, and besides it there was no other.

And just when this feeling began to seem unbearable, he was plunged into fresh distress by finding that it was giving way as the former one had done to another. There stole over his heart now a humbling, prostrating consciousness of deep personal defilement. It was not merely that his sins, the errors of his life, put on new forms of seriousness, neither was it his persecutions of the Methodists only, though these came back to him again with added terribleness; it was an awful sense of guiltiness, a consciousness of personal sinfulness isolating, crushing, and condemning. For the first time in his life he knew what it was to be a sinner.

He became querulous, absent-minded, and deeply melancholy. He could neither eat nor sleep; and he became convinced that he would not be able to conceal his condition much longer from those about him. He was not concealing it as it was. Kinty became undisguisedly concerned, and urged him every day to see the apothecary. Mr. Ebenezer prescribed thyme tea, decoction of valerian root, and water-cress broth, whilst Mr. Josephus had the manner of a man who had been disappointed about something, and was peevish and taciturn. Nancy was almost at her wits' end, and alternately coaxed him into telling her what was troubling him, and sneered at him as a "pluckless dare-naught" and a long-faced Methodist. Goaded by her taunts, Mark made more than one effort to break the spell that was upon him.

One night he stayed at the shop after hours and entertained Kinty and Mr. Ebenezer with all the rollicking old country songs and catches he could think of, and then sat over the fire when he got home and watched his fiddle burn before his eyes. At another time he plunged into an ale-house and sat down to a gaming-table, remaining and playing until there was no one left but the landlord.

He followed this up by going for three successive nights to the same place, and ended by having to be carried home dead drunk. But this escapade so intensified his sufferings that he vowed to have no more of it, and took to attending the services both at the church and the Dissenting meeting-house, settling down eventually at the latter place, and vainly trying to make up his mind to unburden himself to the minister.

By this time, also, he had formed the habit of reading a Bible ; neither he nor his sister possessed such a thing, and he had to borrow one from Kerry, now an avowed Methodist. For a time these religious exercises brought him relief ; but they exposed him to much chaff, both from his master and his sister ; and presently he discovered that they were increasing his misery, though he dared not give them up. To these he eventually added the practice of reading church prayers in private, morning and evening.

By this time summer had come, and he was still in the same unsettled condition with regard to his prospects, whilst his private troubles were fast becoming unbearable.

He had been settling down of late into a dull, heavy misery from which it seemed impossible to arouse himself ; but one day, at the latter end of May, he received two pieces of intelligence which fairly stirred him : one was that Kinty was going away, as the country roads were now as good as they ever were in the year, to visit an aunt in Derbyshire, and the other that Mr. John Wesley would preach in a field at the end of the town next day at two o'clock.

For some time Mark could not tell which of these two announcements disturbed him most, but very soon the greater had entirely driven out the other, and he knew that the crisis of his life had come. Kinty was petulant and sulky about his indifference to her departure, and he found her studying him with perplexed and almost angry looks once or twice. But he had no room in his mind even for her, one thing filled his thoughts and one only—the man who was coming on the morrow could give him relief, could end the awful night in which he lived. Dare he make use of him? and what would be the result if he did?

He had grown almost accustomed to sleepless nights by this time, but that evening seemed all too short for the struggle that was going on within him. Daybreak brought no relief, and he went to the shop with the conflict still raging in his breast.

The coming of the great leader of this wonderful religious movement stirred Helsham even as the visit of his brother had not done. Mr. Josephus was ready immediately he arrived at the shop with a proposition for disturbing and mobbing the coming man, and Mark had to make an excuse about the condition of his leg and the state of his health, to escape being pressed into the opposition.

At two o'clock punctually the preacher was in his place, and half Helsham was there to listen to him. Mr. Josephus, disgusted with, and vowing vengeance against Mark, was induced to accompany his niece once more, and he chafed and fumed and cursed under his breath as he noted that the crowd, in its eagerness to hear, forgot to oppose, and hung eagerly on the lips of the meek-looking little gentleman who was addressing them.

Presently the sermon was finished, but there was no outburst of emotion as on previous occasions, and the party from the hat-shop was just turning away when a slight movement in the crowd near the preacher attracted their notice; a moment later they saw Mark Rawson step up to Mr. Wesley and put out his hand.

And it was in this way that the knowledge was conveyed to those who were so much concerned in it, that as far as he was concerned the die was cast.

CHAPTER XV

AT BAY

AT John Wesley's invitation Mark accompanied him to the house of an old lady, who was aunt to the young maltster and a quakeress, and who, since his expulsion from home, had provided that young convert with a shelter.

In a few choking words Mark explained his condition, and the long weeks of misery he had endured ; and after two or three questions, the great Evangelist, ignoring entirely his abject confessions and his connection with the persecutions, proceeded to speak to him of the great and sufficient Sacrifice made for all human guilt, and then with words of gentle but most comforting encouragement dismissed him.

Mark went down the steps from the quakeress's house like one in a dream, and when he had got out of the little front garden and into the lane, he stood wavering for a moment, as though uncertain where to go. Then he turned his back upon the town, and ignoring alike the time of day and the claims of business, he started in the direction of home. Just before he reached it, however, he turned aside and passed over a little stile to the left, and skirting the flax mill yard struck for the fields beyond.

And as he went he dwelt eagerly upon the few words Mr. Wesley had said to him in parting. He was still supremely miserable, and yet as he walked along he was conscious of a change; not *the* change of which the Methodists most perplexingly made so much, but an alteration in the direction of the index-finger of his mind.

For many a weary week now it had pointed with immovable and inexorable fixedness to his own heart, and its deep and awful defilement; but now he was conscious that he was looking almost constantly away from himself to the great Atonement, and especially to Him who was that Atonement. The idea gradually filled his whole mind, and he could think of nothing else. It was a perfect day; the sun shone with warm, glad rays, the soft air was filled with the music of birds and the fragrance of flowers, all nature seemed to be full of hope and joy, and in spite of himself he was conscious that it was exerting upon him a healing, comforting charm.

Slowly, as the sun breaks through the fogs, he saw the face of the great redeeming Christ forcing its way through the thick mists of mournful, morbid sorrow in which his soul had so long been enveloped; he was conscious of a movement within him, as of the lifting of a great load followed by such a sense of melting softness, that in a moment the fountains of the great deep were broken up in his heart, and he flung himself upon the ground and buried his face in the long grass with a sob that shook his whole frame.

But presently the old anguish came back in a new and more agonising shape ; his sin was no longer sin against the great stern Judge of all the world, no longer against society, or even, as he had so often felt lately, against himself, but against this great pitiful, suffering Christ, whom he had crucified afresh by his folly and selfishness.

The anguish of that moment was excruciating ; the worst horrors he had as yet endured seemed as nothing to it. He clutched wildly at the grass under his fingers, thrust his face deeper into the ground, and was struggling with an almost irresistible impulse to cry out, when all at once he was conscious of singing, and as he held his breath and listened there came to him, he knew not how or whence,

> " Would Jesus have the sinner die ?
> Why hangs He then on yonder tree ?"

Mark would scarce have moved to save his life. This was the answer to his prayers ; this was the message of God ; this was mercy and salvation.

It was a sweet girlish voice with curiously tender cadences in it, as if the singer knew who was listening and was trying to help. Mark drank in the simple words and felt they were life to him, and then, after hearing the last line of the verse

> "They know not that by Me they live,"

repeated, after the Methodist fashion, twice or three

times, he recognised the voice, and lifting his head caught sight of the little maiden who had sung in the loft on that now ever-memorable night. She had the scar of the bruise made by the falling candlestick still on her brow, and was singing in unconsciousness of any human presence, when Mark suddenly started to his feet with a wild, joyful cry, and before she could recognise her companion he had snatched her up in his arms, and whilst kisses were rained down on her fair little face he was calling her the angel of God and the messenger of peace.

With old-fashioned puritan-like prudishness the abashed little singer rebuked him for what she called his unregenerate familiarity, and then made him sit down amongst the flowers at her side in the hedge bottom, and invited him to tell her, " How it was with his soul."

She listened to his long story with glistening eyes and little cries of sympathy, and then she told him her own experience, and sang him more hymns, and again asked him how he felt. Mark's ignorance of theological terminology and the agitation of his heart rendered him unable to satisfy the little inquisitor, and so, after cross-questioning him with quaint precocity, she announced that he had been " under conviction, but was now a servant of Christ's, but only under the law," and eagerly exhorted him to " press forward " until he should get into " perfect liberty."

Then she rose to go, but seemed to hesitate

as if she would like to say something more, but feared to do so. At Mark's encouragement, however, she suggested that she should pray with him, and they knelt down under the hedge, whilst she clasped her thin hands and turned up her face toward the ocean-blue above them, and began to speak to her Maker on behalf of "the brand plucked from the burning."

Mark followed her simple petitions with an oft-repeated "yea," and when they parted, though he felt nothing which he could conclude meant what the Methodists called conversion, there was a rest and peace of heart so strangely sweet and precious that he found it difficult to believe that religion had anything better for him.

For some time longer he remained in the fields communing with his Maker and his own wondering, tremulous heart; but presently thoughts of the duties he was neglecting came back to him, and he was astonished to discover how comparatively unimportant these and the hopes and ambitions they represented had become to him. All the same, he realised that it was necessary to decide at once upon his future course of action, and he resolved to return to the shop and face the matter out whilst he was supported by the uplifting and inspiring influences which now possessed him.

If he went home and told his sister, there was no knowing what she might say or do; and though he felt himself absolutely firm in his purpose, he feared lest her pleadings should move him, and determined to get the matter settled before he saw her. Every step he took, however, seemed to increase the difficulties of his position, and when he turned into the High Street and caught sight of the shop, his heart began to beat in anticipation of the storm which he knew awaited him.

As he entered he caught sight of the pudgy face of Mr. Ebenezer pressed against the little window of the parlour door, but it disappeared as he stepped across the threshold, and he went round the corner of the screen and hung up his hat.

"T'ou 'rt waited for i' th' parlour," said the shopman, and he raised his eyebrows as a significant hint of impending trouble.

With a choky little cough and a sinking heart, Mark ascended the three steps, knocked timidly at the door, and, pushing it before him, entered the room.

Mr. Ebenezer sat in his usual place, with his wig over his brow, ostensibly reading one of his indispensable pamphlets, but peeping over the top of it with timid, anxious looks; whilst Kinty, carefully dressed in a quiet-coloured, lace-tuckered dress over a crimson quilted petticoat, from under which there peeped out a pair of dainty Spanish-leather shoes and a hint of bright-clocked stockings, sat on a low seat near him. Her arms were bare to the elbows, and she was making an elaborate pretence of being absorbed in her sampler.

Mr. Josephus occupied a chair opposite his brother, and sat with his back to the door; but as Mark entered he wheeled round, and, struggling evidently to keep down his anger, demanded harshly:

"Where hast been these two hours?"

"Speaking wi' the preacher and walking in Cridley fields," answered Mark, lifting his eyes for a moment and then dropping them under the glare of his enraged employer.

"So," cried Mr. Josephus, springing to his feet and tossing up his head haughtily, "it is a point i' the new religion to clatter wi' preachers an' take the air i' master's time, is 't? An excellent pretty religion, of a truth."

"'Twas a matter of life and——"

"Matter! matter!" shouted the furious Josephus, "'twas a matter o' treachery, sir! treachery to this house! 'Twas snaking i' th' grass! 'Twas running wi' th' hare an' hunting with hounds. 'Twas two-faced hypocrisy, i' Gad!"

Mark felt his temper rising, and bit his lip to keep back hot words, glancing the while at Mistress Kinty, who, however, still kept her head down and gave no sign. Ebenezer's face was close against the print he was pretending to read, and a low, deep sigh escaped him.

Josephus strode to and fro before the empty fireplace, jerking his head about until the tail of his wig flapped first on one shoulder and then on the other, muttering curses under his breath, and finally he pulled up and snarled:

"Hast naught to say, sulky? Out wi' it, man! Thou'rt a Methodist, a scurvy, snivelling Methodist, eh?"

"Please God, sir, I am!"

"What!" and though the hatter had made the accusation himself, he was evidently utterly amazed at Mark's open avowal of it, and gazed at his servant as though the statement he had made was incredible. An indescribable sound came from behind Mr. Ebenezer's pamphlet, and his spectacles fell upon the floor, whilst even Kinty ducked her head suddenly over her work.

There was a long, uncomfortable pause, during which Mr. Josephus's dropped jaw slowly returned to its place, and he nipped his small mouth together with hardening resolution.

"Boy," he said at last, "flout thy mangy Methodism here and I'll beggar thee." And then as Mark seemed about to speak, he lifted his hand, and cried imperiously: "Begone! Go thy ways to thy belated work, and when the shop is shut bring hither the keys, and, mark me! consider to chuck up this Methodism, and all shall be o'er-looked; but if thou wilt not, by the Lord Harry, thou shalt trudge!"

"Master——" began Mark.

But the irate hatter rapped out an oath.

"Begone, begone, insolent Jack-pudding! Wilt affront me to my very face? Begone!"

As he backed to the doors Mark lifted his eyes to the young mistress, and just as he was disappearing she raised her head and looked at him.

There was cautiousness, self-restraint and a curious sort of scrutiny in her look, but as far

as he could see not a gleam of sympathy, and
with a fresh sinking of the heart and a quiver
of the lip he retired to the little office.

As he stood there at his desk his heart
grew heavier within him every moment, and his
brain throbbed distractedly. The strong consolation that had come into his heart in the Cridley
fields seemed to have left him, and a terrible
sense of loneliness crept over him, benumbing and
paralysing all his powers.

He did not even then remember that he had
had no food since dinner; but this and the
dejection of his mind seemed to take all the
manhood out of him. Kinty's parting look
perplexed him, and in his condition at that
moment perplexity was almost worse than actual
distress.

Mr. Ebenezer's manner was very disappointing,
and he discovered now, that when he had
balanced his situation on previous occasions, he
had always had some sort of reserved hope that
when the worst came to the worst the old
gentleman would be his friend. Well, the worst
had come, and come in its bitterest form, and
his old friend had never moved a finger for
him.

As for his sister, he knew that when the struggle
for which he was now waiting was over, he had
to go home to one which would be in some
senses more dreadful still. And where now was
his religion? He had understood, nay, he had
actually seen that this new form of Christianity
had made weak people amazingly strong, and

lo! he had never known what real weakness was until that moment.

He could only conclude, therefore, that he had been deceived in the hope that the peace which came to him that afternoon in the fields was *the* peace, and he was there, with the great air-castle of his life tumbling to pieces at his feet, without a solitary compensation even from the thing for which he had sacrificed it all. And as he thought he prayed; and as he prayed he felt that he was only growing sadder and sadder every moment.

It was a bitter hour, and he shuddered and shrank within himself as he contemplated the ordeal through which he was called to pass. Then it occurred to him as a curious circumstance that he had spent his time thus far in timid self-pity, and had never addressed himself to the great question which he must immediately decide. He had to bring his mind back again and again from fruitless self-commiseration, and even then he found it strangely difficult to fix his mind on the great issue. His brain seemed dull and stupid in that direction, and try as he might he could not come to anything like consecutive thought.

Meanwhile, the time slipped relentlessly by, and beyond a dull, listless inclination to let things drift, he was conscious of no decision which would help him in his trial.

Presently he awoke to the fact that the shopman was putting up the shutters, and a few moments later he stood at his desk with the keys in his hand, and the answer to the great question still to find.

Twice he turned to the parlour door, and twice he drew back again; but at last with a reckless plunge he knocked and pushed it open before him. The brothers were still in the places in which he had left them, and though it was midsummer, their faces were turned towards the fire and their backs to him.

"The keys, sir," he said huskily, and stepped up to Josephus and held them out.

Josephus was smoking, and without turning his head he bade the young journeyman hang them up in their accustomed place, and when he had done so he pointed to a chair, and said gruffly:

"Sit, boy, sit!"

Mark dropped dejectedly into his seat, and waited with beating heart for his master to commence. Mr. Ebenezer was taking snuff in great pinches, and purposely avoided catching the younger man's eye, and Mark, suddenly remembering, glanced anxiously round the room and discovered that Kinty was not present.

Josephus smoked moodily on for some time, and then, turning slightly round, he said, in a rusty, almost pathetic, tone:

"Boy, thou hast gone far to making thy masters old men to-day."

The most unwonted tenderness of this remark touched a chord in Mark's sore heart, and he stammered out:

"Nay, master; nay, nay!"

Josephus shook his head in a melancholy regretfulness, and then went on sorrowfully:

"Thou hast served us excellent well these eight long years, excellent well."

This was the first frank acknowledgment that Mark had received from his senior master, and coming at this moment it quite unmanned him; but before he could command himself to speak soberly the old man went on:

"We never had a thought to part from thee, let alone in anger."

At any other time this almost unnatural lapse into tenderness would have excited Mark's suspicion, and perhaps also his contempt; but now it came with almost overwhelming power to him, and he felt all his purposes slipping away, a sense of ingratitude and selfishness came upon him, and with twitching mouth and broken tones he cried:

"Oh, masters, forgive me! forgive me for a senseless ingrate!"

Mr. Ebenezer snatched off his wig and recklessly wiped his eyes with it, and Mark looked from one to the other of the brothers, wondering in the self-depreciation so new and still so easy to him if he were the base wretch he felt himself to be.

Suddenly, however, Josephus changed his tone, and leaning over the elbow of his chair, and punctuating every word upon the young fellow's knee as he spoke, he said earnestly:

"Boy, there be twelve hundred guineas i' that shop an' trade."

And then, after waiting to watch the effect upon his hearer, he went on :

" And it's waiting for some fine fellow to take up with."

The room seemed to be swimming round, and Mark's heart rose into his mouth. Here was the great prize for which he had so long schemed and waited actually thrust at him. He made an effort to speak, but though he opened his mouth, no sound came forth, save the cracking of his parched lips.

Josephus was watching his young servant with keenest interest, and when he did not speak he went on :

" An' there's a parcel o' petticoats goes to this bargain, an' the hussy has t-w-o t-h-o-u-s-a-n-d g-u-i-n-e-a-s."

Josephus's voice sank into a thick, portentous whisper as he uttered the last words, and, rising from his chair, he stood with his back to the fireplace and gazed at Mark with eager impatience.

But the poor fellow had nothing to say ; the temptation seemed to have defeated its own purpose by its very strength, and so many thoughts struggled together in his brain that he found it impossible to arrange them into speech. The master was fast losing control of himself; such incredible stupidity he could not understand at all, and at last he rapped out :

" Well, man, hast naught to say ? "

Mark drew a long breath, looked at his master as though he were not sure even yet that he had heard aright; but at last he found power to say:

"Dear master, I shall esteem you for ever for what you have just said. I love young mistress with my whole soul, her dear idea will remain with me for ever; but—but—what says she upon this matter?"

"She! Tut, tut, man, fear not for that. Thou hast but to forswear the Methodists, and——"

But Mark had suddenly risen to his feet. The mention of the name of the hated sect brought him back with prompt swiftness to himself, and then, for the first time, he knew what he would do.

"Master," he said slowly, "you lifted me to heaven and dashed me to hell at a stroke. All that a grateful servant could do will I do to pleasure you and Mr. Ebenezer. All that man may do for woman will I do for my dear mistress, but in the sight of my God this that you ask I cannot do."

There was a dead silence, broken only by certain mysterious mutterings from Ebenezer, who had picked up his wig from the ground where he had previously thrown it, and was now holding it upon his head with clutched fingers, as though he were in a storm that was blowing it off. Josephus had gone white with passion, his little eyes fairly blazed with baffled rage, and he glared at Mark as though he would scorch him. Presently, however, he obtained some sort of control of himself and asked with ominous calmness:

"Is that thy final answer?"

And Mark, with bowed head and drooping eyes, answered slowly:

"My final answer."

Ebenezer's attention seemed attracted at this moment by something behind Mark; but before the young Methodist could glance round the storm broke. With a furious dash the enraged Josephus sprang at the parlour door and flung it open, and then, oblivious of the fact that the shop was locked up, he snatched at Mark's little cocked hat, and flung it through the doorway, shouting wrathfully:

"Go! ingrateful cur! Canting Methodist, go! and never show thy dirty jib inside these walls more!"

And then he shrank back with a baffled cry, and Mark felt a soft little arm slid into his; and before he could realise what was happening, he heard a high, clear woman's voice saying:

"Where he goes, I go."

And looking down, lo! Kinty, with white face and glowing eyes, stood at his side, looking triumph and defiance at her nonplussed and crestfallen uncle.

CHAPTER XVI

KINTY'S CONFESSION

MARK looked round on the scene before him with a rush of feeling that almost dazed him. Mr. Ebenezer had jumped to his feet, and with his wig gripped firmly in his left hand, stood gazing around with wonder and delight on his ruddy face, whilst his brother, abashed and confused for the moment, stepped back to his place near the fire-grate, and stood glaring at his daring niece.

"Begone, bold hussy! this is no place for thee," he cried, waving his hand to dismiss her. But Kinty, clutching Mark's arm more firmly, drew herself up, and cried:

"My place is by the side of my man! my brave, true man!"

Mark, scarcely knowing either where he was or what he was saying, bent over to persuade her to let him go; but she ignored him altogether for the moment, she had evidently not finished what she wanted to say.

"Yea, uncle. Yea, truly; I *am* a bold, bad hussy! I've been spy-holing and eavesdropping, and have heard it all. You would thrust your niece down a young man's throat, would you? I thank you for't; you did me honour, and I'll thrust myself down enow. *You* thought him a weak-backed Jack-pudding, I thought him a greedy self-seeker; but he's a MAN! a man, I say; and I love him!"

"But, woman, he's a Methodist! a canting, whining Methodist!" shouted Josephus.

But with a royal sweep of her free arm, and a most unladylike snap of her fingers, she cried:

"I heed not! I mind not what he may be; Methodist, Episcopalian, or—or—— What do you call 'em, Uncle Tebby—Muggletonian? he's a man, a strong, brave man; and that suffices."

According to all precedents, Mark ought to have snatched his brave little defender in his arms at this stage; but so many and so exhausting had been the emotions he had endured that day, that he seemed incapable of any new sensation, and stood there dazed and bewildered.

Josephus was getting desperate; the authority he had exercised unchallenged so long seemed to be about to slip away from him, and he must assert it now or lose it for ever. Besides, he was a shamefully ill-used man. He had swallowed his pride, and made a most condescending overture to his own apprentice, only to have it flung in his teeth, and the Methodism his narrow soul hated, flaunted before him as something to be proud of. He foamed at the mouth, stamped on the floor, shook his clenched fist at the rebels, and seemed ready to quarrel even with the inoffensive Ebenezer.

"Wilta begone, knave! bundle? Take thy scurvy carcase off!"

"Master," began Mark, recovering speech at last, "I will go. I would not bring strife into this beloved household. I will go—— "

But here, with demure face and steady eyes, Kinty looked up at her uncle, and repeated:

"Where he goes I go."

"Thou brazened baggage! Thou impudent trollop!" and with a furious curse the enraged man sprang at the lovers with the evident intention of separating them by main force; but before he could reach them, Ebenezer, who, whilst he had been speaking, had glided softly round the table, interposed his portly form, and gripping his brother by the arms, forced him back into his seat.

"Let a-be, man, let a-be!" he cried, panting from his unwonted exertions. "'As you brew, so shall you bake.' ''Tis a good horse that knows its own stable.'"

And then he stooped down and searched upon the floor for his wig, and having carefully put it upon his head, he beckoned the two young people to seats, and commenced the longest oration he was ever known to utter. He recalled to Josephus's mind the fact, almost always forgotten in the house, that he was master equally with his brother—though this part of his speech was more roundabout than the rest, in consequence of his evident desire to put the point as delicately as he could, and, finding no way out of the confusion into which he thus got, he finished that part of his discourse by lamely quoting the proverb about the number of people it takes to make a bargain.

Then he enlarged, with many a snuffle and many an awkward hiatus, upon the affection they both bore to their niece, and the obligation they were under to the memory of the dead parents of that young lady. From this he passed to a review of the years Mark had been with them in the business, and the faithfulness and diligence of his service.

Next he took up the subject of the Methodists, frankly avowed a more than passing partiality for that despised sect, and asserted that it was the unjustifiable cruelty of others towards them that had first excited his sympathy. Then he proceeded to point out that a man's religion need not interfere with his duties to his employers or his friends, and stoutly maintained that by recent observation he could prove that Methodism was making bad servants into good ones, and bad citizens into patriots all over the country, and especially in Helsham.

He paused many a time in this novel effort of his, and quoted proverbs to support his arguments at every step; but when he came to speak finally of the long years he and his brother had lived together, and the comfort and amity in which they had always dwelt, interlaced as his statements were with pathetic little declarations of his own great regard for Josephus, he fairly broke down and ended with a number of choky, spasmodic little sobs which were drowned in louder sounds of the same kind which came from Kinty and Mark.

There was a pause for a moment or two when he concluded, and whilst he sank into his chair, and for lack of handkerchief began to rub his eyes once more with his wig, Kinty raised her face and looked anxiously in the direction of Uncle Josephus. What she saw there must have encouraged her, for, relinquishing Mark's arm, she cast herself upon her knees before her uncle, and sliding her soft little hand into his as it lay on his lap, she began to stroke it coaxingly and kiss it.

Josephus looked moody still and excessively uncomfortable; but she pulled at his arm until his face was near enough to salute, and then pressed her hot lips upon his and began to plead. Every term of affection she could command was brought into service; she called him all the pet names she had used in her childhood, and vowed it would break her heart to have to leave him.

And, after all, poor Josephus was but a man, and had somewhere a heart which the earnest little pleader found means of reaching, and so presently he stooped down and kissed her hair and bade her go to bed.

"But Mark, uncle? dear brave Mark, what of him?"

Uncle Josephus shook his head and sighed heavily, and Mark was just commencing to beg her not to consider him, when she cried:

"Let me tell you, uncle, let me tell you how

I was brought to love him. I liked him ever for himself, but I could not abide his hot temper and pride. Besides, I feared he was ambitious, and wanted my few guineas, and I mistrusted him. And when I saw him swallow his manhood to become a cruel hunter of heretics I despised him. But one day I heard say that he had defended the Methodists out o' pure pity, and that pleasured me. Then I saw him strike down the sottish Barny for mobbing the poor preacher, and I loved him, for I saw he was a man. Sin' then I've watched him shrewdly, and seen his manhood struggling with his ambition. I've seen him sink, and I've seen him rise, but to-night I've seen him conquer. 'Twas a poor compliment he paid me, uncle, but I loved him for 't; an' when he wouldna sell his manhood even for silly Kinty I loved him wi' all my heart."

But at this moment there came a sharp ran-tan at the side door, followed by impatient shouts from some one either drunk or very excited. Mark and Kinty sprang apart, the two brothers turned to each other with looks of startled surprise, and after a moment's pause Josephus curtly bade Mark go to the door.

"Have a care, boy! Parley wi' em!" cried Ebenezer, hurriedly adjusting his wig and backing to his chair.

Mark, disappointed at the interruption, but remembering the danger of the times, stepped backwards, and cried:

"What is 't? Who's there?"

Another curse and a heavy lunge at the door.

"Open, 'prentice. Open i' th' King's name."

"'Tis the mayor," cried Mark, between relief and astonishment. But almost before he could unfasten the heavy wooden bars the door was pushed roughly in upon him, and he was jammed against the wall, whilst the maltster, accompanied by two serving-men, strode into the parlour.

"Curse me, Man Kirke! Art kalling [chatting] here with Papists and lousy Methodists whilst the country's i' danger, and the jabbering French are marching upo' London!" And the irate magistrate glanced first at Mark and then at Ebenezer, and finally fixed a savage glare upon Josephus.

"Nay, nay, worship; not so bad neither. Sit, man, and tell the news." And the hatter stamped on the floor for ale.

"Sit! Sit, says ta, and the country ruined? The French King and his army down on us, and the barelegs [Highlanders] crying for Charlie!"

But his worship dropped into a chair for all that, and glanced with looks of surly suspicion at Mark and Ebenezer.

Knowing that this blustering mood was not the maltster's most serious one, and that therefore the news he brought might be safely discounted, Mr. Josephus nodded to the others to leave the room, and stamped impatiently upon the floor again. Ebenezer, still nervously arranging his wig, got up and sauntered towards the staircase for bed, and Mark and Kinty withdrew shyly into the dark shop.

"Tut, worship! 'Tis but an idle buz," Josephus was saying as the others vanished.

"Buz! 'Tis God's truth, Kirke! The Mounseers are coming, and twenty thousand men in ships. Brickett, the aletaster, got the news from the driver of the north coach at Wetgate. By the Lord, I'll hang every Papist in the town, and pitch every Methodist Jacobite into the mews-pond" (horse-pond).

Mr. Josephus was divided between interest in the news and impatience for liquor, and so he strode to the head of the kitchen stairs.

"Kerry, Kerry, thou maggot head! A tankard A tankard wi' thee?"

As there was no response, he began to grope his way with muttered curses down the steps, and whilst his back was turned, his worship stole on tip-toes to the corner behind Mr. Ebenezer's chair. There he picked out a bundle of pamphlets, hastily scanned their titles, and then skipped back to his seat with a grunt.

Mr. Josephus returned, followed by Kerry with a can of small-ale. The domestic had evidently retired to rest, and now appeared with blinking eyes, protesting face, and hastily assumed garments that too imperfectly concealed her charms. She was proud of her small-ale, and the thick foam on the mouth of the tankard certainly justified her; but the mayor glanced at it in sulky scorn and pushed it away from him.

Josephus made wild signals behind his visitor's

back for Kerry to bring something better, and
she presently returned with a dirty leathern
bottle of old October, which she dumped down
on the table in evident anger. The sight of the
stronger liquor pacified the mayor somewhat,
and after a prodigious pull he drew his chair a
little nearer to that of his host, and proceeded
to supply such details of the battle of Fontenoy
as had reached him, and then abandoned himself
to doleful vaticinations of an approaching Jacobite
rebellion; but it was clear to his host that he
was keeping something back, and kept glancing
towards the shop door with growing impatience.

Then Kinty returned to the parlour, having
dismissed her lover for the night. She began
to adjust out-of-place articles of furniture, but
as their visitor's restlessness increased, Josephus
curtly ordered her to bed. After listening intently for her receding footsteps, the maltster
drew his chair still closer to the hatter's, bent
his tall frame forward, and tapping Josephus
on the knee, he dropped into a thick whisper,
and demanded:

"Dost know there's treason i' this old house?"

Josephus stopped in the act of recharging his
pipe, stared at his visitor with indignant resentment, and cried:

"Tut, man! the lad's honest; his Methodism
will pass, he's no Jacobite, man!"

"Lad! 'tis not the lad. 'Tis the other, I tell
thee!"

Josephus rapped out an oath, and sprang
angrily to his feet. But the mayor rose with

him, and still staring hard into his face, he
went on:

"'Tis he got 'em the flax mill, man; he's the
owner on't."

Josephus went white and then swollen-red with
indignant repudiation.

"I tell thee, Kirke, I've seen the deed; the
mill is his, man! But for him the rascals 'ud
'a' been stamped out o' the town."

The hatter could not speak; that he should
have to listen to such insinuations in his own
house, and from his closest friend, was intolerable; and that Ebenezer's silly dabbling
in curious creeds and movements should have
made such insinuations possible, only added fuel
to his wrath.

But the mayor, who, now they were alone,
had dropped his half-drunken bluff, was carefully watching his man; and so, when at last
Josephus ceased to storm and curse, he leaned
forward still farther, and said, in the same husky
whisper:

"Kirke, who's the head o' the Helsham
Methodists?"

"Who? Why, Bridge, the rascally tinker;
not Ebenezer. 'Tis monstrous, man!"

"And what was Bridge i' '15?"

Josephus's jaw dropped in sudden recollection.

"An' what wants a tinker wi' horse-pistols, an'
hangers?"

Josephus stared stupidly.

"An' what wants a tinker wi' two saddle-horses?
Where got he 'em? Who paid for 'em?"

A long, uneasy silence; and then, seeing how profound an impression he had made, his worship changed his tone and went on:

"Teb is more fool than rebel; but the canting rogues have got him by the nose, and they'll lead him into th' muck. As for that Methody pup o' mine, he's like to grime my good name; but, by the Lord, I'll have him pressed first."

The thought that his friend was, after all, as much involved as himself mollified Josephus somewhat, and he began to talk more freely. And as they talked they drank the old October, and became more and more confidential. A common sense of danger drew them together, and a common hatred of Methodism made them regard it as the cause of all their perplexities.

As they conversed, the mayor noticed that his companion never alluded to young Mark, and did not even take the bait when it was thrown out to him. A straight question or two set Josephus explaining, but his language was so vague and apologetic, that his visitor's suspicions were aroused; and so, bit by bit, he discovered that there was more than a possibility of Mark's Methodism being condoned, and of his being accepted as nephew-in-law and partner at the hat-shop. He felt that he ought to go warily here, but he was angry and in drink; and so, losing all control of himself, he stamped on the oak floor, cursed the Methodists to everlasting destruction, and, finally, concentrating his indignation on the amazed Josephus, he called him every evil name he could think of.

Why this particular development of the case should so inflame his worship, the hatter could not see; but presently a loose word or two gave him the clue, and also revealed the real object of the magistrate's visit.

Josephus became alert and curious again, and asked a tentative question or two.

"That baggage of a Sue of ours has been visiting her rascally brother in spite o' me, and she tells her mother that he's fancying thy niece again, and weakening on his confounded Methodism. In short, if he can have the wench he'll come home again, and throw over the Conventicle."

Now in the rebellion of '15 both these men had been ardent Jacobites, but now, old and prudent, and with a strong sense of the value of worldly position, they were only too anxious to avoid the possibility of suspicion; and here, it seemed, they were being involved in spite of themselves.

For two hours they talked; now in portentous whispers, and now in protesting shouts; every aspect of the complicating case was discussed, but they reached no definite conclusion. Josephus was experiencing strong, mental recoil, and thanking his stars for the lucky interruption which had saved him from giving a consent that might have been dangerous. And yet he saw how serious were the difficulties. If he explained himself to Ebenezer, that worthy might turn stubborn, especially as Kinty's happiness was concerned. He had a mortal dread also of that young damsel's tongue, and went cold as he thought what the impetuous and love-sick Mark might do if driven to extremes.

Moreover, though the mayor's fortunate arrival had stopped his consent on his very lips, he could not but feel that the other parties to the affair would regard the matter as settled. He put his position to his confederate; but his worship brushed his scruples aside, and insisted that he had only to consent to the marriage of Kinty with his son, and leave the rest to him.

Midnight passed, the cracked bell in the court-house tower struck one, but no decision had been arrived at; and at last the two parted with the understanding that they were to meet next morning at the mayor's office and come to some arrangement. But when the magistrate had been gone some twenty odd minutes and Josephus was preparing to carry his perplexities to bed with him, a stealthy rap at the passage door arrested him, and, opening it, he stood face to face with his friend.

"I've got it, neighbour. Leave all to me. A fine ripe plan, egad! I'll do the Methodist's business, and save the wench also. Leave it to me, and do nought till you see me."

And before Josephus could reply, he had vanished again into the night.

CHAPTER XVII

THE MAYOR'S STRATAGEM

MARK RAWSON had never spent a sweeter half-hour than the one he passed in the dark hat-shop with his lady-love. They were too excited and too much interested in each other to pay any heed to what was going on in the parlour ; and though a word or two did reach them now and then, it was usually something about politics, and therefore supremely uninteresting.

Presently Kinty grew uneasy, and urged him to depart by the front door, assuring him again and again that their fortunes were better left at that particular juncture in her hands. Mark exhausted every excuse he could think of for remaining, but at last took a reluctant though demonstrative leave. It was very dark in the narrow street for the time of year, and somehow he felt strangely depressed as he strode along.

When he reached home, however, he entered softly, lest he should awaken his sister, who still occupied the little room under the thatch. Then he had to struggle with a wish to call her up and tell her the great joy that had come to him that day; but conquering the desire, he groped to the side of his own truckle bed, sniffed at the pungent odour of a recently extinguished rushlight, and, feeling about on the little table, found a bowl of skimmed milk and a hunk of barley-bread, and sat down to eat and think.

One after another the events of that most marvellous day in his history passed before him, and one moment he was overflowing with gratitude to God, and the next burning with intense admiration at the noble stand made by Kinty. And still there was always that strange misgiving; the interruption caused by the arrival of the mayor seemed, in his over-wrought state of mind, ominous. He tried to laugh and reason himself out of the feeling, and at last he dropped upon his knees in prayer.

But do what he would the feeling was there, and, in fact, grew heavier every moment. Long and anxiously he sat thus in the darkness, one moment resolving to call his sister up, and the next deciding to reserve his joyful tidings until he could tell her all. But depression and foreboding grew upon him, some one he must talk to, and the clear-eyed, practical Nancy was just the one to see the rights of a difficulty complicated to him by superstitious fears. And so he was just about to step to the foot of the little ladder and awake her, when he noticed that it was growing lighter, and at the same moment a heavy footfall struck his ear, and he turned aside and took a peep through the blindless window. It

was some early labourer going to the fields doubtless. The footsteps came nearer, but it was not
light enough to see much, and so he was just
selecting the best bit of glass in the knotted
window, when he sprang back, with a cry he
could not suppress:

"Good God! 'tis the mayor!"

His worship was coming straight to the cottage,
and so, remembering the sleeping woman upstairs, Mark stepped to the door and softly
opened it. The maltster pulled up a couple of
yards away.

"Good lack! up a'ready?"

"Ay, worship. But what's your will, sir?"

Astonished and suspicious, his worship drew
back a little, and then, dropping his voice into a
loud whisper, he cried:

"'Tis said thou'rt a Methodist Jacobite!"

"Nay, worship, no Jacobite, please God."

"Tut, man, ye are all traitors. 'Tis found
out, I tell thee. Methodism is a popish plot,
no less."

"God forbid! We're all loyal, we honour the
King."

The maltster looked cautiously around, took
a step nearer, hesitated a moment, and then,
sinking his voice, said:

"Ay, but which king?"

"King George, sir; no other. Give me occasion,
and I'll prove it."

With another suspicious glance around His
Worship took a step nearer, stopped, and sprang
back with a fierce:

"Nay, then, ye're traitors all!"

Mark came forward eagerly, and, provoked as the mayor intended he should be by his insinuations, he cried:

"Let me prove it! Give me a task an' I'll show you all."

Eyeing him over studiously from head to foot, the magistrate wavered a little, or pretended to do so, and then said softly:

"Man Rawson, I could make a man o' thee, an I could but trust thee."

"Trust me and try me, whatsoever it be."

The mayor shook his head.

"Man, I could do thy business with the Kirkes an' fix thee for life."

"Then tell me, master, and trust me to do it."

Still studying his man dubiously, the maltster sank his voice again, and asked:

"Canst ride a horse?"

"Nay, master."

Disappointed, but still eager, his worship continued:

"Dost know the way to Nettleton?"

"Nay, I was never farther that gate than the Pilbury cow-downs; but I could find it."

Nettleton was a river port of evil fame some forty odd miles away, with no road to it but country lanes, and sheep or bridle-paths. Mark guessed that the mayor had an errand for somebody, but why him? Why not send one of his own or the town's servants? Besides, on foot it would be a three days' affair, and at this juncture of his affairs it was not to be thought of for a moment, at any rate not until he had seen his masters again.

But his visitor was impatient and curiously angry.

"Loyal, ay truly! Ye're traitors, and, by the Lord, I'll make you dance."

Mark steadied himself; it came into his head that here might be an opportunity of rendering service to the Methodists to whom he owed so much, only his restless suspicion was too strong just at that moment, and so instead of offering to serve his worship he blurted out:

"Why fix upon me, worship?"

"Why, good lack! Am not I giving thee a chance to clear thyself and thy Methodists? How can I protect ye till I have true proof of ye?"

"But you have servants, master."

"Hoots! send them, and let every spying Jacobite in the country know! 'Tis secret service, man; I must have a man unknown and safe."

In struggling indecision Mark looked hard at his visitor and sighed. The mayor was plainly inconsistent with himself, and that aroused his suspicions; if on the other hand he refused—but here the impetuous maltster broke in.

"Ay, ay; ye're traitors all, but by the Lord, I'll——"

"Master," interrupted the young hatter, "what of my employers?"

"Tut, man! have I not come from the shop direct? Thy master commands it."

Mark still hesitated; he could not tell this blusterous man why he so much wanted to be free that day. It was a fine thing that was offered him if all were straight and square about it, but somehow his heart seriously misgave him, and to go without any satisfaction about the thing that was nearest his heart seemed impossible.

He was still staring at the impatient magistrate and pondering, when a dark figure flitted for a moment out of a narrow passage, and he beheld the tall form of Goody Wagstaffe who, with puckered brow and uplifted finger, was warning him.

"But, master," he cried, more to gain time for thought than anything else, "ye accuse me in one breath an' would trust me i' the next!"

"Man, am not I loth to think ill of thee? Take this message and that will certify me, and the Methodists shall have protection."

Goody was still darkly signalling, but Mark could make nothing of it, and in the tenderness of young spiritual life was strongly tempted by the idea of sacrifice for the sake of his fellow-religionists, and so at last he said hesitatingly:

"I'll do your bidding, master, an you'll promise to protect us."

Goody was now gesticulating wildly, but as the mayor promptly closed with the offer and then turned round, as he fumbled in his fob, she had to vanish.

"Here's a couple of crowns for thee. Get thee gone on the instant. Nay, man," he added, as Mark began to demur, "I'll let the hussy inside know thou art safe. Take this packet to one Tester at the sign of the Wooden Mallet in

Labour Lane, and get it truly delivered to him by noon to-morrow, and then take thy pleasure and see the town."

It was a strange business, full of suspicious circumstances, but the sweet sense of service to his religion overcame everything, and so, though his heart sank with disappointment and uneasy fear, he stepped softly into the house, put on his coat, possessed himself of a stout oak staff, and then turned and looked with strange longings at the familiar objects around him.

As it was now about daylight and a youth was passing with a herd of lean cattle, the mayor followed his young companion into the cottage. But the moment the animals were gone he became all impatience for Mark's departure, and as he was not too certain of his man he walked along with him until they were out of the town. Then he stopped and repeated his instructions, assured Mark that he would make all right both at the hat-shop and his own cottage, and then stood in the rutty lane and watched him up Wetgate bank until he disappeared over the hilltop.

Meanwhile, Kinty was lying awake in bed, not even desiring to sleep. Her brave little heart warmed again as she thought of the heroic stand made by her lover, and though a characteristically whimsical regret arose within her now and then that the days of her maiden liberty were ended, that was soon swallowed up in glowing pleasure at the wonderful turn events had taken.

Most heartily did she ban the mayor for his untimely intrusion, and again and again she put back the bed-curtains to look for the slow-footed dawn. She must have dozed off some time, however, for about six o'clock she suddenly sat up with a startled cry of "Mark! Mark!" and found the tears standing on her cheeks and the daylight streaming in through the corners of the hangings.

"I saw him tossed," she murmured, as a deep sob quivered upwards to her lips, "I saw him tossed, and the bull had the maltster's face! Oh, lack a day! what can it foretend?"

Nervous reaction from the excitement of the previous evening was doubtless affecting her, but she knew nothing of such things and dressed in fretful uneasiness. The maid, struggling with flint and tinder-box, was surprised to see young mistress astir so early, and the journeymen hatters, as they dropped down the front steps into the workshop, were puzzled somewhat to see Mistress Kinty open the kitchen door to scrutinise each new-comer.

Mr. Ebenezer came down into the parlour humming a country catch, and though he was evidently struggling to keep his face under control, there were funny twitchings about his mouth corners, and his eyes overflowed with amusement.

"Ho, ho! give a man luck and throw him i' th' sea," he murmured, apparently to himself, as Kinty, duster in hand, began to flit about the room on morning duties, and when, on hearing the old proverb, she dashed at him with a hug and a kiss, he chuckled delightedly and went on,

" Set a beggar on horseback and he'll ride," egad !
Kinty merrily shook her duster at him, which
set him off crowing again. "Hoots, woman !
Ah, ' A man's a man still if he hath but a hose
on his head,' and ' A man may be learned without
a long wig.' "

But it was getting time for both Mark and
Uncle Josephus to appear, and Kinty felt herself
growing restless.   Presently she went to the shop-
door and glanced down the street, lingering there
a few moments with growing impatience, and
when she returned she found Uncle Ebenezer
busy chalking on the plain stone mantelpiece
with a piece of ruddle:

"AT THE SIGN OF THE MONMOUTH CAP,"

KIRKE & RAWSON,

HATTERS,

"BEST IS BEST CHEAP."

Kinty laughed at the obvious *double entendre*
of the added motto, but hastily rubbed the in-
scription out as she heard Uncle Josephus coming
down the creaking stairs.   Her first glance at
him drove the blood from her cheeks, and when,
with tightening mouth and flashing eyes, he flung
the door going into the shop open and bawled
" Mark !" her heart sank. The shopman called
back to say that the ex-apprentice had not yet
arrived, and Josephus, after consulting a big

tortoiseshell-cased watch, turned to stare in moody wrath at the fireplace.

Ten minutes passed. Kinty, with trembling fingers, was assisting the preparations for breakfast. Mr. Josephus drew up to the table with a smothered snort, and then, rising hastily, went to the glass-door again, and ordered the shopman to " go after the scurvy laggard."

Still Kinty held her peace ; the more so as there were most unwonted indications of wrath upon Ebenezer's usually sunny face. Her colour came and went rapidly, the food seemed to choke her, and she could scarcely draw her breath. " Oh, why should the thoughtless Mark be late on this of all mornings ? " Ebenezer ate rapidly as though to check his rising wrath, Josephus sat stiff and stern and did not so much as look at his food. The shopman had had time to go to Mark's house, he must surely have met him before this ! What could be detaining them ?

" He has o'erslept himself, belike," she murmured apologetically, and was surprised at the huskiness of her own voice.

Josephus laughed, but there was scorn and rage in his voice.

" Curse me, brother ! " and Ebenezer, purple with sudden anger, sprang to his feet ; but at that moment the door was burst open, and the shopman, with wonder and alarm on his face, cried out :

" He's gone, masters ! He's not so much as been abed ! "

Kinty rose with a sharp cry, Ebenezer opened

his mouth in amazement, and Josephus flung himself back, with a hard, crackling laugh, and cried :

"Buss me, but the rascal's shrewd! Oho! not such a pudding-head as he looketh! Ho! Oho!"

"Uncle! speak you thus of my lover?" and Kinty, with quick self-recovery, stepped forward, with eyes flashing and mouth set and hard, and then turning abruptly to the shopman, she demanded, "His sister, what saith she?"

"She can tell naught, mistress, she is gone to the flax mill to find him."

"Go! quick, man!——"

But before Kinty could get any further the shop door swung back, and Nancy Rawson, staggering forward, cried, as she flung up her arms :

"Oh, lack-a-day! He's gone!"

"Thou liest, vixen!" roared Ebenezer.

"Oh, master, 'tis true! I met the mayor's man but now, and he tells me that he has stolen Crackey Leech's mare and rode off to the Pretender!"

There was a moment's astounded silence, and then a sudden babel of tongues.

Ebenezer fell on the sobbing Nancy with fiercest objurgations, Josephus danced about the room, uttering malicious little laughs, and Kinty assailed the shopman with incoherent exhortations to go and search for the missing one in all likely places ; whilst Kerry, coming upstairs with a dish of salt pork, threw meat and wooden platter from her hands, and, dropping into a chair, began to shriek in sympathy with the excitement about her.

But the very confusion steadied the intrepid little mistress of the house. Mark's absence had deeply alarmed her, especially after her dream; and that common terror of the times, the press-gang, made her dread what might have happened to her lover.

But the news Nancy brought, by over-shooting the mark, really relieved her; and so she bundled the tearful Kerry downstairs, hurriedly whispered something to Ebenezer which sent him out through the shop with his wig, as usual, in his hand, rebuked the sobbing Nancy, and then, stepping up to her uncle and facing him, she cried:

"Uncle, those that hide can find. Where is Mark?"

The old hatter, showing his dingy, broken teeth in malicious triumph, made answer:

"Gone to the north to Charlie."

"North, south, east, or west, I'll to him!"

"Wench, he's a traitor! a Methodist Jacobite rebel!"

"And so am I, Methodist, Jacobite, rebel!" and, in the height of her angry defiance, she snatched up a wooden cup, and raising it above her head, she cried shrilly, "To the King! to the King that's robbed of his own!"

But in the very act of defiance her head dropped, the mug slipped from her suddenly nerveless fingers, and, with a rush of passionate tears, she flung herself on the settle, and sobbed as if her heart would break.

The scared horror on Josephus's face slowly faded out, he watched the weeping woman with glazing eyes, hesitated, looked stupidly round, and then, snatching at his cocked hat, vanished.

CHAPTER XVIII

REVIVED LOVE

NEITHER of the two young women left thus in the parlour were of the class that wastes time in useless lamentation, and so in a few minutes they were deep in debate on the anxious situation. That Mark had gone to the Pretender was too ridiculous to be believed, but the fact that he was missing was not to be got over, and the charge involved in the only explanation of his disappearance which they had heard had a sinister significance, and showed but too clearly that Mark had enemies, and enemies of a most unscrupulous kind.

Kinty, of course, knew much more of the exact position of affairs than her visitor, but her more complete information only increased her perplexities, and even when she had briefly summarised the proceedings of the previous night for Nancy's enlightenment, they neither of them saw any further into the mystery.

But they could not be still, something definite must be ascertained, even though it increased their troubles; and so presently they separated, Nancy to interview Big Barny and the Methodists, and Kinty to make inquiries in other directions.

Nancy's researches only increased her alarm, for the Methodists, knowing nothing definitely of Mark's conversion, and remembering his previous attitude towards them, were reticent and suspicious; and Kinty, whose love for the apprentice was, of course, unknown in the town, was regaled with such wildly improbable stories that she grew heart-sick until it suddenly occurred to her to interview the wise-woman.

It was well into the forenoon when she turned into the lane leading to Goody's tumbledown mud-and-wattle cottage, and she pulled up with a little cry of dismay when on coming in sight of the house she discovered that the rickety shutters were closed, and Goody was either abroad or ill in bed.

Hoping against hope—for the wise-woman had mysterious ways—she approached the door and knocked. But there was no answer, and when she repeated her summons, she noted that the string, which was Goody's substitute of a latch, had been drawn inside, and there was no smoke issuing from the drunken-looking mud chimney. She was neither more nor less superstitious than any other girl of her rank and time, but all the gruesome stories she had ever heard of Goody on the one hand, and the Methodists on the other, returned to her in a flood, and she began to shake with vague uncanny fear.

Evils of a devilish kind had perhaps overtaken her hapless lover.

" Good day, mistress !"

With a start and a little frightened cry, Kinty

whisked round, and there stood gaunt Mother Wagstaffe, glum and weird-looking as ever. Kinty felt a sudden cold chill in the presence of this awesome creature, and she shrank away with a little shudder.

"Affeared, mistress? Ah, Goody has no more wicked spells, she's washed in the blood of the Lamb."

With quick revulsion of feeling Kinty burst out:
"Oh, Goody! Where is he? Tell me, where is my lover?"

"Thy lover?"

"Ay, Mark the 'prentice, I took him but last night, and now he is gone, Goody."

The wise-woman stood looking at her visitor in a manner that sent the blood back to her heart; and then, without answering, she stepped to the door, opened it by some mysterious and complicated means, led the way inside, carefully closed the door and shot the bolt, and then, turning round, she demanded:

"Dost love him truly, mistress?"

"Ay, dame, oh ay; but where——"

"An' does he love thee?"

"Ay, does he! But tell me, good woman, where he is. I dreamed a bad dream of him in the night. Oh, Goody, I saw him tossed with a bull."

"Mistress!" and the dame almost shrieked out her exclamation.

"I did, dame! Oh, tell me not 'tis an evil dream!"

The light went out of the wise-woman's eyes,

her chin dropped upon her breast, and in a low husky voice she groaned:

"Good lack! I dreamed the like myself!"

There was dead silence; Kinty's heart went cold, then relieving tears rose to her eyes, and she was just about to speak when Mother Wagstaffe drew herself up, dropped her crooked walking-stick, and with her black eyes glowing and her sallow face shining, with strange inspiration she began in the tone and manner of an ancient Jewish prophetess.

"'He shall give His angels charge concerning him; He shall cover him with His feathers, He shall hide him in His pavilion. There is no enchantment against Jacob, neither is there any divination against Israel. He shall deliver his soul from going down to the pit. A thousand shall fall at his side, and ten thousand at his right hand, but they shall not come nigh him; only with his eyes shall he see the destruction of the wicked!'"

This weird rhapsody was more terrifying to Kinty than a torrent of curses would have been, the succession of unfamiliar Scripture quotations sounded like an incantation, and she gasped for breath and gripped the arms of a chair to support herself.

But Goody, dropping her strange manner as suddenly as she had assumed it, began to unfasten the shutters, and when the daylight came in it seemed to break the spell, and Kinty sank trembling into the chair upon which she had been leaning.

"But, dame, can you tell me naught? Can you not read his——"

"Why, mistress, I saw him go!"

"Dame!"

But another idea had evidently entered the subtle brain of the old-time witch. She made a quick step forward and stood right before her visitor, looking keenly down upon her with a calculating, studious stare.

"Tell me, mistress, has he aught to fear from the mayor?"

"Nay. Yea, oh, yea! He is—what do you name it?—converted, and 'tis said the Methodists are all Jacobites!"

Goody frowned and shook her head.

"Mistress," she said slowly, "the mayor got him from his bed at break o' day and sent him—O God!—to Nettleton!"

"Nettleton!"

And Kinty with a new horror on her face, sprang to her feet, and the two stood looking almost fiercely into each other's eyes. They had neither of them the least suspicion of the real motive of the mayor's action, but they saw clearly enough that his worship wanted to get rid of Mark, and if so it would be perilous to bring him back even if he could be found; for the Government wanted men badly just then, and Mark would make an ideal recruit either for army or navy.

"Perhaps 'tis but an errand he hath gone upon," said Kinty, with a faintness of voice that belied her words.

"And what then of our dreams?" was the chilling reply.

Kinty shuddered, and then with a fresh thought she said eagerly:

"But can you not divine, Goody? Can you not break the evil spell?"

"Toots! Get thee behind me, Satan!" But with change of tone, the weird creature went on: "I can do better than that, mistress. I can *pray*. Ay, an' I can move the Methodists to pray." And then softening suddenly she asked, "Can you pray, mistress?"

But to Kinty this was mere solemn trifling; the old beldam was demented with her new religion. She was for instant action; something must be done and done at once, so presently she asked:

"Went he riding?"

"Nay, afoot."

"Then he can be overtook?"

"There be many ways to Nettleton, mistress, and none of them simple."

"But a horseman could o'er-ride him and stop him going near the town."

"And what then?"

"He would be saved; he could come back."

But even as she spoke the momentary eagerness died out of her voice, and she was not surprised when the old woman shook her head sadly and answered:

"'Twould but be walking into another trap."

"But there's the law."

"There's no law, mistress, for the Methodists."

"But the mayor's son is a Methodist."

"Ay, that is why he so hates us all."

Kinty sighed heavily, but the necessity of action was strong upon her, and seeing no further help in the dame she moved disconsolately to the door.

"I cannot rest! I must do something!" she cried with querulous pathos.

And Goody, as they parted, put her hand out, and touching her respectfully, said:

"God is above, and young Mark is His servant, so fear not."

But as Kinty was hastening away, she called her back, and said:

"Pray for him, mistress. Come and join us to-night at the flax mill."

Kinty shrugged her shoulders and hurried off. She had a grudge against the mill and against the people who resorted there: but for them her lover would have been safe.

During her hurried walk home she decided that her next application should be made to Uncle Josephus if she could find him. She could not think that he knew anything about the mayor's proceedings, but at any rate she would learn what view he took of the matter.

He was in the parlour unexpectedly when she arrived, but so changed in this short forenoon that she felt a fresh pang of fear. His sneering, malicious manner had given way to one of nervous apprehension, and as she entered he sprang at her, crying:

"Hussy, where is thy uncle?"

"I know not," she began loftily; and then,

though she noticed his extreme concern, she went on recklessly, "Gone to Nettleton, belike!" and stood watching the effect of her shot. She was more than justified, for Josephus went positively green.

"Nettleton? why Nettleton?" he shouted.

But seeing how the first chance shot had told, she repeated the attack.

"Nay, uncle, you should know best."

"Baggage!" he yelled, but with sudden change of manner, he seized his hat once more and dashed out through the shop.

Breathless and bewildered, Kinty sat down to collect her thoughts. Why, her reckless guesses seemed to have hit the mark! Uncle Ebenezer gone? There was some comfort in the fact, at any rate; at his age there was no danger of his being pressed, and for his years and bulk he was still an expert rider, and might easily overtake her lover. Only there were so many possible roads to Nettleton, and a man on horseback would scarcely go the same way as a foot passenger.

Perhaps he had not gone, after all; his habits were such that there was really little cause as yet for fear, and as her head began to throb and her lips to quiver, she leaned on the table, buried her face in her hands, and sobbed again.

That proved an awful day for the distracted girl, fits of helpless depression were followed by fits of fruitless activity. She dare not go down to the kitchen, for Kerry was in a state of collapse, and would overwhelm her with useless lamentations; neighbours came in every hour or so to madden her with suggestions probable and otherwise, but chiefly the latter. Uncle Josephus never came near her even for his meals, and not a word could be learnt about dear old Uncle Ebenezer.

Towards evening, however, her fears were confirmed, Ebenezer had gone off to Nettleton, and was by that time probably far on his way; and we in these times can have no conception of the feelings of a lonely girl in those days of dangerous travel under such circumstances.

As the day drew to its close and no relief came, a feeling of helpless loneliness crept over her. Nancy called twice, but brought no fresh news except that the Methodists had lost their suspicion of Mark, and were rejoicing over him as a brand plucked from the burning.

Her sense of burden and loneliness deepened after Nancy's last visit, for it came to her gradually that Uncle Josephus, however near he had been to yielding the night before, was now of quite another mind, and she could not for the life of her think of any reason for the change. Perhaps it was no change, and she had been deceived when she thought he had relented. Even if Mark came back, therefore, there would still be that difficulty to surmount, and it seemed harder and more dreadful in her present depressed condition.

Utterly wretched and full of fearful forebodings, she began to long for something, she knew not what. There must be help and sympathy somewhere, surely. Oh for some one who knew and would understand! It was the mute blind groping of a stranded soul after God, but she did not know.

Then another thought stole upon her; the only people who were in sympathy with her present feelings were the despised Methodists. Yes, she would go and join them in their prayers. She knew not the time of meeting, but guessed it would be some time after sunset, and so a little before eight o'clock she stole out of the back door, and a few minutes later gently pushed the heavy flax mill door before her and entered.

The worshippers, about a score in number, were assembled at the farther end of the room singing, and as she was seeking a shy place behind the door, Mother Wagstaffe came towards her and led her forward. The others did not turn round to look at her, but stood with closed eyes and rapt faces absorbed in their melody, which was read out to them in fragments of about two lines by the tinker.

Kinty kept her eyes down, but as the singing concluded, and the others were going to their knees, she was dimly aware that she was being observed, and, glancing timidly up, she caught the mayor's disinherited son eyeing her with burning looks. But she was in no mood for coquetry, and in a few moments young Giles was forgotten as she drank in the spirit of the supplications that were being made.

A strange spell fell upon her; these people were praying to a real God, and they prayed much as they talked. They spoke to their Maker as though they could see Him, and asked in definite terms for the one thing that was upon their hearts. They called Mark "the new-born babe," and asked that he might be "snatched from the jaws of the lion."

And the most amazing but fascinating thing was that they believed that they were being heard, and that God would do literally what they asked. If this was prayer, and her heart told her it was, she had never before understood it. Gradually she warmed towards these simple people, she felt as though they were building a sheltering wall around her absent lover, and when the meeting closed she rose from her knees with wet eyes.

"I never thought to see you here!"

Kinty turned with a little start and met the ardent gaze of the young maltster. She was abashed for the moment, but her heart was full, and so she bowed her head and walked on.

Drawing closer to her and dropping his voice almost to a whisper, he asked:

"Are you feeling the drawings of the Spirit? are you seeking after God, sister?"

"Nay; I am seeking my lover, Mark Rawson, my lover!"

Giles flushed to the eyes and looked like one stunned.

"Your lover? Mark the 'prentice?"

"Yea, Mark the 'prentice! Know ye aught of him? What hath thy father done wi' him?"

But he was thinking hard on other lines, and so, ignoring her question, he said:

"But he cannot be a Methodist and your lover!"

"Cannot he! but he is i' faith, and a right forward one, too."

And she laughed wistfully as she recalled certain lover-like proceedings in the dark hat-shop the night before.

"But a Methodist may marry only in the Lord."

"Let him but come safe back an' he shall marry me as he lists."

"But, mistress,"—and great beads of perspiration began to appear on his face,—if—if—— Why, I had to give up father and mother and you, too, to save my soul!"

"And I thank you for't, Master Giles, and so will Mark."

A battle royal was going on within the young maltster, the presence of the girl he had deliberately given up for his soul's sake had most unexpectedly revived the old Adam in him; his whole nature went out to her, he had never felt that he loved her until now. His dull eyes gleamed like balls of fire, he was driving his nails deep into his clenched fists, a sickly pallor spread over his face, and at last he stammered out:

"If one man may risk his soul for a woman, why not another?"

The theological point involved took Kinty out of her depth, but the idea suggested reached the old spirit of banter within her, and so, though her heart was cold and heavy, and they had by this time reached the market-place where

groups of people stood, she made a pretty little
gesture of dismay, and cried:

"Mercy, Master Giles, but I cannot marry
two men!"

The untimely frivolousness of the answer did
what serious argument might not have accomplished. The young maltster felt first offended
and then rebuked, and so recovering himself with
a great effort he turned the conversation by
asking:

"But what has my father to do with it?"

Kinty opened her eyes wide, and then checked
herself. Evidently he knew nothing of his father's
motives, and if the Methodists did he would have
heard of them. Perhaps Goody would not wish
the fact that she had seen the interview between
Mark and the mayor known. At any rate, it was
as well to be careful, and so she answered:

"Does he not hate and persecute all Methodists?"

But he was studying her intently. Certain
overtures he had recently had through his sister
made him aware that if he wished to be reconciled
to his father the way was open, at least upon
certain terms. Mark was now out of the way;
he had doubtless gone, like many another in
those times, to feed the greedy god of war; for
it was no uncommon thing just then, when the
authorities were unscrupulous and bounties for
recruiting high, for a strapping young fellow to
disappear, and when he did so nobody thought
twice as to his whereabouts.

In a short time the bewitching young beauty
at his side would doubtless forget her lowly

lover and even be thankful that she had escaped a misalliance. The first glow of new religious life had waned somewhat of late, and if he could get reinstatement in his father's favour, recover the prospects he had forfeited, and obtain Kinty, the matter was, at any rate, worth considering. And so, as they had now reached the hat-shop, and he noticed that the neighbours were observing them curiously, he took a ceremonious leave and went away.

And that night there was another young soul in the throes of fiercest moral conflict, and as the sun broke over Purstone Hill another well-built young Helshamite rode out of the town end towards that place of ill repute—Nettleton.

CHAPTER XIX

ADVENTURES BY THE WAY

No sooner had Mark Rawson turned the crest of the hill after parting with the mayor, than he became the prey to distracting fears. There was something worse than cruel in his being sent away from the town on the very day that was to see the consummation of his life's dreams, and he could not overcome the feeling that the circumstance was somehow ominous.

He was angry with himself now, for not having awakened his sister, and he pulled up, and was strongly tempted to run back and tell her both what had befallen him at the hat-shop, and on what errand he had been dispatched. But the mayor had undertaken to explain all that was necessary to her, and if he should see him returning he would most certainly be angry.

As he reached the corner of Baking Lane, it occurred to him to run round to the back door of the hat-shop, and scribble a message on the flag before the kitchen door; Kerry could not read, but she would be sure to call her mistress's attention to it. And yet why waste time? Mr. Josephus knew all about the matter and there was really no cause for the foolish fear that troubled him.

Then he remembered the strange conduct of the wise-woman. Why had she signalled so earnestly? Well, he was near, two minutes' walk would bring him to her door, why not see her and settle that point, at any rate? Slipping down the lane, therefore, and along the " Beck " side under the willows he approached the cottage and knocked.

There was no response; the door was fast and evidently the old woman had not returned. For several minutes he lingered about in the hope that she might appear, but at last he gave it up and went back into the road. Then his reflections began to pull him in another direction ; calculating time and distance, he realised that starting so early, it was just possible with push and good luck to reach Nettleton that night, and then with the money provided him by the mayor, get some sort of ride back on the morrow.

It would be an unheard-of feat, but surely he had reason enough for more than ordinary effort, and so in a few minutes he was scudding along the road, staff in hand, at a fine swinging pace. The callow morning air braced and freshened him, activity also contributed its recuperative influence, the keen edge of his disappointment wore off, and even his misgivings became less heavy.

As he passed through Freedale hamlet sounds of waking life began to stir. He could hear the striking of flint and steel in the cottages, and now and then he met a haymaker going to the fields. For an hour longer he trudged along, his spirits rising with every mile he travelled.

It was too early to be very hot, and the roads for the locality were fairly good. He stumbled occasionally in the deep grass-hidden ruts, passed now and again the ruins of rough country vehicles which had been stranded in the rainy spring and abandoned, more than once he had to turn aside to avoid putrifying carcases of animals lying on the roadside; but altogether he thanked his stars that he encountered nothing worse, and about eight o'clock he entered the faded old town of Higher Wincott, where the present road ended, and where also he came to the limit of his topographical knowledge.

Calling at an inn, he found some difficulty in ascertaining his nearest way forward, but a horse-dealer came to his assistance and bade him take the fields to Wincott Bottoms, then cross the pack-saddle moors to Munderham. But "The Bottoms" proved a labyrinth, and the moors apparently endless, and when a little before noon he came in sight of Munderham his hopes of reaching Nettleton that night had sunk to zero.

It was now exceedingly hot, and though he bared his neck and carried his coat on his arm, he was perspiring profusely and had become footsore and overpoweringly sleepy. As it was noon and the beginning of the haymaking season, he was not surprised to find the little village quiet; but when he pulled up for a moment the stillness become noticeable and he observed that grass was growing up long and rank between the cobble-stones of the street, and most of the cottage window-shutters were closed.

He seemed to have walked suddenly into a veritable deserted village. Looking wonderingly around he spied a little alehouse farther on, and made at once for it. But this also was closed up, and he was just gazing perplexedly round, and wondering what it all meant, when a footstep fell on his ear, and wheeling round he came face to face with one of the most hideous-looking objects he had ever beheld.

It was a man, certainly, but the hungry, cadaverous face, the glittering green eyes, the stubbly unshaven chin, and the tufts of coarse iron-grey hair that projected through the holes of a tattered wig presented to Mark's horrified gaze one of the most grotesque and terrifying figures he had ever seen.

"Laugh!" cried the wretched object with a fierce grin, and glaring savagely into Mark's face. "Laugh, man! there hasn't been a laugh heard i' old Munderham these two months! Laugh, stranger, laugh!"

"Whaa-t! What is't?" cried the traveller awestruck.

"What is't! the vengeance o' God! 'Tis wrath and hell, 'tis the plague!—H-u-s-h!"

The sound of slow rumbling wheels was heard on the cobble-stones, and the weird creature snatched at Mark's arm and drew him into the shadow of the doorway.

The young hatter had already half-guessed the

terrible truth, and a moment later there came into sight a rude springless cart led by two mournful-looking men. A dingy piece of cloth was thrown over the load, but as it passed, one terrible glance told Mark all he needed to know; and with a gasp and a horrified cry he sprang from his repulsive companion, darted down the deathly street, and did not stop until he had left the place a mile and a half behind him.

He had walked into a plague-stricken village, paralysed and decimated by the ravages of small-pox. In his scare he had paid no heed to his directions, and now found himself sorely puzzled; and as he stood reflecting and getting his breath, he heard the sound of hoofs coming towards him. But when the approaching horseman saw him emerge from the Munderham lane, he shouted, pulled up, wheeled round his horse, and dashed hurriedly away.

Hot, hungry, disheartened and drowsy, Mark threw himself into the long grass by the wayside with a fretful moan, and lay there in the sun wondering where he would get food, and when his journey would be completed. It was clear he could not get to Nettleton that night, and he was so stiff and sore that he would have been glad to get shelter and rest anywhere.

What was the secret purpose of his journey, and why had he been required to take it just at this time? And as he wondered and sighed, he grew drowsy, and though he roused himself once or twice he was soon overpowered and lay in the deep grass fast asleep.

It was late in the afternoon when he awoke, and an hour's walk brought him to a cottage where a woman sat in the doorway working a spinning-wheel. She gave him food promptly enough, and then offered ointment for his bleeding feet, accompanying her ministrations with vague references to the balm of Gilead.

She was a Methodist it turned out, and when Mark had told her of his own recent conversion, and such details of his present journey as he thought prudent, she informed him that he had come many miles out of his way, but that at the next village five miles farther on he would find a Methodist webster who would give him shelter for the night.

He could scarcely move his stiffened limbs when he rose to depart, and cried out more than once with pain ; but a little exercise eased matters, and he pushed on towards Gunnell. The road dipped sharply into a valley, and he began to pant with the stifling closeness of the air. The sides of the valley were well wooded, and he came every now and again into delightful bits of shade.

A sound of distant hoofs made him look round, and there some distance above him on the hillside was a horseman on another road, but evidently making in the same direction as himself. The traveller was coming down the hillside at a fine rate, and was soon some little in advance of him. He seemed to be talking to his horse somewhat excitedly Mark thought.

Presently the rider plunged into a shady bit

17

of wood, and the young hatter had almost forgotten him when he heard a cry, a succession of dull blows and the discharge of a pistol. He pulled up, listened a moment, gripped his ashen staff and, weary as he was, dashed forward.

The cries and knocks increased as he ran, and he shouted in response, and then coming into the straight he beheld the horseman with riding-whip in one hand and horse-pistol in the other struggling with two ragged footpads in the road, whilst a third ruffian was in the very act of mounting the stranger's horse.

"Help! help!" bawled the rider.

A shock went through Mark, the voice was strangely familiar; he shouted again and sprang forward. Yes! Oh heavens! yes, the horseman was Mr. Ebenezer.

With an amazed yell Mark smote the nearest footpad with his staff, and began to belabour him about the head and shoulders until he turned upon his new assailant. Mr. Ebenezer discovering his helper, sprang back, roared out a volley of mingled oaths and proverbs, and the roughs were just being beaten off when there came a crash in the wood behind, a succession of oaths, Mark was smitten heavily on the head by some blunt instrument and fell senseless to the earth.

When he came to himself all was quiet again, only Mr. Ebenezer, with face all smeared with blood and tears, was looking anxiously down upon him, and he had only time to observe that his old master was coatless, when all went dark again.

"Lack-a-day! ' A fool's bolt is soon shot.' ' Who reacons without his host must twice reacon.'"

Mark raised his head, and then became conscious that his own outer garment was gone, as well as his master's.

" Hoots, man, I've found thee! ' 'Tis an ill wind that blows nobody good.' Thou cam'st i' th' very nick, lad. Ah, lousy rascals, ' Twixt cup and lip is many a slip.'"

" But, master, where are our coats ? "

"Tut, man ! heed not the garments ; near is my coat, but nearer is my skin. The rascals gave thee a bat [blow]."

" But, master, the letter ! the letter was in my coat ! "

" Nay, nay, man ; thy wound, what of it ? "

Thus reminded, Mark put his hand to the back of his head and drew it away again all wet with blood. The sight sickened him, but with a great effort he staggered to the rotting stump of an old tree and propped himself against it. Ebenezer, rapping out energetic oaths on their vanished assailants, bound up Mark's head with his snuffy old handkerchief, muttering as he fumbled with the unwonted exercise, " Need makes e'en the old wife trot." But he gave no sign that there was anything amiss with himself, and it was some time before the younger man discovered that his companion also was injured.

In a few minutes Mark comprehended what had happened. The two who were assaulting Ebenezer had been reinforced upon his appearance by others out of the wood. They had achieved their purpose only too successfully—pistols, saddle-bag, money, coats were all gone, Mr. Ebenezer's outer garment having disappeared most mysteriously ; for he would not admit for a moment that he had been knocked down and stripped whilst unconscious.

A sudden sense of the Divine protection fell upon Mark as he leaned against the tree trying to realise the situation, and he dropped upon his knees and began to return thanks to God. Ebenezer watched these proceedings, first with astonishment and then with a dull stare, and when at length the younger man rose and looked round he found his companion kneeling with his face to a wayside bush and his wig gripped firmly in one hand, repeating the Apostles' Creed with headlong rapidity.

With his head singing and swimming Mark felt that the first thing to do was to get assistance, and so they started forward to the next village. It had grown a little cooler, but as they soon emerged from the shelter of the trees, and strange sharp pains in the scalp began to distress him, he doubted whether he could travel the uncertain distance to the place of refuge. Mr. Ebenezer, however, was optimism itself, and laughed at the difficulties Mark saw.

"Tush, man! we canna always have good news from Holland. Robbed? Ay, but we're safe enough now; 'naught's never in danger.'" But here he became incoherent and reeled in the road, and Mark insisted that he was hurt and was concealing it.

The old fellow stoutly denied any such thing, but

almost immediately staggered again, and Mark was just insisting on knowing the truth when his master gave a faint whoop, and pointed forward; and following the direction indicated, he beheld a broad shallow stream crossing the bridgeless road, and they both pushed onward for a drink.

Mark arrived first, and with a sigh of satisfaction threw himself down, and sank mouth and face in the cooling waters. Ebenezer was following and dropped on his knees, and began to crawl towards the stream. Mark drank deep and dipped his face again and again, and was just rising from his knees, when, glancing round, he found his brave old companion lying half length in the stream, apparently in a dead faint.

For the next twenty minutes Mark with swimming head was struggling to bring his master back to consciousness, and when at length he got him to sit up, he noticed that the sun was sinking fast and night would be soon upon them. They were at the lowest point of the road, and the shoulder of the hill hid the village beyond from view. It must be nearly two miles off, Mark calculated, and how they were to reach it in their present condition he was unable to see.

Mr. Ebenezer seemed to prefer a prostrate condition and lay on his back muttering the Creed, and Mark, in utter exhaustion, had to struggle with an overwhelming desire to fling himself down by the old man's side and give up. But Ebenezer raised his head and sat up in a listening attitude,

Yes, some one was coming, for there was a sound of hoofs, and Mark prayed it might not be the return of the robbers. The still evening enabled the sound to travel easily, but several minutes passed before the traveller hove in sight. The strain of listening must have drained Mark's strength, for the next thing he knew he was lying on his back, and John Snaith, the Methodist preacher, was rubbing his limp hands.

An hour later he found himself reclining on a comfortable long settle in the inglenook of a large kitchen, a rosy-cheeked, meek-looking woman was attending upon him, and a rubicund yeoman, half-farmer, half-tradesman, was deep in conversation with Snaith.

A lugubrious groan and a muttered " When the bad is highest the good is nighest " made him aware that Mr. Ebenezer was somewhere near, and raising his bandaged head he beheld his old master seated in a corner chair, with his arm bound up and a face as white as a sheet, whilst two gentle-looking damsels were waiting upon him; one, in fact, being just in the act of helping him to a pinch of snuff.

Mark soon found he was in the best of hands, and when at last he was able to sit up and eat, he told as much of his story as he thought prudent, and then listened with growing distress to Mr. Ebenezer's account of his disappearance from Helsham, and the alarm which it had caused.

" But the mayor ! said he naught of where he had sent me ? " he gasped.

In an energetic but unprintable monosyllable,

the old hatter consigned his worship to woeful regions, and then gave Mark to understand that he had been put upon the scent by Goody Wagstaffe, and that he thought him well rid of the letter which he swore meant mischief to its bearer.

The rosy old dame mildly deprecated both the old fellow's language and his surmises, and as Mr. Ebenezer was without the clue to the mayor's motives held by the reader, and John Snaith added exhortations about "thinking no evil" and "speaking evil of dignitaries," the old man was in danger of losing his temper; and so, to divert his attention, the women began to urge the necessity of rest, and in a few minutes our two adventurers were lying side by side in a cool room, soft linen sheets about them, and soft pillows under their aching heads.

CHAPTER XX

STRANGE PENITENTS

A STEADY snore soon proclaimed the older man asleep, but Mark found it impossible to soothe his excited mind. Had the mayor played him false? and if so, why? Was the losing of the letter a Providence, as his old master insisted and even Snaith seemed to think? Why, at any rate, had not the magistrate explained his absence, as he promised, and what, oh, what were they thinking of at that moment in Helsham?

He dozed now and again, and woke with frightened starts, but when at last slumber seized him he slept heavily, and lay tossing and moaning about until bright daylight filled the room, and sounds of returning life could be heard from all parts of the house. Ebenezer was still snoring, but Mark was soon back in the incidents of the previous day and the anxieties connected with them.

He had lain thus, and was debating with himself his best course of action when a sound of distant singing floated softly into the room. Yes, he knew the tune, some Methodists were evidently worshipping somewhere not far away.

A goodly company, too, by the volume of sound ;
why should he not join them ?

But when he tried to move, his limbs seemed
fast to the bed, and the least effort gave him
pain. He groaned and sighed and waited a
while, but at last the sweet morning, the alluring
melody, and his own restlessness, were too strong
for his aching bones, and he got up and hastily
dressed. He was met at the foot of the stairs
by the mistress of the house, who protested
that he must remain in bed for one day, at
least.

Mark admitted his soreness, and then, dropping
into a cautious tone, informed her that he was
a recently converted Methodist, and longed to go
to the service. Then the dame called one of
her daughters, and bade her accompany their
guest and see that he took no harm. With
demurest smile the damsel, fair-haired and pretty
almost as Kinty herself, led him through the
farmyard, along the side of an orchard, and
across a field to a shady nook, where he beheld
some sixty people gathered for worship.

Some of them had their reaping-tools in their
hands, and others held the bridles of horses.
John Snaith was praying when Mark came up
to the edge of the little dell, and so he accepted
the timidly offered assistance of his fair companion's arm, and watched the newcomers as
they arrived.

The Scriptures were read next, another soft,
tender hymn was sung, and the preacher commenced his sermon. The girl at Mark's side was

soon listening with rapt attention, but he found it difficult to follow the preacher at all. Do what he would, his eyes wandered over the assembly, and his thoughts returned to the absent ones at Helsham.

For some fifteen minutes the sermon proceeded, and Mark was just beginning to get interested when he caught a movement out of the corner of his eye, and, slightly turning his head, he observed three men steal sheepishly up to the edge of the company, look round with sly, suspicious glances and finally settle down to listen.

There was something about the last of the newcomers that seemed familiar, and yet as he looked at him he could not decide what it was. He checked himself and turned his thoughts to the preacher, but a moment later he was eyeing the stranger again with an earnest, struggling sort of look.

Suddenly light came, and he started forward with an astonished cry. It was not the man, nor his face, but he was wearing Mark's own coat. A chill crept over him as he stared along the dell-side. He turned to speak to his fair companion, and then, glancing back at the stranger, became so fascinated in watching him that he forgot coat, sermon, and everything.

Snaith was discoursing on the Judgment, and he had just commenced to give lurid and terribly realistic descriptions of the last great assize, and the wearer of the stolen coat, with his big mouth wide open, and his eyes bulging out in growing fear, was drinking in every word. Now and then he licked his coarse lips, unconsciously took a step nearer the preacher, pulled nervously at his frowsy beard, and gave every sign of being interested to the point of helplessness.

Mark, forgetful of everything else but what he saw, held his breath and watched. The stranger began to grind his teeth, and great beads of perspiration stood on his forehead. The preacher's voice had fallen to a whisper, not a sound could be heard but the sibilant accents of the sermon, and Mark, stiff and spellbound, saw the footpad move like one mesmerised towards the centre of the ring.

Nobody saw, nobody heeded. The whispered descriptions of the Great Judgment were holding every heart in thrall. Suddenly the preacher flung out a sentence, high, shrill, terrific; the man Mark was watching sprang into the air with a shriek, loud moans broke out on every side, and, a moment later, the thief was grovelling at Snaith's feet, crying for mercy to an accompaniment of cries and groans and tears.

The scene, though repugnant even to Mark's untutored instincts, thrilled, repelled, and even frightened him, and he was just sighing in an effort of self-assertion when there was a roar and a crash, kneeling worshippers were toppled incontinently over, a well-known figure dashed into the ring, and with shouts of "Rascal! thief!" Mr. Ebenezer was seen fiercely dragging Mark's coat from the back of the kneeling penitent.

With a startled glance the thief looked up, and, recognising his assailant, realised that the preacher's warnings were being fulfilled with swift and most appalling literality ; Nemesis had overtaken him indeed, and with another yell he threw his arms round Ebenezer's legs and began to cry out for mercy.

The old hatter kicked and sputtered, and finally, with a lurch and a roar, toppled over on the top of his prey and lay on the soft grass, proclaiming vociferously that " Old birds were not to be caught with chaff."

The appearance of Mark, who now sprang into the ring, completed the wretched footpad's terror, and as he was now joined by his two companions and his coat was in Ebenezer's hands, he grovelled there in ragged, dirty shirt, through the plentiful rents of which a dirtier skin was visible, and cried for pity from God and man alike.

It took all John Snaith's powers of command to obtain anything like order, and when this was at length accomplished he dismissed the worshippers to their work and invited Mark and the footpads to stay behind.

The congregation, standing in little knots on the edge of the dell, watched the proceedings with intense interest. The three penitents were notorious characters, and their capture by the Methodists was regarded as a most signal triumph. Mr. Ebenezer, still upon the grass, was alternately denouncing the thieves and fortifying himself with proverbial philosophy, and Mark began to search the pockets of his recovered coat for the letter.

At this moment, however, the farmer came down the dell-side and, after saying a word or two to Snaith, he turned to Mark and his master and invited them back to the house. But Mark demanded his letter, and Mr. Ebenezer, declaring he would have the villains gibbeted, bawled out for some one to fetch the constable.

Snaith checked the old man somewhat sternly, and assured Mark that the letter and all other matters should be adjusted as far as might be if only they would return to the house. Ebenezer announced that " A bird in the hand was worth two in the bush," and was not to be pacified, and it was clear to Mark that the old fellow was very much overwrought.

At length they prevailed upon him to depart; but he went away muttering threats of vengeance against Snaith if the culprits escaped him. The women of the house placed food before them; but to Mr. Ebenezer this was a species of corruption and bribery, and he tramped about the kitchen denouncing the three penitents as highwaymen and the Methodists as villainous Jacobites and balderdash.

Then he tried to induce an old man-servant, who sat in the chimney-corner making wooden spoons, to fetch a magistrate, and, failing in that, he sat down in a pet, sulkily refused to eat, and kept up a series of mutterings to the effect that " A bird in the hand is worth two in the bush," and "Save a thief from hanging, and he'll cut your throat."

Presently Snaith and the farmer entered the kitchen.

"The letter! What of my package?" demanded Mark eagerly.

"The men know naught of any letter, they have not even seen it."

"But 'twas in the pocket! Where are they?"

"The men are gone."

"Gone?"

"Gone?" shouted Ebenezer, and with a savage laugh he went on, "So, so! 'Set not the fox to watch the geese.' Scoundrels are ye all!"

Mark had risen from the table with a flushed, angry face, and Ebenezer, clutching at his wig with his uninjured hand and waving it about, began to denounce the Methodists as villains and vagabonds.

"Silence!" commanded the preacher sternly. "Old man, thy language ill becomes thy years. The men are true penitents, and will return."

"Return! return, says ta!" and rushing at Mark the excited and indignant old fellow seized him by the arm and began dragging him out of the house. "Come forth, come forth! We've gotten 'out o' the frypan into the fire.' 'Set a thief to catch a thief.' Rascals are they all! Come forth, man!"

But Mark, in spite of his distress about the letter, was interested. Could such wretches as these be influenced by religion? To see three such scamps genuinely penitent and bringing forth fruits that were meet would be a marvel indeed.

In spite of his confident language, however, Snaith seemed strangely anxious and restless. The men, he explained, were not really criminals, but mere broken men, who had turned poachers and hen-roost robbers out of sheer starvation. Their attack upon Ebenezer was their first serious plunge into crime, and he was anxious that they should have a chance of justifying his kindness and faith in their sincerity.

Mark hastened to assure the preacher that if he could only recover his letter he would be glad to forgive the rest; but his old master obstinately announced his intention of having the "rascals" gibbeted, and laughed to scorn the idea that they would be such "pudding-heads" as to put themselves within the power of the law.

> " 'Love can bow down the stubborn neck,
>   The stone to flesh convert;
> Soften and melt, and pierce and break
>   The adamantine heart,' "

quoted Snaith, but it was evidently quite as much to confirm his own wavering confidence as to convince the mocking hatter.

And, as if to justify his faith, the back door opened and in stepped the three culprits. They had hastily washed their faces and there were fringes of wet hair hanging over their brows and marginal dirt-stains round the edges of their cheeks.

A strange stillness fell on the company, surprise and wonder appearing on every face. The men drew up in the middle of the room and looked inquiringly around, shame and high purpose curiously blended in their faces. The wearer of Mark's coat, who was now a picturesque pillar of dirty rags, glanced shyly round upon the company and then down at a pistol in his hand, and groaned.

"Lord, help him," said Snaith fervently, and the tears stood in the women's eyes, whilst Mark had sudden difficulty in seeing through his.

The footpad stepped up to Ebenezer and laid the pistol before him.

"Glory!" cried Snaith under his breath.

The thief hesitated a moment with quivering mouth, and then quietly laid a purse by the side of the weapon; the preacher breathed out another deep ejaculation.

Then, turning to his companions, the penitent took from them saddle-bag, straps, and a small wallet, and laid them before the old hatter. With fascinated eyes the lookers-on watched the proceedings in dead silence, and when the chief actor hesitated for a moment the preacher said, in low stern voice:

"Keep back naught of the price, brother. Remember Ananias and Sapphira."

The thief looked up in perplexity, he evidently did not understand the not too obvious reference.

"Go on, brother, make an end; hold naught back."

The penitent seemed still at sea, and so Snaith added urgently:

"The horse, brother, what of the horse?"

Light came into the dull face, and dropping his head again, he said humbly:

"The horse is in the yard, master, and the constable."

"The constable?" cried two or three at once.

"The constable!" echoed Snaith. "Nay, then, I meant not that; this is righteous overmuch."

Two of the culprits were glancing nervously towards the back door, and they heard Snaith's protestations with most evident relief; but their spokesman, labouring to swallow something, opened lips that cracked as they separated, and answered huskily:

"But we want the peace of God, master."

Snaith looked round on the company with a flash of holy triumph, and burst out "Praise God!" and then, stepping forward, he explained to the culprit that Mark and Ebenezer were willing to pardon their offence, and that, unless they had the guilt of some other crime upon their souls, there was no need to give themselves up to justice.

The two assistants murmured words of gratitude, but their leader shook his head wearily and repeated:

"We want the peace of God."

With the flash of a new thought in his eye, Snaith strode to the back door, and returned with a little pock-marked, wiry man, who had "officer of the law" written large on every

feature of his fussy face. The women uttered
cries of protesting pity, Mark sprang to his feet
and caught at the preacher's arm, but Snaith
threw off the grasp, and, stepping back, said:

" Officer, do thy duty! "

" In the King's name," began the little constable ;
but before he could get any further, he was
sent spinning against the pot-rack, and a husky
voice cried :

" Touch 'em not! " and Mr. Ebenezer, his red
face all smeared with hot tears, thrust himself
between the culprits and the man of law, and
turning suddenly round, flung his free arm round
the neck of the man who had worn Mark's
coat, and hugging him convulsively to his breast
he cried :

" Bless, bless thee, for a man and a Christian ! "

Joyful little sobs broke from the women, the
thieves looked round in perplexity, Mark tried
to speak but could not, and Snaith, looking on
with folded arms and glowing eyes, laughed in
the excess of his triumph ; for he was beholding
and demonstrating to others the marvellous trans-
formation which the Gospel could produce upon
even the most hopeless cases.

But the constable had picked himself up, and
began to assert the majesty of the law, and so
Ebenezer, who seemed to have taken command,
picked up his restored purse, pushed a guinea
into the irate officer's hand and thrust him incontinently out of the house, then turning to the
penitents he emptied all the silver left in his
fob before them, slapped them heartily on the

back, and invited them to return with him to Helsham.

And then, as a sort of winding up of the ceremonies, he grabbed at Mark's arm and cried, whilst the tears rose into his eyes again :

"Boy, these rascals have made me a Methodist. State Church, man ! State Church is balderdash ! "

CHAPTER XXI

KINTY'S AWAKENING

DISPIRITED and exhausted by the trying experiences of the day, the old feeling of loneliness descended upon Kinty again as she entered the house after parting with the young maltster. Uncle Josephus in his hardest mood would have been welcome just then, and she peered into the dark corners of the unlighted room with a weary, sinking heart. She was too preoccupied and miserable to think of calling for a light, and so after groping about a little, she found Mr. Ebenezer's chair, and with a sobbing sigh sank into it, impulsively kissed the hard polished arm, and then dragged herself upstairs.

Under ordinary circumstances her anxiety about her uncle would have kept her astir, but she had reached the point of suffering where sorrow loves to feed upon itself, and she found herself seeking the very loneliness which oppressed her so much.

Listlessly she took off her cloak and hat, and as listlessly sank upon her knees to repeat her ordinary evening prayer. She went through it as mechanically as she had done a hundred times before, and was just rising again when her pressing sorrows overcame her, and, sinking back, she laid her head upon her hands and began to think. Oh, for some one to talk to, some one who could comprehend; some one to whom she could open her heart!

Tears of soft self-pity began to flow, and kneeling there in the still twilight she realised for the first time in her life what it was to be an orphan. For years she had reigned a happy giddy queen over the hearts and home of two old bachelors, and now, when a full-grown woman, she had a sudden aching longing for the parents she had never known.

For a long time she knelt thus, yearning pensively for she scarcely knew what. Suddenly she opened her eyes with a startled look; a curious self-consciousness came over her, awesome stillness seemed to enwrap her, and she held her breath in a sort of half-trance. At first it was as though some faithful old clock had stopped ticking; but that feeling gradually died away, and a chilly sense that some one was near came over her.

She dared not move or even breathe; a moment more and she must have either shrieked or fainted. But just then a soft humming cadence, a snatch of music that came and went and slipped away when she tried to catch it floated into her brain and began to entice her. "What was it?" "Where had she heard it?" Ah, yes; the flax mill came slowly back before her mind, the rapt faces of humble Methodists appeared and went again, the chill vanished, a gush of warm tingling emotion, like a soft south wind on frozen land, passed over her, and she found herself repeating with swimming eyes and quivering lips:

> "In darkest shades if Thou appear
> My dawning is begun."

This was the daybreak of Kinty's spiritual life, had she known it; it was not an orthodox one—real awakenings seldom are—but it was hers, and as she murmured the sweet words over and over again, the far-off, hazy, lord-chief-justice-of-the-universe deity of her former days faded for ever away, and into the vacant place there came a real friendly fatherly God, who was tempting her to tell the full tale of her woes into His sympathetic ear.

And so she began to pray. It was a simple, confused, altogether earthly prayer, the petition of a maiden for her absent lover; but she seemed to know that it was entering into feeling ears, and told out her love and apprehensions with guileless *naïveté*.

Meanwhile Mr. Josephus was being greatly exercised in his mind about the absence of his brother, and whilst we must do him the justice of admitting that much of his concern arose from genuine anxiety for his old comrade's welfare, we scarcely need say that it was intensified by uneasy fear of what Ebenezer might discover.

His brother was very fond of Mark, and hated all foul play, and if he found out—— But Josephus did not care to contemplate what might happen in such a contingency. He drank more heavily than usual that night, and never knew how he got to bed; but when he came down next morning, somewhat late, he found the mayor waiting for him.

Turning away from the breakfast-table without so much as looking at his food, he seized a tankard of ale, filled his worship's pot, took a long pull at the liquor, and then sat down in surly silence opposite his visitor.

The mayor, who was watching him with ill-concealed impatience, grabbed at the vessel offered him, and then as he raised it to his lips he looked over the top, and burst out:

" The rascal's absconded ! "

" And what of Tebby ? "

But his worship was on the rack, and so with sudden heat he jerked out:

" Hang Ebenezer ! I speak of the boy—my *own* boy. He's gone, man."

The hatter's jaw dropped in dull, stupefied amazement.

" Gone ? How ? Where ? "

" Gone to Nettleton ! Gone after thy lousy apprentice ! Gone to the devil ! "

And the magistrate, now on his feet, poured out a volley of oaths and curses that shocked even the case-hardened Josephus.

Relapsing each into his chair, the two conspirators stared hard at each other. They were elderly, experienced, and for their times intelligent men; but as they glowered glumly into each other's face each man was telling himself that there was something uncanny in the whole business. They were being played with by some mocking Nemesis which was leading them on and laughing at them.

Kinty came into the room just then on some domestic errand, and so, waiting until she had gone, the maltster said:

"Dance and Jerry are gone to Nettleton, Podger to Derby, and Dick along the south road, but, curse me, I cannot rest!"

"No lad is safe nigh to Nettleton these times, 'prentice or gentleman," replied Josephus with serious conviction.

"Tut, man, my son! The scoundrels 'ull never put finger on my son."

"What of Grigsby's boy?"

Young Grigsby was the scapegrace son of a wealthy brewer, and had been pressed within a mile of his father's house, and so far neither money nor influence had succeeded in recovering him. Josephus, in his many perplexities, had a sneaking sort of satisfaction in the fact that his friend was now in the same boat as himself; a view of the case which the mayor hotly resented, and all the more so as his own heart strangely misgave him.

"Hoots! these are times, truly!" he snarled. "No man can go safely now." And once more he banned the Methodists as Jacobites and disturbers of the country's peace.

For half an hour longer they talked the thing over, but the guilty fact they held between them caused all sorts of miserable apprehensions. They were the prey too of a peevish fretfulness which made them hyper-sensitive, and so they parted to avoid quarrelling.

Afternoon brought a clergyman traveller into the town, and this worthy, interviewed at the Hanover Arms, reported that he had met a young fellow at the Luggerholme cross-roads, who was inquiring the way to Nettleton.

"He rode hard," he added, "but he cannot come to the town before dark, and not then if he misseth the way again."

His worship cursed his son under his breath as he wandered to the door, listened absently whilst the landlord questioned the cleric about Mr. Ebenezer, and then, with another bitter burst of blasphemy, he hastened away. But at nightfall he drove out of the town-end in a heavy, old-fashioned carriage, accompanied by two armed men-servants, on his way to that place of sinister mesmeric attraction—Nettleton.

And, as the father went out of Helsham, the son, on a lame and jaded mare, was turning the brow of Snelson top and going wearily down the hill towards Nettleton. Though evening was gathering in he could still see the town, some three miles below him, and the sluggish, leaden-looking river beyond. Wherever he had come that day he had made inquiries after Mark, but without success, and that for the very sufficient reason that for the last twenty miles he had chosen a much nearer road than the one taken by his rival.

It had been a hard ride, and he was almost

ill with soreness, thirst, and hunger. He was approaching a little hedgeside alehouse, and though eager to get to the end of his journey, he pulled up and shouted, "House! house!" and then, unable to wait for the response, he flung himself with a groan from the saddle, threw the bridle over a rusty hook near a link socket, and stumbled stiffly into the inn.

"Ale, there, ale!" he cried faintly, and sank into the nearest seat.

It was almost dark, but one of the two persons in the room, brushed hastily past him to fulfil his demands, and Giles was too self-absorbed to notice the other.

"You are spent, young sir," said a gruff voice from the other end of the room.

"Ah, spent enough! How far to Nettleton, good man?"

"Nettleton?" cried the pipe-voiced host, coming in with the ale, "three miles, and down hill every yard. The night is young, sit and sup, sir."

Giles took a long, deep pull at the liquor, wiped his mouth with the back of his hand, and then, throwing his legs on the bench beside him, he turned to the host and asked:

"Know you one Tester i' Nettleton?"

"Ah, marry! 'tis the brazier in Labour Lane," said the landlord.

"Bottom o' the town near to the wharf," added the other man.

But another thought had entered Giles's head, and so he said:

" Any other young fellow asked after Tester here to-day ? "

The landlord reflected, and was just about to reply, when Giles added :

" A lad on foot ; an apprentice."

" Ah, a runaway ? "

And with a sudden quickening of interest, the host came nearer to his customer. Before he could reply, however, the stranger, now almost invisible in the gathering shadows, asked :

" Then you are for Tester's to-night, young sir ? "

" Please God, good man ! "

" Then hand these to him, and tell him that Toby Greener, the chapman, picked them up in the old Gunnell Road."

Giles took what appeared to be a small book and a letter, and was putting them into his side-pocket, when the feel of the volume struck him as being familiar, and so he tried to examine it, and then got up and went to the door for better light.

It was a thin little Methodist hymn-book and on the fly-leaf was written " Mark Rawson: his book." The backs were curled somewhat, and the colour of the binding seemed to have run a little and then dried suddenly.

" Man, where got you this ? "

" In the Gunnell Road, as I told thee ; it was wet when I picked it up ; had lain there all night belike."

With a little gasp and a flutter at his heart, Giles turned up the letter. It had thumb- and mud-marks upon it, but the writing on the outside was his father's! He stared at it with sinking heart and buzzing brain.

" But, Mark? the 'prentice, saw you aught of him? " he cried, springing back into the dim room, and approaching the chapman.

A long shake of the head and a stare of questioning surprise were the only responses.

A thousand wondering questions rushed into Giles's mind. What did this discovery signify? Was it a good omen or an evil one? How had Mark come to part with it? What had happened to him, and where was he now? Would Mark, if he had lost the letter, return home, or had he gone forward into the town?

Perplexity and caution struggling together within him, he first blurted out a string of questions, and then closed up and made reticent and evasive remarks. At any rate, the letter had strangely miscarried, and the question was, what to do next. He only suspected that mischief was intended against the young hatter, and he had started in pursuit of him in order to be near and protect him amid the dangers of the town he was going to ; but if Mark had discovered his loss, he would, in all probability, return home. As he mused he turned the letter dubiously over and longed to open it.

Next moment, however, he felt prompted to hand the missive back to the chapman and let it take care of itself, whilst he returned in search of his rival ; but, detecting in his own heart a sort of unholy regret at the thought that Mark was escaping, and might get safely back to Helsham, he determined to ride on, deliver the note, and return as best he could.

The two men were watching his waverings curiously, and this annoyed him, and so, flinging a coin on the table, he asked the chapman another question as to the exact whereabouts of the brazier's residence, flung himself heavily into his saddle and turned his horse towards the town.

He pulled up several times, however, as he went down the hill and turned back once; but at the end of half an hour he rode slowly into Nettleton, and a few minutes later he led his tired mare down a cobblestone yard towards a low squat door in the far corner of the court.

It was as dark now as it ever would be that night, and the yard was still and empty. There were no lights in the little diamond-paned windows looking into the court, but a dingy swing-bracket overhung a door in the corner, and so he made for that. As he drew up under the sign and reached out his hand towards the heavy old knocker, however, he was conscious of a sudden fit of fear and drew back with most painful misgivings.

Why, he was walking into the very trap out of which he had come to rescue his rival! Goody had insisted, with that strange, prophetic manner of hers, that harm was intended to Mark, and his knowledge of the circumstances of the case confirmed her contentions; and here he was carrying the very instrument that was to accomplish Mark's ruin!

Then he remembered something else and glanced down at his garments. Since his conversion he had adopted the simpler style of dress affected by his fellow religionists, and now, dusty and disordered as his clothes were, there was little to distinguish him from an ordinary apprentice. The risk was too great; he would go back and spend the night at the Green Man, where his father at any rate was known, and then consider the situation during the night and act as his judgment directed in the morning. As for the letter——

"Soft, soft, my lad."

He jumped back with a frightened start and his heart began to beat rapidly. He gripped the rein of his horse tightly and peered suspiciously round, but nothing at all could he see.

"Tarry, tarry, lad! I'll be with thee in a twinkle."

Ha, there it was. In the window just at one side of the door and right above his head was the grinning face of a cross-eyed, cadaverous, toothless old man, and before he could collect his thoughts the door near him opened, the wearer of the face he had just seen emerged, accompanied by two men-servants carrying horn lanterns.

"The Green Man, neighbour! Which is the Green Man?" cried Giles in flurried, caught-in-the-act manner.

"Green Man! Ho, ho! yea, truly; this is the Green Man and the Red Man and the Blue Man? The Green Man, Gobbs? The Green Man, Gobbs?"

"The Green Man," answered the servant addressed as Gobbs.

"The Green Man," echoed the other, who, as he spoke, glided round in the gloom and laid a stealthy hand on the outer rein of the mare.

Giles did not see this latter performance, but the manner of the three increased his suspicions, and so stepping a pace back he said:

"But this is no hostel, master!"

"Yea, verily, the best hostel and the cheapest; the 'prentice's hostel—and the slip-master's hostel," and the old wretch came nearer, thrust his ugly face in Giles's, and leered horribly.

But Giles was getting seriously alarmed.

"Out, man!" he cried. "Take you me for a runaway 'prentice seeking hidey-hole! I am a tradesman's son from Helsham, and want a decent inn."

The old fellow's bantering manner changed suddenly, and snatching a lantern from Gobbs he came near, scanned his visitor from head to foot, and then asked suspiciously:

"Know you one Twist i' Helsham?"

"Ay, marry; he's the mayor and my father!"

"What! Tut-tut-tut! Ha, well-a-day! Enter, young sir, enter!"

And taking Giles by the elbow in a respectfully caressing manner, he tried to lead him into the house. But the young maltster's suspicions were not so easily laid.

"Nay, nay, good man; I want the inn."

"What inn? My old friend's boy go to an inn! Nay, nay! Enter, young man!"

Still far from easy, Giles allowed himself to be led indoors, and was ushered into a passage, and from thence upstairs into a dimly lighted but comfortable room. Everything looked so cosy and decent that he began to be ashamed of his own fears, and when he had been fussily pressed into a chair and had answered a string of eager questions about the well-being of his father, meat was placed before him, and he was pressed to eat in the most cordial and respectful manner.

Still struggling with his uneasiness, Giles drew up to the table and ate ; watching and carefully studying his host as he did so. But the old fellow's manner was now respectfulness itself, the ill-looking servants had disappeared, and the air of homely cheerfulness that pervaded everything had a most reassuring effect.

The old brazier seemed not to notice his guest's taciturnity, and rattled on merrily about the rumoured invasion by the Pretender, the doings of the much-talked-of Methodists, and the prevalence of crimps and press-gangs in the town of Nettleton. His manner when he spoke of these last was artlessness itself, and Giles began to reproach himself for evil-minded suspicions.

Then he began to ask wary questions, and soon found that the brazier had seen nothing of Mark, or, in fact, of any Helsham person, and this discovery set him off into a debate with himself as to whether he should present the letter ; and the fact that the old fellow showed no curiosity as to the object of his visit seemed encouraging. The brazier lolled back in his chair with a little sigh of lazy indifference, and Giles began, in spite of his inward restlessness, to feel somewhat drowsy. The conversation dragged a little, there were several long silences, and Giles had not yet settled his problem when the old fellow, in the tone of one who talks for the sake of talking, said:

"Thy father send no message for me?"

Giles gave a little start, and noticed that the brazier was watching him now with curious intentness. There was no help for it, he could not lie about the thing, and so he fumbled in his inner pocket and produced the packet.

Tester took it and examined the outside with absent indifference, then he arose, slowly lighted another rushlight, carried the note to a window-sill, set the light down and opened the message; Giles the while watching him intently. It seemed to take a lot of deciphering, for the old man was some time before he could comprehend it. The letter ran as follows:

"To John Tester, at the sign of the Wooden Mallet, these. The bearer is a King's man most evident, and I send him to thee for my own greater comfort and the peace of this good town. Let him be shipped post haste."

Two or three times the brazier perused this brief epistle, carefully keeping his face averted so that Giles could not watch him. Then he coughed thoughtfully and strolled back to his seat. "Curse the Pretender and all his rascally followers!" he muttered, as he dropped upon a long settee, and Giles, supposing that the exclamation had reference to the subject of the letter, felt no little relieved.

But the conversation flagged now more than ever, Tester answering very absently, and, as he twice caught the old fellow eyeing him sharply when he turned his head, Giles's uneasiness returned, and so to try his man he arose, wearily stretched himself, and announced his intention of going to the Green Man to sleep.

To his surprise the brazier offered no more serious objection than decent hospitality required, and respectfully offered to escort him to the inn himself, which, he explained, was on the far side of the town. Then he excused himself for a moment and went downstairs, and Giles, still suspicious, heard voices talking in undertones, and finally the sound of footsteps going out of the courtyard.

Tester, however, was quite talkative when he returned, and retained Giles for several minutes longer, whilst he told him amusing stories of the jolly landlord of the Green Man. Then he led the way down into the yard, still extolling that wonderful host.

At the corner of the lane he was so absorbed in narrative that he pulled up, and, apparently forgetful of the time and the errand they were on, took hold of Giles's coat, whilst he finished his tale. Then, suddenly remembering himself, and with the shy apologies of a garrulous old man who is wearying his friend, he made a sudden dash forward. A little way down the lane he took a sharp turn into what seemed a backyard, but which led them out upon the wharf.

Then Giles remembered that the chapman had said the Green Man was near the wharf and felt reassured; but in a few moments Tester doubled again into another dim passage. It looked so dark and ugly that after a few steps Giles held back and finally stopped, but as he did so his companion, doubling his hand, made a peculiar hooting sort of whistle; two dark figures sprang out in front, a door Giles had not seen opened behind them, men from front and back sprang upon him, gagged and bound him, and then he felt himself raised on rough shoulders and, struggling and kicking, carried off towards the wharf side.

Once he threw himself out of their hands and fell heavily to the ground; but they were too many for him, and in a few minutes he found himself thrust into a dark, stinking cabin, and when the day broke he was far out at sea.

By strange mischance, or series of mischances, he had walked into the trap which his father had laid for Mark Rawson.

CHAPTER XXII

THE RETURN

AND whilst her lovers were thus experiencing perilous adventure, Kinty was consuming herself with anxieties, and found her only relief in stealing away to her little bedroom and pouring out her troubles into the Divine ear. She was too preoccupied to observe how great a change this denoted in herself; the exercise was intensely and increasingly comforting, and, in the same unconsiousness, her heart was going out more and more to the despised Methodists, who were the only persons who seemed to understand and sympathise with her.

The men who had gone out in search of her uncle returned, but could give her no comfort, no trace of the old man having been met with by any of them. Her only consolation was that they seemed very confident that nobody would think of harming so well-known and good-natured a person as Ebenezer Kirke.

At dusk she crept out to the Methodist prayer-meeting, but what comfort she derived from that was speedily taken away when she learnt on her way home that the mayor himself had gone after his son. This, she noted with a sinking heart, was regarded by her friends as a most serious sign, and had it not been that Goody Wagstaffe, seeing her woeful plight, accompanied her homewards, and expressed unfaltering confidence that God would protect His own, she must have given way to utter despair. Goody would give no reasons; she was mysterious and reticent, but very sure, and for once Kinty's superstitious trust in the old wise-woman was of service to her, and she did her best to believe.

But the next day her fears grew stronger every hour. Uncle Josephus ate nothing and carefully avoided her, and the one solitary glimpse she got of him showed that he was haggard, unshaven, and more than half-drunk. Goody came twice, and Kerry was sent every hour to inquire for news; but neither of them brought the least scrap that relieved the tension, and dull, heavy grief settled down on her soul.

Twice during the day she roused herself in dazed wonder. This was never Christiana Kirke! and she rushed off to do she scarcely knew what. But beyond interviewing and almost quarrelling with the Methodist carpenter, who preached resignation to the Divine will, she accomplished nothing, and there came over her a bitter realisation of how helpless a thing it was, under such circumstances, to be a woman.

It was Saturday, and the Methodists, who were expecting John Snaith to preach on Sunday, had arranged to hold an all-night prayer-meeting on behalf of the absent young men. During the afternoon flying rumours which raised high hopes or excited cruellest fears, were carried to Kinty, and at dusk, the arrival of a rickety, lumbering waggon from Nettleton itself sent her scudding off to the Blue Griffin to question the driver.

She found the fellow, the profits of whose trade were obtained quite as much from the secret conveyance of uncustomed goods as from legitimate traffic, surly and taciturn at the inconvenient attention which his coming was receiving. He had, it appeared, bluntly refused to answer any questions, and when Kinty arrived he was revenging himself by giving harrowing descriptions of the dangers of the town from whence he had come.

It was "as full as a fitch," he declared, of Government men, pressmen, soldiers, and even marines, and Kinty, at the edge of the crowd, listened to his oath-embellished communications with a shudder, and then, with Goody Wagstaffe's assistance, got him aside into the stable, and, slipping a gold coin into his hands, drew out of him all the information he had to give.

He had neither seen nor heard of any of the missing ones, either in Nettleton or on the way ; but if any strange young fellow had gone at this particular time into the ill-reputed town, they might say good-bye to him, for he was by this time serving the King on the high seas.

Then Kinty broke down utterly, and, leaning against the cobwebbed wall, sobbed as if her heart would break. In vain the softened teamsman drew on his imagination and told clumsy stories of hair-breadth escapes which likely young fellows had had, even in Nettleton. Kinty was inconsolable, and drew with the perversity of despair only the worst possible conclusions from the driver's extempory romances.

Goody led her away to her own little cottage and coaxed her to drink a little small-ale, and even eat a morsel of rye bread, and at last they went together to the all-night prayer-meeting. And by this time Kinty's persistent despair had infected her companion, and her optimistic predictions grew faint and feeble, and Kinty, seizing on these as proofs that the worst was to be expected, abandoned herself to utter hopelessness.

But the atmosphere of the flax mill chamber was softly, quietly hopeful. A bright Methodist battle-hymn was being sung as they entered, and Kinty's sore, dead heart awoke again and went out in melting gratitude to these pathetic manifestations of sympathy. For over an hour the singing and praying proceeded, the numbers of the suppliants being gradually increased until the room was nearly full.

And as the numbers increased so did the confidence and fervour of the worshippers. Lamentations, prayers for resignation and patience grew fewer, whilst notes of hope and confidence became louder and more emphatic. Following every word that was said or sung, the cold hopelessness melted within the struggling girl; warm gushes of thankful affection towards these strange friends of hers welled up within her, a sense that there *was* help if it could be got, stole into her heart ; the reality, the nearness, the sympathy of God became clear to her, and she found herself following the broken simple petitions with smothered but deep " Amens ! "

Then a sense of passionate longing came over her. Oh to be God's ! to be God's own child and secure for ever ! In a short time she had forgotten where she was, forgotten her condition, forgotten even her lover, and was crying with the deepest that was in her

> " Rock of ages, cleft for me,
> Let me hide myself in Thee."

Suddenly another voice broke upon her ear, and she heard, in the strident tones of Goody Wagstaffe :

" Thou *art* God. Thou *wilt* answer prayer. Thou *wilt* keep from the snare of the fowler. Thou didst save Peter out of prison, and Paul from shipwreck. Save our friends. Save those dear lads, and save them now. Thou canst, Thou wilt. I believe——"

There was a loud bang at the door, a shout and a clamour of voices, and Kinty, springing to her feet in sudden awakening, felt strong arms thrown about her, a pair of blazing eyes met hers, her glad cry was smothered with passionate kisses, and she was folded to her lover's breast.

Goody's prayer came to an abrupt conclusion. There was a confused babel of triumphant voices,

and when Kinty looked shyly round, there a few
yards from her stood Uncle Ebenezer and John
Snaith, encircled by a company of tearful,
laughing Methodists, and behind them three
frowsy ragged ruffians who were looking on in
confused astonishment.

But that had taken place in Kinty whilst she
was on her knees which was more even than
the happy return of her lover, and in a few
moments, unconscious of all else, swimming eyes
were looking into swimming eyes, and Mark
was hearing the sweet tale of how her troubles
had almost unconsciously brought her to her
God.

Breaking off, however, in the midst of her story,
she dashed across the room and flung herself into
the arms of her uncle, who, in spite of one bandaged
limb which she had not noticed, hugged her close
to his breast, and proclaimed through quivering
lips that, " When the bad is highest, the good is
nighest."

Congratulations and exclamations of wondering
gratitude to God were heard on every side, whilst
Mr. Ebenezer shouted out incoherent little scraps
of information about his recent experiences which
only perplexed the excited listeners.

Presently he remembered something else, and,
leaving the Methodists to continue their rejoicings,
he took Kinty by the arm and marched her off
homewards, Mark following at her side and the
ex-footpads bringing up the rear.

But Mr. Josephus had heard the news, and now
came rushing down the street without either hat

or wig. The meeting between the two brothers was touching to behold; but when Josephus, releasing the fat palm of his brother, turned eagerly to Mark and Kinty, and joining their hands together there under the still stars, stammered out, "Bless ye both!" Ebenezer made the dark street ring with "Yoicks! Tally ho! Hallelujah!" and then, springing forward to meet a half-dressed figure that was rushing towards them, he hugged the amazed serving-maid to his breast with his sound arm, and proclaiming loudly that a "Bird in the hand is worth two in the bush," hurried her along to the hat-shop.

Next day word came to the town that the mayor had arrived in Nettleton to find that his worst fears with regard to his son had been fulfilled; but it was only some time afterwards that it was known how Giles had been overtaken in the very snare laid for Mark.

When his worship returned home it was observed that he had not a word good or evil to say of the Methodists, and, in fact, manifested a superstitious fear of them which was significant of much.

It took three months of incessant negotiation to procure the young maltster's release, but he arrived in time to assist at a modest little wedding at the hat-shop, where Mr. Ebenezer surpassed all former efforts of proverbial moralising, and announced amongst other things that his brother and he were about to build a chapel for the Methodists.

Mr. Josephus somehow took a great fancy

that day to John Snaith, and in one of his most confidential moments informed the preacher that the best day in the history of old Helsham was the day that saw "The Coming of the Preachers."

THE END,

Printed by Hazell, Watson, & Viney, Ld., London and Aylesbury.